THE HOUSE OF VANDEKAR

She felt cold and shivered. How ironic that of all the lovely rooms at Ashton she should find herself booked to spend the night in this one. She looked around her slowly, wondering if there was anything left of the woman who had lived here, any aura that had survived the transformation. Nothing. There was no atmosphere, no sense of the past. Perhaps unhappiness and bitterness did not survive. Only her grandmother's magnificent apartments could provide an answer. Alice. She spoke the name aloud. Alice watching her from the canvas in the hall downstairs. She could feel her come to life. If there was any ghost at Ashton, it would be Alice. Not, please God, the other one, the sad little wanton who had flitted past her room on the last night of her life. She had left no impression behind her . . .

'Maybe,' Nancy said aloud, 'maybe you meant me to come back.'

David was waiting downstairs. She went out into the corridor, the corridor of her nightmare, brilliantly lit now, warmly carpeted, welcoming. She closed the door and went down to face her past.

D0048937

Also in Arrow by Evelyn Anthony

Albatross
The Assassin
The Avenue of the Dead
The Company of Saints
The Defector
The Grave of Truth
The Legend
Malaspiga Exit
No Enemy But Time
The Occupying Power
The Persian Ransom
The Poellenberg Inheritance
The Rendezvous
The Return
The Silver Falcon
Voices on the Wind

THE HOUSE OF VANDEKAR

Evelyn Anthony

ARROW BOOKS

Arrow Books Limited
62-65 Chandos Place, London WC2N 4NW

An imprint of Century Hutchinson Limited

London Melbourne Sydney Auckland
Johannesburg and agencies throughout
the world

First published by Hutchinson 1988
Arrow edition 1989

Printed and bound in Great Britain by
Courier International Ltd, Tiptree, Essex

ISBN 0 09 960400 0

For my husband
with my love

1

The child opened her bedroom door: it was easy to unlatch and made no sound. There was a light in the long corridor outside and the massive clock at the foot of the stairs struck two. A woman was coming down the corridor, floating dreamlike on the surface, her red hair gleaming under the light. The child heard a whisper. 'Diana – in here, darling,' in a voice she didn't know. The man was always in shadow, while the woman's face was clear and the negligée drifted round her slight body like a cloud. There was a smile on her face and her eyes were bright, but her look was furtive. Once she paused, one hand pressed to her mouth in fear, as if she heard something. It was a long, long corridor, with no end in sight, as in all nightmares; there were deep patches of shadow where the lights did not penetrate.

The child drew back, watching unseen, and the woman passed by. She did not see the one who followed her, but the child did. Only a shadow, moving out of the radius of the light, a blur of menace that frightened the child so that she wanted to cry out a warning, but no sound came.

Nancy woke, shocked out of sleep by the terror of that old childhood nightmare. Her heart beat too fast; fear made it difficult to breathe for a few seconds. The man beside her didn't notice. He was concentrating on driving through the rain storm. She hadn't dreamed of it for years. Why now? It never varied. She used to wake screaming when she was little, terrified by the shadow without a face that haunted her since she was eight years old. A shadow that was as real as the woman it pursued that night.

7

Over the years it happened less and less. Time and distance kept it at bay and she herself repressed it, as she had repressed her name and her past life.

It was all over now, nothing left but the nightmare, if and when it came. But the fear and the guilt were still there, lying in wait for her. She hadn't cried out in real life; she had cowered behind the door and crept back into bed, a little girl afraid because she had seen what wasn't meant to be seen by anyone that night.

'David,' she said, 'are we nearly there? I wish you'd tell me where we're going.'

'No chance,' he said, and squeezed her hand for a moment. 'You'll have to wait and see. You were asleep for a bit. It won't be long now, about half an hour.'

It was her birthday and her lover had planned a surprise. 'I'm taking you away for the weekend. Somewhere really special,' he had said, 'No, I'm not telling you where. Just pack a few nice clothes and I'll pick you up at six.'

They had been together for six months. It was the first serious love affair for Nancy since a disastrous episode with a married man in New York which had left her hurt and disillusioned. From that time on she had concentrated on her career and, until David Renwick came into her life, that career was all-important. He wasn't typical of the kind of men she met. Their worlds were very different. Her friends were in antiques, the art world, the auction houses, part of the wide circle of interior designers. Renwick was a self-made millionaire with interests in development and property. Renwick's Estate Agents had expanded into a big public company from the tiny agency he had set up with borrowed capital. At thirty-five he was a well-known subject for the gossip columnists, something of an enigma in a world where self-promotion was part of the business.

She had met him at a dinner party given by a rival colleague who was also a friend. Renwick had engaged his company to decorate his new house in Holland

Park. She hadn't expected to like him. Her friend said he was demanding and cost-conscious, but the order was enormous and he had to be kept happy. Nancy was prepared for an arrogant money man with an inflated opinion of himself. Instead she found him charming, intelligent and very attractive. Power and great wealth could endow a man with spurious sex appeal. There was nothing phoney about David Renwick.

The attraction was mutual and he made no secret of it. He didn't waste time: he insisted on driving her home and took her out every night until she asked him to stay. He was so good to her, she thought, and good for her. There were no complications. No wife or ex-wives. They were lovers because they wanted to be, and she knew how important their relationship had become when he said for the first time that he loved her. They'd been together for nearly three months before it happened. Marriage wasn't mentioned. Nancy resisted his suggestion that she give up her flat and move into the new Holland Park house. She teased him by saying she couldn't live with someone else's decor, and he accepted her refusal. She wasn't ready to make the commitment even though he was. He knew how to be patient. He looked at her and smiled.

Not his usual type at all. He liked brunettes, he liked them petite and not very clever. She was tall, had bright red hair and was decidedly intelligent.

He wanted this birthday to be special for her, because he had something special in mind for them both. That was why he had chosen this particular hotel. He was enjoying keeping the destination a secret. He wanted to surprise and delight her. It would be her sort of place. She was that sort of woman. Although he didn't know much about her personal life, he could tell that at a glance. He had had a lot of girlfriends. He liked beautiful girls and beautiful girls liked him. Not just because he was rich, as one indiscreet young lady put it, but he was a fantastic screw as well. The remark ended their affair. Since meeting Nancy he had dropped his other women friends.

The gossipmongers had got bored and stopped watching him. Other men had the headlines now. David didn't mind. He hadn't cared about the publicity when it was directed at tarts calling themselves models and socialites who were both. But Nancy was different. He didn't want the muckrakers getting after her. He slowed in the driving rain – there was a signpost nearby and he didn't want to miss the turning. 'Light me a cigarette, darling, will you?' he said, to distract Nancy's attention. She missed the notice and he turned the car through a blur of wrought-iron gates. There were speed bumps along the drive and he slowed to 20 miles an hour. Great trees arched overhead, dripping silver rain. The headlights searched the way ahead, twisting and turning for over a mile. She was peering through the whirring wipers, trying to see out. And then they rounded the last corner and the house rose up before them bathed in floodlights. Two wide wings embraced the central building. Its grace and symmetry had thrilled him the first time he saw it in a photograph. The reality was far more splendid.

'Here we are, darling,' he announced. 'Ashton! Quite a place?' The car had drawn up in front of the steps leading to the portico.

'Yes,' Nancy answered.

Someone opened her door, holding an umbrella. She got out. She heard a man say, 'We'll put the car in the garage, sir, and bring up your luggage. This way, please.'

They walked up the steps and through the open double doors into the hall.

'If you'd like to sign the register, sir?'

She took a few steps forward while David went to the desk. The lighting was subdued in the enormous hall. A room, not a hall, with a big open fire blazing at one end. The tapestries still moved as if there was a draught, and at each side were suits of armour, oiled and gleaming. The one nearest the stairs had a grotesque German animal helmet that used to frighten the children. And there, by the fireplace, was the portrait.

David came hurrying back to her, taking her arm. 'Like it? Fantastic isn't it?'

'You're in the Fern Suite.' A young man in footman's livery preceded them to the main staircase, massive and dark, with carved sentinel figures on each newel post. For a moment Nancy touched the banisters. She didn't mean to, but she moved ahead, passing them both, leading the way.

'It's here,' she said, and turned to the right a few yards down the corridor.

'Yes, madam.' The footman sounded surprised. He opened the door and stood aside.

They were in a high-ceilinged room, lavishly decorated, with a handsome half-tester bed facing the windows. There were flowers and an ice bucket with champagne. David had thought of everything. He tipped the young man, who thanked him and said, 'Your luggage will be brought up in a moment, sir.'

Nancy went to the window and drew back the curtains. There, in the distance, was the shimmer of the man-made lake and the famous Bologna group of Cupid and Psyche embracing in the driving rain, haloed in a single spotlight.

Behind her she heard him say, 'You've been here before.' She turned away, letting the curtain fall.

He was standing, staring at her. He looked angry and disappointed. 'You *have* been here before. It's only been open for four months. Who brought you here?'

'No one.' Nancy said quietly. 'No one, David. I was born here. This was my Aunt Fern's bedroom. My real name is Vandekar. Alice Vandekar was my grandmother.'

The day had begun well. Her office was in Culver

11

Place. When she arrived that morning her personal assistant had brought in a handsome potted plant with best wishes for her birthday from the staff.

She had engaged a young man. She liked him and so far there had been no clash of personalities between them. He didn't mind taking orders from a woman. She had gathered a good team of designers around her and a small but dynamic sales force. She kept the tradename Becker because it was prestigious and added the one she had adopted for herself. Percival. Becker & Percival Interior Designers.

'Tim,' she said to her secretary, 'Get Mr Rowland on the line, will you? I want to talk to him about the Grosvenor order – and I'd love a cup of coffee.'

The morning had passed quickly; the plant looked very well on her desk. How nice of them to remember, she thought. Lunch with two French buyers, both new clients with some very big companies on their books. An order for exclusive Becker Percival designs would expand her European business into something really serious. So far the company had only nibbled at the French and German textile industries. If it went well over lunch and during the afternoon, she might end up with a head start over some of her larger competitors.

Lunch did go well. Nancy had learned in America that it's better not to entertain at all than to watch the expense account. They lunched at the Savoy; she had made sure of a good table overlooking the river and she was well known there. People noticed if you were treated with deference as an old customer. The French were very status-conscious. It all contributed to the aura of confidence and success. And the fact that she spoke perfect French, and could manage passable German also impressed them. She didn't explain that it was the result of having a French governess from the age of ten. That side of her life was permanently camouflaged. It belonged to the past, like her real name. It had nothing to do with Nancy Percival.

She left the office early. One order was assured. She

had made the first major breakthrough into a market that regarded British designers with caution. David was collecting her at six. He was never late. She had a bath and changed. Her mood was buoyant and excited. She wondered where they were going that was so special. Somewhere where she would need nice clothes. Not a green-wellie-and-waterproof weekend. That wasn't David's style. He worked out and kept fit; he played squash and tennis, but she'd learned early in their relationship that a typical English weekend in the country was his idea of hell. He hated going for walks; he disliked getting muddy or wet or cold. He didn't shoot and he had never put a leg over a horse. 'I'm Urban Man,' she remembered him saying. 'If I'm going out of London I want a nice centrally heated hotel with a big colour telly in the bedroom. And I don't want to talk to anybody either. Except you.'

She picked out a black dress. Dinner on her birthday would be something special. He hinted that much. She was feeling excited; there was a fluttering sense of anticipation she hadn't felt since she was a child, coming downstairs to find the dining room festooned with balloons and everyone assembled in their party dresses for tea. How odd that she should think of that. But it was her birthday and birthdays were always celebrated with great pomp, even the children's.

She reached into the back of the cupboard; she took out a packet sealed in tissue paper and opened it. Diamonds flashed in the palm of her hand. Why not? Why not wear it on that special night? It was all she had left now, hidden away in a shoe at the back of the cupboard. Everything else had been sold to raise money to buy out Becker. But not this. She didn't know why she had kept it back. It was by far the most valuable. She had forgotten how big and pure the diamonds were. The brooch commanded attention – it was so much larger than life, even for a piece of Edwardian jewellery. Like the woman who had first worn it. Too large, too aggressive for the other one, who had felt troubled and ill at ease with it pinned to her shoulder.

Then the bell rang and she realized David was outside and she wasn't ready. She put the brooch into her bag.

'Settle back,' he told her. 'We've got a long drive ahead. Had a good day?'

'Wonderful,' she said. 'Rowland rang up with a moan about the Grosvenor's project.'

'Stupid old fart,' he remarked, concentrating on the traffic. 'I don't know why you don't fire him. There are plenty of good people around who'd do his job.'

'Maybe,' she said. 'One day he'll go too far and I will. But not yet. He's very, very good, that's the trouble. Now let me tell you the really big news...' And she told him about the French order.

'Don't overreach yourself, that's the only danger.' It was good advice but he wasn't fooled by his own motive. He didn't want her to be too successful. He had other plans.

'Let's have some music,' she suggested, and he put on a tape. He had no appreciation of music, he just liked a soothing noise, and all the better if it sounded familiar. Nancy let the bland background harmonies and the rhythm of the windscreen wipers lull her into leaning back and closing her eyes.

And then the dream began. The child was hidden in the doorway watching, as the dainty figure floated towards the lover who whispered his invitation. 'In here, darling...' The guilty glance, the strange excited smile... And then the one who followed, hiding its evil from the light, a creeping shadow among shadows. The child's cry of warning that would never be heard.

David said harshly, 'You owe me an explanation, Nancy. What the hell is all this about?'

'You shouldn't have brought me here,' she said. 'You should have told me.'

14

'How was I to know?' he countered. 'How was I to know you weren't who you said you were? That this place had anything to do with you?'

'I'm sorry, that wasn't fair of me. David, let's go home? Leave things as they were – we've been so happy.'

'I'll still want that explanation,' he said. She had never seen him angry before. He wasn't a man to be taken lightly. He felt a fool. He felt deceived. He was right; he was entitled to know the truth about her.

'All right, David,' she said at last. 'All right. But please, leave me alone for a while. It isn't going to be easy for me. I'll change and come down as soon as I can.'

He went out without another word, and without looking at her.

She went to the windows again and drew the curtains fully back. The rain had stopped. The marble lovers were locked in their embrace for ever, a symbol of love where there had been so much hatred. The room was unrecognizable from the bedroom her Aunt Fern had shared in loveless union for so many years. It had been cluttered with ornaments and photographs, lacking in the flair and taste that characterized the other suites.

She felt cold and shivered. How ironic that of all the lovely rooms at Ashton she should find herself booked to spend the night in this one. She looked around her slowly, wondering if there was anything left of the woman who had lived here, any aura that had survived the transformation. Nothing. There was no atmosphere, no sense of the past. Perhaps unhappiness and bitterness did not survive. Only her grand-mother's magnificent apartments could provide an answer. Alice. She spoke the name aloud. Alice watching her from the canvas in the hall downstairs. She could feel her come to life. If there was any ghost at Ashton, it would be Alice. Not, please God, the other one, the sad little wanton who had flitted past her room

15

on the last night of her life. She had left no impression behind her.

Nancy changed into the black dress. It made her look even paler and her red hair more fiery. She pinned the big circle of diamonds to her shoulder. 'They suit you,' the long-stilled voice echoed down the years... 'You've got to be tall to wear them.' As she was tall.

'Maybe,' Nancy said aloud, 'maybe you meant me to come back.'

David was waiting downstairs. She went out into the corridor, the corridor of her nightmare, brilliantly lit now, warmly carpeted, welcoming. She closed the door and went down to face her past.

David chose a seat near the fire. The portrait of the famous Alice Vandekar looked down at him. He studied it. My grandmother, Nancy had said. It didn't mean as much to him as it should. His childhood hadn't been spent in surroundings like these. You didn't know much about millionaires in the back streets of Deptford. But then Nancy didn't know about that. She'd never pried into his background. Now he knew why. She hadn't asked questions because she didn't want to answer any. He ordered whisky. A couple in evening dress passed by; they looked at him and smiled. He looked away. There was a private dinner party in the French Room, the waiter explained, putting his drink down beside him. David didn't respond.

'Thanks,' he said. 'Get me a brochure from the desk, will you?' He'd read it before, but then he was interested in the photographs, the facilities and the prices. He had skipped the history of the house and the Vandekars. Now he read the introduction carefully: a famous house, built in the early eighteenth century on the site of a seventeenth-century royal hunting box. Bought in 1935 by Hugo Vandekar after his marriage to the American beauty Alice Holmes Fry, the house had been used as a convalescent home for RAF officers during the war. After the war it became famous for its lavish parties and gatherings of celebrities in politics and the arts. Alice Vandekar was one of the noted hostesses of the post-war period. Members of the royal family were entertained there, and signed photographs of the King and Queen and the Duke and Duchess of Gloucester, with many famous figures of stage and political life, were still on loan to the house. The furniture was mostly original, purchased when the house was sold by the Vandekar executors.

That didn't tell him much. But he had a feeling that something was left out. It was all a little too bland. What happened to the Vandekar millions? Why was the house sold?

'Hello,' said Nancy.

He looked up and put the booklet down. He saw a blaze of diamonds on her dress. He felt as if he'd been looking at her a few minutes earlier.

'I tried not to be too long,' she said.

'That's all right. What would you like to drink?'

'The same as you, I think.'

We were meant to be celebrating, he thought. Champagne, a special dinner. I've got a birthday present upstairs that I was going to give to her. It wouldn't look much beside that brooch.

'I've been reading this.' He held out the booklet. 'It doesn't say a great deal.'

'I don't suppose it does,' Nancy said. She didn't read it. 'Have you looked at the portrait?' She got up and went to stand in front of it.

David followed her. A member of the staff watched them from the other side of the hall. He was used to people admiring the picture. It was one of the focal points in the whole house. A beautiful work of art as well as a memorial to a fascinating woman.

'She was very beautiful,' Nancy said. 'It doesn't flatter her.'

The painted figure was just below lifesize, the work of a fashionable portrait painter in the fifties who said that the sitter had inspired him to do his best work. The woman was very slim, with a sensual body draped in a blue dress that was moulded to the breast and thigh. She was very blonde, with a white skin and dazzling blue eyes that seemed to follow you. The neck was exaggerated, a little too long, the bare arms and shoulders highlighted against the dark background. The expression was challenging, proud and provocative. She wore no jewellery except a glittering dab of light at her breast.

'There's a strong look of you,' David said. 'Isn't that the same as you're wearing... the same brooch?'

'Yes,' Nancy answered. 'She gave it to my mother as a wedding present and my mother left it to me.' She stood staring up at the picture. 'She hated cowards,' she said suddenly. 'She wouldn't be proud of the way I've run away. Let's sit down, David.'

He drank his whisky, waiting for her to speak. There was a look, a definite resemblance between that self-confident beauty in the portrait and the woman he had been going to ask to marry him that weekend. 'My real name is Vandekar. Alice Vandekar was my grandmother.' No wonder he sensed she was different.

'Why did you change your name?'

She looked at him, and he realized she had been far away, thinking of someone else. 'Vandekar's a famous name. You say you were born in this house. Why were you running away, Nancy?'

'It seemed the only thing to do,' she said. 'I wanted to make a new life, forget everything. I've just told you, I was a coward. You really want to know about my family? About me?'

'I really want to.' There was no give in him at all.

'It's a long story,' Nancy said quietly, 'and things may never be the same for us again... We all lived here together, my cousins Ben and Phyllis – they were my aunt's children – and my father and mother. This was our home, whether our parents had houses in London or not. Alice liked having the grandchildren.

At least she liked having me near her. I was always her favourite. But then she simply worshipped my father. You're still angry, aren't you?'

'No,' he said. 'Just curious. I've lived with you for six months and I don't know anything about you. It's a funny feeling.'

'I'm sorry. I wasn't deceiving you. For all these years I've been trying to deceive myself. If you want to understand, David, you've got to know about my grandmother. Let me start with Alice.'

2

June was truly glorious that year. Everyone agreed that the season opened with a spell of lovely weather. May was warm and delightful, so different from the dismal chilly late spring of 1933. Yes, 1934 was going to be a vintage year for people who wanted to enjoy themselves. The debutantes were pretty, some outstanding. One or two, like the young beauty from Boston, Alice Homes Fry, were a gift to the society columns. There were balls and cocktail parties and luncheons every week. The Derby, Royal Ascot, Henley, Cowes; country-house parties at weekends and nothing in the world to worry about except love affairs and which invitation to accept. For the rich, that is.

But Alice Holmes Fry, who had arrived in proper style on the *Queen Mary*, with her mother as chaperone and a ladies' maid, had just enough money to last the year in England. If she failed to catch a rich husband she would have to go home to Boston and take what she could get. Americans were sought after and popular; many were very rich and the less well-endowed bachelors with expensive houses to keep up and diminishing resources circled around the little pool of heiresses like hungry crocodiles, teeth bared in ingratiating smiles. They didn't trouble Alice. The Holmes Frys were Boston aristocracy; they had a well-documented Founding Father among their ancestors, but they weren't rich. Alice's father had seen to that. Gambling and women had eaten away what remained of a substantial inherited fortune. When he died there was not much left beyond a modest trust which had eluded him. Alice was twenty-two.

It was her idea to go to England. Her mother was described by friends and family as a sweet woman, by which they meant she was weak with her profligate husband and too stupid to see their ruin approaching. But Alice knew better. Alice knew it wasn't weakness or stupidity. Her mother loved him. And she always spoke of him as 'your dear father', even though he had died in another woman's bed.

Mother and daughter were so different, but they couldn't have been closer. Phoebe Holmes Fry was small and dark and inclined to plumpness. Alice, she thought proudly, was so like her father, with his bright blond hair and those amazing blue eyes. No wonder the women had run after him – it wasn't really his fault. Alice had his height and slender build, his magnetism, so that people clustered around her.

'Why go to England, sweetheart? You've got some nice young men just dying to propose, but you won't let them.'

'Mother,' Alice had said, 'they're dull and I'm not in love with any of them. I want someone special. There's no one special here.'

At least not interested in me. Daddy's final curtain exit hasn't helped my chances, but I'm not going to say that. She mustn't be hurt. He hurt her enough for a whole lifetime, the bastard. If we go to England I'll meet the sort of man I want. I know I will.

They booked into the Ritz. 'But sweetheart,' her mother had protested, 'we really can't afford to stay there!'

'We can't afford not to,' was Alice's answer. 'We must do it in style, Mother, or not at all. We've got to rent a house, where we can entertain, and it's got to be in the right part of the city. We've budgeted. We've got a year. Don't worry – everything will be fine, I just know it.'

'I don't know where you get all that confidence,' Phoebe said. 'Certainly not from me. Maybe your dear father...'

Alice turned away and said, 'Maybe.' She didn't want her expression to be seen.

They had personal introductions, and part of the expenditure was a fee to a lady of ancient lineage and very modest means who promoted and presented young ladies like Alice at Court. They met for tea in the Ritz two days after their arrival. Lady Margaret was slightly lofty in her attitude towards them. Phoebe felt intimidated, Alice irritated. She might be a duke's daughter, but she was getting paid.

When the plans were laid, the sandwiches and China tea and little cakes removed, she found a chance to remind her of it. A quartet was playing tunes from the latest musical successes in the West End. *Evergreen*, with an actress called Jessie Matthews. Alice wanted to see that.

'I think we've discussed everything,' Lady Margaret said, and gathered gloves and handbag. She was a tall, rangy woman who had once been good-looking in a rawboned way. The Court presentation had been arranged through the American Ambassador. She would accompany Alice to Buckingham Palace to make her curtsey before King George and Queen Mary. The invitation to the ball at Ashton had been difficult, but the Rushwells were old family friends and Lady Margaret had vouched for Miss Holmes Fry.

'How kind,' Phoebe said gently. 'You've taken so much trouble.'

Lady Margaret bestowed a wintry smile. They would never know, these rich Americans or, worst of all, their social-climbing English counterparts, how humiliated and depressed she felt at selling her friendships and her family connections in this way.

'Indeed you have,' Alice said, and her smile was very sweet. 'If I make a really good match, we'll just have to double your fee.' Then she shook hands and took her mother back up to their rooms.

'That wasn't at all tactful,' Phoebe said. 'Didn't you see how red she went when you said that about the fee?

22

You shouldn't have mentioned that, Alice. People like Lady Margaret don't like being reminded about money. I was most embarrassed!'

'I'm sorry, Mother. Sorry you were embarrassed, I mean. I thought she needed reminding, that's all. Don't worry. She won't change her mind. You mustn't let people like that walk over you. They're not doing us any favours. Isn't it wonderful about the Ashton ball? They say it's the most beautiful house in the whole of England!' The irrepressible enthusiasm had burst through again.

Phoebe couldn't help smiling. Darling Alice did have a temper, that was the trouble. She'd telephone Lady Margaret later and be extra nice. 'Who says?' she demanded. 'You haven't met anyone yet.'

'No, but it's in all the books on the grand country houses. I've seen a picture of it too. It's enormous. You see, I've been reading up on all these places and the families so I won't seem ignorant. They think all Americans are hicks. Not this one! Mother – telephone messages – we forgot! See if anyone has called already.'

'Nobody knows we're here,' her mother said. 'We've only been here for two days.'

But Alice was right. There were two messages, and one of them made Alice clap her hands and laugh with excitement. 'Cocktails with Lady Furness? Mother, isn't she . . .'

Phoebe held up a hand. 'Yes, she is, but you're not going to say it.' The mistress of the Prince of Wales. A fellow American who'd known Phoebe when they were girls. 'That's very sweet of her,' she said.

'I didn't expect to hear from her so soon. She'll be very helpful to you, sweetheart. She knows everyone.'

'I can't wait to see her,' Alice said. 'Even if I'm not allowed to say why.' She bent down and hugged her mother. 'Clever you to think of writing to her. I make all the noise but you do something really smart and never say a word. It's going to be wonderful; I'll be a great success. I'll make you proud of me.'

*

Hugo Vandekar was bored. He was staying in a boring house party in a chilly Victorian pile 15 miles from Ashton. The food was indifferent and the girls uninteresting. He wished he'd refused the invitation. He much preferred business to society. It was his mother who urged him to meet new young girls. At thirty-one and head of the family since his father died, she felt it was time he got married. She had confided to friends that she was in mortal fear of some smart divorcée snapping him up. Morals were so slack these days.

Hugo was very eligible. He made no claim to aristocratic birth – his grandfather had come over from Amsterdam and built a shipping empire, which had extended to include coal mines and industrial property. Hugo's father was equally shrewd. His forte was the stock market. He had made an incredible fortune after the Wall Street crash in 1929, picking up stock for nothing and waiting patiently till the American market recovered, and had started a private banking house in the city. He had died three years ago, but Hugo had been involved in the family business since he left Oxford. He was ready to take control. He had a younger brother, Phillip, who worked with him.

After a few duty dances, Hugo slipped away from his house party and sat drinking champagne in a small library near the main hall. The band was resting between numbers and there was a chattering noise, like a mad bird colony, emanating from three hundred people with nothing of importance to say.

'Are you lonely or just bored?'

He looked up quickly. She was blonde and very beautiful, but it was the boldness about her that surprised him. She stood with one hand touching her hip and stared down with amusement.

'I'm certainly not lonely,' he countered. American – he recognized the Boston vowel sounds.

'Then you must be bored. Or drunk. Are you drunk?'

He couldn't help it. 'Good heavens,' he said, 'of course I'm not drunk. What a thing to say!'

'Well, my partner is,' Alice responded. 'And that really *is* boring. You haven't seen him, I suppose? Freddie Cavendish – tall and dark with a moustache?'

He knew Freddie Cavendish by reputation. He was usually drunk at parties. 'I'm afraid not.'

She laughed. 'Oh well. I guess I'll have to go look somewhere else.' She disappeared back into the babble beyond. He got up and followed her.

She hadn't found Cavendish, but he noticed she was instantly surrounded by a hedge of young men. Someone said, 'Hello, Hugo – how are you? Didn't know you were here . . .'

'Very well,' he answered, not taking his eyes off the blonde girl. 'Do you know who that is . . . that girl over there in the blue dress?'

'Oh, you mean Alice Holmes Fry. Super, isn't she? A real stunner. Always getting quotes in the papers, you know.'

'I don't read the gossip columns,' Hugo said. He was disappointed. She hadn't seemed the type to court publicity. Every American girl said how thrilled she was to be in London and how divine it all was.

'Naughty little thing,' his companion went on. 'Says anything that comes into her head.'

'So I noticed,' Hugo answered.

'Are you interested? Do you want to meet her?'

'I've already done so. Excuse me.'

Alice saw him coming towards her, but pretended not to notice till he was right beside her. Then she turned and smiled. 'Why, hello.'

'I'm Hugo Vandekar,' he said.

'I'm Alice Holmes Fry.' She held out her hand. She gripped quite firmly, rather like a man shaking hands.

Hugo Vandekar. Millions and millions. And good-looking too. 'I didn't find Freddie,' she said. 'Maybe he's gone home.'

'More likely he's asleep somewhere. Come and

dance with me.' He slipped a hand under her arm to ward off anyone with the same idea. 'OK,' she said. 'Let's go.'

She was a very good dancer, but then so was he. They danced for most of the evening and he took her in to supper. She talked and laughed with infectious gaiety. Hugo was rather serious and proud of it. She made him feel that everything was fun. 'And this house,' she went on over supper, 'isn't it just gorgeous? I've been to a lot of parties since I came over – Belvoir and Clivedon for instance, but this is the most beautiful place I've ever seen. Don't you think so?'

'I've never thought about it,' he admitted. She was beautiful. He'd never seen eyes of that piercing blue before. Or that gold-coloured hair which was pinned and braided in defiance of the fashion for a neat bob. He wondered suddenly what she would look like naked, with that hair falling round her like a curtain. 'Have you been on the terrace?'

'No.'

'Then I'll take you out. It should be lit up and that is quite dramatic.'

'Oh, just look at that,' Alice said. She had forgotten him for a moment. They stood on a broad terrace. Other shadowy figures moved or stood entwined in the lee of the house. The moon was out – it glinted on a huge silver sheet of water in the distance, while a statue of nude lovers embraced in a single spotlight. It didn't seem erotic to her. It hadn't seemed so to Hugo either when he'd seen it a dozen times before with other women. Now he wanted to touch this girl so much he had to move away in case he lost control and took hold of her.

Alice said, 'Someone was saying the Rushwells were pretty hard up. They might have to sell it one day.'

'It's true of a lot of people. They never think of replacing what they spend. There's always a day of reckoning if you're careless.'

She thought, that's rather a cold thing to say, but

decided not to say it. 'I feel sorry for them,' she said. 'It would break my heart to lose this if I owned it. Shall we go back to the party?'

'Of course. Before we do, will you have dinner with me in London?'

He hadn't tried to kiss or maul her – that was a relief. He was more of a gentleman than some of the men she'd met.

And she liked him. She really did. 'I'd love to. I'm staying at the Ritz with my mother until we find a house. Give me a call there.'

Two months later he asked her to marry him and she accepted. The newspapers loved her for the quote that became famous.

'Only a very special man would do for me. Specially handsome, specially clever and specially rich!'

Mrs John Vandekar was furious and Hugo roared with laughter.

It was her wedding day. 18 April 1935. She woke quite early. The last day she would wake in a rented house in someone else's bed. The day that was going to make her the happiest girl in the world. She got up and pulled the curtains back. The sun shone. 'Happy the bride the sun shines on,' she said out loud, and laughed. It was so exciting; she had no nerves about the occasion, only feelings of elation. She'd promised her mother to make her proud, and she'd kept the promise. It would be the wedding of the year. St Margaret's, Westminster. A reception at Londonderry House, lent by the marchioness as a favour to the Vandekars. And the greatest coup of all, the future king of England would attend. She opened the door to the dressing room. Her wedding dress was draped over the dummy, a long sheath of white satin, demure and yet provocative because it fitted like a skin. Hartnell had made it. They hadn't sent a bill. That would come when she was Mrs Hugo Vandekar. A plain tulle veil and a wreath of silk lilies of the valley. No borrowed tiaras, no diamond necklaces. Just the circle of perfect stones which Hugo's mother had given her. Unwillingly, Alice suspected. But Alice was marrying the eldest son and it was a family tradition.

It was only eight o'clock. What a long time to wait – how could everyone be sleeping when she was awake and pulsing with energy and excitement? And hungry too. She rang the bell for her breakfast tray.

Phoebe came in later. Unlike Alice, she hadn't slept well. She was so happy for her darling girl, but a little sad for herself. It would be lonely without Alice. But Hugo was such a fine man, responsible and sensible, and *so* much in love it was quite touching to see him and Alice together. He'd take care of Alice – she needn't worry about her daughter in his hands. And Alice, bless her, would continue to brighten his life. She was extraordinary, Phoebe thought, seeing the empty breakfast tray and the clear, bright face without a trace of nervous tension. She struck sparks off people, like an electric charge. Hugo had said to her once, 'You know, Alice makes me feel as if the sun was shining. She has this marvellous gift for enjoying life and making people enjoy it too. I can't thank you enough for her.' And he'd bent and kissed Phoebe's cheek. For a remote man, sparing with his affections, this was a great compliment. She had blushed with pleasure.

'You're awake so early,' she said. 'And breakfasted already? I couldn't eat a thing!'

'Don't be so edgy, Mother – you'll only feel faint in the church if you don't eat. There's nothing to be nervous about. And I want you to enjoy everything as much as I shall.' Alice reached over and squeezed her hand. 'I couldn't have done it without you. You sold your things to raise the money to come to England . . . I know all about it. I'm going to buy them all back for you, Granny's necklace and earrings and anything else you sold to Tiffany's. No, don't look like that, I found the bill of sale before we left home. You shouldn't be so

28

careless leaving things about!' She giggled suddenly. 'Poor Hugo's going to be broke by the time I've finished with him. Shall I call him and say hello?'

Phoebe was shocked. 'No, of course not. You can't just talk on the telephone as if this were an ordinary day! He's got to see you coming down that aisle looking like a queen. You're not to think of calling him.'

'He's probably on the phone to his broker,' Alice said.

'Oh, Alice... you mustn't say things like that.'

'I say it to his face. All he thinks about is money and me, or me and money, I hope. He laughs. Mother darling, if I'd been some mealy-mouthed minnie, he wouldn't have looked at me. I put up a fight and he thinks it's marvellous. He loves it. And I love him.'

She threw back the bedclothes, pulled on her dressing gown and poked her feet into her slippers. She had beautiful feet and long, elegant legs.

'You really do love him, don't you?' Phoebe said. 'It's not just because he's rich and you've got carried away?' She'd asked the same question when they became engaged. Alice had loved her for it then. How many mothers, faced with such a rich son-in-law and permanent security, would have risked asking such a question.

'I do love him,' she said. 'And I'm not the kind that gets carried away, believe me. He's everything I want. He's clever, he's interesting, he's got the best sense of humour, we never stop laughing, and I'm going to love being married to him. He wants a family; I want to be the best wife in the world to him. We're going to be blissful together. I know it. Now Mother darling, I'm going to run my bath. I'll see you later. And mind you eat something!'

It was Hugo's wedding day. His valet woke him with tea at seven and he asked about the weather.

'It looks like a fine morning, sir.'

'Good. We can't have it raining today, can we?'

'No. Certainly not, sir. Shall I bring breakfast later or would you like it now?'

'Now, I think. And some aspirin.'

The valet smiled. 'They're on the teatray sir. In case you needed them.'

His bachelor party had gone on well past midnight and ended in a nightclub, where Hugo had refused to celebrate his last night of freedom by taking one of the pretty dance hostesses upstairs. But he had drunk a lot of champagne, followed by brandy, and he had a headache. It was a fatal combination. He was usually very careful not to start the day with a hangover. He hadn't wanted to sleep with the girl. One of his friends had taken her on instead. He'd laughed off the jokes at his expense. He couldn't explain that his hunger was for one woman and no others could rouse him. If the wretched girl had stripped off in front of him, he wouldn't have reacted. All he could think of was holding Alice in his arms that night, undressing Alice, pulling the long hair down and spreading it through his fingers. He wanted her so much it was like a sickness. From the moment on the terrace at Ashton she roused a passion he had never experienced before. Many women had come and gone through his life. He had fancied he was in love with some of them. He indulged a powerful sexual appetite without any scruple. He knew that his money was an attraction to women, his bachelor status even more so. He had pursued and been pursued but never caught. Alice had not attempted to catch him. He had been entrapped by her independence and her gaiety. And by the sexual aura of which she seemed quite unaware.

His mother didn't like her, Hugo knew that. His brother Phillip was admiring, but he was still too much his mother's boy to have a favourable view of Alice. Hugo didn't care. He didn't care what anyone thought because this was the girl he was going to marry and that was the end of it. And she was strong. He had watched the contest between his mother and his fiancée, and Alice won without much difficulty. He loved his mother, but his father only tolerated stupid women and Hugo's mother was very stupid. Alice was clever. Strong-willed, impulsive, highly intelligent. A challenge that would rise up and face him all through their married life, he realized that.

He was marrying her that day. The ritual and the snobbery didn't concern him. Nor did the service. He was not religious. Nor, he was sure, was she. He knew she was a virgin. Not because she told him, but because he'd known too many impostors to be deceived. Alice was innocent in her own way.

He didn't even think of taking her to bed. He was keeping that, whetting his own appetite and hers by deliberate self-control. He didn't want a hole-and-corner seduction to spoil the climax of their wedding. He wanted to conquer that provocative sexuality and prove that he could master it. And her. Then offer her the world.

It was indeed the wedding of the year. The society columnists went into ecstasies over the bride's dress, the handsome bridegroom; they gushed over the distinguished guests – twelve hundred of them – the splendid reception at Londonderry House. It was lavish, glittering, romantic. The superlatives flowed like the champagne. And then the final accolade. The Prince of Wales attended the reception.

Alice and Hugo were standing together; the receiving line had come to an end at last. Alice had shaken so many hands her own felt numb. The Prince arrived late; Hugo's mother had begun to panic that he might not be coming. But there he was, advancing towards them. Alice curtsied. She didn't get a chance to examine him properly. Lady Furness, who'd been so kind when they first came to London, wasn't his mistress any more. Her good friend Wallis Simpson had replaced her. He murmured a few words – he had a flat, rather metallic voice. She watched him move into the crowd. People made way for him. He joined a small, very slim woman in an exquisitely cut blue dress.

'What did he say to you?' Alice wanted to know.

'Nothing much,' Hugo answered. 'Just said how charming you looked, wished us happiness.'

'He said that to me. I looked charming, I mean, not you! Is that her – in the blue?'

'Yes, it is. Don't stare, darling. We should move round and talk to people. And he's wrong. You don't look charming. You look beautiful.' He raised her hand and kissed it. She looked up at him and he saw the expression in her eyes. For a moment he trembled. His wild one, he called her. She was gazing at him with real love. That look promised everything.

She said, 'Why darling, you've got the shakes. You must have been a naughty boy at your dinner last night!'

'It's tonight I'm thinking about,' he whispered.

'Me too,' Alice said. 'Won't it be wonderful to be just on our own – just the two of us? I guess we better mingle. It'll soon be time to cut the cake.' Hugo watched her as she entered the crowd. He was so proud of her. She hadn't faltered throughout the long wedding ceremony. She had carried herself with dignity and grace, and he'd never forget that look, more valuable to him than any vows.

The bridal suite was booked at the Amstel. Amsterdam was a beautiful city, one of the most romantic in the world. And so special to him. He wanted to show her the little house by the Zeeden Bridge where three generations of Vandekars had been born and died before old Adam moved to London and began to build a trading empire. Alice would love it. He could see her talking to a group of young men. Men were fascinated by her. He would have to be careful with Alice. Only a fool would be complacent.

'Hugo.' He turned. His younger brother was beside him. Phillip had been his best man. They had never been rivals. Even as very small boys, Hugo's dominance was accepted.

'Well, you did it,' Phillip said. 'You've actually got her to the altar! I must say, she's a stunning girl. I've been sent over to tell you it's time to cut the cake. Mother and I have been talking to La Simpson. She makes the Little Man dance attendance on her like a bloody waiter. I've got the notes for our speeches. I'll put yours on the table for you.'

'I'll get Alice,' Hugo said. He could sympathize with his future king's obsession. He wanted Alice with him every moment.

It was a wonderful wedding, ending, as all wonderful weddings should, with a laughing departure in a flurry of rice and real rose petals. Mrs John Vandekar waved them away, with her son Phillip beside her. She said goodbye to her daughter-in-law's mother. She was just a little tired, she explained, and her doctor had insisted that she go home to Sussex and have an early night.

Phoebe accepted the lie with her usual simplicity. It had been an emotional day, she agreed. But wasn't it just wonderful? Weren't they the handsomest couple, and so much in love? Tears brimmed in her eyes.

Mrs Vandekar said yes, indeed, and please excuse her but her chauffeur was bringing round the car and she had a long drive ahead of her. She was not going any farther than the house in St James's Square, where a dinner for thirty close friends and relatives had been planned long before. She disliked sentimentality and that silly woman's wet eyes had irritated her. Mrs Vandekar was practical, sound and not at all clever. She felt that Hugo had made a thoroughly bad choice. But he was the head of the family and she would have to make the best of it. She wished he had settled on a nice English girl. These American women were so assertive. She looked quickly at her younger son. Phillip was a good boy. A lightweight, his father called him, but then he was such a harsh judge of his sons.

Phillip was a dear, and he wouldn't marry anyone she didn't approve of, she felt quite confident of that.

She slipped her hand through his arm. 'I shall miss Hugo,' she said. 'But, thank goodness, I've got you. I don't like her, Phillip. I don't know what it is about her, but there's something... I do hope Hugie will be happy with her.'

'Mother,' said her younger son, 'don't worry about Hugie. He can take care of himself. Give Alice a chance. She's very American. She'll mellow. And she won't let him walk all over her either, and that's no bad thing. Now cheer up, we'll have a jolly good party tonight.'

The flight was exciting. The plane bumped in air pockets and Alice clung to her new husband and laughed. Nothing frightened her. She had no nerves, no anticipation of disaster. Everything was an adventure. Looking at her flushed cheeks and bright eyes, as they lurched in some really unpleasant turbulence, Hugo thought what a splendid man she would have made, and then thanked God she wasn't.

As it grew calmer and they came in to land at the airport, he pointed out to her the gleaming network of canals, shining like silver ribbons through the city. 'I love it,' he said, 'I come three times a year. I feel it's part of me, I feel as if I am coming home whenever I see that view.'

'Well, you're part Dutch, darling, so it's not surprising,' Alice said.

He hadn't told her where they were going till they were driving to the airport. She had rather hoped for Paris. Amsterdam made her think of tulips and those round, red-skinned cheeses. But Hugo said the Amstel was one of the greatest hotels in Europe, so that would be nice.

It didn't disappoint her. Neither did the charming old city itself as they drove through. She exclaimed over the quaint gabled houses fronting onto a sweep of canal. There were windowboxes everywhere, filled with tulips – what else? – but it was colourful and neat, like a picture-book town.

The Amstel was as grand as he had promised. They had a suite overlooking the canal and there were great banks of flowers in their rooms. Trunks and suitcases were brought up. Hugo wouldn't let her bring a ladies' maid. The hotel had offered to engage someone suitable, and they had. A pleasant Dutch woman with reasonable English came to help her change out of her travelling suit. Champagne was waiting in their sitting room.

Hugo had changed too. He wore a short silk dressing gown. He gave her a full glass. 'To us, my darling,' he said. 'I'm going to make you the happiest girl in the world.'

He was fast asleep. She could hear his deep breathing in the darkness. As soon as she could, she eased herself away from him, inching to the very edge of the bed. She couldn't bear to touch him. He was naked and, despite all her protests, so was she. When he slept she was able to cry. She let the tears run down her face until the hollows at the base of her neck were wet.

She wasn't hurt. He had been so considerate, so gentle, assuring her over and over again that the horrible things he was doing would be lovely for her too. 'Just relax with me, my darling, don't tighten up against me . . .' She had wanted to strike out at him, tear herself free. But she couldn't. This was the much-vaunted wedding night, this disgusting ordeal.

She couldn't blame him or say that he had been rough or selfish. His gentleness and restraint had made it worse. In trying to arouse her, he prolonged the agony.

Men had kissed her, tried to take liberties. Her first admirer was a cousin who had fumbled with her clothes when she was seventeen and retreated with a slapped face.

It was easy to fend off what she didn't like: she had her reputation to consider and a good, rich marriage as her aim. She wasn't ignorant. She knew all the facts and viewed them without enthusiasm or alarm. Other girls said what a man did to you was thrilling, and she accepted that it probably was since so many people made fools of themselves on account of it. Sex made the world go round. She remembered that axiom and felt sick. Really sick, so that she slipped out of bed and into the bathroom, heaving into the basin. Nothing came up.

She saw herself in the bright looking glass. A dishevelled, naked stranger stared back at her. Her mouth was sore, her chin and neck irritated by his rough skin. There were red blotches on her breasts, marks all over her.

She felt dirty, sweat-stained and defiled by his emission into her body.

She said out loud, in a voice full of anger, 'Goddamn it, I need a bath!'

It was 4 a.m. and there was no hot water. She plunged into the bath and scrubbed herself in the icy water.

He'd want to do it again. And again and again. Two weeks' honeymoon – she remembered him apologizing that it was so short, but he had so many business commitments. God, if it had been a whole month, like most people took . . . She rubbed herself dry and got warm. The icy bath had pulled her together. She couldn't panic. She mustn't let him see how much she hated what he was pleased to call lovemaking. It wasn't his fault; she kept that in view. She just didn't like it. That wasn't so unusual. Lots of women put up with their husbands. Some were downright glad when their husbands had affairs and stopped bothering them. 'Shut your eyes and think of England.' How she'd laughed at that.

Those stuffy, toothy women with their smelly dogs and horses. What attractive man would want to wake

36

up and find one of *those* on the pillow? It all sounded so easy. All you had to be was beautiful, like her, smart and quick-witted, and a little daring, and the Hugo Vandekars fell into your lap like ripe apples off a tree. Fell into your lap was right. Ugh.

She left the towels on the floor and picked her way back through the darkness towards the bed. Her nightdress was on the ground where he had dropped it. She put it on. The pure silk georgette felt cold but at least she was covered. She felt protected again. He hadn't woken. She curled up to get warm, careful not to make contact with him.

You'll have to put up with it. I won't. You've got to. You've got to face the facts. He's your husband. You can't say no. Maybe, but I can think of an excuse. I can say no sometimes, for God's sake. What am I – a piece of meat?

She lay wide awake in the darkness, until light crept round the curtain edges.

Hugo found the bed empty when he woke. He sat up, calling for her. Poor sweetheart, he knew she'd found it difficult. He wanted to make it up to her, show her that from now on it would be easier. She came out of the bathroom, wrapped in frothy white georgette and lace, her hair hanging like a river down her back.

'Alice,' he said and started to get up and come towards her. 'What have you been doing? Are you all right?'

She kept her eyes on his face. She didn't want to look at him and see that whole bloody business was starting again.

'Oh, darling,' she said. 'Darling, I'm so sorry. I don't know how it happened, but I've got the curse!'

He accepted the lie. He loved her and he argued with himself that perhaps he had expected too much. She had always been rather a prude. Imagining how he would teach her the pleasures of making love had excited him. There had been no pleasure for her, and he felt guilty. That guilt bought her a little time.

She was too high-spirited, too febrile. She laughed and talked and wouldn't sit still. She wanted to go everywhere, see everything. And at night he let her fall asleep beside him and then gently took her in his arms. She must come to him in her own time. He must build up her confidence.

He took her to the house where his grandfather was born. It was privately owned but they were allowed to wander round. Hugo held her hand. She seemed quieter, more relaxed. 'He was a clever old devil,' he said. 'I can't remember much about him, he was so old when I was born. I didn't know my grandmother, but my father said they were devoted. When we have a son, I'd like to call him Adam, after the old chap. Would you mind, darling?'

'I think it's a lovely name,' Alice said.

She thought the house was dark and cramped, the furnishings heavy and too ornate. But she wouldn't let him know. He loved it all and it was part of him. A son, he'd said. She didn't want to think about that. For three days she'd kept them both at running pace. He drank rather a lot in the evenings. Sometimes she thought he looked unhappy. That added to her anxiety. He didn't deserve to be miserable. She loved him. She wanted to make him happy. But the one thing that would do so filled her with a sick disgust.

They went to the Ryksmuseum, and she forced herself to tease him to raise both their spirits. 'I don't know what all the fuss is about. I don't think Rembrandt's all that special. Now there, over there, darling... that's what I call a painting!'

'Yes,' he said, 'I think most people would agree with you.'

Vermeer's picture of a girl reading a letter was so fresh and alive that Alice said. 'You could reach in and touch her, it's so real. And there's such peace. Such a lovely serene feeling. I wish I was like that.'

He smiled at her. 'I don't think it would suit you.

Perhaps when you're a very old lady surrounded by children and grandchildren. You might sit still and pretend to be serene. But not for long, darling. Let's go back now, shall we? We've been sightseeing all day.'

They dined in the hotel. He ordered champagne to be served in their room. He gave her a glass when they came upstairs.

'How are you feeling, my darling?'

'Well, a little... you know.'

'Drink that; it'll make you feel better.'

I can't pretend any longer, Alice thought. I know by the way he's looking at me. I knew all through dinner. If I drink, maybe it'll help...

He took her on his knee. He stroked her breast and slid his hand into her lap. 'Hugo,' she started to say, but he kissed her and his hands went on moving over her body, sliding under her skirt, pulling at her under-clothes to expose her. With a fierce effort she pulled away and jumped up.

She lost her head as he came towards her. She bumped into the table and the champagne glass fell on the floor and broke.

'No!' she shouted. 'No! Don't come near me! I've told you, I can't!'

He didn't see the fear in her eyes. He heard the angry cry with its note of revulsion and lost his temper.

'You can,' he said 'And by Christ you will!'

His fantasy became reality. He mastered her only because he was the stronger one. She tore at him with her nails – he didn't even notice. When it was over she wept and sobbed herself to sleep. The seduction he had planned degenerated into a furious rape, fought out by both of them. At one point she had screamed at him, 'I hate you! I hate you!'

When she woke the next morning the bed was empty. She was sore and bruised. She hoped she had hurt him. Some of her nails were broken. She burst into tears. 'Oh, my God, my God, what am I to do?' He'd behaved like an animal, holding her down on the bed, making her submit. For a few moments she gave way to hysteria, weeping and throwing herself against the pillows.

She couldn't stay, she couldn't face him. 'Mother, Mother,' she cried as if she were a frightened child again calling in the dark. Slowly she grew calmer.

Exhausted emotionally, Alice stopped crying. The panic ceased. She couldn't run away. She couldn't walk out and go back to London. How many days since that wedding, she and Hugo playing the star parts before the world – go back and admit that it was a disaster? Be whispered about and scorned, because, of course, the truth would come out.

'She can't bear sex, you see ... Poor Hugo. I heard she wouldn't consummate the marriage ...'

She could just imagine what they'd say. What a scandal, what a juicy divorce it would be, with the press leering at them both.

She got up. She said out loud, 'No. No, I can't face that. I won't. I don't know what the hell I'm going to do, but I won't run away. And now, Alice Holmes Fry, you're going to bathe and go down to breakfast.'

Hugo had been walking. He left the Amstel early in the morning and set out to walk through the city. It was bright and clear; industrious Dutch housewives were already sweeping their doorsteps. They said good morning as he passed. The shops were opening; barges processed down the canal, followed by sweeps of scavenging seagulls. There was a bite of sea air in the breeze.

It was a glorious day in the making and he was more unhappy than he had ever been in his life.

He was so ashamed. Frustration and rejection had made him behave like a brute. Finding her sleeping beside him when he woke, he had been stricken with guilt. But he didn't touch her. There was no use apologizing or trying to explain. There was no going back after what had happened. He got up to walk the streets and try to think what to do.

And on that walk, alone among the busy morning crowds, Hugo recognized one inescapable fact. The girl he loved was frigid. Not inexperienced, not shy – God knows Alice wasn't shy – but frigid. Revolted by sexual love and unable to conceal it. The vibrant personality, the flirtatious, provocative manner hid a cold, inhibited core that saw human intercourse as a disgusting ordeal. She hadn't realized it before they married; he didn't doubt that. They were both taken unawares. He stopped at a little café. The sun danced on the surface of the canal, a wharf cat slunk past him, fat on discarded fish entrails. He drank some coffee and tried to imagine what would happen when he went back and they came face to face.

They could get a divorce. It would take time and he would have to provide evidence. The real reason couldn't be told. He wouldn't do that to Alice, or to his own family. No scandal. Nobody benefited in the end. He pushed the cup away, called for the bill. He'd been wandering for over two hours. He had to go back. Perhaps she would be willing to talk to him. Perhaps even now something could be worked out, because he loved her, and at times, despite everything, he believed that Alice had loved him.

Inside the hotel foyer he hesitated. He was surprised by his own cowardice. He went into the dining room to delay the moment and found Alice sitting there.

'Good morning,' she said, 'I've just ordered breakfast.'

He approached her slowly. 'Alice ... I've been out walking ...'

'I thought you must have,' she said. 'Aren't you going to have breakfast? All that air must have given you an appetite.'

He sat down. 'What can I say to you? What are we going to do?'

She paused for a moment, opened her bag and lit a cigarette. He had never seen her smoke before evening.

She inhaled, puffed out the smoke and then said, 'I'm not going to do anything. We're married. That's the end of it. I'll try and adjust, if that suits you.'

'What does that mean?' he asked her. She was so cold and artificial he began to feel angry. 'I hate you,' she'd said. There was no passion left in her now, not even the humanity of hatred. She had withdrawn completely.

'Adjust to married life,' she said. 'I don't like it, but unless you want a divorce and all the messy details coming out, we should be able to reach some kind of agreement.'

'I see,' he said. 'A business deal, is that what you mean?'

'You needn't make it sound like that. We've made a mistake. Either we admit it and suffer the consequences or we try to work something out. I'm willing, if you are.' She stubbed out the cigarette with such force it broke in half.

He said in a low voice, 'Alice, you're my wife and I love you. I'm sorry about last night, but that won't alter the real problem.'

Alice interrupted him. 'I don't want to talk about that. Never, please. Why don't we just go on as if nothing had happened? We'd planned to go to the Hague today – why don't we go?'

'And when we come back,' he countered. 'What do we do – ask for separate rooms? I won't do that. I won't pretend in public and have you say no to me when we're alone.'

She looked at him. The beautiful eyes were red-rimmed under the heavy make-up. For a moment he saw her misery and it matched his own.

'I won't say no to you,' she said. 'But that's all I can promise.'

Two days later, as they were dressing for dinner, Alice said, 'Amsterdam is fun, but I would like to spend a few days in Paris.'

'We'll go tomorrow,' Hugo said. 'I'll ask them to telegraph to the Crillon for a suite.'

She turned and smiled at him. 'Thank you, darling. You're an angel.'

He chartered a plane and they landed at Orly the next afternoon. They went shopping in the morning and he bought her a sable coat from Revillion and a diamond bracelet from Cartier. They dined and danced at Maxim's. And Alice kept her promise. She let him make love as often as he wanted, and it seemed that this only increased his desire.

The more she eluded him, the more sexually infatuated with her he became, the more he indulged her and lavished attentions upon her. They never discussed what was happening. They paraded in public, at the races, the opera, held hands and smiled, and refused to admit that their marriage was a disaster.

They went on to the South of France because Alice suggested it. They gambled at the Casino in Cannes, where Hugo won and Alice lost. 'You're always so lucky with money, darling,' she said.

The press was waiting when they landed at Croydon. The morning papers carried photographs. 'Mr and Mrs Hugo Vandekar, the millionaire banker and his beautiful wife, returned from their honeymoon yesterday.' Alice read the papers in bed the next morning. Hugo's mother Beatrice had retired to the hideous Victorian family home in Sussex, leaving them the house in St James's Square while they looked for somewhere of their own.

Hugo had left very early before she woke. And last night he had said he would sleep in his dressing room. 'I have a lot of work to catch up on, sweetheart, so I'll be up very early and I don't want to wake you.'

Alice had laughed and said brightly, 'Seven o'clock sounds like the middle of the night to me! You go off to your stuffy old bank, darling, and I'll just miss you till you come home.'

She went to bed alone and slept long and deeply.

She felt different. Everything familiar about herself was changed. She was living a lie and acting a part, and her body was not her own any more. It belonged to someone else. She didn't cry any more when Hugo was asleep. It was possible to endure him because now he made no attempt to arouse her and expected no response. The pattern of their life had already taken shape. She gave him what he wanted and in return he indulged every extravagant whim.

She rang for breakfast. There was a silver vase with a single white rose on the tray. That was Hugo's idea, no doubt. She felt suddenly irritated. She looked at the girl who had brought the tray. 'Who ordered this? This silly vase with a flower in it?'

The girl blushed. 'The housekeeper, madam. Mrs Vandekar always has a rose on her breakfast tray.'

'Well, I'm Mrs Vandekar now,' Alice snapped, 'and I don't! Take it away please.'

So long as they were living in this house it was going to be run her way. Anyone who didn't like it could go elsewhere. She was sorry she'd been rude to the maid. She recognized her as a parlourmaid and wondered why she had brought up breakfast. In the strict working practices of domestic life, that was not her job.

Alice decided she wouldn't waste time. She'd call her mother – it would be lovely to see her, but she'd have to lie and pretend that everything was wonderful. She wouldn't think about that. A few words would assure Phoebe that all was well – she was the most trusting soul in the world. Then she would call the house agents and start things moving.

After only one night in the Vandekar house, Alice found it getting on her nerves. That dull old woman's hallmark was everywhere, from the dreary decorations to the heavy furniture and pictures. Light and grace and elegance were what she wanted, a house she could mould into a home of her own. It had to be Hugo's money, but it would be her individual style.

She rang the bell again and the same girl appeared.

'Would you run my bath, please?'

'Certainly, madam. How do you like the water?'

'Warm, not hot. And don't put in any bath salts or essences. What's your name?' The girl had a calm, direct manner that Alice liked. Servility annoyed her.

'Parker.'

'I mean your Christian name.'

'Lily, madam.'

'OK, I shall call you Lily. How long have you worked here?' Alice went on talking while an idea formed.

'Eight months. I'm under parlourmaid, but the young girl Mrs Cooper engaged as chambermaid gave notice the day before you and Mr Hugo came back. That's why I brought your breakfast tray this morning.'

'I'd like you to bring it every morning,' Alice said. 'Do you know how to take care of clothes? Can you sew?'

'I'm a good dressmaker – so was my mother.' What's she on about, Lily Parker wondered, but nothing showed in her face.

'Then I'd like you to look after me,' Alice announced. 'I'll tell Mrs Cooper that I'm taking you over. For as long as I'm staying here anyway.'

'Very good, madam,' Lily said. She went in to test the bathwater. 'I'm taking you over...' She hadn't been asked. What would have happened if I'd said no, she wondered. Sacked, most likely. 'I think the water's just right,' she said.

'Thank you, Lily.'

Lily went out, closing the door. She did everything with a quiet dignity that Alice liked. She had a direct way with her and looked you in the eye, without being impudent or familiar.

Lily didn't hurry back downstairs. What would Mrs Cooper think when she heard she was losing her. Not too pleased, she felt sure. But if she did the job well and made herself indispensable to Mrs Hugo, she might take a big step up the ladder. Next to the housekeeper and the nanny, no one had more prestige than the ladies' maid.

Lily Parker didn't know it, nor did Alice as she stepped into the bath which was exactly the right temperature, but their lives would interlock for over half a century.

'You mustn't give up hope, Mrs Vandekar.'

'Sir John, if what you say is true, what's going to change it?'

He shook his head. So many rich and famous people came to his consulting rooms; few had a more tragic or intractable problem than this beautiful young woman. And beyond the bald statement of the facts, there was no cure he could offer.

'You could go to an analyst,' he said. 'But the treatment can take years and there's no guarantee of its success. I've had a number of patients who found it actually made their symptoms worse. An intelligent person like yourself can do as much to help herself. You have an aversion to sex. Coming to terms with your feelings and accepting them may relax the tension for you. And perhaps you won't judge him quite so harshly after a time. That would help you too.'

Alice got up. 'If you're suggesting that I forgive my father, please don't bother. Thank you for seeing me.'

'Goodbye, Mrs Vandekar. Don't hesitate to come again if you feel it would help.' They shook hands. He noticed the firm, unfeminine grip. 'Goodbye, Sir John.'

And the set of that determined jaw. Not much there of the gentle, compliant mother she'd described so affectionately. Ironically, more like the father she hated. And that hatred had distorted her sexual development. He felt very sorry for her. Sorrier still for the husband. It was just possible that pregnancy might help, but he doubted it.

Outside the consulting room Alice paused by the

46

receptionist. 'I'd like to pay the bill now, if that's possible.'

'Yes, of course.' A number of Sir John's patients didn't want his account going to their homes. She made out a bill and Alice wrote a cheque.

'Thank you, Mrs Vandekar. Shall I make another appointment?'

'No thank you.'

She watched Alice go out. Who would have thought it? All that money, all that publicity. What was the problem, she wondered. Not drink surely. She didn't look the type. There was a vogue for cocaine sniffing among a certain group. She wasn't one of those either. And she looked too self-contained to suffer from what was commonly known as nerves. Oh well – she allowed herself a twinge of complacency – money and good looks didn't always equal happiness. She went into the waiting room and asked the next patient to come through.

Alice had come in a taxi. When she walked out into Wimpole Street it was drizzling. She hadn't brought an umbrella and there were no taxis. She walked quickly, pulling up her collar. She felt slightly sick now that the ordeal was over. His explanation made sense in a way, and no sense at all in another. Why had she been afflicted? Other women had broken homes behind them, disreputable parents, scandals. Why weren't they affected? Perhaps many of them were. She didn't know. She didn't want to think about it any more. I'm glad I went, she said to herself. I'd have felt a coward if I hadn't. But now I wish I hadn't. I wish I could forget everything he said and I said. It's made me feel like hell, sick and shaking all over. I can't tell Hugo, I can't tell anyone. Oh, there's a taxi . . . 'Taxi!'

I don't want to go home, not yet. Where can I go to calm down . . . ? 'Gunters, please,' she said. It was the first place she could think of. She could sit down and have tea. It was quite early – there wouldn't be anybody there.

But Alice had just sat down at a table when two women she knew came into the elegant tearoom and, seeing her, hurried over. She couldn't escape, so she steeled herself to smile and agreed to join them. And then, in the middle of the flow of lighthearted gossip about clothes and parties and mutual friends, she heard one say, 'You know Johnny Rushwell's decided to sell Ashton? Isn't it a shame? But he told my mother they just couldn't afford to keep it up.'

'Ashton?' Alice repeated. She couldn't believe what was being said. 'You mean it's for sale?'

'Yes, darling. I told you. There's not much money in the family and it's so expensive to run. By the way, have you found a house yet?'

'No,' Alice said. 'Not yet. Nothing that we really like.' She wasn't really listening any more. She felt unbearable excitement, where a little time ago she had been sickened and depressed. She forgot about the consultation with Sir John Edge. She couldn't believe that the wonderful house that had fired her imagination that night was actually coming up for sale. 'Darlings,' she said, 'I must run. Can I have the bill, please?'

The rain had stopped and the sun was breaking through. And there was a taxi drawing up at the most famous tearooms in London with a man and a girl getting out. Alice gave them a brilliant smile and took it over. Ashton. It was fate. When Hugo came home she rushed to meet him with the news. Guess what – the wonderful historic house where they'd first met – it was for sale! Wouldn't it be marvellous to own it and live there? Oh Hugo, isn't it exciting! Her enthusiasm swept his objections aside. And besides, he hadn't seen her look so animated and happy for a long time. Of course it was too far from London, but they could surely get a smaller place, even a flat . . . Oh, couldn't they call up the Rushwells and at least make sure it was true, and then maybe they could go down and see it?

He hadn't the heart to say anything but 'Yes, darling, telephone if you want to,' and she rushed away to ring immediately.

Scenting a prompt solution to their financial problems, Lord and Lady Rushwell invited Alice and Hugo down for that weekend.

Previous plans were cancelled on both sides, and as they drove up to the house in daylight Hugo had to admit that Alice was right in one respect. It was breathtaking in its beauty. The pale stone glowed almost white in the sunshine, the tall windows diamond bright. Its symmetry was completed by two sweeping wings, and the majestic portico at the centre of the main block rose three storeys high. The gravel drive was not well kept – he noticed potholes here and there – and there was a sinister crack along one pediment near the roof. It would need money, a lot of money. But nothing could quell Alice's enthusiasm. 'Think of the wonderful parties we could give,' she whispered as they toured the rooms with their host. There was a good shoot and hunting with the Leicestershire... and of course it needed completely redecorating, but if he left that to her she'd perform miracles...

They could indeed have lavish house parties; they could impress his friends in the United States and make useful business connections. He believed in the American economy and was arguing in favour of moving many of the family's interests out of Europe. He distrusted the political trends in Germany and despised France, which seemed unstable and corrupt.

A house like Ashton could certainly pay for itself in terms of prestige and making powerful friends. And he knew that Alice was determined to have it. She didn't try to hide her feelings. She praised everything, and Lady Rushwell blessed her for it. Bad enough to leave the grand old house she'd come to as a bride. How much more painful to hear it criticized in an attempt to

49

negotiate the price. They were given one of the nicest bedrooms, with a glorious view over the parterre and the lake.

Hugo took Alice in his arms. 'Yes, darling,' she said, 'of course,' answering the silent question. He made love to her, and afterwards she sat up and switched on the light. She had tried so hard. She had thought of everything the wise old specialist had told her, but there had been no miracle. 'You know, I think if we lived here, we could be very happy.'

Hugo didn't answer. He felt deflated and depressed. She'd tried; she'd come as close to shamming as it was possible, but he wasn't deceived. He couldn't touch her, no matter what he did. He held and used an empty body, from which she had escaped until it was over. Now she talked of being happy, as if this house could ever change her. If she tried to bribe him into buying it, he would never forgive her.

'Why happier here than anywhere else?' he asked.

Alice looked at him. 'Because we could make it a home, build it up together into what we wanted. We need something like this, darling, to bind us a bit closer. I think it would help.'

He said, 'We'll talk about it tomorrow. Good night.'

In the morning, after breakfast and morning service in the chilly little Norman church, they asked the Rushwells to excuse them while they went for a walk. It was mid-September and the glorious reds and golds of autumn splashed the landscape with fiery colour. They didn't walk far. They stopped arm in arm by the lake. Two hundred years before a Rushwell ancestor had dredged and excavated and diverted a river on his estate to provide this marvellous water view from his house. Hugo thought suddenly, I could teach a boy to sail here.

'Well?' Alice tugged at his arm. 'I can't stand another minute of it – the suspense is killing me. What do you say?'

He looked down at her. Still so young, so filled with

eagerness and energy and yet with the sad wisdom of a much older woman.

'We need something like this to bind us closer.' There was no bribe, no false promise in that, just an honest belief. 'Please,' she said, 'Please say yes, Hugo. Oh, I'm just mad to live here!'

'If you really want it and you think we could be happy here, then I'll buy it.'

'Oh darling!' She hugged him, and suddenly her eyes overflowed with tears. 'You're so good to me. And I'm so sorry –'

He held her for a moment. 'You're never to say that again,' he said quietly. 'Now find a handkerchief and stop being a silly girl. Let's go back and tell the Rushwells. They're probably dying of suspense too!'

Alice moved in to supervise the redecoration of the house. Everything needed modernizing. She installed herself in a suite of four rooms and directed the builders, electricians, plumbers and painters to do exactly what she and Hugo wanted. And she brought Lily Parker with her.

Lily had been looking after her since that first morning. The housekeeper's protests had been brushed aside. Lily was going to be her personal maid and that was the end of it. There were plenty of parlourmaids – she could engage someone else. And Alice averted a fuss with her mother-in-law by writing a sweet letter explaining why she had upset her domestic arrangements. Attack, as Alice knew, was the best means of defence. Hugo was very busy; life was a hectic mixture of social engagements and the absorbing project of Ashton. He let her do whatever she wanted. In the evenings they would sit together and pore over the plans, discuss the layout of the rooms, even the colour schemes.

'It'll take at least a year,' Hugo remarked.

'Oh no it won't! Not if I'm there to see they don't sit around and slack. Would you mind, darling? I ought to go down and be on the spot. You could join me at weekends. I'd make sure it was cosy for you.'

'If you think you can manage,' he said. 'Won't you be wretchedly uncomfortable with all that noise and mess going on around you?'

'I'd rather be there and get it done in six months than hang around halfway between homes like we are now,' she said. They had handed back the St James's Square house to Beatrice Vandekar and moved into a furnished house off Berkeley Street. 'I can take Lily with me. And someone to cook. You bring Clay down at the weekends. We'll manage. And I'll come up to London if there's anything important.'

'It might be better to leave Clay behind,' Hugo said. His valet was not likely to enjoy picnicking in a half-finished house.

'OK, Lily can look after you too.'

'She is remarkable, isn't she? Nothing seems to fuss her.'

'Only me,' Alice laughed. 'I can fuss her all right.'

Hugo looked up. 'I wouldn't get too intimate. It doesn't do with English servants.'

She came and sat on the arm of his chair. 'I know. But she'd never take a liberty. She's no doormat either, and I like that. Now and again I just tell her to shut up, and that's it. My God, look at the time – we'll be late. The curtain goes up at eight-thirty. I must fly upstairs and change.'

He followed her. He had his own suite of rooms. His evening clothes were laid out. They were going to the ballet. She was so happy, so busy, and the house had drawn them together. She'd been right about that. There was no time to be unhappy, except in the sad aftermath of making love. She'd kept her promise. She never said no. She didn't lie or make excuses. She was so honourable in her commitment to the terms of their agreement that he didn't know whether to admire her or hate her for it. But he still wanted her too much to stop or analyse.

He fantasized that one day he would be able to arouse her. He imagined ways of bringing her senses to life, but only succeeded in arousing himself. Perhaps it would be best if she went to Ashton. It would give him a chance to concentrate on his business. And to look around. Perhaps another woman would make it easier . . .

'I won't have time to bath,' Alice announced.

'It's run and ready,' Lily countered. 'You can't go out without bathing, madam, you're all hot and sticky.'

She was too, Alice conceded. Running upstairs had made her sweat. It was a quick bath.

Lily held out the big bath towel and helped her dry. Alice had no inhibitions about her maid seeing her naked. Women didn't worry her. It was nice to be cosseted.

'Madam,' Lily looked at her, 'I think you're putting on weight!'

'Oh, shut up, Lily. Of course I'm not.'

She was dressed and made up. Lily draped a fur-lined cloak over her shoulders. 'You look very nice, madam,' she said.

Alice smiled back at her as she left the room. 'Thanks to you. Don't wait up, I can get out of this by myself, thank goodness.'

When she was gone Lily began to tidy the bathroom and the bedroom. That was not her job but she disliked someone else coming in and handling her lady's things. She wouldn't let the housemaid touch the bed or fiddle with things on the dressing table. That was her domain.

She had been six months with Alice and now Alice couldn't do without her. She was proud of the way her lady looked and proud of how much that was due to her efforts. And it was very personal, working for Alice. She shared in the excitements. That amazing day, for instance, when they came back late on a Sunday evening and there was Alice bubbling like champagne, instead of being quiet and low, like she usually was at the end of a weekend with him there all the time. 'Lily,' she'd said, 'We're going to buy the most wonderful house in England! And I want you to come and live there with me!' Life had become varied for her because it was full of activity for her mistress. 'What shall I wear today, Lily?' was a regular question. 'Depends where you're going, madam.'

The answer could be anything, from a dinner at Kensington Palace to lunch with girlfriends at Claridges. And then there was Mrs Holmes Fry. Lily liked her. She was a gentle soul, not at all a firecracker like Madam. Lily did an alteration once or twice and was so nicely thanked she didn't mind being asked at the last minute. 'You can do this for Mother, can't you, Lily? After all, you're one of the family now...' She was such a devil, really, Lily admitted. She knew just how to twist your arm. And then make you feel as if she'd done *you* a favour. She worked long hours and got told to shut up if she protested about anything, but Lily couldn't imagine going back to her old humdrum life. She was even excited about going to Ashton. She couldn't wait to see the sparks flying when her lady got to grips with the workmen.

And I'm right, Lily insisted, checking the room before she went off duty. She is putting on weight – that dress isn't as loose as it should be. She stopped halfway through the door. Of course. Of course, that was it. She ought to know, seeing she looked after Alice's undies and washed everything delicate herself. Alice hadn't had her last curse. Nearly two months. And hadn't noticed, like as not, Lily decided. Thinking of nothing but that blessed house. Well. She'd just have to slow down, that's what. She lived on her nerves as it was, rushing about all day long. She looked tired in the mornings, really poorly sometimes. Lily thought Mr Hugo was nice enough, but he must be a bit of a pig in that way, or her lady wouldn't look down in the mouth first thing in the morning. Not for long – she soon perked up though. Well, she said to herself again. Never a dull moment around here.

A week later Alice started feeling sick. Phoebe hurried round. 'Oh darling, why didn't you tell me? How long is it?'

'Mother, I didn't know,' Alice said impatiently. 'I'm not certain till I see Dr Harris, but it seems most likely.'

Phoebe said gently, 'Aren't you pleased? Isn't Hugo delighted?'

'He doesn't know, I'm not saying anything until I'm sure. With any luck it may just be very late.'

'Alice, you sound as if you don't want it to be a baby. What's the matter? You said you were longing for a family.'

'Not in the middle of trying to move! Mother, for God's sake, I want to get Ashton ready. How can I do it if I'm pregnant and being sick as a cat?'

Phoebe didn't argue. Alice was obviously upset, poor child. Remembering how ill she'd felt herself, Phoebe sympathized. But there was more to it than that. It wasn't just the house and the upheaval. Alice wasn't pleased at all. 'Alice, is there anything the matter?' Phoebe said.

The denial was too fierce and too quick. 'Matter? What are you talking about? Everything's just wonderful – we've got this wonderful house and everything's going so well. All I want is to get on with it and not be hampered . . .'

She lit a cigarette. She wished her mother would go. I can't tell her. I can't confide in her because she just wouldn't understand. She let my father walk all over her and never said a word against him. And I don't want to make her unhappy. She'd worry and she'd ask me about it every time I saw her. She smiled. 'I'm sorry,' she said. 'I didn't mean to be sharp. I guess I felt sick and it's all a bit sudden, if it is a baby. Don't worry, darling. I'll be fine . . . I've an appointment with Harris tomorrow morning. I'll call you as soon as I know. Now let's have lunch. I want you to come to Partridges with me this afternoon. They've got a set of chairs that would look wonderful at Ashton.'

'I can't have it,' Alice said. 'It's impossible.'

'Mrs Vandekar, I'm afraid that I don't understand. What's impossible about your having a baby?' Dr Harris was polite, but his expression was unfriendly. What was she saying, this rich, spoilt young woman in perfect health? Impossible? He sensed what was coming.

'I can't have a baby at this particular time,' Alice said flatly. She could feel his hostility. 'We're moving, with major renovations to be made. I'm fully committed for the next six months. I've got to be free to carry out those commitments. For my husband's sake, as much as anything.' She was angry and frightened, so her attempt to sound pathetic failed.

'There's no commitment higher than motherhood,' he said. 'If your life was in danger or there was a genuine risk to your health, I might listen to you, but you're extremely healthy and strong and you should have a very easy pregnancy. All you need to do is be careful for the next few weeks. After that, you can get on and do up your house and lead an active life.'

'I don't want it,' she said. 'I want you to help me.'

He moved his chair back and got up. He was still very polite. 'I'm sorry,' he said. 'I don't give that kind of help. But please don't hesitate to call on me if you're worried about anything. And do try to look forward to it. I know so many women who'd give anything in the world to be in your place, Mrs Vandekar.'

Alice stood up. 'I wish they were,' she said. 'Thank you, Doctor. Good afternoon.'

It was cold and wet outside – dull winter weather, depressing the spirits further still. I don't want the baby, I'm not going to have it . . . why should I? I don't want to be sick and fat and housebound. Oh God! She cried in the car on the way home.

Be careful for the next few weeks or else. She saw Hugo's hat and stick on the hall table. She didn't want to face him. He knew nothing about it, and he was not going to know anything, in case . . .

She ran upstairs. Where was Lily? She had to talk to someone. She went down the passage to the ironing room.

Lily was pressing her evening dress. She looked up, saw Alice's face and stopped. 'What's wrong? Aren't you well, madam?'

Alice leaned against the door. 'You know damned well I'm not. Leave that, will you, and bring me a cup of tea.'

Lily cleared the cup away. She had made Alice lie down and taken off her shoes. 'You mustn't upset yourself,' she said. 'It won't do any good.' The philosophy of endurance came naturally to her. Pregnancy, poverty, sickness – these were part of life for Lily and Lily's family. You put up with it and did the best you could. And children were a blessing. Some children, at any rate. No good saying that to her lady; not while she was in this mood. 'I'll get you another cup,' Lily said. 'Then you have a rest before your bath. I've to finish your dress, remember.'

'To hell with the dress,' Alice said. 'And I don't want tea. Lily, what am I going to do? That damned doctor wouldn't help me.'

'Help you do what, madam?'

'Get rid of it.' Alice pulled herself up. 'That's the last time I'll go to him! If you'd heard him – there's no higher commitment than motherhood!'

'That's because men don't have the babies,' Lily remarked.

Alice looked at her. 'Lily, you don't know anybody do you?'

Lily went red. 'No, madam, I don't! What, have some back-street abortionist sticking knitting needles into you! I've a good mind to go and call Mr Vandekar.

'You do that and you'll be out on the street in five minutes flat!'

'Not five minutes,' she answered. 'It takes longer than that to pack, madam.'

'Oh, shut up, Lily!'

'Yes, madam,' Lily said. 'I'll come back when I've pressed that dress. You'll have your bath at the usual time?'

Alice turned away. 'Yes. You're not going to say a word about this to anyone. Nobody is to know for the time being. We're going down to Ashton next week and start the ball rolling.'

Lily knew when to argue and when not. Now was not the time.

'Yes, madam,' she said. 'You can rely on me.'

'You're wearing yourself out,' Hugo told her. 'You look absolutely exhausted. I insist you come back to London.'

'No,' Alice said. 'I'm perfectly all right. If I leave now, things will just grind to a halt. Christmas was what made me tired.'

'Alice, if you won't think of yourself, then for God's sake think of the baby. You've been told to rest.'

'Oh, I'm so sick of being told to do this and do that, and Lily nagging me and mother telephoning and now you! Nothing can hurt the baby. It's just ridiculous making all this fuss. Do get me a drink and stop badgering me.' She turned away from him angrily. Nothing can hurt the baby. Right up to three months she'd run up and down stairs, soaked in hot baths, exhausted herself at Ashton until the decorator she had engaged had walked off the job saying she was giving him a nervous breakdown. But nothing went wrong. The morning sickness stopped, the baby remained firmly growing inside and refused to be dislodged. When she told Hugo he was delighted, and drove her mad by fussing. He wanted the child, of course. He talked about a boy as if the sex was not in doubt. They had spent Christmas in Sussex with his mother and that weedy brother Phillip in that terrible cold, ugly monster of a house. Everyone gave her presents and gushed over her. She grew larger and ill-proportioned and the baby kicked her in the stomach at night and woke her up. She was bad-tempered and demanding. She sacked Lily, who refused to take her seriously, so she sacked the builders, who did.

Yet Ashton grew, even as the baby grew. Except that as she became uglier the house became more beautiful. Walking through the rooms, seeing the plans become a reality, Alice recovered her spirits. She even found a kind of tranquillity. The house was nearly ready and, in spite of everything, it was under nine months. The last set of curtains were hung, the pictures and furniture in place.

Hugo drove down from London. He put his arm around her. They walked from room to room. Through the magnificent hall, into the long green drawing room – that was her masterpiece, she thought, that lovely airy spacious room with the Gainsborough portrait hanging at one end, where the light caught it.

'Do you like it?' she asked Hugo. 'Are you really pleased with what I've done?'

'It's perfect,' he said. 'I thought you'd kill yourself doing it, but it's perfect.'

'Wait till you see the dining room,' Alice said. 'I've been saving that up. Oh Hugo, I can't wait to have this baby and get back to normal. Think of the parties we'll give here!'

He didn't answer. She didn't want the child, he knew that. Maybe after it was a reality she'd feel that it was more important than the house.

In the first week in May she gave birth. It was a long and very painful labour. The child was a girl and she was christened Fern.

Ashton was too remote, so Alice agreed they should have the christening ceremony in London, at St James's, Piccadilly. There were six godparents.

'Not a commoner among them,' Alice announced to her mother. 'I guess you think I'm a snob.'

'I hope not, darling,' Phoebe answered. Alice was too thin, and too restless. The birth had been difficult, poor Hugo had been frantic with worry, but the baby was so sweet, poor little thing.

Fern Alexandra. Lovely names. Phoebe said gently. 'I'm so glad it's a little girl. I've always wanted a granddaughter and she's so pretty already.'

Alice put an arm round her. 'I'm glad you're glad,' she said. 'She'll be lucky to have you. I know I am. It's just a pity she's not a boy.'

'Hugo doesn't mind. He's crazy about her – surely you know that?'

'Of course I do. He hangs over the cot making goo-goo noises like some kind of idiot – Mother, don't you see it means I've got to have another one? Nine months of feeling like hell and looking worse and then that awful business at the end...'

She lit a cigarette. The ashtray was full of stubs. She had chain-smoked since the birth. She saw her mother's anxious face and said. 'Oh – I shouldn't have said that. Don't take any notice of me, I'm just het up about this christening. All these hundreds of people and all the arrangements to be made. I wish we could have had it at Ashton.'

She seemed happy when she was there, more relaxed. The house was always full of people and Alice loved showing it off. Phoebe felt she was too obsessed by it, but again she said nothing. So far as she could see, Hugo was an adoring and indulgent husband. Alice was beautiful, rich, gifted with wit and personality. But not happy. Phoebe had suffered enough herself to know that.

'Mother, I've got a fitting this afternoon – I've got to rush. I'll call you tomorrow.'

'You go ahead, darling,' Phoebe said. 'I'll just go up and see little Fern before I leave.'

It was the prettiest nursery imaginable. Pink and

white, with a cot swathed in tulle and ribbons. The nurse engaged by Alice had impeccable references and long experience of looking after children from a few weeks old. Alice could safely leave the welfare of the little girl to her.

'Good afternoon, Mrs Holmes Fry.'

'Good afternoon, Nanny. Is she asleep?'

'No, just lying quietly. She's such a good baby, never cries.'

Phoebe bent over the cradle. Under the canopy of pink and white flounces the baby looked at her. She was dark, like Hugo, with a round, rather fat face and big blue eyes that were already changing colour. She didn't cry much, that was true. A placid, quiet little thing.

'She's a little dear,' the nanny said. 'One of my nicest babies.' She leaned over and touched the child's cheek. The baby smiled. The mother never went near it, except when Mr Vandekar came up. The grandmother showed more affection than *she* did. But she was typical. Spoilt, selfish young madam. 'I want someone who'll take complete charge,' she'd said. 'I don't know anything about babies and we lead a very busy life.'

Poor little thing, with a mother like that who didn't even come to see it. She'd make up for her. She'd give the little girl lots of love, like all her other babies. She saw the grandmother out. Nice woman, even if she was American. She went back to the cot. 'There, my little lovekin, we're going to turn over and have a nice little nap.'

It was a very prestigious job, with a very good salary and conditions. She lifted the baby and cuddled her for a moment. 'Who's my best girl, then?' she murmured.

Alice's baby looked at her and smiled.

By the time Fern Alexandra was two years old, the little king with the yellow hair had abdicated and married his American divorcée. The jazzy parties became old-fashioned, like the rattle of cocktail shakers. The little king's Fort Belvedere was given up to ghosts. Bright and brittle lives had lost their glamour; the country and the Empire were safe from constitutional crisis. There was a new king and his consort, with two small daughters, and Britain felt secure again.

Mr and Mrs Hugo Vandekar were just as popular with the society columnists. Alice was photographed and written about, her witty sayings were repeated; invitations to Ashton became more and more prized as the splendour of the parties she gave increased.

The Vandekars were a bright spot in a darkening year, with rumours of Nazi Germany's build-up of armaments and men. To Alice the talk of possible war was tiresome pessimism. Anyone who mentioned such things and spoiled the fun at Ashton wasn't asked again. And Hugo didn't discuss it with her because there was another woman, and he talked to her about everything.

Fern Alexandra grew up with Nanny in her nursery. She was a happy child. Quiet and a little slow, perhaps, but docile and sweet-natured. Nanny's love enveloped her; she saw people called Mummy and Daddy but they came so briefly into her life that they had little substance. Daddy played with her and she grew to like the smell and feel of a man. It was reassuring. Mummy came in and out, like a bright sunbeam that vanished moments later. She didn't know the smell or the feel of her, because she stayed on Nanny's knee and clung in case Mummy tried to pick her up. There were grannies, who patted her and brought soft cuddly things to play with. She still clung to Nanny in case they tried to separate them. But she was very happy.

The Munich crisis put an end to one of Alice's best-planned weekend parties at Ashton. Two cabinet ministers and their wives, long pursued by Hugo and finally netted by Alice, cancelled at the last moment.

Hugo had come down from London early on Thursday. The way to manage his enormous interests was by dint of inside information at the highest level. He had courted Chamberlain's colleagues with that end in view, and because Alice understood his reasons she targeted the wives. She was difficult to resist, even for ladies so highly placed. She was so beautiful and so well known, and, of course, so rich. But above all she could be so charming. Men and women were equally vulnerable and her reputation was untouched by scandal. She flirted and amused, but there were no whispers of a lover. The same was not said of Hugo. Some of her women friends were able to be sorry for her, and that made her even easier to like.

'What am I to do?' she demanded. She threw the telegrams down and faced Hugo. 'We've got the Adams and the Reedlands and the Spanish Ambassador – what are they going to think that our two most important guests have cancelled? This is just the damnedest thing to do!'

Hugo looked at her. She was twenty-seven, mature and lovely as a young woman, but she seemed suddenly no more than a petulant, silly child. Have I done this, he thought, seeing the scowl and the telegrams bunched into little tight balls and thrown on the floor. Have I turned the intelligent, original girl with all her American flair and independence into a spoiled, useless creature who can't see anything beyond her weekend party? He felt more angry with himself than with her.

'They've cancelled because the Prime Minister has decided to fly to Germany and see Hitler. He's trying to avert a war. It's just possible that Charlie and Rachel Adams and the Reedlands *and* the Spanish Ambassador – who I didn't want to ask anyway – will understand. I only wish you did too.'

Alice stared at him. 'Well, my God! And who's been baiting the hook for those two old bores for nearly a year? You have! "I want to invite them here," that's what you said to me. "I want you to be especially charming to Lady Tritton – see if you can get her to lunch." God, Hugo, what a hypocrite you are! You're just as furious as I am, except you won't admit it – and *I've* taken all the trouble. Why did he have to go to Munich just at this time anyway? Next week would have done just as well.' She opened one of the cigarette boxes that were kept in every room and lit a cigarette.

Hugo stopped blaming himself. That last remark was a deliberate provocation. He still slept with her – he hadn't completely got over that miserable hunger when she was close, but she could make him lose his temper quicker than anyone else. He grabbed her by the arm. 'There's going to be a war. Don't you understand? Don't you care? I wanted those old bores, as you call them, because I've got responsibilities all over the world and I have to protect them. That's why I'm disappointed. You're just annoyed because your bloody house party's been upset!'

Alice wrenched her arm away. 'Responsibilities my foot! Money's what you mean. I don't care about Chamberlain or Munich and I don't believe there's going to be a war! And if there is, you'll just get richer!'

He stepped away from her. 'If there's a war, I'll be fighting while *you* get richer. Now I'm going upstairs to see Fern.'

'Go ahead,' Alice shrugged. 'Have a nice long talk with Nanny. Ask her what she thinks about Munich!'

He slammed the door.

She lit another cigarette. 'I'd better tell Lily,' she said out loud. What she meant was, where's Lily, I want to tell her what's happened. But she couldn't admit that, of course.

'I wouldn't mind, if I was you, madam,' Lily said.

'You're not me,' Alice said. 'You haven't made all the plans and written all the letters inviting people and worked out all the menus.'

Lily put her head on one side. 'Oh, there, there. You've a housekeeper and a chef and lord knows how many servants in this house taking care of everything. Why don't you put the others off then?'

'Oh, shut up, Lily! Go and get me a drink and stop nagging.'

'I'm not nagging,' Lily insisted. 'Why don't you put them all off? It'd look better, you know. People shouldn't be giving parties at a time like this.'

'You're nuts,' Alice said. She knew vulgarity pained Lily. 'You'd think we were at war already. What do you mean, look better? Who cares what I do?'

'Nobody, most likely. It just looks better, as if you and Mr Hugo were serious about it. Like the rest of us.'

'You mean you? Lily, what the hell does any of it matter to you? You won't be affected.'

'I have three brothers, madam. They'll go off and fight if there's a war. And England's my country. I mind about it.'

Alice rubbed her arm. Hugo had held on so tightly that there would be a bruise. It brought back ugly memories of a night in Amsterdam. 'I asked for a drink,' she said. 'I've half a mind to take your advice, you know that? I've half a mind to ring round and cancel everyone. That'd teach him.'

'Make it a whole one and do it,' Lily said. 'I'll get you a nice martini made up.'

Alice went on rubbing her arm. Suddenly she didn't feel like entertaining people. The motive had gone.

Perhaps Lily was right. She had this straightforward common sense that saw the obvious. Maybe she should cancel her party, not just to spite Hugo, but because it was the right thing to do in the circumstances. The telephone rang. She picked it up. 'Yes, oh, yes, Your Excellency. Oh, well, of course I understand. You couldn't possibly be out of touch here at such a time. Well, I'll make a confession to you . . . I was just about to call you and our other guests and suggest we made it another time when let's hope things are more settled. Yes, I do pray he will. So much does depend on it . . . Yes, I will tell my husband. Goodbye.'

Lily came back with a dry martini on a salver. She knew how to mix Alice's favourite drink and kept the ingredients in her sewing room.

'That's the Ambassador,' Alice explained. 'He's cancelled too. Give me that, Lily, and get me my address book, will you? I must get on and call the rest of them before anyone else calls me.'

'Yes, madam,' Lily said. For a moment she and Alice smiled at each other, like conspirators. Alice tried the martini, found it excellent as usual, and reached for the telephone.

There was a report in the press the next morning that the famous society hostess Mrs Vandekar had cancelled one of her lavish parties as a sign of concern over the Anglo-German crisis. It was the beginning of her reputation as a patriot.

'Darling, don't cry.' Phoebe hugged her. Alice hardly ever cried; when she did it was noisy and uninhibited. 'I've got to go home,' her mother went on. 'If there's going to be a war, I might not get back for ages. Please, don't make it so difficult for me.'

'There *isn't* going to be a war,' Alice insisted. 'It's just a lot of scaremongering! Why can't you wait a bit longer? I'm going to be so lonely without you, Mother...'

Phoebe reached out and put her arm round Alice's shoulders. 'Darling, listen to me. We've been very close since you got married. I'm always coming down to Ashton and I love it here. But you're settled now. You have Hugo and dear little Fern, and this wonderful house you've made so beautiful. You're a famous person, my dear. Your life is full. You don't need me any more and you shouldn't. I want to go home. I miss the States. I'd have gone sooner except you wouldn't hear of it.'

'Don't make me feel guilty,' Alice said. 'It's not fair. I know you miss home. Damn it, so do I at times.' She wiped her eyes angrily. 'OK, my life is full. But I've made it full. I've made it so busy I haven't time to think. And I've always had you. I just had to lift the telephone and you were there.'

'Yes,' Phoebe agreed. 'We'd lunch together or go to exhibitions of dress shows, but you never talked to me, did you? Alice, I've known there was something wrong. But you wouldn't open up to me. You've got everything any woman could want, and still you're not happy.'

If I tell her the truth, Alice thought, she won't leave me. But she'll be unhappy for me. It'll ruin everything. She won't understand either. I can't do that.

Her mother said, 'Is it Hugo? You don't love him, do you?'

At least she could be truthful about that. 'I thought I did, but it hasn't worked out that way. We get on fine, you know that, but he's so occupied with business and we have people here all the time.'

'I'm sorry,' her mother said. Tears came into her eyes. 'But you've got Fern, darling... She's so sweet...'

'Mother,' Alice interrupted, 'I'm not maternal. I'm not like you. To me she's a fat pudding of a child who screams when I try to pick her up. Maybe I'd feel different about a boy, I don't know. Anyhow, she's all right. She's got Nanny, and Hugo dotes on her. She doesn't need me.'

'Are you going to have another baby soon?'

'With all this talk about war, it seems a bit silly,' Alice said hastily. 'Mother, why don't you wait till the summer? Would you like me to come with you? Hugo wouldn't mind. Maybe if you were at home for a month or two and we saw a lot of people, you'd change your mind and come back with me.'

No, her mother thought. No, that's not the answer. She's running away from her problems, and she's too brave to do that. I mustn't help her. 'Alice,' she said gently. 'I'm going, and I'm going alone. I've booked my passage on the *Mary* and I'm sailing on 20 June. I so want you to be happy. You deserve to be. I wish you loved him; he surely loves you.'

'I know,' Alice said. She turned away. 'Maybe I'll never know what I've missed. Maybe I'm just spoiled.' She had managed to smile when she looked at Phoebe again.

'I don't think so,' her mother said. 'Love is the most important thing in any woman's life. And one day you'll find it.'

Alice gave a ball at Ashton on the night her mother sailed for the United States. She excused the extravagance by saying that if there was going to be a war, and it really did look like it, it was her swan song. Everyone was going to have the best evening to remember, something to keep them warm in the cold climate of war. The remark was a Fleet Street invention, but it took hold of the public imagination. People saw the party as a gesture of defiance to the looming enemy. Her mother was leaving, and Alice set about spending a fortune to cushion herself against the parting.

Lily saw Alice's red eyes in the mornings and recognized that the hectic schedule was a form of self-defence. Mrs Holmes Fry was a sweet and gentle person – Lily had grown fond of her too. Madam would miss her terribly when all the fuss about the ball had died down.

She dressed her on the night of the ball. Hartnell had made the dress. It was sea green, and pearl and crystal embroidery sparkled among the sweeping folds of the organza skirt. 'Nothing on the bodice,' Alice had insisted, resisting the designer's penchant for over-decoration. 'I'm not going to look like the fairy on the Christmas tree.' If anyone else had said that he would have refused to make the dress. But Alice got away with it. No tiara either. Tiaras were not for commoners. No jewellery except the big circle of diamonds.

She had never looked more beautiful, Hugo

thought, as they stood receiving their guests after dinner. Her hair was swept up off her face, and hung down in the smooth pageboy style which was so fashionable. Plain diamond stud earrings and the family brooch competed with the gleam and glitter of her skirt as she moved, shaking hands, smiling, greeting people with a vivacity that danced and sparkled.

He couldn't contain his pride in her at that moment. He knew how much she dreaded parting with Phoebe, and he had never been jealous of their love for each other. And although he deplored it in principle, he had let her have her way and give the last great ball to take place in England before war was declared, as he knew it would be. Ashton was her creation. Sad that she should turn to a house for comfort, adorning it, showing it off in a blaze of publicity, rather than seek comfort from him or the child in the nursery. But that was not her way. A bang, not a whimper. Defiance and high spirits and extravagance were her weapons against human pain and human loss. He was proud of the magnificent house, lit up like a great white palace for miles around. But sad too. He would much rather have spent that evening quietly with her at home.

There was dancing to the music of Carrol Gibbons. Alice loved to dance; whenever Hugo looked for her she was on the floor, the man holding her laughing and enchanted. He suddenly remembered the night he met her in that same house. At a ball given at about the same time. He remembered how bored he had been until she came into what was then the library. He turned away from the scene in the splendid hall, from the gyrating couples and the cream-smooth music, and made his way back to the same room. It felt like a pilgrimage, but he didn't know why he made it. Perhaps I'm going to be killed in this war that's coming, he thought, and was surprised to find the idea didn't trouble him.

But it was changed, of course. The Rushwells'

shabby book-lined room was now an elegant boudoir, with grey silk walls and the fine plasterwork ceiling picked out in Wedgwood blue. Alice's room, with her stamp imprinted on it, her desk and her chairs and her photographs of Hugo and herself on their wedding day, of Phoebe, of Fern in her christening robe...

'Hugo? Darling, I've been looking everywhere for you.'

He was standing by the window looking out on the incredible floodlit garden, the famous Cupid and Psyche snow-white against the night sky. He turned, and there she was. Celia Forbes, his mistress for the past two years, dark-haired, sleek, thin as a rake. She had a beautiful smile, and she was wearing the diamond necklace he had given her. A handsome elegant woman of wit and sophistication, with a strong sexual appetite. Alice knew the Forbes but had no suspicions about Hugo's liaison with Celia. The Forbes's were not among their close circle of friends and that was just as well.

'What are you doing in here all alone?' she asked. 'Come and have a dance. Aren't you enjoying yourself? It's a marvellous party.'

She came up and slipped her arm through his. She was in her early thirties, married for the second time. She had never said she loved Hugo or expected him to say he loved her. It wasn't a business relationship; more a passionate friendship. He gave her jewellery and paid for a Lagonda car as a birthday present. She was a wise and discreet companion in whom he confided with absolute confidence. Except about his personal relations with Alice. She had never even tried to pry. She was bored to tears with Forbes, as she called him, and assumed that Hugo's spritely American wife had begun to pall on him too. She liked having a lover and she needed the attentions of a man.

'I must say, Alice has excelled herself. Everything's been thought out, down to the last detail. So clever to get Carrol, too. I adore his music, don't you? How about that dance?'

'Would you mind if we didn't?' he said. 'But we could have a quiet glass of champagne.'

'Why not?' she agreed. 'I'll wait here. What a pretty room this is. I've never been in here before.'

'It's Alice's room,' he said. 'I'll get our drinks. I won't be long.'

She sat down, arms locked behind her head, studying the decor. Very pretty. A little overdone perhaps. All that silk on the walls and the strong blue. She didn't like Alice. Forbes thought she was marvellous, but then he would. What a fool not to keep a husband like Hugo amused. She wasn't interested in stealing him, admittedly because she knew she couldn't, but one day someone would come along who was more ambitious... She lit a cigarette.

There was going to be a war. She could feel it. There was a restlessness; almost a feeling of frustration because it was inevitable and yet it went on threatening, never happening. Forbes was looking forward to it. Talking about rejoining his old regiment. He'd been terribly attractive as a Lifeguards captain. That uniform did wonders. Pity he was a non-stayer. Now almost a non-starter, she thought and smiled at her witticism. But he wasn't a bad stick. Quite sweet really, and very undemanding. He didn't ask about the jewellery, except once, when he saw Hugo's necklace. 'Oh, come into money, have we?' 'No, darling, just something I decided to invest in.' He'd never mentioned it again.

'Sorry I was so long.' Hugo came back with two glasses. 'I couldn't find a waiter and there was a frightful crush round both bars. Here we are.' He sat beside her.

She touched her glass against his and toasted him. 'Here's to our next lunch in London,' she said. 'I've missed you.'

'I've been very busy,' Hugo said. 'But next week we

could see each other. I've missed our afternoons together.'

'So have I,' Celia Forbes said. She put down her glass of champagne and bending forward, kissed him on the mouth. And that was what Alice saw when she opened the door. Celia had her eyes closed; it was Hugo who glanced up and saw his wife standing in the doorway, staring at them. For how many seconds, he didn't know, but the door slammed and Celia jerked away.

'My God, what was that?'

Hugo stood up. He wiped his mouth and there was lipstick staining his handkerchief like blood. 'I'm afraid that was Alice,' he said.

'Oh my God,' Celia repeated, and she laughed. 'That's awkward. Is she likely to make a fuss – surely just a little kiss... you can explain it away can't you? Say I was tight, I don't mind. I don't want to make trouble for you, darling.'

It can't be helped,' he said. 'We shouldn't have sat in here. It's the one room she'd probably come to if she wanted a rest for a bit. Oh, goddamn it. Come on, we'd better get back to the dance. I'll see if I can find Alice.'

'Of course. I'll get myself a partner and get on to the floor. I do hope she won't make a song and dance about this. Sorry, darling.'

'Don't be,' he said. 'It was just as much my fault.'

He couldn't see Alice. He searched for her on the dance floor, and through the dining room where the buffet was laid out, and on through the tented supper room erected on one side of the house. She was nowhere. He hesitated. If he went upstairs, that nosy personal maid would see him. He was never quite sure about Lily. Alice relied on her too much. He decided to wait until the party was over. See what she said. She might ignore it. Under their peculiar circumstances, many wives would. Fidelity on his part had not been part of the bargain made in Amsterdam. He asked the wife of the Foreign Secretary if she would like to dance and guided her round in a romantic slow-tempo Carrol Gibbons speciality. He noticed with relief that the distinctive green and silver dress was floating somewhere among the crowd, and steered towards her. She didn't look at him – she was gazing into the admiring face of a very handsome young Conservative politician, famous for his hats and for having resigned over Chamberlain's capitulation at Munich. When the music stopped he excused himself and went over to her.

'Alice,' he said, 'I've been looking for you. Anthony, you must forgive me, but I haven't had one dance with my wife the whole evening. She's been too popular!'

'I'm not surprised. What a wonderful party you've both given!' Anthony brought Alice's hand to his lips and kissed it. He was very attractive to women. Alice thought him charming, intelligent and fun. He sensed that, while she was flattered and amused by him, she was not at all interested in him. He supposed she must be very much in love with her husband. Lucky devil, Hugo Vandekar.

Alice and Hugo began to dance. They didn't speak for some time. Then Hugo said, 'I'm sorry. It didn't mean anything. I've been looking everywhere for you.'

'I went for a walk,' Alice said. 'The gardens were looking so lovely. We ought to have the floodlighting more often.'

'Don't be angry with me,' he whispered. 'I promise you, it meant nothing to me.'

'She is the biggest tart in London,' she said, smiling at someone as they passed. 'How did you manage to jump the line, Hugo? Paid her bills? Hello, Joan, how ravishing you look –'

'Alice, on this evening of all evenings, I don't want you to be upset. Come and we'll walk in the gardens together. Please, darling. Let me talk to you.'

The music ended and there was a swell of applause. It was the hit song of the moment and no pianist could play it like Carrol Gibbons.

Hugo held her hand too tightly; she couldn't get away without attracting notice. He could feel how angry she was. Anger was in the flashing smile and the hurried walk as they made their way out onto the terrace. There Hugo stopped. 'Do you remember standing here with me that first night when we met? I fell in love with you then. And you fell in love with all of this, didn't you?'

'And you bought it for me.' Alice finished for him.

'I don't know whether to be glad or sorry.'

She stared at him. 'What do you mean? Isn't it what you wanted too?'

'No,' he said. 'I didn't want a house, however beautiful. I wanted you, Alice. I'll always want you. Celia Forbes doesn't mean a damn to me. I'll never see her again after tonight. That's a promise. But will you do something for me?'

She said slowly, 'What is it? What do you want me to do?'

'Go to a doctor and talk about this thing. There must be a reason. Don't you see, it's the only thing that stands between us and our being happy? Really happy. Ashton won't do it. Children won't either. I know you don't give a damn about Fern. Money won't and parties like tonight won't. There's going to be a war; God knows what the outcome will be. People are talking about six months, a year perhaps. I don't believe it. I think we're in for a terrible time. We may not even win. Alice, my darling, it's our one chance. Will you see a doctor?'

There was a breeze and she shivered. She turned round and he saw that she was crying. The harsh flood-lights made her face look hard and ashen.

'My father died fucking a common whore. That's what sex means to me. I don't need any doctor to explain it.'

He was so shocked he let go of her and she swung away from him. She went on, gripping the balustrade, intent on self-destruction. 'I'm not a fool, Hugo. I'm not a cheat either. Do you think I'd leave it and not do anything about it? How do you think I felt, letting you climb on top of me and feeling I wanted to rush into the bathroom and be sick? Having Fern and knowing you'd want another child. Of course I went to see someone. He called himself a nerve specialist. He said there was nothing to be done. He said my father was the cause of it. Talking about it is supposed to cure the thing, isn't it? Well, it didn't cure me. Don't give up Celia. You're entitled to her. I was just hurt and jealous for a moment back there, and I've no bloody right to be. Now I'm going back in for what's left of the party.'

And she went, leaving him alone. He didn't try to stop her or follow.

The dawn was rose and gold above the rooftops when the last of their guests drove away. Alice said, 'Good night, Hugo,' and went upstairs. She didn't wake Lily. She tore the back fastenings to free herself from the green and silver dress and kicked it aside.

She didn't sleep; she lay and listened to the sounds of the house coming to life as the staff began putting the rooms in order. The caterers would come later and take down the tented supper room. It had been much admired, with real candles in the chandeliers and those wonderful green and white flower arrangements everywhere. Just like a flower garden, darling... The voices mocked her, the faces smiling and mouthing compliments ran like a newsreel before her closed eyes. Such a success. Such a miracle of planning. How did you ever find the time to get it all arranged? The celebrities, thick as daisies on the ground. The money, my dear... She'd heard that whispered as she passed. It must have cost an absolute fortune... But they're stinking rich anyway.

She sat up, knowing that Lily would soon be coming with her tea tray.

'I'll have to offer him a divorce,' she said aloud. 'We can't go on like this. It isn't fair to him.' And she managed a smile when the knock sounded, took her tea from Lily and said what a marvellous evening it had been.

She dressed and went down to find Hugo and tell him. He must have his freedom. He could have Fern too, if he liked. All she would ask for was Ashton and enough money to maintain it. But he wasn't in the house. The butler said he had left early for London. When she telephoned the bank he was engaged and didn't return her call. Or the second call she made. In the early evening his secretary called. Mr Vandekar had flown to Paris on urgent business. He would contact her from the Crillon.

Alice didn't wait. She asked for the number and was put through. He always used the same suite. They had stayed there during their honeymoon. She heard the internal phone ring twice and then a woman's voice said, 'Hello.' Again, 'Hello . . .' His business in Paris was Celia Forbes. Alice hung up.

When he came back three days later she didn't ask him for an explanation. He didn't offer one. There was no mention of a divorce, and he moved permanently into his own suite of bedroom and dressing room. Alice didn't comment. She showed him the letters from their more illustrious guests, thanking them for the great ball at Ashton. It was, as one writer expressed it, the end of an era for them all. Its bright memory would give them courage in the trial to come.

On 3 September war was declared. The sirens sounded over London within the next few minutes. It was a false alert, a presage of the phoney war, so soon to become all too real when the German armies overran Belgium and France fell in 1940.

A number of the Vandekars' friends were killed at Dunkirk. Hugo joined the Grenadier Guards and was posted to the War Office. When Alice asked what he was doing, he said it was an administrative posting and he would do his best to get out of it. Phoebe wrote worried letters from the States asking Alice to come over before Britain was invaded and to bring Fern with her. Such terrible things were happening in Europe, and if the Germans came people like the Vandekars would be specially singled out. Alice wrote back and said simply that neither she nor Fern would be in any danger. Didn't her mother know that the rich were always able to buy themselves out of trouble? The cynicism troubled Phoebe and she approached Hugo next. His reply was kindly but direct.

His wife and child were safe at Ashton, untouched by the Blitz devastating London and the ports. She had no need to worry about them and there was no question of any member of his family fleeing to America.

He came home at weekends. Celia Forbes's husband had been killed fighting a doomed rearguard action in France. It was common knowledge that Hugo was supporting her. She had joined the Ambulance Service and spent her time in London, driving through the fiery hell of night-time air-raids.

Alice stayed at Ashton and watched indifferently as Fern grew up with Nanny hovering protectively over her. The war seemed far away from the peaceful beauty of Ashton. Hugo in his uniform seemed like someone dressing up for a play. He didn't discuss his work because her questions showed that Alice wasn't really interested. People came down for odd weekends but there was little carefree gaiety. Alice joined the local WVS and rolled bandages and made smalltalk. Boredom and frustration made her short-tempered. One day she said to Hugo, 'I can't go on sitting down here, wasting my time with all these old frumps from the village. I'm so bored I could scream. I want to go to London. I want to *do* something. Something positive to help.'

'You're not going to London,' he said flatly. 'You're not putting yourself in danger just because you're bored. Fern needs you.'

'Fern doesn't know me from a bar of soap!' she retorted. 'You don't want me up there because of Celia! It's all right for her to be a bloody heroine driving ambulances through the Blitz, but I've got to sit here doing nothing.'

'Celia has no responsibilities. She has a reason for being a bloody heroine, as you put it. Forbes was killed, remember. She minded about that.'

'Did she really? Good for her. I thought she might have been relieved. It's left the way clear for the two of you.' Alice lit a cigarette. 'Not that I mind, don't think that. I said you were entitled to her, didn't I?'

'Yes,' Hugo answered, 'you did, and I took you at your word. I'd still give her up if you asked me to.' He turned away, not wanting her to see his face. Or to know how much she could still hurt him.

'Oh, don't start that again,' she said. 'I didn't mean to be bitchy. I'm just on edge. I love being at Ashton but I want to do something useful instead of just sitting here. I'm sure people criticize me for it behind my back. I'm sure they do.'

'Well,' Hugo said after a pause, 'if you're serious, there is something that might answer all the problems. I haven't mentioned it because I didn't think you'd welcome the idea.'

She looked at him in surprise. 'What is it? Come on, tell me.'

'It's been suggested that we turn the house into a convalescent home,' he said.

'Ashton? Make it a hospital with a lot of people taking over and running my home?'

'I thought that would be your reaction. Before you dismiss it, I have to warn you, it can be done with or without our consent. I'm going down to see someone in hospital at Horton. Why don't you come down with me, Alice? You might change your mind and we can offer Ashton without having it requisitioned anyway.'

Alice hated illness. She was healthy and strong,

78

inclined to be impatient with anyone who wasn't. The quickest way to bore her was to mention sickness. But the hospital ward at Horton was different. Hugo's friend, a man she'd never met, was a Hurricane pilot who had broken both legs after baling out. He was cheerful and kept making jokes. But there were others. Men so badly burned they were swathed like mummies. Men in pain, semi-conscious, men hidden behind screens, and she knew what that meant without being told. Mostly RAF, Hugo said. A lot of casualties among the pilots. Bombers limping back with wounded and dying crew members aboard.

Driving back in the car she said nothing. He saw her take a handkerchief out of her bag and wipe her eyes; she couldn't help herself. He reached over and squeezed her hand. How often had he said to himself that he hated her, and yet he couldn't bear to see her cry. 'It was pretty awful, but at least you know what's involved.'

'They were so young,' Alice said. 'Some of them looked such babies. I feel the most selfish, spoiled creature. Moaning about being bored. God, Hugo, what kind of a person have I turned into? What's happened to me?'

'I don't know,' he said quietly. 'You have changed, Alice. We both have.'

She looked at him. 'Then I'm going to damn well unchange. We'll turn Ashton into the best damned convalescent home in England. That's going to be my contribution to this bloody awful war.'

'Thank you,' he said. 'I'm glad. Knowing you, you'll do exactly that.'

'I must say,' the ward sister remarked, 'She's amazing.' She sipped her cup of tea.

Lily said, 'She is a bit, I suppose. I've been with her for five years now, so nothing surprises me.'

'When she said to Matron she wanted to help, we all thought she'd read to the boys, stop for a chat with some of them, that sort of thing. When Matron suggested it she fair bit her head off. "I mean *help*," she says. "Not fool around playing Lady Bountiful." I haven't seen many people stand up to Matron, I can tell you. But she got her way!'

'She always does,' Lily agreed. 'I've told her she's wearing herself out and she just tells me to shut up. There's no half measures with my lady. When she does something she does it.'

Lily was so proud of Alice. From the moment the first group of patients arrived, Alice had taken charge of the non-medical side. The RAF welfare officer decided it was easier to collaborate with this dynamic and determined woman than to fight her. And she worked without counting the hours or the cost. She wrote letters home for the men too hurt or apathetic to do it for themselves. She telephoned relatives, she arranged concerts and film shows, buying a projector and setting aside a room as a cinema. And, of course, influence secured the latest films, the concert pianist who came down to play for them, a well-known comedian who never gave his services without a fee but succumbed to her bullying and blandishments. And she volunteered to sit during the night and watch anyone who needed it. Some, having suffered psychological damage, couldn't sleep, and she would sit up talking to them or playing cards till the nurse on duty came in the morning. The men recovering from burns were her special care. No matter how hideous the scarring, Alice didn't flinch. Often, when the bandages came off, the victim would ask if she would be there. The young men blinded were always asking what she looked like. The nurses said truthfully that she was blonde and very pretty. Bit like a film star.

Hugo was proud of her too. She was usually so tired by the weekends that they would spend the days quietly in their own wing of the house. Even then she would rush down to see this boy or that to make sure he was all right. Hugo was proud of her, but nothing had changed between them. They slept apart, and their one child grew up in her nursery alone. Hugo began to spend more and more of his time with her. Fern was a sweet child, and he loved her. Docile and trusting, a little too dependent upon the old Nanny, who didn't discourage it. As soon as Fern was old enough, they should engage a nursery governess and let Nanny fade into the background. There would never be another child unless he could persuade Alice that it was cruel to deprive Fern of a sister or brother. He didn't expect her to listen. She was too absorbed in her work. All the love she had withheld from him was being lavished on the maimed and the helpless.

In the meantime he suffered and her daughter was neglected. But he was still proud of Alice, and praise for what she was doing was reaching far beyond the confines of Ashton. If she went on like this, Alice Vandekar would be a legend by the time the war ended. And there was no sign of that.

Christmas 1941. Russia had been invaded; the war in North Africa was going badly, and Hugo had finally arranged to join an active service unit. He hadn't told Alice. She was too preoccupied with making Christmas something everyone at Ashton would remember.

There was a huge tree set up in the hall, cut down on the estate. She and some of the young airmen had spent two days decorating it. There were individual presents for everyone. Luxuries like chocolates and whisky were begged from her friends, supplies of food well beyond the stringent rations. Nobody asked where they came from but everyone knew who paid. She had arranged a carol service on Christmas Eve. Hugo had ten days' leave. They gathered in the hall around the splendid tree, young men in Air Force blue, some in wheelchairs, others standing. It was a moving sight, sad and yet heartening, because there was hope and there was joy, even among those for whom life would be a travesty. Hugo looked at Alice and thought, she has created this for them. She has made this possible; by the sheer force of her own will, she's given them hope and given them joy. They'll remember her for the rest of their lives. Some of them will love her for the rest of their lives. And for them, there'll be no disillusion.

They spent Christmas Day with Fern and Nanny. There were no lavish presents, except toys for the little girl. She seemed uneasy, glancing nervously at her mother. Alice didn't seem to notice. They made an effort to be jolly, but it was forced and flat, and Hugo watched as the old woman monopolized his child. Alice seemed relieved not to be bothered. Something had to be done. The environment was bad for Fern. She needed young company, a proper family. He would have to talk to Alice about it before his leave was over. His unit was scheduled to sail for North Africa in the New Year.

When Fern had gone back to her nursery, shepherded away with her toys, hand firmly clasped in Nanny's, he poured himself and Alice a precious ration of drink and decided to face the issue. But the internal telephone rang. Alice answered it.

'It's for you,' she said. 'A Group Captain Wallace.'

'Oh? I wonder what he wants.' James Wallace was one of his colleagues in the job he had just left. 'Hello. Yes, fine thanks. Very nice. Did you? Good. What can I do for you, Jim?'

Alice looked up. It was a long, one-sided conversation. Hugo was frowning. She'd never heard of Group Captain Wallace before.

'Of course. Yes, don't worry, we'll look after him. I'll tell my wife. Right. Goodbye.'

'Tell me what? she asked.

'There's a special case coming in the day after tomorrow. One of our chaps. He's had a rather bad time, and Jim Wallace asked me to see he gets extra care.'

'Why's he special – and what does "one of our chaps" mean? I don't understand.'

'We've been dropping agents into France,' Hugo said. 'Part of an experiment for something bigger we've been working on. This man was one of them. Unfortunately he was captured. He got away but he's had a pretty rough time. He needs a good rest, so they're sending him here.'

'Do you mean a spy?' Alice stared at him. 'Is that what you've been doing? Intelligence? You told me it was administration.'

'That's what they told me, in the beginning. Not a spy, a saboteur. Trained in explosives. His name is Nicholas Armstrong. Take an interest in him, will you, Alice? He's not like the others. And he can't talk about what he's been doing either.'

'Of course. I'll ask to be notified when he arrives. What do you mean, a rough time?'

'He was caught by the Gestapo,' Hugo said. 'Now Alice, I want to talk to you about Fern.'

Lily was waiting up for her mistress. Her family lived too far away for her to travel home for Christmas. By now she'd grown apart from them. She spoke and thought differently; she'd adopted many of Alice's habits and attitudes without realizing it. She felt strange among her relatives and, since her mother died, she had seen less and less of them. The war was a good excuse.

'Would you like a cup of hot milk, madam. It'll help you to get to sleep quicker.'

'Thank you, Lily. That would be nice. Why don't you have one with me?'

Lily stared at her for a moment. 'I couldn't do that,' she said. 'I couldn't sit down in here with you. It wouldn't be right.'

'Oh, shut up, Lily. Get two cups of hot milk and don't be such a damned snob!'

We ought to get rid of Nanny, he'd said. She hadn't argued. Yes, OK, as soon as she could find a nursery governess, but she wouldn't be young, she pointed out. All the young women were caught up in war work. Unless they had another child. She was shocked into silence. His face showed nothing, his tone quite noncommittal. Another child – she had repeated it. Surely this wasn't the time to think of such a thing. How could she possibly start a pregnancy when there wasn't a spare moment at Ashton? It's unfair on Fern, he'd interrupted. She's growing up lonely and isolated. We owe it to her not to condemn her to being an only child. Of course, if she agreed, he'd end his affair with Celia. Alice saw an escape route and took it.

'Aren't you being a little unfair on *her*?' she said. 'Sacking her after all this time.'

'I have my priorities, Alice,' he answered, 'and so has she. She's changed a lot since the war. I think she carries on more for my sake than her own. If she felt that you and I were trying to start again, she'd be genuinely pleased.'

'Would she really?' Alice remarked. 'She sure has changed. Hugo, I think you're fussing about Fern. I also think she plays up to you. I agree she needs somebody new – Nanny runs round like an old hen after the child. It's making her silly and self-important. I'll see what I can do. We'll have to pension the old girl off, you know.'

'I know,' he said without looking at her. 'I've got something else to tell you,' he continued. 'I'll be going abroad quite soon. God knows when I'll get home again.' He didn't add, 'Or if I get home.' He couldn't have said anything to rouse her pity. 'Will you think about having another child? Just think about it in the next few days before I go.'

Alice hesitated. She could feel herself freezing up. To start again. To endure that miserable, horrible experience after years of being left in peace. She felt almost panicked. I can't. I can't go back... I don't want another child. I don't like the one I've got . . .

'Can't we wait until the war is over? Then I'll try. I promise you, Hugo. Don't ask me now.'

'Here's the milk, madam,' Lily said. 'I've put a spoon of honey in it. I drank mine – it was getting cold,' she added. 'You look tired, you know. Why not have a sleep in tomorrow?'

'I'm not tired,' Alice insisted. 'Mr Hugo wants me to replace Nanny.'

'Glad to hear it,' Lily said. 'She smothers that poor child. Won't let her do this or that, keeping her a baby so she can hang on to the job!'

Alice knew Lily and Nanny disliked each other, but this surely wasn't fair. 'She dotes on Fern, and you know it. It's going to be very hard on her. I'll have to find a nursery guv, but God knows where. That milk was lovely. Do you think Fern's lonely? She seems happy enough to me.'

'I think she needs other children instead of that old woman mollycoddling her. She'd grow up faster too. There's a nice little village school. Why don't you take her down there for a morning or two and let her mix? Do her a lot of good. If she makes friends she could have them up to tea sometimes.'

' Mr Hugo wouldn't consider it,' Alice said. But then he wouldn't be there after next week. It was a very sensible idea. Trust Lily to think of something practical. If Fern had playmates and if she found a nice woman to teach her and run the nursery . . . 'I think we'll manage something,' she said. 'Good night, Lily, and no nonsense about waking me. Tea at the usual time.'

'Good night, madam. Sleep well.'

Lily checked the curtains and switched out the main light. She saw Alice settled down and covered up, and the bedside light went out as she closed the bedroom door. She was glad that old bitch would be leaving. If her lady knew how she criticized and carped about her behind her back, she'd have sent her packing long ago.

But Lily never told her. Her mistress had enough on her mind, with her boys to look after, without hearing what a rotten mother she was and how frightened the dear little child was whenever she had to go down and see her.

Why should she like the child, anyway? Lily didn't. She thought she was a sly little thing, spoiled and pampered, and always whining to get sympathy. She twisted her father round her finger too, even at that age.

Lily went to bed and read a novel for an hour before she turned out her own light. She loved wartime romances.

3

'Mrs Vandekar?'

'Yes, sister?'

'You wanted to see Flight Lieutenant Armstrong when he came in. He arrived this morning. Dr Ferguson has seen him and he's settled in.'

'Oh, yes,' Alice remembered Hugo's concern about this particular patient. 'Which ward is he in? I'll go along at teatime.'

'He's in Spencer,' the sister said.

Alice was surprised. The rooms in the south and north wings of Ashton were reserved for the worst cases who needed special nursing. 'Why's he in there?' she asked. 'Is he badly wounded?'

'Only his hands,' was the reply. 'He's more of a mental case – the director at Princess Mary's hope the change of environment will help him. He's made some progress, but he probably won't speak to you. He's very withdrawn. I'll tell nurse you'll go at about four o'clock, shall I?'

'Yes, thank you,' Alice said.

The nurse accompanied her to the special ward. 'I'm afraid you won't get much change out of him,' she said. 'Hasn't said a word since he came in. His hands are in a terrible mess, I've never seen anything like them. He's been in some German POW camp, sister said. Here we are.' She knocked and opened the door for Alice.

'Good afternoon,' she said, her voice rising on a bright note. 'You've got a visitor. Mrs Vandekar's popped in to see you.'

She looked at Alice and made a face, as if to say, 'Much good it'll do trying to chat to *him*,' and then went out.

He was sitting in a chair by the window with his back to the room. He hadn't moved or looked round.

For a moment Alice hesitated. Then she walked up and stood in front of him. 'Hello,' she said, and gave him her best smile. 'I'm Alice Vandekar.'

Slowly he raised his head. He was sallow and emaciated, with huge deep pits under the dead eyes. And they were dead. She'd never seen such emptiness and numb despair in a face before. The injured hands were lying in his lap, hidden by white cotton gloves. He just looked at her and didn't speak.

'Won't you say hello to me?' Alice said. No answer. Just that terrible vacant look. 'Oh God,' she said under her breath. 'What do I do now?' Leave him? Say goodbye and go? But that was to admit defeat. He must answer in the end. He couldn't just sit there and ignore her.

She brought up a chair and sat down. 'OK,' she said. 'You've been very sick and you don't feel like talking. But you won't mind if I talk to you for a bit, will you? It might even cheer you up. Sitting alone is so damned gloomy.'

At the end of an hour she came out. The nurse was sitting reading in the corridor.

'Any joy?' she asked.

Her manner irritated Alice. She felt tempted to say yes, we got along fine, but she didn't. 'Not yet,' she answered. 'It'll take time, but we'll win in the end. I'll be back tomorrow.'

The nurse shrugged and went back to her book. She was so sure of herself, just because a lot of the boys had crushes on her. Well, she'd be wasting her time with this one.

Alice couldn't stop thinking about him. 'He's so lost,' she said to Lily. 'I can't explain it. God knows I've seen people crying and shot to pieces with nerves, but never anyone like this. It's as if he won't admit he's alive. But somebody must be able to get through... And it isn't going to be any of the nursing staff, that's obvious. I think they've written him off already.'

'You've been going in to see him for a week now,' Lily reminded her. 'And he's never said a word to you, has he, madam?'

'No,' Alice admitted. 'But he knows I'm there. I saw him move when he heard me come in. That's something. I know I'll get him to talk to me. I know it!'

'Well,' Lily said, 'if anyone can, you can. But don't fret about it. Some of these cases you can help and some never get better. I saw Miss Prince in the village today. I mentioned about Miss Fern going down to the school for an hour one morning and she said that would be very nice. She said they'd be delighted if you brought her along. I hope you didn't mind my mentioning it.'

'No, of course not,' Alice said. 'I'd forgotten about it. I'll see Nanny tomorrow. She can go with Fern.'

Lily busied herself with her sewing. Her lady came to her room to talk as often as she sent for Lily. It seemed to draw them closer. 'She won't like it,' she said, threading cotton through the needle. 'She'll put the child off going, if you ask me. Would you like me to take her if you're too busy?'

'Now that would really upset Nanny,' Alice remarked.

'I suppose so,' Lily agreed. 'She might even give her notice if you insisted, madam.'

Alice stared at her and then burst into laughter. 'Why, you cunning – Lily, I'm surprised at you! What a good idea! She'd have to stay till I got someone else, of course, but it might just get rid of her. I'll tell her tomorrow morning. My, you're devious. I'll have to watch out for you!' And she laughed again, while Lily only smiled and went on sewing.

'Hello,' Alice said. 'It's me again. You must be sick of listening to me chattering away. If you don't want me to come, you've only got to say.' Was there a flicker in the eyes – she held her breath for a moment, not daring to believe it. 'If you really are fed up with me, just nod your head,' she said. 'I'll go away and I won't come back. Just nod, that's all you've got to do. I won't mind, I promise you. But I'll miss you. I'll miss coming in to see you. Shall I go away?'

Every day for fourteen days, an hour, sometimes longer, of reaching out to him. He didn't nod. He shook his head. Tears came into Alice's eyes. She didn't try to hide them. She let him see them, and she touched him for the first time. She put her hand on his arm for a moment.

'I'm so glad,' she said. 'I'm so glad you want me to come. And one day you're going to say so. I'm going to call you Nicholas from now on. I know your name, and you know mine. I'm Alice. I'm your friend, and I'm going to help you to get well. Oh, damn it all, I can't stop crying I'm so happy you shook your head. Wait till I tell that boot-faced nurse!'

Hugo hadn't been home since Christmas. He'd telephoned and she'd talked to him about Nick Armstrong. He said yes, it was a tragic case, but he refused to give her any details. 'It's confidential stuff,' was all he said. 'We had to give the details to the medical officer at Princess Mary's, but I can't discuss it with you, darling. Just carry on visiting the poor devil, I'm sure it helps.'

'It'd help a lot more if I knew what had happened to him,' Alice snapped. 'If the army doctors know, and I imagine that includes Dr Ferguson, I don't see why you can't tell me!'

'Because it's classified,' he said. 'How's Fern?'

'She's fine,' Alice answered. 'Nanny's given notice, by the way, and Fern's going to the village school till I find a governess.'

She didn't give him time to protest before she made an excuse and rang off. 'Classified information my foot,' she said out loud. 'If you won't tell me, I'll find out some other way.' And then she snapped her fingers in impatience. Of course. Dr Ferguson would have the details on his medical records. And those were right under her nose at Ashton.

The doctor's office was kept locked at night and when he went off duty during the day. But in the housekeeper's room there were duplicate keys to all the rooms in the house. The doctor's office was a storeroom on the ground floor near the old butler's pantry. All she had to do was get the key and look up Nicholas Armstrong's file.

It was 3 a.m. and she hadn't been able to sleep. Dr Ferguson kept his records in a green metal filing cabinet. Alice opened the door to the office with the duplicate key, locked it behind her and began to go through the A's. There were only three Armstrongs and then she found what she wanted. Nicholas François Armstrong, age twenty-eight, admitted to Princess Mary's Hospital suffering from malnutrition, exhaustion and clinical depression as a result of torture while in Gestapo custody. A lot of medical terms she didn't understand. All nails removed from both hands. She shuddered. Severe psychosis induced by trauma. Alice read those terrible sentences over and over. Bald statements of fact which condemned Nicholas François Armstrong to a life sentence.

They'd certainly tried at Princess Mary's. Drugs, electroconvulsive therapy. He had just retreated further to escape them.

Ashton was his last chance, a gamble that a change from the secure environment of a hospital might jolt him into self-awareness. Hospitals where the windows were meshed as a precaution against suicide were the same to him as the cell in the Avenue Foch. She paused, and suddenly realized that she was trembling. She knew the Avenue Foch from pre-war trips to Paris. A lovely wide boulevard lined with trees, mansions masquerading as town houses. She'd been to smart parties in the Avenue Foch. Now one of those lovely old houses had been turned into a torture chamber . . . If Armstrong didn't respond at Ashton, then he would return for further treatment at Princess Mary's with a view to long-term stay in a civilian mental hospital.

Alice closed the file and put it back. He was responding but not fast enough. Not nearly fast enough to escape the fate closing in on him. A shake of the head, a movement in response to her approach – they wouldn't save him. She had to make a breakthrough before those critical three months were up. She had to help him, no matter what the risk. Either way, he had nothing to lose.

She spent the rest of the night awake, thinking what she could do. There was a clue in that report, and it was nearly dawn when she realized what it was. 'Jolt him into self-awareness.' That was it. Bring him face to face with the terror he was trying to escape. And not by letting him sit in self-imposed silence, cut off from the world. She didn't wait until her usual teatime visit. She went to the Spencer room that same morning. As she went in she met the sister.

'Good morning, Mrs Vandekar. We weren't expecting you until this afternoon.' It was phrased as a question and a pleasant smile went with it, but Alice noticed a glint in her eye. They felt she was spending too much time with this one man, and her persistence was becoming a reproach to the nursing staff.

'I've decided,' Alice said, 'to come more often. Thank you, Sister,' and she walked into the room and closed the door.

He was sitting in his chair in the same position by the window. She had an idea. Everyone spoke to him in English. For the past few months he'd been hearing the same words in the same language and refusing to respond. 'We'll try French,' Alice said to herself. 'We'll see what that does.' She was fluent, although Hugo mocked her strong American accent.

She took her place beside Armstrong and again she laid her hand on his arm.

When she spoke to him he jumped. 'Of course, this is your second language, Nick. How stupid, I should have thought of it before. That's why you went to

France, isn't it? You could pass as a Frenchman.' She moved closer to him. 'It was a wonderful thing to do,' she said softly. 'You were very brave. You've got to be brave now. And I'm going to help you. I'm going to talk to you about France.'

That evening she went to find Lily. She was flushed and her eyes were wide and bright with excitement. Lily looked at her and felt a funny pang of alarm. She'd never seen her with that look. Never.

'Sit down, madam' Lily said. 'I'll make you some tea'.

'I don't want tea,' Alice said. 'I've got something wonderful to tell you. Lily, I think he's going to be all right!'

Lily didn't need to ask who she meant. She never talked about anyone else these days.

'Why?' Lily stared at her. 'What's happened? Has he said something?'

'Yes,' Alice announced. 'That's what he said. "Yes." It's the first word he's spoken in God knows how long. I talked about holidays, places I'd stayed and people we knew, and then I'd drop in something special, something I knew he'd recognize. He didn't like it. He looked so upset and disturbed at times, poor darling, I couldn't go on. So I went back to talking about the opera and the races and that sort of nonsense. And then it was time to go, Lily, and I said what I've said every single time, almost out of habit. "Shall I come tomorrow?" And he said, "Yes." That was all. *Oui*. Oh, I could have died, I was so thrilled.'

'What did you do, madam,' Lily asked. 'What ever did you do?'

Alice clasped her hands. 'Nothing. Nothing at all. I just behaved as if it was the most normal thing in the world. And then I went and found the nurse on duty, it was a new one on the corridor, and told her to tell Dr Ferguson. Lily, I feel like a million dollars tonight!'

'And so you should,' Lily agreed. 'I have always said if anyone can help that poor soul, it'll be you.'

Alice said, 'I'm suddenly tired. I've been on top of the world and now I could just drop. And I haven't been up to say good night to Fern. I'd better go or I'll have that old hag's reproachful looks tomorrow. God I can't wait for her to leave!'

'She says she won't leave her little darling until she sees there's someone responsible to take over,' Lily said. 'And she's worked that child up over going to the school with me till she cries all the way there!'

Alice said firmly, 'Shut up, Lily, stop making trouble. I know you hate her. I'll go upstairs and say goodnight. And I wouldn't mind a nice strong martini waiting for me when I come down.'

Nanny was sitting by the fire, knitting something long and navy blue. She was always knitting for sailors. She got up rather slowly and said, 'Oh, Mrs Vandekar, Fern's in bed. It was so late we thought you weren't coming.'

'I'll put my head round the door anyway. Fern? Are you asleep?'

'No, Mummy.' There was a slight whine in the voice these days which always irritated her. She went into the bedroom. Her daughter lay flat under the covers, still as one of her own dolls. She had wide dark eyes like Hugo's and they watched her mother warily. Alice came over and sat on the edge of the bed. 'I've come to kiss you good night,' she announced. 'Then you must be a good girl and go to sleep.'

'Yes, Mummy.'

'Did you have fun today?' God, can I do with that martini, Alice thought. But I'm so happy. So happy. Just one little word in a rusty voice. I've never heard him speak before in all this time...

'I hate it, Mummy,' she heard the child say, and came back to reality. 'They don't play with me. Do I have to go?'

Alice looked down and saw the tears brimming and the turned-down little mouth that never roused her pity. 'Yes, you do,' she said. 'You can't just quit on something because you don't like it. You've got to try with people, Fern. The children are shy, that's all. They'll get to know you and you'll get to know them. It'll be good for you.'

'Nanny says they're rough and nasty,' Fern whispered.

'Oh, does she?' Alice said quietly. 'Well, you listen to what I tell you. Never mind what Nanny says. You're going to school in the mornings and you'll learn to play with the other children. You've been stuck in this ivory tower up here for long enough. Now I've got to go. Good night, darling. Sleep well.' She bent and sealed the child's forehead with a brisk kiss.

Fern didn't lift up her arms or move. She stared at her mother's back as she walked out and closed the door. Nanny was leaving. Fern had cried and cried when she told her, and then poor Nanny had cried too. Her mother was too busy looking after the young men in the house to care about her own dear little girl, Nanny had declared in a bitter monologue which Fern could hear. And that jumped-up maid of hers, dragging the poor child down to that dreadful village school full of common children. She was sure some of them had nits in their hair, and Fern would catch them. She had fine tooth-combed the long dark hair every night, and Fern wondered in horror what she was looking for.

Her mother was horrible, she thought, blinking back her tears and glaring at the closed door. She was being cross with Nanny. She could hear their voices in the night nursery. Poor Nanny, being sent away. I hate her, the child thought, and then slid down in the bed in guilty fear at the enormity of thinking such a wicked thought. I wish Daddy was here. He wouldn't make me go to that school.

'Mrs Vandekar, I hope you won't take this the wrong way.'

Alice crossed one leg over the other. She regarded

Dr Ferguson with a slight smile and a cold eye. 'Of course not. Why should I?'

'You've done invaluable work,' he began. 'All the chaps here are devoted to you. Nobody could have done more, apart from turning your house over to us so generously. But I'm afraid Flight Lieutenant Armstrong is in a different category to the others. I'd like to talk to you about him.'

'I thought you might,' Alice said. She lit a cigarette. 'Please go ahead.'

He cleared his throat. She was tireless and devoted to the men in his care. But with Armstrong she was exceeding her brief.

He had to be tactful but firm. He sensed that she wasn't going to be easy. 'He's a special case,' he said. 'Mentally wounded, if you like. He's the first patient in this category to come here, and I have to say I wasn't happy about it from the start. But he's got quite influential friends in his branch of the Service, which doesn't seem to follow normal RAF rules. He needs expert medical help. I'm afraid your visits seem to be upsetting him.'

'Dr Ferguson,' Alice said coldly, 'When Flight Lieutenant Armstrong came here he hadn't spoken a word to anyone since his escape from France. He has actually *talked* to me. You know that.'

'He's said the odd word certainly. That's a great tribute to your patience and persistence. But it seems you're trying to probe into his past experiences. Am I right in suggesting that you're trying to get him to relive them?'

Alice looked sharply at him. 'I didn't know your nurses listened at the door,' she said.

He reddened, but there was no denial. 'Let me try to explain.' He resented her rudeness but he was still trying to be polite. 'Armstrong was practically catatonic when he was brought into Princess Mary's. You know what that means, I'm sure.' She nodded. He went on, 'He wouldn't respond to any stimulus. Some rather severe treatment helped that, but he is still very precariously balanced. His refusal to communicate is a safety valve. It's amazing that you've got him to speak the odd word. There might just be some hope for him in the long term. But you are taking a risk with his sanity, Mrs Vandekar. I know it's from the best motives, but I must ask you to stop. Stop your visits, just for the timebeing.'

'You're saying I'm doing him harm?'

'I'm afraid so. You're meddling with something you don't understand. He could collapse completely, and all the work done in hospital would have been wasted.'

'I understand one thing,' Alice said. 'He's hiding from the world because there's something he can't face. You've done nothing to help him. He should be in a ward, not isolated from other people. He needs human contact, not some nurse bustling in and out again. And that's what I've given him.' She paused – nothing she said was having any effect. And she couldn't let him know she'd seen his files.

'He needs time,' Ferguson said. 'He's not ready to face anything yet.'

Time, as Alice knew, was what Nick Armstrong had not got. But she couldn't say that either.

'He will never be ready,' she tried once more, 'unless there's someone there to take him by the hand and hold it tight when the crunch comes. I believe I am that person.'

His face was set like stone. 'I'm afraid I must insist,' he said. 'Your visits must stop. The nursing staff have noticed how disturbed he is. I've seen evidence of it myself. I'm sorry, Mrs Vandekar, but my patient's welfare comes first.'

He stood up to end the conversation. Alice didn't move.

'What happens if he asks for me?'

'He won't,' Ferguson said. 'He won't notice. He's looking inward, protecting himself.'

'If you're wrong and he does,' she persisted, 'you'll tell me? You'll let me see him?'

'Yes. I promise you. But don't delude yourself. It won't happen.'

Alice got up, stubbed out her cigarette. 'Very well. I'll stay away. But you've promised.'

'I have indeed,' he said. 'Thank you for being so understanding.' He thought she looked as if she might break down in tears. He didn't want that – it would be most embarrassing.

'Because I've accepted what you say, it doesn't mean I agree with it,' she said, and walked out of the office.

He tipped the ashtray into the waste-paper basket. He was not used to being challenged by a woman. He decided that Alice Vandekar needed a strong man to put her in her place. No, he admitted, he didn't really like her in spite of all the good work she had done. And it was obvious that she had become emotionally involved with Armstrong. She didn't realize it, but there was a deeper motive than the desire to comfort a sick man. A very dangerous situation all round, especially so when dealing with an acute neurotic. The sooner he could get rid of Armstrong and restore normality, the better. At least he had a few days' grace to sort it out. And she wouldn't break her word. She wasn't the type to do that.

The next few days seemed as if they would never end. Alice drove herself to exhaustion but she couldn't sleep and she couldn't stop thinking about Nick. Once she found herself drawn to that long winding corridor in the south annexe, passing his door. She had to force herself to hurry on. The thought of him sitting alone, slumped in despair in front of the window, tortured her. She'd seen him for so long sunk in the twilight of guilt and fear. He wouldn't notice, that pig of a doctor had insisted. Don't delude yourself. How she hated him, with his stubbly red moustache and his pompous voice talking down to her. She shouldn't have agreed; she should have fought harder . . . She blamed herself

98

and agonized for the lost and lonely man abandoned in his room. But there was nothing she could do. Ferguson's threat prevented her. 'He could collapse completely . . .' She had to endure the misery and the uncertainty, and pray that Ferguson was wrong and Nick would prove it. But nothing happened. By the end of the week she gave in and confided in Lily. She was in floods of tears.

Lily was horrified. She couldn't believe that the weeping girl was her sturdy, independent mistress. She'd been proud of her resilience, her gutsy reaction to trouble and sorrow with the other men. She'd never seen her so upset, not even when her mother went back to the States. Lily wondered how this poor creature had come to mean more to her mistress than any of the hopelessly disfigured or the wheelchair-bound for life. She was shocked and she didn't know what to make of it. Or she didn't want to know. But she saw the pale, tear-stained face and her heart ached for Alice.

'Lily, he'll just go back to a mental hospital and stay there for the rest of his life if something isn't done to help him! What am I to do?'

Lily thought for a moment. Then she said, 'How do you know he hasn't asked for you, madam?'

'What? Ferguson promised.'

'Who's going to tell Dr Ferguson,' Lily countered. 'That nurse who went running with tales – tell the doctor she was wrong, my foot!' Alice's favourite expression came out before she could stop it. Neither of them noticed.

Alice said, 'I promised I wouldn't see him. I can't go back on that.'

'You can't go in, but there's nothing to stop me,' Lily declared. 'Let me go and see how he is. I'm not frightened of any nurse. At least it'll set your mind at rest.'

'Oh, Lily. Would you do that? Would you see him today, right now?'

Lily looked at her wristwatch, a present from Alice

one birthday. It was gold, with a pretty little strap. 'It's lunchtime,' she said. 'Wait till the afternoon rest period. I'll pop in then. And don't you worry, madam.'

Alice sat down on the window seat. The lovely landscape unrolled below, the marble lovers locked eternally in their embrace.

'I'll never forget this,' she said, not looking at Lily. 'You don't know how miserable I've been these last few days. Not seeing him. Worrying about him. He may think I've just got bored and given up on him.'

'I'll tell him you haven't,' Lily promised. And she said again, 'Don't worry. I'll see to it.'

The rest period lasted from two until 3.30. There was no one about when Lily knocked on the door in the south annexe. Nobody answered so she opened it and went in. The man sitting in his chair looked up briefly and then turned away. Funny-looking type, not what she'd expected. Dark as a Spaniard, black hair and eyes and all. Thin as a scarecrow too. Fancy her lady getting so worked up about him.

'Good afternoon, sir,' she said. 'Can I get you anything?'

'No.' The voice was flat. He turned his head away.

Lily took a deep breath. 'I'm Mrs Vandekar's maid. She sent me to see how you were.' She stood there – it seemed impossible to wait much longer.

Then his head turned towards her. 'Where is she? Why hasn't she come?'

'What on earth are you doing in here!' The nurse had come up behind her. She caught hold of Lily's arm.

Lily shook it off. 'You shut up,' she snapped, 'You never told the doctor, did you? Well, I'm telling him if you don't. Now, sir, do you want Mrs Vandekar to come and see you?'

'Yes.' It was said very low. He brought up a hand and wiped his eyes.

Lily saw the tears running unchecked down his face. She gave the nurse a venomous look.

'Oh, you bitch,' she whispered, 'you bitch! Wait until my lady hears about this!'

'Mrs Vandekar, I've decided to move Flight Lieutenant Armstrong back to Princess Mary's. It's the best thing for him.'

Alice drew a deep breath. 'So they can send him to an asylum? Oh no, Dr Ferguson. No, you're not going to do that.'

He was infuriated by her tone; her angry denunciation of his nursing staff was the last straw. Armstrong should never have been foisted on them in the first place. He belonged with the mentally sick. 'I've already made the arrangements.'

Alice flushed scarlet. 'Then you can unmake them,' she said. 'Unless you want to be posted out of this nice cushy billet. And don't think that I can't arrange it. One telephone call to my friend Lord Warrington complaining about your behaviour and that will fix you. For good!'

'How dare you threaten me!' he exclaimed. 'How dare you try and blackmail me!'

'I don't give a damn what you call it. But I don't threaten anything I can't deliver. How would you like to go to North Africa, Doctor, and see the war at the sharp end for a change?'

'You're unbelievable. You're a lunatic yourself!' He got up. 'Get out of my office!' he shouted.

'It's not your office, it's my house,' she shouted back. 'You leave Nick Armstrong alone. I'll be responsible for him. I'll nurse him myself, and if anything goes wrong you can blame me. But he's not leaving here. Now call up and cancel those arrangements.'

'I will see you damned before I do.'

'Very well,' Alice said. She walked over to the desk and picked up the telephone. She dialled and, after a pause, said, 'This is Mrs Hugo Vandekar. I'd like to speak to Lord Warrington. Thank you. Peter – how nice to talk to you . . . Oh, very well, busy, you know.

We've a lot of patients at the moment.' She gave Ferguson a glare. 'Not at all, it's a great privilege. But I'm having a little problem with one of the medical officers here . . .' She heard the door slam as the doctor walked out. 'Well, it is rather embarrassing, but I wonder if you could help. It's a patient we've got, he's such a sweet boy and he's had such a bad time. I'm afraid this man Ferguson doesn't concern himself with battle-fatigue cases. He thinks they should all be in asylums. Yes, seriously, I've begged him not to send this particular boy away, but he won't listen and it's upset me dreadfully. He *is* rather special to me, Peter, and I've spent such a lovely time with him, reading and getting him to take an interest in things again. Now it's all going to be wasted. You wouldn't have a word, would you – just for me? Oh, you are just darling. I'm so grateful. Flight Lieutenant Armstrong – I'll go and tell the poor chap he won't have to move – he'll be *so* relieved. Everyone's been terribly upset about it. You really will? Oh, thank you, Peter. You're my favourite man.'

She put the receiver back. Peter Warrington was an old friend, one of the prewar circle who spent many happy weekends at Ashton. As Minister for Health he had inspected Ashton after it had been open for six months and had told Alice he would mention the wonderful work being done there to the Prime Minister. She walked back to the south annexe. If Peter Warrington said he would intervene, then the lines to Army Medical Corps would be buzzing.

'Hello, Nick,' she said. He looked at her with his empty eyes. 'Aren't you going to say hello?' she prompted. 'If you don't speak to me, I won't be allowed to come and see you, you know. Did you miss me?'

'Yes.'

'Oh, thank God,' she said under her breath. 'I missed you too. How have you been feeling? Are you all right?'

'Yes.'

'No, you're not,' she said brightly. 'You've been sitting here glooming away feeling sorry for yourself. That's going to stop. I'm looking after you from now on. You don't need a nurse, except to dress your hands. I can do that for you if you like. One day you're going to stop wearing those silly gloves.'

He drew a sharp breath and hid his hands under his arms. 'No,' he said, 'no.'

'I know they look bad,' Alice said gently. 'It doesn't matter. They'd heal quicker if you didn't cover them. Nothing like that matters except your getting well.' She came and knelt close to the chair.

'You don't know,' he said, and his mouth twisted in private agony. 'You don't know . . .'

Alice reached out and put her arms round him. 'Oh yes I do,' she whispered. 'I know everything. You just trust me – everything's going to be all right. I promise.'

The new medical officer arrived within the week. Alice didn't see Ferguson before he left. The nursing staff knew that he had been replaced because of a row with Mrs Vandekar; it didn't make her popular but it made them wary. She had taken charge of Armstrong. She did everything for him herself, moving down into the south wing to be near him at night.

Some odd and ugly rumours began circulating among the nurses. He was a real basket case, they said, but Mrs High and Mighty had decided she was going to cure him. They couldn't say she neglected the others. Somehow Alice found time to do everything she'd done before. She read to men whose eyes had been affected, she played cards, she organized the weekly film show, she was there for anyone who asked. But she spent most of her time in that room, taking her meals with him, reading poetry which she discovered he liked. She only found it out because he would volunteer whole sentences sometimes. There were good days when she was full of hope, and bad days, when she hid her anxiety from him. There was no need to force the pace, no threat of a return to a mental hospital. Dear Peter Warrington had seen to that.

Alice left the war and his experiences lying fallow in his mind. Her task was to bring him back to normality, to make contact with life and people, and then bring him to the edge, holding fast to him when the moment came. 'Nick,' she said one morning, 'the sun's shining. It's quite warm outside. I'd like to walk round the garden. Will you come with me?'

When he didn't answer, she went on, overriding the refusal before it came. 'I'll get a warm coat, there's one in the cupboard here. We'll just take a few turns and then come back. It'll do you good. Come on, put this on. There.' She buttoned it for him. He was taller than she was, but so frail and so uncertain in his movements that Alice held his arm and guided him out into the corridor and through into the gardens.

It was a warm day for early April, a time of year when Ashton drew on its cloak of glorious spring colours. Daffodils in great swathes, the patchwork of primulas under the trees. If only he could recognize its beauty, she thought. If only he could forget his nightmare and look out and see how wonderful life could be because of a beautiful day.

There was a walled garden, sheltered from winds and passers-by. She took him there and made him sit on a little seat in the sun. 'You should have seen this place before the war,' she said. 'Now it's a mess, because you can't get enough people for the gardens. They're all one-legged or something.' She laughed and slipped her arm through his. He still wore the gloves, but one day she would persuade him to take them off. 'It used to be a sunken rose garden,' she went on. 'The scent was almost too much when they were all blooming. But I'll get it right, when things are normal again. There'll be no more weeds, Nick, just masses and masses of flowers.'

'I'd like to see them,' he said.

'You will,' Alice said. 'I promise.' He was having a

very good day, she thought, and her heart filled with a deep joy. There was a brightness in his eyes she hadn't seen before.

'I can't stay here for ever,' he said.

'You can stay as long as you like,' she said.

'I'd like that.'

'So would I.' She mustn't let him see how moved she was. He became agitated and distressed if he sensed she was unhappy.

'I don't want to go back to the hospital. I heard them say . . .'

The brightness was gone. He was fearful again, and Alice responded almost fiercely. 'You're not going anywhere you don't want to,' she declared. 'You're staying with me, here at Ashton. For the rest of your life, so far as I'm concerned.'

There was a long silence. She thought they had better go in. His walk out into the garden was miracle enough for one day. But there was another to come.

'You care about me, don't you?'

'Yes,' she agreed. 'Very much.'

'I don't deserve it.'

'I think you do.' It can't go on, it's too good to be true. He's talking to me about himself. Only once before when he wept in my arms and mumbled about his guilt, and since then nothing. Oddments. I like Browning. That gave the clue to poetry. Some classical music. This pudding tastes of apples. Fragments of the personality, but always superficial, always guarded. Maybe the moment was coming.

'Nick,' she said. 'We're going back to the house now. But we've had a lovely morning, haven't we?'

He nodded. He looked sad, and yet he was trying to smile at her. 'Yes. Lovely. Thanks to you.'

'There'll be lots of lovely mornings and lovely days,' she said quietly. 'I want you to believe that. And one day I'm going to ask you to do something very brave. Just for me.' She helped him up. 'Will you do it?' She held him by the arms looking up at him.

'I'll try,' he said.

One of the nurses saw them walking slowly back towards the house. She told of the incident at lunch. 'You have to hand it to her,' she said. 'She's bringing him back to life, no mistake about it. Out walking arm in arm they were. When I came here he was like a zombie.'

'Yes,' one of the physiotherapists said, 'it's amazing what true love can do!'

'Go on –' the nurse said. 'I've heard all that stuff about her sleeping next door, but it's a lot of nonsense.'

'I'm not talking about sex,' the other girl insisted. 'I'm saying she's madly in love with him. Good luck to her, I say. Let's hope he doesn't say thanks and bye-bye and walk off to the wife when she's got him well.'

'He's not married, is he? There's never been a wife down here to see him.'

'They're *all* married,' the physiotherapist said sourly. She had had bad experiences with glamorous servicemen in need of treatment. 'Pass the bread, please. And the mousetrap. Thanks.'

'Now, Nick, we're going to have tea in here for a change. This is my boudoir – that word's such a silly affectation. It makes me think of someone dripping around on a day bed. It's my sitting room, that sounds better, doesn't it?'

He looked around him; the colour of the grey silk walls and the cool Wedgwood blue was very soothing. 'It's beautiful,' he said.

She guided him to a deep sofa, piled extravagantly with embroidered cushions. 'You sit there,' she said. 'I'll light the fire.'

'No. I'll do it.'

She gave him the matches. 'All right. Lily's going to bring us some tea.'

He knelt by the grate, the loose gloves making it difficult for him to take the match out and strike it.

She longed to take the box and do it for him, but

every independent move he made was progress. He wouldn't let her go on her knees to light a fire; not long ago he'd have sat passive and withdrawn while she did so. 'That's fine,' she said. 'It'll burn now. I love a fire at this time of day. It starts to get cool around now. Come and sit beside me.'

There was a knock on the door. Lily came in with a tray.

'Good afternoon, sir,' she said. 'Madam, I managed a few sandwiches and some biscuits. I hope that's all right.'

She saw the brilliance of Alice's smile. 'That's perfect. Thank you, Lily.' She looked so content, sitting there with him beside her. So happy. Like an old married couple. Lily chided herself for making the comparison.

Alice poured. The cups were her own, delicate porcelain. She thought, he's going to find it difficult to hold the cup. I've brought him here to get him away from that room and its associations. Maybe this is the time to do it.

She glanced quickly at him. He had fleshed out a little; he looked frail and ill but the ghastly pallor and leaden eye had gone. It was such a risk, her courage faltered. If it went wrong... You're being a coward, she thought. A coward because you're scared for yourself.

'Nick,' she said, 'you can't hold my best china in those damned gloves. Please take them off.'

It was the longest moment of her life. It seemed as if everything was frozen. The clock stopped ticking, the fire didn't crackle. She held her breath.

He was looking at his hands. He held them out. 'I don't want you to see them,' he said.

'I shan't mind,' Alice said. 'Please take them off.'

Slowly he pulled at the one on his left hand, finger by finger.

She didn't gasp. She bit so hard into her lip that she drew a tiny bead of blood. 'Now the other one,' she said softly. 'The other one, darling.' She didn't realize she'd called him that. 'There,' Alice said, and kept her eyes on his face. 'Now you won't break my favourite cup.'

He was sobbing in her arms. She rocked him to and fro as she had never done with her own child. 'Hush,' she murmured, 'Hush, don't cry like that. It's all right, everything's going to be all right now.'

'I told them,' he was saying, over and over, 'I couldn't stand it. I tried, but they kept coming in and starting all over again.'

Alice held tightly to him, imagining the flickering images and the ringing screams of pain. The poor mangled hands were clutching at her. All the nails were ripped out, the fingers twisted and broken.

'I was half drowning...' he said, 'in the bath... I tried to drown but they pulled me out... Then they tied my hands down.' He pulled away from her and crouched, moving backwards and forwards in the agony of his grief.

'I gave in,' he said through his rough weeping. 'I betrayed the others. I betrayed my own wife... Oh God, I wish I was dead. I wish I was dead.'

She slipped down to the floor and knelt beside him. She put her arms round him. For a moment he resisted and she panicked. If he rejected her now, if he turned back in upon himself with the burden of that dreadful guilt... But she felt him come to her and lean, and she cried silently herself because she knew the worst part of the battle for his life was won.

'My darling,' she said, 'my darling, trust me, let me help you. I'll do anything, anything in the world.'

She didn't hear the knock; she didn't hear the door open. She cradled him in her arms, while Nanny and Fern stood there, staring at her. There was a bandage round Fern's knee. She'd been knocked over in the playground and Nanny had marched down to show Mrs Vandekar the result of making the child go to that dreadful school.

Nanny stood rooted, unable to believe her eyes.

Making love to one of the young men. Right in her own sitting room. She gave a loud gasp and tugged at Fern to take her away. But Fern had seen too. Her knee was cut and needed two stitches. She felt sick with the pain and worse still because Nanny fussed and exclaimed while the doctor was treating her. Now Mummy was putting her arms round somebody, kissing him. It was shameful and bad, and Nanny was saying things under her breath.

Fern burst into more tears. 'I'm going to be sick,' she said. And she was.

Alice didn't know anyone had disturbed them. She didn't hear the door close. The teatray was untouched. The fire burned low, and in the end Nick was calm enough to look at her and say, 'How can you forgive me? How can you ever forget what I've done?'

'Because you didn't do it,' Alice said quietly. 'You didn't betray anyone. You thought you did because that's what they told you.'

'That's a lie,' he said. 'You're saying that. They said that in the hospital. I know what happened. I know they killed Janine...'

'Nick,' she said, 'do you trust me? Do you think I'd lie to you?'

'If it would help me, yes you would.'

'It wouldn't help you,' she answered. 'Only the truth will help you now. Don't you see what's happened? You've broken the spell! You knew what would happen if you took off those gloves, and you still did it. You want to face what happened, and that's why you're going to get well. Now listen to me. Listen and believe what I'm saying.' She raised her hand and touched his face. 'If you did give way under torture like that, I wouldn't care a damn. I wouldn't try to lie to you. I'd tell you to accept it and then forget it. Better men than you have cracked for far less. But it didn't happen that way. And I can prove it to you.'

'How?' he asked her.

'Just give me a few days,' Alice asked him. 'Hold

yourself together, and I'll prove the whole story is a lie.'

After a moment she said, 'The tea's quite cold.'

'Don't leave me,' he said, 'I don't want to be alone.'

'You won't be,' Alice promised. 'You're coming upstairs and you'll stay the night with me.'

'Lily, I'm going to London. You've got to look after Nick today.'

Lily had come in with her mistress's morning tea to find her asleep in the armchair and the flight lieutenant in her bed. She didn't doubt Alice's explanation for a moment. She merely protested at not being told. She could have given up her bed to madam, and watched over him during the night.

Alice thanked her. 'I've been quite comfortable – I slept on and off. You can keep him company today. I've got to see someone in Mr Hugo's office.'

'Oh? Can't Mr Hugo help?'

'He won't,' she said shortly. 'But there may be someone else who will. The man who sent Nicholas down here. He was in the RAF himself. If I can find him . . . Lily, you mustn't look at his hands. Don't say anything, for God's sake. Just chat, or read to him, and see that he eats. He'd better stay up here till I get back.'

'Is he bad again, then?' Lily asked.

Alice's tired face lit up. 'No, Lily. He's come through. He's himself now. You'll see. But I've something vital to do for him, and then he'll be able to take up living properly again. Oh, it won't be soon, but in the end he'll be really well.'

Lily nodded. 'I said you'd do it. Don't worry about him, madam. I'll take care of him.'

'I know you will,' Alice said. 'You've always taken care of me. Now run the bath and put something out for me to wear. Something pretty. I'm going to have to work on this Group Captain Wallace.'

When she was shown into his office in Baker Street, Alice was surprised to see how old the Group Captain was. He was well into his fifties and quite grey.

A call to Hugo's old number had got her transferred. Wallace was very friendly, and said of course they could meet if she felt he could help Nick Armstrong. No, he wasn't at the War Office, he was in an overspill, an old building in Baker Street. Close to the Waxworks, he said, making a joke of it.

He was surprised by how beautiful she was. He wasn't a man who had read the society columns before the war or was interested in the frivolous lives of the very rich. He had been a don at Oxford. He had served in the Royal Flying Corps at the end of the First World War; his rank reflected his seniority in the newly formed intelligence unit proposed by Churchill. SOE – Special Operations Executive. Set Europe ablaze, the Prime Minister had commanded. Men like Nicholas Armstrong were spirited into occupied France to do just that. And a great many of them, women included, were captured. Unlike Hugo, Wallace saw no reason to withhold the broad outline of what had happened. Armstrong was one of a group landed by felucca on the Mediterranean coast. Their job was to make contact with the French Resistance and organize them into groups. They were to sabotage important German targets, establish networks of other groups throughout France, and be prepared to suffer torture if they were taken alive. Armstrong was a very exprienced operator and this had been his third mission in France. On this occasion he and several others had been captured by the Gestapo. He was on a train bound for Mauthausen concentration camp when the Resistance derailed it. In the confusion he had been rescued and was eventually picked up by the felucca and returned to England. She must have seen for herself the wreck he had become after his ordeal.

'Yes,' Alice said. 'I saw it. And I also saw that nothing positive was being done to help him. I had a fight with our medical officer because he wanted to send Nick back to Princess Mary's. After that it was a mental hospital. Probably for life. I wasn't going to let that happen to him. And it won't now. He's so nearly well, Group Captain Wallace. He's put up such a fight to get back to normal!'

'I have a feeling you've done quite a lot of fighting for him,' Wallace said. Such a pretty woman, and such a determined one, in spite of the ultra-feminine approach to him. He saw through it immediately. He admired her, and her dogged refusal to give up on a hopeless case awoke his sympathy. He didn't give in easily either. He wondered what his colleague, the austere and serious-minded Hugo Vandekar, made of this singular devotion to another man.

'Was his wife on this mission with him?'

He raised his eyebrows. 'His wife? Good God, no. Why do you ask that?'

'Because he thinks she was,' Alice replied. 'He thinks he betrayed her to the Gestapo. He told me ... They killed Janine. That's what he said!'

Wallace frowned. 'It's a delusion, of course. His wife's in England. In London, as a matter of fact.'

Now it was Alice who stared. 'In London? Why hasn't she been to see him?'

'Because she's left him,' he said. 'She's living in some style with one of our American allies. A Colonel Chuck Wallace. Same name as mine, but no relation, I assure you.'

'Does she know what happened to him?'

'Indeed she does. Of course, nobody realized he was harbouring this appalling delusion. How did you find out?' He looked at her with the steely appraisal he reserved for potential recruits to his organization. Not only a very determined woman, but a very intuitive one to have succeeded where the army psychiatrists had failed.

'He told me when he broke down,' she said slowly. 'It was terrible to see him. He cried and cried. I've never seen a man tear himself to pieces like that and I've been with burns cases when they looked in the mirror for the first time. It all came flooding out. How he'd been nearly drowned, and then they ripped his hands to bits. He said he'd told them everything, betrayed everyone. Including his wife. She was dead, he said. I can't believe this. Why? Why should he think that?'

Wallace thought for a moment. 'God knows. God knows what they said to torment him. Anything, and when you're half mad with that kind of pain, you'll believe anything.'

Alice said quietly, 'Did he give the others away?'

'We'll never know,' he answered. 'He was the only one rescued from that train. Personally I doubt it. Good God,' he said angrily, 'if only we'd known this we could have saved the poor devil so much agony.'

'I promised him proof,' she said. 'I didn't know I'd even get any. But I promised. I knew from the medical records there was something driving him crazy, but I didn't know exactly what.'

'I'm surprised you were allowed to see them.'

'I wasn't. I found them and looked them up.'

'I see,' he said. 'I think I'd better contact his wife and see whether she'll agree to visit him. She wasn't particularly anxious to go down to Princess Mary's actually. She certainly didn't persist when the doctors said no. But this may be different.'

'If she's any kind of a human being,' Alice said, 'she'll come to Ashton tomorrow.'

'I hope so,' he answered. 'But guilt does funny things to people. Usually it makes them run away. Thank you for coming to see me. And thank you for what you've done for Nick Armstrong. I've known him for a long time. I recruited him, you see, so I've been feeling rather guilty myself. He's a fine man. He won't disappoint you, Mrs Vandekar.'

She was driving back when she remembered what he had said. She wondered what he meant by it.

Fern's knee turned septic. It was swollen and she ran a temperature. That accounted for her being sick, or so the doctor diagnosed.

113

Alice stood with him by the bed; it was kind of him to look after the child when he had so much to do with the patients. He was an elderly man, called back from the reserve, and she liked him as much as she had hated Ferguson.

Nanny hovered in the background. Her days were numbered. The local schoolmistress had a sister, now retired from teaching. Lily had brought her up to be interviewed and Alice had engaged her. She seemed pleasant and competent; too old, unfortunately, but not the type to smother Fern and hold her back. Fern heard she was coming and began to be sick again.

'Hot poulticing,' Dr Banks said, 'Plenty of warm drinks and rest. It's only a local infection but quite nasty. The vomiting will settle when the temperature comes down. Now you be a good girl and you'll soon be well.' He smiled at Fern and patted the top of her head. He had grandchildren of his own, and she looked so pathetic lying there, flushed in the face and sunken-eyed.

'I want Daddy,' she murmured.

'Of course you do, but Mummy's here,' he said. 'Daddy'll be home soon, I expect.' He turned to Alice. She was looking impatient. That is a pity, he thought. A great pity if she isn't sympathetic. But the young mothers of today are a different breed. Especially with all that money and staff to take over their responsibilities for them. He sighed. 'Are you expecting Major Vandekar on leave?'

'He phoned to say he'd be back at the end of the week,' Alice said. She moved away from Fern's bedside, so she wouldn't hear. 'It's embarkation leave, I'm afraid.'

'Well, we won't let the little girl know about that,' Dr Banks said firmly. 'I think it would help if you settled her down tonight instead of her nurse. Read to her for a bit.'

'Yes, of course,' Alice agreed. She glanced back at

114

Fern. The child was staring at her. Meeting Alice's eye, she closed hers tightly.

'Wouldn't it be better if she just went to sleep?' Alice suggested.

'Try reading to her for a little while. I'll look in tomorrow and see how she's getting on. And if you're worried, just phone and I'll come straight up. Good night, Fern. Good night, Mrs Vandekar.'

Alice suppressed a sigh of irritation. Two days of waiting – two days of suspense, keeping Nick's spirits up. It was Wallace who'd advised her not to tell him his wife was alive, but to present him with the *fait accompli* by bringing her to Ashton or him to London. So Alice kept the secret and waited for news from the group captain. It had come that very afternoon. Janine Armstrong had been contacted and was ready to see her husband. Her only stipulation was that she could bring her American colonel with her. Otherwise she couldn't get petrol for the drive. Tomorrow. They were coming tomorrow.

Alice turned back to her daughter. Nick was downstairs in her sitting room, waiting for her to join him. If he was left alone he faltered, sinking back into numb despair and self-blame. Just one more day and she could bring the living proof of his innocence into the room.

'Now, Fern, what would you like me to read to you?'

'If you're busy, Mrs Vandekar, I can read to her.' Nanny was bristling with hostility. She had a new way of looking Alice in the eye these last few days, not attempting to conceal her dislike. Even something more than dislike; Alice supposed it was resentment at leaving and forgot about it.

The offer was tempting, but she resisted it. She had neglected Fern and felt a brief pang of guilt. The old hag was just dying to be able to criticize at the last gasp. 'No thanks. Just give me the bedtime book and I'll stay for half an hour. I don't want to tire her out.'

Alice sat by the bedside. *What Katy Did.* She remembered reading that herself. Surely to God there was something more up to date in the nursery . . . She found the bookmark and started to read.

Fern lay very still and watched her mother from under her lids. She wasn't listening to the story. She couldn't get rid of that horrible picture in her mind. It kept coming back and making her stomach heave. Her mother kneeling on the ground . . . A strange man all entangled with her, and her mother kissing him. She had never seen her kiss her father. She received the brisk touch of the lips on her cheek or her brow, and that was what she saw happening to the man. Nanny had cuddled her afterwards. She hadn't even scolded her for being sick in the corridor. Whatever her mother was doing, it was so terrible that Nanny kept on nursing her on her knee and saying frightening things like, 'Don't you worry, my poor pet . . . You just pretend you never saw anything . . .'

Her mother didn't want to stay with her and read the book. Fern didn't want her to stay. She knew the story backwards and had never liked it. Nanny said wasn't it a lovely book and went on reading it time and again. With the chill precocity of an only child, Fern realized that it was because Nanny liked it herself. She hated the bouncing, clever heroine who was always pretending to be a boy and getting into trouble. There were girls like that in school, pushing and shoving her whenever they got the chance. She thought, I wish Mummy would go away, I know what will make her go. She raised her head from the pillow and said in a threatening voice, 'I think I'm going to be sick!'

Alice stopped reading. She looked at her daughter and saw something cunning and unchildlike for the first time. 'No, you're not,' she said. 'You're not going to be sick at all. You're making it up. What's the matter with you, Fern? Is it because Nanny's going? Tell me. Come on, I won't be cross.'

'No.' The voice became a whine. 'I just feel sick.'

'If you go on saying that, you will be,' Alice retorted. 'Listen to me, darling. Nanny's too old to look after you now. You need someone who'll be more fun, who'll teach you things. OK, you had a nasty fall at the school and cut your knee, but it'll get better. Isn't there anyone you like there, any little girl you'd ask up here to play?'

Fern shook her head. 'No,' she whimpered. 'They're all horrible. I want the bowl, Mummy. Please!'

Alice stood up. She closed the book. 'I'm going to get you some different books to read,' she said. 'This one is so old-fashioned you must be bored stiff with it. You don't really want to be sick, do you? If I kiss you good night and tuck you up, you'll go straight off to sleep. You'll feel better in the morning.'

She fluffed up the pillows and drew the bedclothes over her, securing them under the mattress. Fern felt as if she was weighted down and unable to move.

'There,' Alice said. 'That's what I do for the poor wounded airmen when they're not well. I'll come and see you tomorrow. Good night, Fern.' She kissed her forehead. It was hot and sweaty. She felt the child draw away at the contact and was surprised. It was usually she who avoided touching Fern; she couldn't pretend to find cuddling her attractive. Now Fern was recoiling from her.

To her amazement Fern asked a question. 'Do you kiss the wounded airmen good night too, Mummy?' What an extraordinary thing.

Alice said firmly, 'Good heavens, no. Whatever gave you that idea? You don't kiss grown-ups, silly. Only children. Now go to sleep.'

She closed the door and hurried downstairs. Fern wriggled and pulled at the bedclothes until they were loose. She lay and looked at the ceiling. Nanny would be in soon. She forgot about being sick. She said to herself in a slow, deliberate whisper, 'Mummy tells lies. She smacked me once for telling lies. But she tells lies.'

*

'I am sorry we are late. I hope it hasn't inconvenienced you, Mrs Vandekar.'

'Not at all,' Alice said. She hadn't known what to expect. Certainly not this tall, elegant Frenchwoman. Thin as a reed and dark as the husband she had abandoned.

Colonel Chuck Wallace stood awkwardly in the background. He was a stocky, fair-haired man in his forties, good-looking in a Nordic way.

Alice was determined to be gracious. Everything depended upon this woman. 'It's very good of you to come,' she said. 'Your husband hasn't been told. I'm not sure how we should do this.'

Janine Armstrong looked surprised. 'Won't it be a terrible shock to him if he thinks I'm dead and I just walk in?'

'A shock is what's needed,' Alice said. 'That was Group Captain Wallace's advice. He knows your husband very well.'

'It's amazing,' the French accent was very strong, 'extraordinary that he should have such a delusion.'

Alice kept the ice out of her voice. 'He was severely tortured, Mrs Armstrong. His hands were mutilated.'

'I know.' She shook her head. 'I know what they do. I worked for the Resistance. That's how I met Nicholas. I am very sorry for what has happened to him. But that's the risk we all took, I have lost friends and relatives.'

'How terrible,' Alice said. 'I didn't know.'

Janine Armstrong shrugged. 'Why should you? I was sent back to England because the Gestapo were looking for me. Nick went out on this mission. Maybe he thought I was still in France. We were separated by then. Well, if I am going to give him the shock, perhaps we shouldn't delay any longer?'

A very cool, self-possessed person, hardened in a fire beyond anything Alice could imagine. For a brief moment their personalities met, clashed and withdrew in time. She said, 'I'll take you to him. He's down the corridor. Colonel, do sit down and make yourself comfortable. I won't be long.'

Alice paused outside the Spencer room. She knocked on the door. She opened it and stood with Janine Armstrong hidden behind her. Nicholas got up and came towards her. She said quickly, 'You've got a visitor. I promised you, remember?' Then she stepped aside and let his wife enter the room. She closed the door and, with a hammering heart, went back to her sitting room to wait.

The colonel sprang up when she came in. 'No, please,' she said, 'sit down. Would you like some tea, or a drink perhaps?'

'A drink, mam,' he said. 'I guess I'm more nervous about this than Janine.'

'I've only got gin,' Alice explained. 'We've used up our whisky ration. You're from the South, aren't you?'

'Kentucky's my home state,' he said. 'And where are you from, mam?'

'Boston,' Alice said. She gave him a drink and poured one for herself. 'My mother's there now. How long have you been over here?'

'A year, almost. I'm with the Eighth Air Force. Not flying, I'm too old for these machines they have now. I fly a desk instead.'

He had an engaging smile. She began to like him. 'I wonder what's happened,' she said. 'I wonder if I should go and see? He's been so desperately ill. Mentally shattered. Colonel, would you mind if I leave you a minute?'

'Why don't I come too? It's just as important to me. I love Janine. I don't know what her seeing him will do to us.'

Or to me, Alice thought suddenly. I could lose him if she decided to go back.

They met her coming towards them down the corridor. She looked very pale and her mouth had a tight set to it.

'Janny.' Wallace brushed past Alice and went to meet her. 'You OK?'

'Oh yes, I'm fine, don't worry. And so is he, Mrs Vandekar. He got over his shock quite quickly. He cried for a minute or two, and then he called me a whore and told me to get out. He'll recover quickly now.'

There was no need for Alice to pretend any longer. 'Thank God for that,' she said.

'We'll be going now,' the colonel said. He had his arm round Janine's shoulder. 'I don't want Janine upset any more. Whatever those guys did to him, it hasn't stopped him being a bastard.'

Alice opened the door and went into the room. Nick was waiting for her. He didn't speak, he held out his arms. Alice went to him. He held her close and she felt him kiss her hair. 'I don't want to say anything,' he said. 'I don't want to talk about her.'

'You don't have to,' she whispered. 'She's gone. And you're free now. Free to get well and live again.'

'I love you,' he said to her. 'Kiss me.'

There was no miracle, no blinding revelation. She gave him her body without expectation. He needed her as much then as when she had first found him, silent and beyond hope. She loved him, and that made it possible to submit to a passion that she couldn't share. But there was no stiff repugnance. No feeling of disgust and degradation when he made love to her. Just a tender satisfaction that she was able to make him happy. No shame, no guilt either. Just the joy of seeing him peacefully asleep beside her. She brought him back upstairs to her room and no longer pretended to Lily that she was sleeping in the chair. She just said, 'Don't bring tea tomorrow. I want him to sleep.'

'Yes, madam,' Lily said, and saw them looking at each other.

'I'm glad, she thought. I'm glad she's happy. Hugo

telephoned at the end of the week to say he was coming home on embarkation leave.

'It won't be for long,' Alice said. 'It's only ten days.'

'It'll seem like ten years,' Nick told her. 'He'll be with you, holding you . . .'

Alice stroked his hair. She didn't mind him nestling against her naked breasts. 'Don't worry about that. We haven't slept together for years. Not since Fern was a baby.'

He raised his head. 'I can't believe that . . . No man would live in the same house with you and not want you, every day and every night.'

'I didn't want him,' she admitted. 'It wasn't Hugo's fault. It was mine. You know, my love, I'm not much good at it. You just don't complain, that's all.'

'You're wonderful,' he insisted. 'You need time, my darling, and someone to teach you. Every time you come to me a little more. Don't you know that?'

She whispered, 'I hope so. I want to – I want to make you happy more than anything in the world.'

'You do,' he said. 'You're my whole life. I'm sorry for your husband, but I'm jealous of him too. He's going to be with you for ten days and I can't see you.'

'Oh yes, you can,' she promised. 'I'll find time – he won't be with me every minute. I'll come to you whenever I can. But we can't go to bed. Not while he's in the house. I don't want to cheat him more than I can help, Nick, and I don't want to feel guilty about what we're doing. I don't give a damn what anyone thinks, but I'm not going to hurt Hugo. I've hurt him enough as it is. He'll be fighting in North Africa. He could be killed. I've got to make this leave happy for him, darling. I owe him that. We have all the time in the world afterwards.'

'Mother and Phillip are coming down next weekend,' Hugo said. 'He's on embarkation leave too. Poor

121

Mother's so upset – I thought it would be nice if she had some time with both of us and saw Fern. I hope you don't mind. I didn't want to cut into my leave by going down to Sussex.'

'Of course I don't mind,' Alice said. 'I'll be happy to have them both. I didn't know about Phillip – do you know where he's going?'

Hugo shook his head. He was surprised by her reaction. She didn't like his mother and dismissed his brother as a mummy's boy. And he knew that she never pretended. She smiled at him, as if she could read his thoughts, and said. 'I'll make sure they have a happy visit, Hugo. It must be awful for poor Beatrice, losing both of you at the same time.'

She's changed so much, he thought. The selfishness that was ruining her character had given place to warmth and compassion. The hard edges were blurred, the brittle attitude to life and its purpose had changed so dramatically that it actually showed in her face. She's more beautiful now than when I first met her. And I love her as much as I ever did. I can admit that now, when I'm going to leave her, perhaps for ever, if I'm unlucky. He said, 'Alice, Celia and I are finished. I wanted you to know that.'

'Oh?' He saw a slight flush come into her face. 'Why – any particular reason?'

'I didn't want to say goodbye with that between us,' he answered.

Alice hesitated. 'Did she mind?'

'No. She understood perfectly. She was never in love with me. And I never loved her. It was just an – arrangement.'

'Oh,' Alice said again. I know what this means, she thought, and panic welled up in her. I know what he's leading up to, and why he's got rid of her after all these years . . .

She got up and said quickly, 'Why don't I call Beatrice and say how much I'm looking forward to having her. Wouldn't that be nice?'

He got up too and came towards her. There was something so vulnerable in his face that she stopped trying to run away. He didn't touch her.

'Alice, won't you come back to me... just until I leave? You mean so much to me.'

'It's because you want another child,' she countered. 'You can't feel anything for me after all this time. And after the way I've treated you.'

'I don't care about a child,' he said. 'That can wait until I come back and the war's over. I want you, Alice. I love you – I've never stopped loving you. No other woman has ever meant anything to me or ever will.'

He was so proud, she thought, so reserved. Seeing him beg was too much for her to bear. She had given everything to another man. Her eyes filled with tears as she reached out to him.

'Of course we'll be together,' she said. 'So long as I don't disappoint you all over again.'

He held her in his arms. He didn't kiss her. She couldn't see his face.

'Thank you, my darling,' was all he said.

It was the morning at last. She hadn't slept. The ten days were over, his mother and brother had gone. Some of it seemed like a dream. Beatrice Vandekar looked so old suddenly, and Phillip in his uniform was a different man. He was a pilot, wings on his left breast and a funny moustache. She kept looking at him and thinking, he's going to be killed. I can feel it.

And Hugo going down to the cellar for champagne and opening it to drink a family toast. 'To all of us, and to the end of this damned war.' Fern sitting primly on the sofa, next to her grandmother, with that shut expression on her face whenever Alice spoke to her. That child hates me, she realized, and was shocked. Lily laying out clothes she hadn't worn since war broke out, because Hugo wanted her to look her best, to pretend that things hadn't changed and would never be the same again. 'I want to put the clock back,' he'd said, 'I want to see you and Ashton as I've always known it.' So the silver was brought out and cleaned, the dining room opened up and stripped of dustsheets. They pretended, all of them, and it was as much for his younger brother, Alice knew, as for Hugo himself. They stood in their old-fashioned evening clothes and drank that toast, then kissed each other afterwards like voyagers setting out on a journey with no known end.

And Hugo made love to her and told her how much he loved her. But his need was too strong, too menacing in its masculinity. Nothing changed for either of them. Alice endured it out of pity and guilt, but it was a dreadful ordeal.

She got up quietly so as not to wake him. The house was still; it was just before six and the day nurses hadn't come on duty. Alice opened the window onto their balcony. It was chill and a mist rose from the distant lake. She stood for a moment and shivered. It was so beautiful, so peaceful.

She thought, I may never see him again after today. I can't imagine that. I've hated him, or tried to hate him, and hated myself because of the way things were between us. And I've betrayed him, as he betrayed me.

And yet I can't think of life without him. I can't think what lies ahead for any of us. But I don't want him to be killed – dear God, don't let that happen. Or hurt like the poor boys I've tried to comfort. He mustn't be diminished, mutilated. He wouldn't be Hugo Vandekar any more.

She was freezing in the misty air and she went inside, closing the door. She got back into bed, but she couldn't get warm.

When she woke it was mid-morning. She rang for Lily. 'Look at the time! For God's sake, why didn't you wake me?'

'Mr Hugo said I was to let you sleep. Now here's your tea, madam, and stop shouting at me, I only did what I was told. He left this for you.'

It was a short note. She sat up in bed and still felt

124

cold. 'My darling, I didn't want to wake you. I didn't want to say goodbye. Thank you for making me so happy these last few days. I love you always. Hugo.'

He was gone. God knew when she would hear from him or see him again.

'You can come in for a while,' Lily said, 'But you mustn't stay long. She's not out of the wood yet.' She opened the door and stood aside to let Nick Armstrong into Alice's room. 'Not too long, mind,' Lily insisted. 'She mustn't get tired.'

'Don't worry, Lily. I won't be more than a few minutes. I just want to see her, that's all.'

Half the time, Lily grumbled to herself, I've been running round looking after him as well as my lady. Carrying on and trying to get upstairs to see her, and her delirious and calling out for him... She was exhausted, what with nursing Alice and fighting the real nurse who had been sent in to look after her, and keeping *him* from going out of his mind with worry downstairs. A right pair they were, the two of them. If that was what being in love was, thank God she hadn't come across it.

Alice was propped up on a heap of pillows. She looked very thin and white. But when she saw him she raised herself up and held out her arms.

'Oh, Nick, Nick darling! No, you mustn't kiss me... you might catch it.'

He didn't listen to her. Lily saw them embrace and closed the door on them.

It had been a terribly anxious time. First she'd gone down with a cough and a temperature. Wouldn't go to bed, wouldn't take any notice. Wouldn't, typically, admit that she was very ill until she collapsed in Armstrong's room, and they had to carry her out of there and send for Dr Banks. Nice lot of gossip that caused. Thank God that old bitch Nanny was long gone. The nursery guv was not much better – just as nosy, in Lily's opinion, but slimier, always buttering up her lady and saying what a little sweetheart Miss Fern was. Lily couldn't abide the child. She hadn't even asked after her mother. When she did come down to the sickroom, she just stood there like a pudding and stared. Pneumonia, Dr Banks said. Double pneumonia he said later, and he looked extremely worried. Luckily she was very strong and healthy. But you never knew with these things, once the lungs were attacked.

Lily had sat up night after night with her, listening to the rasping breathing, wondering what she would do if Alice died. Because Lily wasn't fooled. She knew what double pneumonia meant. Her own mother had died of it. And she'd been a sturdy woman with never a day's illness before in her life.

Mr Hugo's mother came down. She didn't seem able to cope, what with both her boys gone to fight abroad. She fussed and flustered around for a few days and then went home again. She seemed old and dithery, and Lily was sorry for her, but glad to see her go. She'd spent a lot of time with that child, and it seemed to affect her.

Alice's mother was telegraphed and kept in constant touch with them. Lily would have been pleased to see her. Mr Hugo was somewhere at sea. His wife could have died without him even knowing. But she wasn't going to die now. Dr Banks said the rales in the chest were fading and her temperature was coming down. 'She's a great fighter,' he said. 'That's been a help, I can tell you. Last week I really thought we might have lost her. And,' turning to Lily, 'it's time you took some time off, or I'll be doctoring you!'

Lily went to her room and had a long private weep with relief. Yes, she was tired out. She hadn't slept a full night through since Alice had been brought upstairs and put to bed. And now she could put Armstrong out of his misery. The last thing her lady needed was for him to have a relapse when she was getting well.

Well, she thought, they were together again. That'd

help the both of them. She looked at her little gold watch. Ten minutes and she'd go back and turn him out. Dr Banks was adamant that his patient mustn't exert herself mentally; she must have complete quiet and rest until her temperature had been normal for at least a week.

'I've been so worried about you,' Alice whispered. 'Lily told me you were all right, but I was so worried.'

'I was going mad, thinking about you,' Nick Armstrong said. 'I felt so bloody useless, just sitting around, not able to see you or do anything. But you're better now, you're out of danger, my darling.' He kept clasping her hands, holding them so tightly that it hurt.

He looked ill, she thought anxiously. Ill and too thin, with those awful black hollows under his eyes. 'Nick,' she said, 'Nick darling, you mustn't worry any more. I'm fine, I just need time to get my strength back. But you've got to think of yourself. You're not to mope, I'll never forgive you if you do. It'll make me worse,' she threatened.

He said hastily, 'I'm not moping, I promise. I'm taking walks every day, and I go in and play cards or chat to some of the chaps at night. I just miss you so much. That's the trouble. If only I could do something.'

'You can,' Lily's voice was brisk. 'You can let madam rest now and come back tomorrow, sir.'

Alice turned her head and looked at her. To Lily's delight there was a brief flash of the old spirit. 'And you can shut up, Lily, and not talk to Mr Armstrong like that!'

She watched Lily usher him out and didn't protest any further. She felt so damnably weak. The least effort tired her out. The emotional tide running high between them had exhausted her.

'I'm sorry, Lily,' she said. 'I didn't mean that. You've been so wonderful to me.'

Lily went very red. 'Somebody had to see that

clodhopper of a nurse didn't kill you,' she said. 'Didn't know how to bathe you properly. I caught her using carbolic soap! Imagine!'

Alice laughed and then began to cough. 'Oh God, Lily, no wonder the British win wars, while they've got people like you . . .'

'And you, madam. Dr Banks says you fought your way through it. A lot of others wouldn't have.'

For a moment they looked at each other. There was no need to say any more.

Alice closed her eyes. 'I guess I could sleep for a while,' she said, and she did, while Lily sat in a chair and watched her.

Alice couldn't think why Dr Banks was smiling. She'd been out of bed for a week and was feeling stronger every day. Then, unaccountably, she nearly fainted after her bath. He was sent for and examined her.

'Your chest is fine,' he announced. 'I'll give you a general check over, just to make sure.' And then he covered her with the sheet and stood there smiling down at her.

'When was your last period, Mrs Vandekar?'

Alice gasped out loud. 'Why, what do you mean?'

'Because I think that little fainting fit has a happy explanation. I'd say you were having a baby.'

He wouldn't let her get up for the rest of the day. She had to stay imprisoned in the bed with Lily standing watchdog over her until Alice screamed at her to get out and leave her alone. Then she threw back the covers and went to her long mirror. She stripped off her nightdress and stared in horror at her naked body. There was nothing to show; she was painfully thin. Except her breasts were heavier. And tender when she squeezed them. There was an ooze of watery milk from one nipple.

'Oh God,' she cried out, 'what have I done? It can't be true! It can't be!' She'd taken precautions with Nicholas. The same precautions with Hugo. She

128

couldn't be pregnant. And then she remembered the first time, the day Janine Armstrong had come to see him and he'd turned to Alice for solace. That's when it happened, of course, of course, she repeated. She dressed again and sat down on the bed in despair.

It was Nick's child. It would be born a Vandekar.

Alice didn't tell Nick. He was still too frail to be burdened. She didn't tell Lily either and this deception was possible because, unlike with her first pregnancy, she wasn't sick. Her illness was an excuse for resting if she felt tired; she put on a little weight and everyone was pleased. Only Dr Banks knew the reason and she had insisted that he kept her secret. She didn't want to be fussed over, she said, and she was convalescing anyway. After three months, maybe four, she would announce the happy news. Happy news. Happy for no one, she thought in despair. She didn't want a child. Nick couldn't be told in case it worried him, and Hugo would be palmed off with another man's bastard. She didn't suggest an abortion to Dr Banks, she knew better than to even hint at such a thing. She didn't know what to do. For the second time in her life Alice was entrapped in a situation which she couldn't control. The first time had been with Fern.

'I won't think about it,' she told herself, in imitation of fiction's most famous heroine of the day. 'I won't think about it today, I'll think about it tomorrow.' But that was so contrary to her nature, that the thought of the child became an obsession. It loomed like a black cloud on the horizon, overshadowing the happy days she spent with Nick coaxing him back to strength and confidence. It spoiled the work she did among the patients, because she felt tired and irritable and couldn't say why. And it raised a barrier between her and Lily for the first time in their association. She had never lied to Lily, and she couldn't imagine Lily lying to her. But she couldn't confide in her because she knew that Lily would guess that Nick, and not Hugo, was the father.

She wrote Hugo long letters and never mentioned the baby that was actually fluttering like a bird inside her. Sometimes she looked at Nick Armstrong and was tempted to shed the burden, to turn to him for strength and comfort for a change. But it wouldn't be fair, she thought; he'd suffered so much. He needed peace and security as much as the love she gave him so unstintingly. And he was changing visibly. The broken fingers had been reset, even the nails so brutally ripped out were growing back. There was a substance to him now, a new enthusiasm for life. He mixed more and more with the other patients. Sometimes Alice suffered an unworthy pang of jealousy when she came down and found him engrossed in a game of bridge instead of waiting for her. He laughed now, and it was strange, strange because for so many weary weeks she'd never seen him smile.

Then one bright day in early July he said to her, 'Darling, Jim Wallace wrote to me. He's coming down to see me.'

'Jim Wallace?' For a moment she couldn't place the name.

'My old boss,' Nick said. 'From Baker Street. Could we give him some lunch?'

'Of course. We can run to that. I'll fix it. When's he coming?'

'He suggested Friday,' he said. He looked bright and enthusiastic. 'It'll be good to see him. I've never told you about him, have I? He's the most remarkable chap.'

'Yes,' Alice agreed. For a moment she was back in the office, facing him across the desk. 'I've known Nick for a long time. I recruited him.'

She said on impulse, 'What does he want, Nick?'

'Just to see me, have a chat.'

'That'll be nice,' she said. 'It'll do you good.'

For a second he hesitated. Then he took hold of her

hand and squeezed it. 'I'm not an invalid any more, you know,' he said. 'Thanks to you, darling.'

It was a pleasant lunch. It had been so long since Alice had been able to order food on a proper scale that when the group captain produced a smoked ham their lunch became a feast.

'A present,' he announced. 'One of my young ladies has a butcher for a father. Very illegal but jolly nice.' He looked at Alice and Nick and beamed a smile at them, as if he were a father surveying his children.

It made Alice feel uncomfortable. She ate the ham and was surprised at how greedy she felt. But she had an odd and frightening intuition as they sat round the table and he began talking intimately to Nick about people she didn't know. Beware the Greeks...

'What did you say?' Wallace broke in, and Alice blushed. She must have spoken her thought out loud. 'Oh – nothing...'

He was genial all over again. 'You mustn't take any notice of us, my dear Mrs Vandekar. Nick and I were just catching up on old friends. Very boring, do forgive me. Perhaps we could go off after lunch and have our shop talk later?' He turned from her and Nick said promptly, 'Yes, why not?'

After lunch she did feel sick. It must be that damned ham, she decided. Junior doesn't like it. She went upstairs and lay down, trying not to think.

It wasn't the ham, and it wasn't the baby, which was quiescent at the moment. It was the instinct that the group captain had come down with a purpose, and that purpose was to take Nicholas away from her. And that Nicholas was getting ready to go. She got up and hurried downstairs. Too late. They'd had their shop talk, whatever it was. He'd gone. And there was Nick, smiling and eager to tell her the wonderful news.

'He wants me to go back,' he said. 'Back to Baker Street. I'm fit enough and he says I could be a tremendous asset. I've got first-hand knowledge, darling. I can really help the people going out. I can

131

brief them in a way that no one else can who hasn't been through it. And he made one very important point.' He paused for emphasis. 'I can prove that it's possible to come back.'

Alice said slowly, 'The others didn't. The other ones who were caught.'

'No,' he agreed. 'But that's war. Soldiers get killed. We're soldiers. Oh, Alice, try to understand. I want to be useful. I want to do something. I can't go on lotus-eating here with you while the people I trained with need my help.'

He put his arms around her. He couldn't see the desolation on her face.

'I love you, Alice,' he said. 'You saved my life. I could stay with you for ever and be perfectly happy. But I wouldn't be much of a man if I stood aside and let my friends fight for me. I wouldn't be worthy of you.'

He made her look up at him and saw the tears in her eyes. 'Don't, my darling,' he begged. 'It's not a real separation. I'll be in London, I'll get down to see you and you can come up to me. I'll get a medical clearance. Jim says I'll have to go back and see the trick cyclists at Princess Mary's, but that won't be a problem. And there's another reason.'

'You don't have to explain,' she said. 'I was just being selfish. I'm sorry.'

'I want to tell you,' he insisted. 'You mentioned the others who didn't come back. I was half crazy, crazy enough to believe I'd betrayed Janine when they taunted me. I don't know how much I did tell those bastards. Jim said we'd been penetrated and I wasn't responsible for giving anyone else away. But I'm not sure, Alice. I'll never be sure. That's why I've got to go back.'

'Yes,' she said. 'Yes, you have. But will you promise me something?'

'If I can,' he said gently.

'You won't let them persuade you to go back to France. You've got to promise me that.'

He kissed her and held her close to him. He stroked the bright blonde hair. 'I couldn't go back,' he told her. 'My cover's blown. I'd be arrested in a matter of hours. So I don't have to promise you, sweetheart. It doesn't arise. I only wish it was possible.'

And when she drew back and stared at him, he smiled down at her. 'You see what a marvellous job you've done. You've given me my courage and my hope. I can face it again, because of you. So you be proud – and no more tears.'

After that it was impossible to tell him that she was pregnant. He had to be free. There could be no moral blackmail exerted to tie him to her.

The next two weeks were a time of extremes for Alice. Extremes of happiness when they were together – even his lovemaking became a kind of comfort – and extremes of misery, when she thought of life without him. Because Alice knew that she would lose him when he left Ashton. The more he made plans to return or for her to go to London, the more she realized that neither would be possible without telling him the truth. The lie would be worse, if he believed that she had slept with Hugo and conceived a child after so many years of separation. So she clung to him for the time that remained and tried not to think of the next few months.

He went to Princess Mary's and she tasted the loneliness to come. Ashton was empty without him, and she couldn't sleep because the baby was moving so strongly inside her.

Dr Banks paid an unexpected call. 'Just to check on you,' he said cheerfully.

Lily had sought him out. She was worried about Mrs Vandekar. Her mistress was off her food and looked unwell. Lily hadn't been let into the secret, the doctor knew. But the time was coming when Alice's condition couldn't be kept secret any longer.

Alice submitted unwillingly.

He listened to the foetal heartbeat and announced that it was strong and everything was fine. Except that she seemed rather peaky. Doing too much, he suggested. She denied it.

By the way, he'd had a call from one of his colleagues at Princess Mary's. Flight Lieutenant Armstrong had passed his medical. Not A1 of course, but enough to resume light duties. He was sure she'd be pleased to hear that. So much was due to her nursing, after all. Yes, Alice agreed, it was wonderful news, and she thought that if he stayed another minute she would burst into tears.

'Mrs Vandekar, I hope you'll join us this evening.' The senior RAF officer was a group captain who had bailed out over the North Sea returning from bombing industrial targets in the Ruhr. There were four bullet holes in him and he'd contracted pneumonia from floating in the icy seas for two hours before Air Sea Rescue picked him up. He was all of twenty-six. He'd been at Ashton for three months and had at last been pronounced fit enough to return to duty. There was a batch of young men ready to leave. Some would be reclassified, others given a medical discharge and a pension. The miserly sums horrified Alice when she heard of them. Before the war she had spent the equivalent of a year's disablement pension on a new evening dress.

'We're planning a little party for you,' the group captain said. 'We wanted it to be a surprise but you can't keep much of a secret around here. So will you come and join us after supper?'

Alice said, 'I'd be delighted. How sweet of you – I don't deserve a party.'

He had a cheery laugh. 'Oh yes you do! The boys won't leave here without saying thank you. And I certainly won't. About seven o'clock, then?'

'Seven will be fine,' Alice felt like laughing and crying at the same time. He looked so ridiculously young, and his breezy manner hid the anguish of having lost three members of his crew. Alice had seen that side of the coin when he first came. He learned how to cry on her shoulder. Now she wanted to cry on his because she was losing Nick and carrying a child that couldn't be acknowledged. But she smiled and thanked him again, saying what fun it would be. He hesitated for a moment. She saw a tinge of red run up into his cheeks.

'You wouldn't put on something specially pretty for us, would you, mam? The boys would love it, if you wouldn't mind.'

'Of course I will,' Alice answered. 'I'll find something special.'

Lily helped her choose a prewar evening dress. It was bright blue, slim fitting – for a moment Alice panicked, remembering how quickly she had outgrown her clothes with Fern. But all was well, the dress fitted.

'You look like your old self, madam,' Lily said. She was a beauty, no mistake. Couldn't look plain if she got herself up in an old potato sack, Lily thought proudly. And that hair was a wonder. Lily had brushed it and dressed it, and found a big artificial silk flower to pin at the back. 'There now,' she said. 'You'll do!'

He wasn't back, that was the trouble. The week had run on to ten days and for the last three days he hadn't telephoned, so of course she had that drawn look from worrying and missing him. There were times, Lily said to herself as Alice went downstairs, there were times when, much as she liked the flight lieutenant, she wouldn't be sorry to see the back of him for her lady's sake. He took too much out of her. No man was worth that.

The men were gathered in the hall below, and when Alice came down the stairs they gave a spontaneous cheer. The group captain came up and took her hand.

'Thank you,' he said and made a gallant little bow. 'You look smashing. Air Force blue, isn't it?'

'The nearest I could find to it,' she agreed.

They'd got hold of some champagne, God knew

how, and toasts were drunk to her and to the staff at Ashton and to Ashton itself.

'We'll always think of it as home,' one man said to her. 'Don't ever let it go, will you?'

'Never,' Alice promised. 'You'll all have to come and see us after the war!'

There was another cheer. She drank two glasses of champagne very quickly and began to feel better. She was flushed and very animated; they were jostling to get near and talk to her. Then there was a call for silence. It wasn't the group captain who made the little speech. It was a rear gunner who had survived third-degree burns to his hands and chest. He was going back to civvy street, as he called it.

'We want to say thanks for everything,' he announced. 'We'll never forget you, and because we're a conceited shower, as you probably realize,' there was a rippled laugh which died immediately, 'we don't want you to forget us. So we'd like you to accept this.'

The gift was tied up with ribbon and she tore the wrapper open. There was a group photograph in a handsome silver frame. It was engraved: 'To Mrs Vandekar. From her boys. July 1942.' Twenty men in two ranks, all smiling at her. Twenty names written by each one at the sides of the photograph. She looked at it and then at them.

'This goes on my desk,' she said, 'where I'll see it every morning. That means I'll think of you every morning. You've given me something I'll treasure. God bless you.'

It was a moment captured in time for many of them; the sight of Alice in her blue dress at the foot of the great staircase would remain when other memories had faded. And she made it permanent by turning and running upstairs with the photograph clasped in both hands, as if she couldn't trust her smile to stay in place.

Lily was waiting for her upstairs. She didn't waste time. 'He telephoned,' she said. 'He's coming back tomorrow morning.'

'Oh.' Alice sat down on the bed. She was still holding the photograph. For a few moments she had forgotten him. A few moments. It was eight o'clock. For all that time she had actually lived independently of where he was and what he was doing. A different kind of love had enveloped her. The kind where sadness was bearable and the spirits didn't flag. 'Look what they gave me,' she held out the photograph to Lily. 'It's inscribed and they've all signed it. Wasn't that the sweetest thing to do? They had champagne and poor Gerry Pitman made a little speech at the end. I had to run or I was going to cry, Lily.'

'Just as well you didn't,' was the retort. 'You'd have had half of them wiping their eyes, I expect. I told you, the flight lieutenant's coming back tomorrow.'

'Yes, you did,' Alice said. 'Did he sound all right?' Banks had said he had been cleared three days ago – why hadn't he come home then? Or telephoned? Suddenly she felt weary. Weary and low-spirited.

'You know he's going back to duty,' she said.

Lily nodded. 'He'll manage, don't you worry. It'll be better for him.'

'It won't be better for me,' Alice said.

'This lot are going, but there'll be a new lot coming in. You'll have plenty to do, madam.'

Alice reached up and took the blue flower out of her hair.

She didn't mean to say it. It was unpremeditated. Perhaps it was the champagne. Or the highly charged emotion of that farewell party. She looked up at Lily and said, 'I'm having a baby.' She waited for the surprise, the reproach for not being told.

Instead, Lily's rather severe expression softened. 'I know you are, madam.'

'For God's sake! How did you know?'

'Because I know you,' was the answer. 'I knew you looked different – in the face, I mean. There was something the matter and then I just thought, of course, that's it. You weren't sick, but you had the

137

same look with Miss Fern. I hope you're pleased about it this time, madam. Mr Hugo will be, I'm sure.'

'It isn't Mr Hugo's,' Alice said flatly. 'And you bloody well know it isn't.'

Lily began hanging up her dress and laying the nightdress across her chair with her dressing gown and the white satin mules underneath it.

'You must write and tell Mr Hugo. It'll cheer him up, wherever he is,' she said.

'Lily!' Alice exploded. 'Didn't you hear what I said?'

The other woman turned round and straightened up. 'No, I didn't,' she answered firmly. 'I never heard anything. Shall I run a bath for you before you go to bed? Helps you sleep, they say.'

Alice didn't say anything. She sat and watched Lily finish tidying up and then go into the bathroom and turn on the taps. She smelt bath essence being poured into the steaming water. 'I hate that stuff,' she shouted, 'you know I do!'

'It makes the water soft,' Lily called back. 'I've only put a few drops. You've got to keep your skin supple, you know, or you'll get those marks . . .'

'Oh, shut up,' Alice called out. 'Come here and listen to me!'

Lily came out. 'I've laid your towels out and the water's just right,' she announced. 'And I'm not staying to listen to a lot of nonsense, madam. I've got things to do for myself before I go to bed. I'll come back and see if you need anything before I do.' She nodded and walked briskly out of the room.

When she did come back Alice was reading. She looked very young with her hair hanging loose. She answered Lily's knock. 'Come in. Oh, Lily, thanks, I was just going to put the light out.'

'I've brought you a little glass of hot milk,' Lily said. 'I begged it off the night sister. We're getting low in the kitchen.'

'Thanks,' Alice said again. She sipped the milk, then

closed the book and put it on the bedside table. 'I was talking nonsense,' she said. 'You're quite right.'

'I know I'm right,' Lily said quietly. 'And don't you fret about Armstrong going. I'll take care of you till the baby's born, like I did last time.'

'Good night, Lily,' Alice said. She let the use of his surname pass unrebuked. The moment of weakness had passed. She'd confessed and the confession had been turned aside.

Lily Parker had shown her what she must do. She switched the light out. Nick would be back tomorrow. 'I'll be happy,' she said aloud, 'I'll make the most of the time we've got left. After that, who knows what may happen.'

She fell asleep and woke refreshed and oddly light in heart. She wasn't bearing the burden any more, because Lily knew. But she was never, ever going to admit it.

Nick had a week's leave. A whole week together, he said, as if they hadn't been inseparable for months. 'Why don't we go off somewhere?' he suggested. 'Spend a few days in a pub on our own. I'd like to take you away, Alice. I don't want to share you with anyone.'

With her head on his shoulder Alice said, 'I'd love that. Just to spend all day with you, not to have to think of anything or anyone else.'

'Then we'll do it,' he declared. 'I know a little place down in the West Country. I used to go there when I was on leave. With the odd girlfriend, I have to admit that.' He smiled down at her. 'But not Janine, if that's what you're thinking.'

'I'm not thinking anything,' she protested. 'I don't care who was there before me. I want to be there with you now.'

'I'll ring them,' he said. 'I got to know the landlord and his wife very well. They were marvellous people. They'll squeeze us in. And, my darling, I've got a petrol ration that'll take us there and back and round the countryside if we want to see a bit of it. It's beautiful down there.'

'Down where?' Alice teased him. 'The West Country covers a big area.'

'Poole, in Dorset. Just outside Poole. It's a picture-book pub, with old beams and horse brasses. Americans love it!' He mocked her in turn.

She laughed. 'I know the kind of place. It's called the Scalp Inn. Every time you stand upright, you take the top off your head! Go and ring up, Nick. See if we can go tomorrow.'

He kissed her. 'It's not very luxurious,' he warned. 'No running hot and cold Lilys around.'

'So long as you don't tell her, that's OK by me,' Alice said. She thought lazily how happy she felt. The parting seemed unreal, as if they would make the week last and last, and the day he was to drive away would never come. He was so happy too, light-hearted and tender with her. He's making the most of what we've got, she realized. Just as I am. And I'm not looking after him any more. Now I feel he's looking after me. I wish I could tell him about the baby. I'd feel better about it, but that wouldn't be fair. It would spoil our happiness. He doesn't want responsibility and I don't either. I want to go away with him for a few days and pretend that there's nothing behind us or ahead.

'Are you sure I shouldn't come with you?' Lily repeated. 'Who's going to look after you?'

'I'm going to look after myself,' Alice said firmly, 'I'm not a damned imbecile, you know. I can turn on my own bath taps and dress myself, thank you. I'm a big grown-up girl, in case you haven't noticed!'

'I doubt there'll be a bath,' was the retort. 'Or any hot water in a place like that.'

'Then we'll go dirty,' Alice countered. 'Lily, for God's sake stop spoiling it for me. I want to go away, I want a break from home. And it's not very long, after all.'

No, Lily decided, it wasn't. She'd be all right. She was so much brighter, less tense since he'd come back. They were like a couple of silly kids, laughing and holding hands, and springing apart when anyone came in. But not quick enough for that creepy child. She'd come down for something and found them side by side on the sofa by the fire, and given them one of her old-fashioned looks. Her mother had laughed it off, but Lily knew better. Good thing if they did go off together for the last few days. She managed a smile and said, 'I'm sorry, madam. I didn't mean to be a spoilsport, but with the baby and everything I didn't want you to rough it. You aren't used to it, you know.'

'Then it's about time I learned,' Alice countered. 'And it's hardly roughing it to be without a personal maid for a few days. What would you say if I was going up to London, for instance, with the air-raids every night?'

'I'll put some things out for you.' Lily refused to be drawn. 'You say what you want me to pack.'

It was a cloudless day when they drove down to Dorset. The pub was just as Nick described it – small and low-browed and cosy as an oak-lined womb inside.

It was another world, and they spent five whole glorious days living in it. Alice laughed when she saw the little bath with the regulation 18-inch line for maximum water painted round it and the tepid trickle that seeped out of the old taps. That was the only time she thought of Lily or Ashton or anything of her real life. She willed the child not to move and remind her and she gave herself to him as often as he wanted. It makes him happy, she insisted, and that's all that counts. I'm not revolted or afraid because I love him, and I can stay outside it, outside my own body, and just give it as a gift.

They explored the countryside. He had a passion for old churches and Alice made fun of him for wandering round reading the inscriptions on the tombstones. 'I never knew you were so morbid! Who wants to read about some old guy departing this life in 1780 or whatever? Come on, let's go and see if there's a pub in the village. I feel like a glass of that disgusting flat English beer!'

'Just because there wasn't anyone in America in 1780, you're jealous,' he grinned.

'There was too,' Alice declared. 'And it wasn't long before we beat the pants off you!'

And on their last evening, spent in the pub with a makeshift supper in the corner of the bar, Nick said suddenly, 'You know what I feel when I think of people living and dying in one village all their lives?'

'Morbid?' Alice repeated and giggled. The beer was flat, but she actually liked the taste.

'No, not morbid at all. I feel a sense of permanence. A sort of security in the lifecycle. No matter what happens to us, there will still be people living and working and spending their lives in places like this. So long as England lasts.'

She looked at him. He was quite serious. 'It will last,' she said quickly. 'We're going to win.'

'Yes.' He took her hand and held it. 'We are. We must, mustn't we? Alice, how would you like to live somewhere like this?'

'How do you mean?'

'Would you find it very dreary after Ashton?'

She put the glass down. 'What are you saying, Nick?'

'I'm asking you to leave Hugo and marry me after the war's over.'

Two people came into the bar. They were elderly men, regulars who had been drinking an evening pint in the same place for most of their lives.

'It would be very different for you,' he went on. 'I haven't any money – and I mean that. I'd have to get a job and we'd have to make do as best we could to start with. There wouldn't be Lily or anything you've been used to for so long.'

Alice said quietly, 'I wouldn't care. I've been

happier here with you these last few days than any time in my whole life. I didn't have any money either. I married it, that's the truth.'

'Think about it, will you?' he asked her. 'No promises, no obligations, darling. Just keep it in the back of your mind.'

'I will,' Alice said. When the war was over. When the child was born and she was free to choose. When Hugo came home and the world stopped turning upside down for them all.

Nick gave her an envelope the next morning. It was sealed down tightly.

'What is it?' she asked him.

There was no laughter in either of them. The idyll was over. Their bags were in the back of the car and he was dropping her back at Ashton and going on to London.

'It's something personal for you from me,' he said. 'I don't want you to open it until you're at home. I wish it was something nicer for you, my darling, but at least it's the only one of its kind.'

'I've nothing for you,' she said, and bit her lip hard so as not to let her eyes fill.

'I don't need anything,' he said. 'I carry you inside myself.'

'I can say the same,' she whispered, but he had started the car and didn't hear.

She stood under the great portico at Ashton and waved him goodbye until the car had turned out of the main courtyard and vanished among the trees. She stood there looking after him, the envelope under her arm, until one of the convalescent officers came up the steps from an afternoon walk and said, 'Good evening, Mrs Vandekar. Getting chilly, isn't it?'

'Yes,' Alice said, and shivered. 'Yes it is.' And she went inside.

She opened the envelope and found a little notebook. She read his poetry that night. He wrote of his love for her and his passion, of his journey through the deepest despair to a shining hope that made it possible for him to leave her at the end. His spirits had soared while he wrote, there was so much joy and strength and pride in the words and the images that Alice read them without tears. The inscription, 'To my darling, who made my darkness into light,' seemed to her as beautiful as anything else in the little book.

And then there was the letter, slipped between the last page. Not a long letter, written while they were staying in Poole. It was headed 'Wednesday morning'. 'My darling. You won't hear from me for a time, but don't worry. I'm not going to be in London after all. There's work for me to do, and that work means silence until it's finished. I love you with all my heart, and when it's over I believe we'll be together. Wait for me. Nicholas.'

'Promise me,' she'd said. 'Promise me you won't let them persuade you to go back.'

It wasn't France. It couldn't be. He'd said himself, 'My cover's blown, I'd be arrested within hours.' He hadn't broken his promise and gone back. Whatever his work was, it must be safe. Not Baker Street but something more confidential – that was why he couldn't contact her. It must be that. She walked up and down, folding the letter into smaller and smaller squares until it began to tear and she didn't even notice. They wouldn't send him back to France. The telephone rang. She swung round, almost running to reach it, hoping perhaps it was him. But it was her mother-in-law, Beatrice, sobbing down the phone. For a moment Alice felt the ground shift under her. Hugo. But it was Phillip, the brother she'd seen in RAF uniform, drinking champagne on the last family reunion. He had been shot down in action over North Africa, missing, believed killed. Beatrice was broken-voiced and almost incoherent. 'Alice, Alice, what am I to do? Oh my poor boy, my poor boy...'

'Where are you?' she asked. 'Beatrice, where are you?'

'London. They phoned me from Sussex and read the telegram over the phone. I can't bear it. I can't bear it!'

'You stay there,' Alice said. 'Don't go back home. Stay where you are. I'm coming to get you and bring you home with me. Hold on, try to stay calm. I'll be with you some time tonight, I guess. I'll beg, borrow or steal petrol, otherwise I'll take the train.'

Dr Banks gave her his petrol coupons and insisted on driving her himself.

'My dear girl,' he said, 'there's no question of your trying to make that journey on your own, let alone attempting to go by train. I'll get you there before the blackout, we'll collect your mother-in-law and set out at once. We don't want to be caught in a raid and have to stay for the night. Besides, I can look after her on the journey if she's in a bad way.'

'Lily! Lily!' Lily heard the urgency and came up the stairs at a run. She'd been down to the village for sewing materials. Alice hadn't been expected back until the evening. 'Madam, what is it? What's the matter? Oh, my God.'

Alice was leaning against the door, white-faced. 'Mr Phillip's been killed,' she said. 'No, don't start fussing over me – get Mrs Vandekar's room ready. Hot-water bottles, light a fire if you can. Dr Banks is driving me down and we're going to bring her home here. She can't be alone in that bloody house in Sussex.'

'Madam, I don't think . . .'

Lily was rewarded by a furious, 'Shut up. Shut up and don't argue. Do as I say for once, will you?'

Alice slammed the door. Lily knew when she was beaten. Not even she would have dared say another word. She went off to do as she was told.

Alice had never liked her mother-in-law. They had tolerated each other over the years and paid lipservice to the conventions. But Beatrice recognized strength

145

and turned instinctively to her daughter-in-law. Phillip had been her favourite, softer than Hugo, more demonstrative even as a child. Losing him broke her spirit – she gave herself into Alice's hands and let grief have its way.

Alice was patient with her weeping and distress; she pitied her without understanding the mother's anguish for a child. She tried to comfort her, to support her, concentrating on making the old lady comfortable and seeing she wasn't left alone.

But Beatrice was disintegrating; she didn't eat or sleep and there was a frightening lack of self-direction. She didn't brush her hair or change her clothes.

Alice conferred with Dr Banks. 'It's very sad,' he said. 'Some people do react like this, especially if it's a favourite son. It's such a pity your husband's away. If he could have got a few days' compassionate leave, it would have helped her. Of course, you could, you know.'

'How?' Alice demanded. 'For God's sake, I've done everything I can think of. What else can I do?'

'You could tell her about her grandchild,' he suggested. 'I think that would make a lot of difference. Give her something to look forward to.'

Alice didn't answer.

He watched her for a moment and then made an excuse and left. There was something odd about the situation, and he had heard enough rumours to guess why the lady was so reluctant to reveal the news. In all probability it was Armstrong's child. But that was no business of his. He'd offered advice on old Mrs Vandekar's behalf and, in his view, on the young one's as well. It was up to her to take it or not. She was strong-willed enough.

Beatrice Vandekar wiped her eyes. Alice sat beside her. Beatrice had taken hold of her hand and was gripping it tightly. 'I'm so glad, my dear. I'm so glad,' she repeated. 'If only my poor Phillip had married . . .'

Alice said kindly, 'Well, this baby will be part of him

too, you know. A little nephew or niece. Think of it like that.'

'Oh, I will, I will,' Beatrice agreed. 'I'm so happy for you and Hugo. And you're so brave to have a baby at such a terrible time. Thank you for telling me, my dear. Thank you for being so good to me.' And she began to cry again.

But there was a difference. Alice sensed it and blessed Banks for his good sense. Beatrice was diverted from her single-minded grief. She was not very intelligent, but she was endowed with maternal feelings that were powerful enough to combat her sorrow. A new baby was going to be born. Hope flickered in her and remained steady, like a tiny flame. She wiped her eyes again and said, 'Does little Fern know?'

'Not yet,' Alice answered. 'You're the first person I've told. Hugo doesn't know either. I wanted to be sure before I said anything.'

'It'll be lovely for her,' Beatrice mused. 'She'll be so happy to have a little brother or sister. I hope it's a boy for both your sakes. Boys are so wonderful, especially to their mothers. My Phillip was always such a darling to me.'

'I know he was,' Alice said. 'But you've got to pull yourself together now. You've made yourself quite ill these last few days. Phillip wouldn't want that. You owe it to him, Beatrice, to get back to normal. You've got to try, from today on.'

'I will try,' Beatrice said. 'Why don't we go and see Fern and tell her?'

'Why don't I get her and she can sit with you for a while?' Alice suggested. 'I have things I ought to do downstairs. You wait here and I'll go up to the nursery.'

Fern opened her drawing book. She had some homework every teatime, but that was finished. She had come back after spending an hour with her

147

grandmother, who was always crying and sniffing and trying to cuddle her. Wonderful news, my darling, she'd said, wonderful news. You're going to have a baby brother or sister.

And there was her mother standing to one side, echoing that silly old grandmother. 'It'll be fun for you,' were her brisk words. 'Someone to play with later on.' She had a nasal voice that Fern hated. But it wasn't soapy and sugary like her grandmother's. If only Daddy had been there. But he'd been gone for ages, leaving her alone with all these women. Soppy Miss Groves, the governess, smarming up to her mother; that horrid Lily, who'd actually slapped her once when she was rude to her; and, worst of all, her mother, her wicked mother, who'd kissed a man and lied about it, and had him to sleep in her bedroom. Fern knew all about that because she had become an expert spy. She crept about the house, listening at doors and watching people who thought themselves alone. She imagined that she was invisible, like a ghost in the story book seeing through walls.

Now they had sprung this horrible surprise on her and told her she was going to be happy about it. 'I'm not,' she said aloud, 'I'm going to hate it. I don't want a brother or a sister.' She drew a circle in her book, stabbed two dots for eyes and a line for a mouth, and then scored it viciously with her pencil. 'I'm going to hate you,' she said again.

There was no word from Nicholas. One week passed and then the next. Alice read his poems and the tattered letter over and over, as if by doing so she kept him close to her. And safe. Because she was becoming frightened. Twice she telephoned the group captain to be told that he was out of London and unavailable. Alice felt the denial was deliberate. She resisted the temptation to go to London and beard Wallace unexpectedly in his office. Nick might be angry if she went so far. She waited, and that waiting took its toll in sleeplessness and worry.

At five months she was able to conceal the baby by careful dressing. Fern had made her swell up very early. There were fifteen new arrivals at Ashton and Alice tired herself out looking after them. She was taking a short walk one afternoon with a young pilot officer who'd been shot in the left leg and was hobbling on a stick. He'd be fully recovered in a few weeks and talked hopefully of going back to flying. For his own sake Alice hoped he wouldn't.

'I think we've gone far enough,' she said. 'If it's a nice day tomorrow, I'll take you down to the walled garden. But you mustn't do too much on that leg.'

He smiled at her. What a smasher she was, he thought. She made you feel better just by talking to you. He'd written so much about her in his letters home, his fiancée had got quite upset. No harm in being a bit in love with her. Impossible not to be really. His leg ached but he had to walk on it. He didn't mind so long as she went with him.

She saw the RAF car parked in the forecourt. A uniformed WAAF was sitting in the driving seat. She helped her charge negotiate the steps up to the entrance, and as they came into the hall a VAD came up to them. 'Hello,' she said. 'Had a nice walk? Mrs Vandekar, there's someone to see you. He's in your sitting room.'

'Oh, thank you,' Alice said breathlessly, then she almost ran in her excitement. Nick was back. It must be Nick.

It was Group Captain Wallace, standing by the fireplace with his hands locked behind his back. Alice stopped dead inside the doorway. He cleared his throat.

Before he could speak she said, 'What's happened to Nick?' He came towards her. She couldn't read his eyes.

149

'Come and sit down, Mrs Vandekar,' he said gently. 'I'm afraid I have bad news.'

She went so white he put out a hand to steady her. Alice brushed it aside. She said, 'He's dead, is that what you mean? You mean he's dead?'

'Yes,' Wallace answered. 'That's why I came to tell you myself. It'll be public knowledge by this evening. I know how much you did for him and how devoted he was to you. I didn't want you to hear it on the news.'

She moved to a chair and sat down. Dead. Nick was dead. She heard him say, 'Are you all right?' and her own voice answer, 'I'm fine. Tell me. Tell me what happened . . .'

He perched himself on the edge of the sofa. Thank God she hadn't broken down and lost control. He was useless at this sort of thing at the best of times. But he owed it to Armstrong. Armstrong had made him promise to see her if anything went wrong. He cleared his throat again.

She had an impulse to scream at him, but just managed to check it. She said, 'You sent him back, didn't you? There was never a job in Baker Street.'

'There would have been,' he said, 'if this had been successful. He was the only person who could do it, you see. He couldn't have gone into active work anywhere in occupied France, that was out of the question. But this was a special mission. Let me explain it to you, please, before you jump to conclusions.

'Six weeks ago we got word that the Gestapo intended moving a batch of Resistance prisoners from Lyons to Paris. That was the first stage on their journey to the Avenue Foch. Among those prisoners were two very important Allied agents. Neither had been able to commit suicide before they were captured. They had vital knowledge, Mrs Vandekar. Knowledge that would have ruined years of patient work in France by our people once the Germans got it out of them. As they would have done in the end. They had to be rescued.'

He paused. 'Would you mind if I had a cigarette?' She shook her head, when he tried to offer her one. Then he went on. 'We mounted a bombing raid on the prison in Lyons. It was very risky stuff, low-level, accurate targeting. Our objective was to blow out the main wall in the exercise area to pinpoint a part of the building which would allow the prisoners to escape. This is where Nick was vital. Nick knew the prison. He'd been held there himself. He knew exactly where we had to aim for and, more important, where we mustn't hit. Otherwise the people we were trying to rescue would have been killed. You can imagine the propaganda value that would have been to the Germans if the French believed we'd gone in and deliberately killed their people to stop them giving anything away.' He hoped she'd say something, but she didn't.

'Nick was the lynchpin of the whole operation. When it was suggested to me I knew we couldn't attempt it without him. I told him what we wanted him to do when he was at Princess Mary's. Obviously he couldn't tell anyone else until the mission was completed. He went in the leading aircraft, and with his direction the raid was a complete success. The prison was attacked and the majority of the French prisoners escaped. Including our agents. The tragedy is, we lost two aircraft. The leading bomber was shot down. It crashed outside Lyons and there were no survivors.'

He waited for a moment. She looked so still and stricken that he was at a loss for words of sympathy. He tried. 'He was one of the bravest men I've ever met,' he said. 'And he wanted to do this. You see, he never really forgave himself for breaking under torture. He couldn't be sure how much he'd given away and who had suffered because of it. He saw this as his chance to atone and he took it. He knew the chances of coming back were pretty slight. But he wanted to go. You must believe that.'

Alice looked up at him. 'I do,' she said. 'I knew Nick. And so did you when you came here that day and told us both a pack of lies. He's dead and he's a hero. I hope you can live with yourself. Now, will you please go?'

'Mrs Vandekar,' he began, but she interrupted. 'Get out. Get out of my house. If you have any decency . . .' As he closed the door behind him he saw her sink to the ground and begin to cry.

She had no sense of time. She wept until she was exhausted and fell into a merciful sleep, slumped on the floor. When she woke, it was so late the room was quite dark.

Nick was dead. The plane had been shot down and there were no survivors.

Slowly Alice got to her feet. She switched on the lamp and huddled onto the sofa. This room, seen dimly in the soft focus of a single light, this beautiful room was the scene of her great heartbreak. And the place where he had held out his arms to her and said, 'I love you.' It seemed to Alice as if her life had begun and ended in that room. Nothing felt real before that moment; nothing will feel real from now on, she thought. Full circle. And so short. Such a short time to know what it meant to be loved and to learn what it meant to lose that love for ever.

The high point of her shock and grief was over. Now there was a dragging pain that would be with her for all the days she could imagine. She sat on until it was pitch dark outside the windows and she felt chilled. She got up, switched out the light and closed the door on the room. It was nearly nine o'clock. She remembered what he had said. It'll be public knowledge by this evening. I didn't want you to hear it on the news . . . She went upstairs, passing Lily's door without stopping. She didn't want Lily; she didn't want anyone. There was a wireless in her bedroom. She lay on the bed and listened.

Details had just been released of a daring raid on a Gestapo prison in occupied France. The same story

Wallace had told her. Highly successful rescue attempt. Tragic loss of a British agent who had directed the bombing from the first aircraft to go in. They gave his name, and she felt it like a blow, hearing it come over the airwaves. How long ago, she wondered, how long had he been lying dead while she read his one letter and the poetry he'd written to her, thinking him alive, waiting for a message that would never come.

'We were so close, my darling,' Alice said aloud. 'Why didn't I know something had happened... I carry you inside me, you said. Isn't it strange that I didn't feel anything? I should have known.'

'Madam.' Lily was standing in the doorway. 'Madam, I just heard the news on the wireless.' She seemed hesitant, as if she was afraid to come in.

'Yes,' Alice said. 'I've known since this afternoon. Group Captain Wallace drove down here to tell me before it was broadcast. He's dead. What am I going to do, Lily? What am I going to do now?'

'Take care of yourself,' was the fiercely spoken answer. 'That's what he'd want. He loved you, God knows he did, but he's dead and you're here. And there's the baby to think of... He shouldn't have gone,' she said suddenly, 'not leaving you like this...' There was a choke in her voice as if she was going to cry.

Alice said quietly, 'He didn't know about the baby. He asked me to leave Hugo and marry him after the war. I was planning to do it, I really was.'

Lily blew her nose. 'It's not fair on you,' she declared. 'After all you've done for everyone. It's just not fair. There's no God, that's what I say, or He wouldn't let it happen!'

Alice turned away and closed her eyes. She was so tired. Poor Lily was upset. She'd want to help her undress, fuss over her and make her comfortable. Alice didn't want to hurt her, but she couldn't have borne that. She said, 'Lily, I'd like to be alone. Just this once.

Tomorrow will be better, but I don't want anyone tonight. So you go to bed and let me be. There's a dear.'

'All right, madam. All right.'

Alice knew she was crying as she went out. She began to drift, lying fully dressed on the bed. The baby gave a little jump and she touched the place with one hand, letting it lie on the spot. His child. Not Hugo's born out of a loveless union on her part, like Fern. A child that was part of him, living through her, carrying him on into a second life. She slept.

It was a scorching autumn. The uncut lawns at Ashton turned brown and the air was close and dusty. The baby grew and Alice wilted; for the first time in her life she felt drained of energy, lethargic and low-spirited. Lily was so worried she mentioned it to Dr Banks, who said Alice was perfectly healthy and that when the weather changed she'd feel much better. A lot of women suffered from nervous exhaustion in that heat. There was nothing to worry about. He didn't mention grief. He didn't have to. Lily saw her many mornings and knew she had cried herself to sleep.

And not only Lily. One day when she was sitting sewing with her door open, she saw Fern come out of Alice's room. The child stood for a moment with an odd expression on her face. Lily stopped her work. Fern began to walk away almost on tiptoe.

As she passed Lily's room, Lily came out and stood in front of her. 'What do you think you're doing, miss? Why are you creeping about like that?'

'I went in to see Mummy,' the child said. 'She's got a very big tummy. That's the baby, isn't it?'

'Yes, it is,' Lily answered, not caring whether Fern was supposed to know the facts of life or not. She was too fly, that one, to be fobbed off with the gooseberry bush.

'She was crying,' Fern stated. She watched Lily from under her lids and saw her start. 'Is it because that

Air Force man is dead? The one who was here that Mummy looked after?'

Lily stood very still.

'I saw his picture in the newspapers,' the silky little voice went on. 'I cut it out and kept it. Miss Groves said he'd been given a medal.' The pale eyes looked up at Lily and there was a gleam of malice in them.

Lily reached out and grabbed her by the arm. She held tight and squeezed hard. Fern whimpered. 'Now you listen to me,' Lily hissed at her. 'You ever say anything about that Air Force man again and I'll give you the hiding of your life, you understand? When I was a kid my Dad used to take his belt off and lay into me, and that's what I'll do to you. So you just remember. Keep your trap shut!' She gave a final savage squeeze and then pushed the child away.

Fern backed off, but to Lily's surprise she didn't turn and run. She was very white and the tears were spilling down her cheeks. 'I hate you,' she said. 'I'll hurt *you* one day . . .' Then, sobbing she fled towards the stairs and nursery.

'Little bitch,' Lily muttered, and went off to comfort Alice.

The call from the United States was for Lily. Alice was resting; she was very big and suffered badly from backache. Not long to go now, thank God. Just let's hope, Lily said to herself, that she has an easy time, not like the last one.

She was expecting the call. 'Mrs Holmes Fry? Good afternoon, madam. Yes, very well, thank you. No, she's sleeping at the moment.' There was a pause while Alice's mother talked. Lily said yes once or twice and nodded. Then she said, 'Oh, it would be such a help to her. It really would. I'd never have written to you but I've been so worried about her. She'll kill me when she finds out, but that can't be helped. When? Oh, good. No, I won't say anything. She'd only try and stop you. You know what she's like, madam. She can't bear anyone making a fuss. Yes, thank you. Thank you so much. We'll see you then.' She hung up.

Thank God for that, she said to herself. It was time Alice had someone to support her through the birth. Old Mother Vandekar was as much good as a sick headache, Lily thought angrily. After all Alice had done for her when Mr Phillip was killed, she couldn't come down and let Alice lean on her for a change. Same thing when Alice had pneumonia. Just flustered round and got in the way. Thank God Mrs Holmes Fry was coming. Even though Lily would probably be blown sky high when Alice found out that she had been responsible. It didn't matter, she thought stoically. I've done the right thing for her.

Alice was reading when her sitting-room door opened. She looked up, expecting Lily with some tea. She hadn't noticed the time and her baby hadn't kicked or stirred since after lunch. It was Lily, but without the teatray and a look of mingled guilt and triumph on her face. 'You've got a visitor, madam,' she announced, and stepped out of the way. Alice's book fell to the floor. She heaved herself up and stared in amazement.

'Mother! Mother, I don't believe it!'

Phoebe came towards her and they were folded in each other's arms. 'Darling,' she said, hugging her daughter. 'Darling, how are you, let me look at you . . .'

'How did you get here?' Alice demanded. She was breathless and overcome with joy.

'Pan Am. They have a flight via Lisbon. I used a bit of influence to get on board, but it was safer than trying a sea crossing,' her mother said.

They were side by side and Alice was grasping her hand.

'Safer? Mother, they've been shooting down civil planes. God, I can't believe it. Why didn't you let me know?'

'We wanted to surprise you,' Phoebe said.

Alice said quietly, 'We, who's we?'

'Lily and I,' her mother said. 'Now you're not to be

cross with her. You'd never have asked me, would you?'

Alice looked grim. 'No,' she said, 'I certainly wouldn't have let you take a risk like that.' She felt her temper rise and suddenly explode. 'How dare she! How dare she take it upon herself!'

The baby gave an agitated lurch in response to her change of mood and she addressed it furiously. 'You shut up in there,' she snapped. 'Just shut up! This is too much – I'm going to sack that woman! I'm going to sack – Oh, Mother, Mother, I'm so glad you came...'

When Lily came back with tea for them both Alice was in Phoebe's arms. She smiled at Lily over her daughter's shoulder. Alice said in a muffled voice, 'Lily, take a week's notice, you hear me?'

'Yes, madam,' Lily said, and to Phoebe, 'Milk and sugar?'

The baby was born on a cold December afternoon at Ashton. Dr Banks delivered it after a short straightforward labour. 'You've got a little boy,' he said. 'Congratulations. A fine healthy baby boy.'

A lusty cry confirmed this and Alice smiled. 'Nothing wrong with his lungs anyway. Can I have him, please?'

The midwife placed the small, bundled-up baby in the crook of her arm and Alice looked down at him. She was still slightly muzzy from the gas and air given in the final stage.

'He's beautiful,' she whispered.

'He's fair,' Dr Banks said. 'Just like you.' He didn't know what Major Vandekar's colouring was. He thrust that thought aside. It was a strong, perfect baby and the mother had come through without too much discomfort. Birth always filled him with a sense of joy. It was a long time since he had practised that side of medicine. He looked on them both, contented and at peace, and smiled. So much of his skill had been devoted to mending the shattered bodies of war's victims. He felt truly grateful and renewed by the experience of bringing a new life into the world.

Phoebe told the staff and the patients the good news. They clubbed together to buy flowers for Alice. Beatrice arrived by the end of the week, and a message was sent to Hugo via the War Office telling him he had a son. They kept the reply from Alice until the child was ten days old and she was allowed out of bed. Major Vandekar was in the base hospital at Tripoli after being wounded. The news had been conveyed to him, and as soon as he was sufficiently recovered he would send a message back.

Influence was a help, no doubt about it. The old friends from the palmy days before the war were in high places and Alice didn't hesitate to call on them. She had no conscience about making use of her position and her contacts. 'Just because some poor women have to wait to find out, that doesn't mean we have to,' she insisted. 'If Hugo's wounded I want to know how and where and how badly. Beatrice, it doesn't do anyone any good to *cry* until we know!'

She was amazing, her mother thought. Bad news seemed to galvanize her.

'I'm damned if I'm going to just accept that message and wait till some half-baked idiot out in Tripoli sends me an answer. If Hugo's badly hurt he must be brought home. And I know just the people who can fix it.'

But it couldn't be fixed. Not even Alice's powers of cajolement and insistence could cut through the red tape and get Hugo out of hospital ahead of time. He had lost his left leg above the knee. When she heard that she cried bitterly. For him, not for herself. She had her precious baby, her health, her spirits and her strength of purpose back. He would come home a cripple. The worst thing that could have happened to such a proud and active man. She grieved for him, and at the same time searched the baby's face for some resemblance to Nick. Some shade in the expression as he grew, some quirk in the infectious, ready smile. But there was none. He was fair as the sunshine, with her blue eyes. He was the image of herself.

He was christened Richard Phillip. Beatrice had convinced herself that he was exactly like her dead son at that age, and Alice gave him the name to please her. She was silly and irritating, but helpless somehow. Adversity had robbed her of whatever solid strength she'd had. She clung to Alice in her sorrow over Hugo. Her one comfort was her grandchildren. She doted on Fern and was besotted by the baby boy.

They all were. Even Lily, who was inclined to be dour and overbrisk with little Fern, won both grandmothers' hearts by her devotion to the boy. He was lovely, she said, admiring him with Alice. Always smiling. Adding firmly, 'Mr Hugo will be so pleased when he sees him. Make up for a lot, having a boy like that.'

Knowing her so well, Alice only said, 'Yes, won't he,' and that was all they ever said. 'He'll love you,' Alice assured her little son. 'He'll be a wonderful father to you, and you'll make up to him for this awful thing, I know you will.' And she would kiss the downy head and hug him.

He was six months old when Hugo came back to Ashton. It was a stranger who walked through the door into the hall to be welcomed by his wife and family. Or rather limped, painfully and stiff-legged, with a stick. For a moment he and Alice looked at each other, but before she could move, Fern had rushed forward with a cry and flung her arms around his waist.

'Darling,' Alice hurried to him. 'Darling, welcome home!' She found Fern between them, holding tightly.

'Alice,' he said, 'how are you? There, darling, let Daddy and Mummy say hello...'

She embraced him; he embraced her. He didn't kiss her as he had kissed Fern. She quelled a pang of jealousy and disappointment. Didn't he know how hard she had worked to get him repatriated? Didn't he know how much anguish they had all felt for him? His mother, poor old thing, and Phoebe, who wouldn't go back home till he returned and was going towards him with that sweet smile of hers, saying, 'Dear, dear Hugo, thank God you're safe home...' That damned child was still holding on to him, gripping one hand while he gave them all a brief embrace in turn.

'Lily,' Alice commanded, and didn't realize the edge that had crept into her voice. 'Bring Richard over here. Darling – this is your son.'

He had to accept him, she insisted. He had to see what a lovely child he was and believe that this was the baby he had begged her to have before he went away. Richard's future would depend upon it. He was the only father the boy would ever know. It seemed a long pause while Hugo looked at the child in Lily's arms. At last he said, 'He's very like you, Alice. He'll be a good-looking chap when he grows up.'

She wanted to take the baby from Lily and say to Hugo, 'Here, hold him,' but she didn't. 'I think there's quite a look of you,' she replied. 'Beatrice swears he's the image of Phillip when he was a baby. He was fair too, wasn't he?'

'Only to start with,' Hugo answered. 'Yes, I suppose you could say there is a look.'

Lily stepped forward. 'Would you like to hold him, sir?'

He held the baby rather awkwardly. Richard gave a gurgling, infectious laugh. Hugo smiled briefly. 'He is a nice little chap,' he said.

'Daddy, Daddy...' That was Fern, tugging at his arm again. 'I've made some lovely drawings ꞏr you; all specially coloured. Come and see them, please come...'

'Of course I'll come.' He looked down at her and the smile became warm. 'But not just yet. Alice, you'd better take the boy,' and he handed him back, which Alice knew was what Fern wanted.

'It's good to be home,' he said. 'You've kept everything going so well, Alice.'

They were alone at last. Dinner had been a strain, with Beatrice talking about Phillip and Fern trying to attract Hugo's attention. He had insisted she should stay up and join them. Phoebe didn't seem to notice anything; she was too kind-natured to see the hostilities behind the façade of his homecoming. But Alice, who had stripped the vegetable garden and used up the month's meat ration to provide a decent dinner, felt left out, almost ignored. For months now she had imagined his return. Dreading it sometimes, then anticipating it with hope of their making a new life together. She had changed so much – surely it would be easier for them to live together. They had the boy, there was a future. The war was going well. But Hugo was not the man who had left her. He was not the angry, hurt husband who had turned from her and found solace with another woman, the man so desperately in love he was prepared to beg for what was his by right. The husband who had gone off to the war, leaving a note for her when she woke up. 'Thank you for making me so happy. I shall love you always.' That man had not come back.

After dinner they went to her sitting room. Several of the convalescents were sitting in the big hall, clustered around the wireless. They smiled at Alice, brightening when they saw her. They knew who the man was, walking on his artificial leg. Lucky sod, coming back to a wife like that...

Phoebe was the first to excuse herself. She bent over her son-in-law. 'Good night, Hugo. I guess I'm a little tired. It's been such a happy day.'

Beatrice followed, taking the hint. Her eyes were moist when she embraced him. 'Thank God I've got you left to me,' she said.

But Fern hung on and said, 'Goodnight, Daddy,' and 'Promise you'll see my drawings tomorrow,' until Alice was stung into impatience. 'Come on, that's enough. It's long past your bedtime, so be a good girl and go right up to Miss Groves, will you?'

'Yes, Mummy.' There was a look of reproach that made Alice feel she had been put into the wrong.

'She's very pleased to have me back,' Hugo remarked.

'We're all pleased,' Alice said, and Fern wasn't mentioned again.

'It's good to be home,' he said again. He stretched in the chair, trying to find a comfortable position.

Alice saw him wince. 'Does it still hurt?'

'At times. It's not too bad. I'll get used to it in time, I expect. I'd forgotten what a charming room this is. Funny, all the good things one takes for granted. The civilized things, like a decent armchair to sit in and a drink in a glass that isn't a tin mug. Silly little details like that.'

He looked so weary that Alice said, 'Darling, would you like a drink? Some of your good brandy. I had it brought up specially.'

'That was thoughtful of you,' he said. 'I think a nightcap would be very nice.'

She got up and poured him a generous measure. For a moment she warmed the balloon between her hands. 'Thoughtful of you.' She could have been a stranger. It wasn't deliberate, she insisted. He had been so hurt himself, he had lost touch with the past.

She gave him the drink and sat close to him. 'You've been through a terrible time, Hugo,' she said. 'But try to realize that it's all over. You're home now, and I want to tell you I'm so happy and relieved. Darling, believe me.'

'I do,' he answered. He sipped the brandy. 'You've hardly changed at all. I used to imagine what you'd look like when I came back. Not that I thought I would. When that mine went up I remember thinking for one split second, this is it. But it wasn't, after all. Just a piece of my leg gone, that's all. Compared to what other people suffered, it wasn't much to bear. So many dead, that was the trouble.' He drank more deeply. He seemed to be talking to himself. 'Not just

162

our own, but so many Germans too. One dead man looks much like another. You forget who's the enemy. You think, Christ, how old was he? And the wounded in hospital. But you understand, don't you, Alice?' He turned and looked at her. 'You've cared for men here who've been burned and mutilated and shocked to hell . . . What happened to Nicholas Armstrong in the end?'

It was as if he had suddenly bunched his fist and struck her.

'He got better,' she said quietly. Her face had flamed with colour. 'He went back to work for your friend James Wallace and was killed.'

'I'm so sorry,' Hugo said. 'You were very fond of him, weren't you?'

'Yes, I suppose so. Why do you mention him, Hugo? Surely I wrote to you about him. He was your protégé, after all.' He knows, she thought. He knows about Nick. It's in his eyes when he looks at me. But, please God, not about the boy . . .

'I heard afterwards that he became yours too,' he said. 'Is there any more of that brandy? I'd get up myself but the bloody stump is rather rubbed after today.'

'I'll get it,' she moved quickly, filled the glass a third full and took a deep swallow of it herself.

He said, 'I've never seen you do that before. I thought you hated the stuff. You always said you did.'

'I've changed my mind,' she answered. 'Here.' She lit a cigarette. Time to think, to decide whether to take up the challenge and tell the truth if that was what he wanted. Or to let the moment slip. She couldn't do anything else. For Richard's sake. In this room, conceived here, with the door locked.

'It's a small world, a war,' he said. 'I shall be quite drunk if I down all this. You remember Dr Ferguson? The medic who was here in the early days?'

'A red-haired Scot? Yes, I remember him. I got him thrown out.'

'So he said,' Hugo remarked. 'He turned up in the base hospital. Wasn't that an amazing coincidence? Very badly wounded. Been in an ambulance that got strafed. He heard who I was and started shouting at me. He was in the next bed, as it turned out. "Your bloody wife," he said. "I wanted to put her boyfriend in the loony bin where he belonged..." He was quite off his head, of course. Babbling and yelling before he passed out. He died later on.'

'Oh?' She felt quite calm now. No panic, just a slow anger coming to the surface. 'Well, don't expect me to say I'm sorry. He behaved disgracefully. He brought the transfer on himself.'

'I expect so,' he agreed. 'Bad judge of character to cross you. I think I'll go to bed now. Can you take this? Thanks so much.'

Together they made the slow and, for him, painful progress up the stairs to their room. 'When the war's over,' Alice said, 'we'll get a lift put in.'

'I won't need it by then,' he said. 'It's just the first few months until you get used to these artificial things.'

Lily had done her best. She had culled flowers from the overgrown beds and arranged them on the dressing table. There was a fire burning, a wood fire, because there was no coal for domestic use. Their nightclothes were arranged on each side of the bed.

Hugo sat down heavily. 'Do you want any help?' she asked him. 'You know I don't mind.'

'But I do,' he answered. 'It's not very pretty when the limb comes off. Would you go into the bathroom until I call out? It won't take long.'

For a moment Alice weakened. Her eyes filled with tears. 'Hugo,' she began, 'oh Hugo, I'm so terribly sorry...'

'About what? My leg?'

'About everything. I'll make it up to you, I promise.'

'Don't worry about that,' he said. 'You've always done your best. I'm glad about our boy. Fern needed a brother.'

164

Alice closed the bathroom door and leaned against it. 'Our boy.' Thank God for that, at least. I'm sorry, Nick, my darling, but he must never, never know. He can think what he likes about you and me, but nothing must hurt Richard. Hugo would be merciless if he suspected that . . .

She heard him call and opened the door. He was already in bed. She came and climbed in beside him. The old, chill apprehension came on her, the fear that, even though disabled, he would want to touch her. He stretched out for the light. 'I'm so tired,' he said. 'So tired I could sleep for a year. Good night.'

The pattern of their life together was formed that night.

Hugo began calling the baby boy Richard Phillip. At times it seemed to Alice that he was clinging to the fancied resemblance to his dead brother, but she dismissed that as the prompting of her own guilty conscience. He paid dutiful visits to the nursery and said what a fine little chap he was, but the child never touched his heart. It was Fern he spent his time with, praising her drawings, teaching her to listen to the classical music he loved, winding the gramophone himself while she sat primly watching him. She was always watching him, willing him to notice her. She was bitterly jealous of her little brother, although she cooed and played with him when Hugo was there.

But Alice wasn't deceived. The hugs were a little too hearty and often the child began to cry. Once Alice surprised her in the nursery, pinching him savagely when she thought herself alone. Alice came up and pulled her away. She didn't say anything. She gave her a ringing box on the ears that sent her sprawling backwards on her bottom. Alice told the young nurserymaid that Fern was never to be left alone with the baby again.

Richard Phillip celebrated his third birthday in a

world at peace. It was a small party, unlike the elaborate affairs organized for Fern when she was tiny. A few local children, no nannies in their smart uniforms. Not the big dining room, its long table spread with a dazzling white cloth, decorated with balloons from the chandelier and heaped with cakes, jellies and tiny sandwiches. An austerity party, Alice called it, making a joke of the meagre cake and teaparty food. A small gathering was held in the breakfast room, with Hugo and Fern and the two grandmothers, the neighbours' small tots of children propped up round the table. The little boy beamed his bright smile at everyone and tried to catch the candles on his cake instead of blowing them out.

Alice looked on with glowing pride. He was her treasure and her joy. She loved taking him round the grounds in Fern's huge old-fashioned perambulator, pointing out this and that to him, as Ashton slowly, very slowly, came back to life. But although the world was very diferent from the one when the war had broken out and she had given her extravagant ball to say farewell to peace, Hugo's fortune hadn't suffered. He was richer than ever. Supplies were difficult, labour impossibly short, but there was so much money at hand to overcome these difficulties that Alice's energy and determination were already working miracles. As she looked at her son she thought, next year it won't be like this. Next year you'll have a big party, like the ones Fern had, and more. And one day you'll have Ashton too. That always warmed her heart. The house she loved would pass to the human being she loved best in all the world. Nick's son.

Hugo had adjusted well to his disability. He had taken up shooting again, rough shooting only, because the great shoot at Ashton was a memory. There were no keepers; the woods had been cut down for fuel; there were no birds. But it would all come back in time. Alice was determined about that. Hugo travelled to the bank in London and stayed in a small flat he'd been able to buy in Eaton Square for a few thousand pounds. An ex-serviceman was engaged as a valet and Hugo was well looked after when he was away. Alice came up sometimes, bringing the little boy and Lily with her. She wouldn't give him up to anyone else's care now. The nursemaid stayed on but it was Alice who bathed him and supervised his food and took him with her wherever she went.

And at last, to her great relief, she was able to get Fern off to boarding school.

'What is it,' she said to Lily once, 'that maddens me so much about that child?'

'She sets out to madden you, madam,' was the answer. 'Everything she does is annoying on purpose. It's not your fault.'

'I feel so mean sometimes. I know she's terribly jealous of Richard, and she drives me up the wall the way she simpers round her father . . . but I should be nicer to her, Lily.'

'You can if you like,' Lily shrugged. 'But you'll be wasting your time.'

Hugo missed his daughter. He was visibly depressed when they saw her off on the school train. 'I hope she won't be too homesick,' he remarked.

'I hope not,' Alice said. 'But she'll get over it. I did – I cried for a bit but I was soon so caught up in what was going on at school I forgot all about home.'

'No doubt, but Fern's not like you,' was all he said, and he remained silent for the rest of the journey back to Ashton.

It was a complete surprise to Alice when he announced that he was going into politics.

'You mean you're going to stand for Parliament in the election?' She stared at him. 'But how can you – Danbourne's held this seat for twenty years? Dynamite wouldn't shift him. They'd never choose another candidate to stand instead of him. Besides, there's no time.'

'I'm not contesting this seat,' he retorted. 'I've been

167

selected for a marginal in South London. There's a strong Labour candidate there and the old Tory member is retiring. There's even a Communist candidate. It should be very interesting.'

'You mean you've been selected and you never told me? Hugo – why not?'

He said quietly, 'Because you would have been masterminding every move, my dear Alice. In the end, they'd have chosen you instead of me.'

'That's very unkind,' she protested. 'I'd have loved to help, you know that. I'm really hurt.' She pushed back her chair from the table.

'Don't be silly.' He waved her to sit down again. 'I didn't mean it like that. I was anxious to succeed on my own account. I didn't want you to know if I failed. Try to understand that.'

'Well, I don't,' Alice answered. She didn't leave though. Politics. How amazing that he should decide to do that. 'Haven't you enough to occupy you with the bank?'

'Not really. I'm not so interested in making money as I was in the old days.'

'You don't have to be,' she pointed out. 'You've got so much it makes itself.'

'That's just why I need something more. England is going to be a changed place from now on. So changed we won't recognize a lot of it. I believe we'll have a Labour government, for a start.' Alice stared at him, horrified. 'We can't! That's impossible! You mean the people would throw Winston out, after all he's done!'

'Yes. He stands for the old order. They don't want that. The men coming into civilian life have quite a different set of values now. I learned that in the army. They want what they fought for, and they don't think they're going to get it from people like us.'

'Oh really? Then what are they going to get?' He was talking nonsense. 'Rubbish,' she insisted angrily. 'Throw Churchill out? Elect a Labour government?'

'I don't know,' he answered. 'That's why I'm not

standing for Labour. I think they have a lot of good ideas and some very bad ones. One will have to wait and see. By the way, if you want to help me in the campaign, my constituency party will be only too delighted. It will mean your separating yourself from the boy. I don't know how you'll feel about that.'

'I'll take him with me,' Alice announced. 'He'll get votes, you see.'

And she was right. Mrs Vandekar, her little son in her arms, became a national figure during the election campaign. She canvassed, she made speeches, she sat on platforms with Hugo and cuddled the boy for the voters to see. 'I want a decent world for my boy to grow up in,' she declared at a meeting, and the press wrote down every word. 'He won't get it with Labour.' It became Hugo's slogan. He won the seat by a tiny majority. He was marked out for future promotion from the back benches.

His enemies, and he'd made a number during the campaign inside his own party, went round saying that he owed his election to his wife. If he heard the comments, Hugo ignored them.

Richard Phillip had his seventh birthday before Alice could fulfil the promise made when he was still a very little boy. Now Ashton was restored to its old glory. The great gardens had been replanted, the splendid borders were ablaze with flowers, and the topiary garden was clipped into its ancient geometric pattern. The green lawns were mowed and cultivated until they looked like baize, and Alice persuaded Hugo to buy an entire collection of eighteenth-century garden statuary that came on the market when a famous estate was broken up to pay death duties. The house had been redecorated, and the last traces of its wartime role had disappeared. All that remained was the silver-framed photograph with its inscription 'To Mrs Vandekar. From her boys. April 1942' that stood on her desk, as she had promised. Hugo bought pictures at her prompting. So many families were being forced to sell up by heavy taxes and a climate hostile to the old order of wealth and privilege. 'That's your bloody Labour government for you!' Alice protested. 'Some good things indeed! I'd like to know what they are.'

'It hasn't stopped you doing your own bit of plundering,' was his reply. Their latest acquisition was a magnificent Van Dyck for the library.

'What's wrong with us having them?' she demanded. 'At least they stay in England.'

'Yes, of course,' he mocked her gently. 'I was sure patriotism was your motive. Don't forget to tell Winston when you get the chance.'

'Don't worry, I won't,' Alice said over her shoulder. And she didn't. The next occasion he visited Ashton he was once more Prime Minister.

Her son's seventh birthday was as lavish in its way as anything given for Fern before the war. The same grand setting, two dozen girls and boys in pretty frilly party dresses and neat little suits, and a conjuror in the library after tea. Richard Phillip blew out his seven candles and showed what nice manners he had, thanking everyone politely, not fighting with any of the boys or teasing the girls. He was perfect, Alice thought proudly, and what a handsome boy he was growing up to be. Everyone said so. Such a pity Hugo couldn't have been there, but he had been made Parliamentary Private Secretary to the new Minister for Agriculture. He had bought his son a watch. Alice had given him a train set, a bicycle and a fishing rod. His father had promised to teach him to fish in the lake during the holidays. Alice was certain to remind him. Only one more precious year remained before he was banished to another English institution, the pre-paratory school. She would lose him after his eighth birthday. No pleas or arguments had moved Hugo. 'All boys go away at that age, some at seven,' was his stock reply when Alice started protesting about its barbarity. 'You sent Fern away, and it's not so traditional with girls. Richard is going and that's the end of it.'

She didn't want to think about that, not on such a happy day. When it was over, and they had shaken hands with everyone, she took her son into the library. She rang for a drink. There was an adequate staff at Ashton now, less than the full complement, but domestic service had acquired a stigma since the war. However, they had an old retired butler who was able to train up the raw material that came unwillingly from the employment agencies, and Lily was as much the housekeeper as anything since a girl had been taken on to look after Alice's clothes. Even so the delicate mending and care of her personal things still fell to Lily, who wouldn't give them up.

'I'd like a drink, please, Thompson. Vodka and tonic. Richard darling, would you like something? Lemonade?'

'Yes please, Mummy.'

'Lemonade for Master Richard,' Alice confirmed. 'Now, we can have a few minutes peace while I put my feet up. Did you have a nice party? Did you enjoy it?'

He smiled at her. He was a demonstrative little boy, and he liked it when she put her arm round him. 'It was lovely. I got so many presents!'

Alice laughed. 'I should say so – think of all the thank-you letters you'll have to write!'

He grimaced. 'I forgot about that. Do I have to?'

'Yes, you do. But not until tomorrow. Who did you like best at the party? James Howard seemed a nice boy; so did that other child, what's his name, you know darling, the one with glasses...'

'Peter,' her son said. 'He's all right. The conjuror was so clever, wasn't he? I tried and tried to see how he did that trick with the handkerchiefs but I couldn't.'

The drinks came. Alice needed hers. Children were more tiring to entertain than any group of adults. But it had been a success for him. He'd been so excited by the conjuror, jumping up and down and shouting out clues when he was asked. He was such a rewarding child; he was pleased with everything. Not at all spoiled, which was a miracle. No thanks to me, Alice said to herself, I've spoiled him to death, but it hasn't made any difference.

'There was one little girl who couldn't come today,' she remarked, 'Lady Brayley's child. She had a sore throat. I'll ask her another time. They've just come to live near here. It's a pity she missed the party. Now it's time you went up and had your bath. I'm going to finish my drink first and then I'll come up and kiss you good night. Off you go!'

He got up immediately. 'Thanks for the party. It was super fun. Is Daddy coming home tonight?'

'No, not tonight. He's so busy these days. But he'll be back on Friday.' If he doesn't go down to his damned constituency, she said to herself. I suppose I'll have to go with him.

'I love my watch,' the little boy said. 'And all my other things. I hope he comes home.'

'He will,' she promised. She finished her drink and eased off one shoe that was pinching. Richard loved Hugo. He was always trying to please him. Sometimes it made Alice really angry when Hugo didn't respond. He much preferred that sullen daughter who was becoming adolescent and even less agreeable to have around. He had given her a real pearl necklace for her thirteenth birthday.

Then she stopped short, checked by her own guilty conscience from making too much of an issue. If all that stuff about blood being thicker than water was true, then perhaps that was the reason. Hugo had never mentioned Nick Armstrong again. Not for nearly seven years. And yet it hung between them, and it always would. She was sure he had a woman up in London, but she didn't care enough to try to find out who it was. She had Ashton and her son and a full life. That was enough.

*

172

'I don't want to play with a girl,' Richard protested.

'Nonsense,' Alice said. 'I told you, she missed your birthday party because she was ill and I promised her mother I'd invite her. How would you like it if you'd just moved to a new house and didn't have anybody to play with?'

'I wouldn't mind,' he insisted. 'I don't like girls, Mummy.'

Alice didn't chide him because she knew why. Girls meant Fern, who was so much bigger and bullied him whenever she got the chance. From the day Alice caught her pinching him when he was a baby, she had kept a close watch on her daughter and the boy.

She said kindly, 'Richard, you're not to say that. It's silly. Girls can be fun.'

He looked up at her with his big eyes and said with the devastating honesty of a child, 'Fern's a girl and she's horrid. Lily says she's a pain in the arse.'

Alice gaped at him for a moment and then burst out laughing. 'Well, Lily shouldn't say that. Fern's your sister. All girls aren't like her. Diana Brayley is only little, but I'm sure she's very nice. So you're not to be rough and push her over, because I'll be there and I'll be very angry with you. OK?'

He hung his head for a moment. She hated being firm with him. Then he brightened. 'OK, Mummy. When's she coming?'

'Teatime,' Alice said. 'You can play afterwards while I talk to her mother.'

The Brayleys had moved into the country quite recently. It was an old and famous name, but denuded of estates and money over the last century, the family had moved out of their enormous house in Somerset when it was requisitioned by the army. At the end of the war it was a wreck, and they were only too pleased to take the miserly War Office compensation and sell it to a builder. Soon he had stripped it of lead, panelling, doors and fireplaces, and left the shell to fall down. They had bought a much smaller farmhouse not far from Ashton. Alice had called on them when they moved in. She found Lady Brayley a pleasant, rather gentle person, who was anxious to make friends and disarmingly honest about their circumstances. She hadn't seen the only child, although Anne Brayley talked about her and said she hoped she'd meet other children in the neighbourhood.

'I can help there,' Alice had offered immediately. 'My son's having a birthday party. I'll send you an invitation. You must bring her over.'

She was in the hall reading when they arrived. Richard was drawing nearby.

'Come on, darling,' she said. 'We'll go and meet them.'

They came out on the top step beneath the portico, and Alice saw the child for the first time, negotiating the big steps up to the house, holding her mother's hand.

The sunlight turned her blazing red hair into a fiery aureole. She was tiny, like a little china doll. Her coat was a bright blue tweed with velvet collar, and her little strap shoes were polished until they shone. She raised a face like a fairy, with big, wide grey eyes and lisped, 'How do you do?' to Alice.

'What an enchanting child,' Alice said, and her mother smiled.

'Oh, not really. She takes after Bill, you know. Red hair comes out in the family from time to time. And this is Richard? How do you do, Richard.'

Alice was proud of his good manners. He made a little bow and shook hands nicely. He and the little girl stared briefly at each other and then looked away.

'Diana, say how do you do to Richard.' For a moment they touched hands.

'We'll have tea first,' Alice said, 'then we can take the children out into the grounds. I've had a swing and some slides put up for Richard. It is so nice of you to come.'

Anne Brayley followed Alice into the hall. Briefly

she noticed the fine tapestries and the valuable furniture and pictures. Very rich, of course. Bill had said they were nouveau, but she envied them.

'Diana's an afterthought, you see. We lost our only son on D-Day. He was just eighteen.'

'I'm so sorry,' Alice murmured. She glanced behind her at Richard, who was walking silently beside the little girl. To bring up a boy and see him grow to early manhood and then to lose him on some bloody battlefield.

'What do you want to play?' Richard demanded. He was determined to be bored. She was such a *little* girl and she kept staring at him with that silly look on her face.

She shook her head. 'Don't know.'

He made a face. His mother would be cross if he didn't do something with her. 'I'll swing you,' he offered. 'Come on.'

She was so small her feet dangled high above the ground; she held to the ropes of the swing and he pushed her back and forth, longing to give it a really good shove and see her fly upwards.

She turned and lisped at him, 'More. Push more!'

Richard gave a wicked grin. She'd asked for it. He couldn't be blamed. 'All right. Hold on tight.'

She went up in a rising arc, high, high above his head. For a moment he panicked in case she fell off. He hadn't meant to do it quite so hard. He expected her to scream, and glanced quickly towards his mother, who was sitting talking to her mother. Instead he heard a gurgling laugh of pure excitement. He was so surprised he forgot to push again and gradually the swing came lower and lower and stopped.

Her face was bright red and she was beaming at him. 'More,' she said. 'More, please.'

Richard scowled. He'd been frightened himself by what he'd done. He was cross that she hadn't realized it was dangerous. 'No,' he said. 'Get off. Come on, get off.'

'Can't,' she said. He went up and lifted her down, letting her drop to the ground with a bump.

'Darling,' Alice called out, 'why don't you and Diana play ball? There's one over there by the slide.' She had seen the incident with the swing and had held her breath until the child was safely on the ground. Luckily Anne Brayley hadn't noticed. She'd been engrossed in her own account of the relief of living in a manageable house after years of the barracks in Somerset.

'How do you manage to keep such a big place warm?' she asked. 'We were always frozen in the winter. People used to come down in their overcoats to dinner.'

'I couldn't put up with that,' Alice answered. 'Americans hate a cold house. Luckily my husband feels the same. We've done a lot to Ashton since the war, and a really efficient heating system was my top priority. How do you like being in the district? It's very social. I expect you've found that out already.'

'Yes, people have been very kind. We've had a lot of invitations. Trouble is, Bill, my husband, doesn't really enjoy entertaining. He makes such a fuss that half of the fun goes out of it.'

'Then you must come to us,' Alice said. 'Hugo and I always have a houseful most weekends. He has a lot of political entertaining to do and I mix in my own friends. We had such a miserable time in the war, didn't we? I guess we're owed a bit of fun to make up for it.'

'That would be nice,' Anne Brayley enthused. 'Bill has the reputation of being a bit grumpy, but I'm sure he'd enjoy himself with you.'

'Then I'll look up the diary and call you,' Alice promised. 'Now, I think it's getting a bit cold for the children, don't you?'

'Oh? Yes, I suppose it is. Bill says I fuss too much over Diana. He says she ought to be brought up to be hardy. I keep telling him she's not a boy.' She laughed rather nervously.

Alice got up and called the children. A boy. In her whole life she'd never seen anything more aggressively feminine than that dainty child. There was no sense of premonition, no warning. She'd seldom seen two more beautiful children than her son and the little Brayley daughter as they ran towards her on that late spring afternoon.

4

'I don't want a party,' Fern protested. 'I don't want to be a deb and waste my time with silly girls and dances. Please, Daddy, you know I've set my heart on going to art school. Can't you talk Mummy out of it? *Please?*'

Hugo patted her shoulder. She was nearly as tall as her mother, although she lacked Alice's grace and slenderness. He loved her so much; they had a bond that couldn't be described, he and his daughter. Perhaps it was the shared knowledge that Alice didn't love them. He often pondered that. The miracle was that now he didn't love Alice. He owed his release to Fern. 'I'll try, but I can't promise. You should have some kind of coming-out, you know, darling. It's expected.'

She moved impatiently. 'Oh, Daddy, not any more! It's different now. It's just a lot of parties and money – anyone can do it. I'd hate it. I'd really hate it. And if I wasn't a success, you know Mummy would be disappointed.'

Hugo put his arm round Fern. 'Your mother only wants you to make new friends. She's such an extrovert, she doesn't understand that you wouldn't enjoy it. She was such a star herself, she imagines it's the same for everyone else.'

'I'm not a star,' Fern said. 'Richard's the star. I'll be a flop, and she'll never let me forget it. He should have been the girl,' she added. 'He's got all the looks, Daddy. He's just like Mummy. Everyone says so.'

Hugo said gently, 'I know they do. But you're wrong about yourself. You're a very pretty girl. You'd be a great success if you wanted to be – don't have any doubts about that. But if you really mean it, then I'll talk to your mother again.'

'I'll go to art college instead,' she promised. 'I'll work terribly hard and then you'll both be proud of me. Do try, Daddy, won't you?'

'Why didn't she come to me?' Alice demanded. 'Why does she have to go whining to you behind my back?'

She had driven down from London after a day spent at two charity committee meetings and a fitting at Dior for three new outfits. She was tired and worried – she had telephoned Phoebe in New York and sensed that she wasn't well. Now Hugo appeared before dinner, campaigning on behalf of Fern. She was not in a sympathetic mood. 'She's so underhand and you encourage her!'

'She's not underhand,' he said. 'She's frightened of you, Alice. You know she is. It's a lot of nonsense, saying she goes behind your back. She doesn't want a London season, and I don't see why she should be bullied into it.'

Alice lit a cigarette, then snapped her lighter shut. 'Bullied, my foot,' she retorted. 'She twists you round her little finger. OK, OK, she doesn't want a dance, she doesn't want to meet people, but she's not damned well staying here making trouble between us! She wants to go to art college, then she goes as soon as the autumn term starts. Now don't let's talk about it any more. I could do with a drink. Ring the bell, will you, please?'

She asked for vodka and tonic, Hugo ordered whisky and soda for himself. 'How was London?' He didn't want to prolong the quarrel. He hated atmospheres, and Alice was adept at keeping a row going these days. She was short-tempered and impatient, even with Lily. The sunshine was reserved for Richard when he came home on exeat from school.

'Tiring,' she said. 'Meetings for the Red Cross and the Palladium Gala. My bloody dresses weren't ready either, so I've got to go up again next week. I called Phoebe today. She doesn't sound very well.'

'Oh?' He liked his mother-in-law. He had been sorry when she'd gone back to the States. Phoebe was fond of Fern, and Fern missed her. His mother had died two years ago. She had left Richard a considerable sum of money. Because of that resemblance, real or imagined . . . 'What's the matter?'

'She wouldn't say,' Alice answered. 'You know what she's like – she doesn't like making a fuss. Hugo, I might fly over before the Christmas hullabaloo starts down here, just to check on her. She says she is seeing a doctor next week. She's losing weight and she feels tired all the time. You won't mind, will you?'

'Of course not. I'd come too, but I can't get away from the House. Try not to worry. I'm sure she'll be all right. Perhaps you could persuade her to come over?'

'That's what I thought,' Alice agreed. 'At least I can see she takes care of herself.'

Fern joined them for dinner. Nothing was said about the future. Fern glanced at Hugo and was given a little nod of encouragement. It was all right, he'd talked her mother round. Looking at Alice's set face, Fern knew it hadn't been without a struggle.

We've won, she thought and kept her eyes down, eating quickly, anxious to get away from the atmosphere. Daddy beat her this time. I will one day. One day I'll stand up to her and get my way. Because I know what she really is. I know what it meant when I found her snogging with that man, bringing him upstairs at night. She's betrayed Daddy. While he was away fighting she was sleeping with that other man. I don't believe Richard is my real brother . . .

'If you gobble your food down like that, you'll get indigestion,' Alice said suddenly. 'And that'll give you spots.'

Fern didn't answer. She put her knife and fork together, leaving the rest of the food on her plate.

'There's no need to sulk,' her mother said sharply.

Fern looked up at her. 'I'm not sulking,' she said. 'I don't want any more, thank you.'

Hugo interposed. 'Your grandmother isn't well,' he said, explaining Alice's bad mood.

'Oh no. What's the matter?' Fern was genuinely worried.

'We don't know,' Alice said. 'She's going to see her doctor, and I may fly over to see her.'

'Couldn't she come for Christmas?' Fern suggested. 'I'd love her to come.'

'I'll tell her that,' Alice said. She felt guilty for having picked on the girl. Fern was fond of Phoebe; it was nice of her to say that about Christmas.

She smiled at Fern, but Fern didn't smile back. 'I didn't mean to snap,' she said. 'I've had a tiring day, and I've been worried about Granny too. Have some pudding, Fern. It's that lemon syllabub you like.'

'No thank you,' her daughter said. 'I don't want to get fat. Or get spots.'

There was no Christmas celebration at Ashton that year.

Hugo and Fern and Richard joined Alice in New York. Early in the New Year Phoebe died in her sleep. With her daughter at her bedside. It was a peaceful end; the cancer that had eaten away her red blood cells was mercifully painless. She had faded so rapidly that the tired sleep passed imperceptibly into a gentle eternity. Alice was holding her mother's hand. She dozed and woke to find it cold and limp. Neither husband nor children were allowed to witness the depth of her grief. As she had mourned the man she loved in solitude so many years ago, so she wept for the loss of her mother alone. She seemed to shrink from human contact; even her son was gently put aside. She couldn't share the pain with any of them. Only Lily, who had seen it happen before, understood Alice's need for privacy.

'We're all so upset,' Fern complained, crying on Hugo's shoulder, 'Why can't we be together? Why does Mummy have to go off on her own?'

181

'I don't know, darling,' Hugo answered. 'It's not easy for your mother to show her feelings. It's been a dreadful blow to her.' But he hugged Fern closer to make up for it.

Richard was very silent. At nearly fifteen he felt it unmanly to cry. It wouldn't have taken much to bring out the tears. He had loved Phoebe, as he loved his grandmother Beatrice. What was worse was seeing his mother tight-lipped and anguished, hiding herself away. He wanted to comfort her. He wanted someone to comfort him. Fern had her father; his father had Fern. He sat on his own and felt a sense of isolation that was very painful.

'I'm going to find her,' he said suddenly in a voice that wasn't quite steady. Father and daughter looked up in surprise, as if they'd forgotten he was there. Then he rushed out and knocked on Alice's closed bedroom door. 'Mother – Mother – let me in.'

She heard the sob in his voice. She opened the door to him and they held tightly to each other. When they came out together, Richard's arm protectively around her shoulders, the polarization between brother and sister, Hugo and Alice, was complete. At Phoebe's funeral they stood on opposite sides of the grave. Fern began her first term at art college, and Richard went back to Eton. Hugo was given a junior ministry that year, and Alice organized and entertained with grim determination. Work was the antidote to sorrow. She owed it to the brave and gentle woman who was gone not to wilt and waste the precious years. The loss of Phoebe had done something fundamental to her relationship with Hugo and with Fern. She didn't have to pretend to love one or even like the other any more. She and Richard were essentially on their own.

Alice never forgot the day Fern announced that she was getting married. It was the weekend when her new portrait was hung in the hall. Hugo had commissioned it for her birthday. Forty-five, she'd complained, and

182

all their friends had chorused in disbelief. The very best age for a woman, one of her admirers insisted, when experience had crowned beauty with dignity and wisdom. Alice had been resisting his efforts to take her out to lunch and then back to his flat in the Albany for years. She just laughed, and said, 'The only thing experience does is give you bags under the eyes, my dear Robert. I made damned sure they were painted out!' It was a famous portrait, the sensation of that year's Summer Academy. It was reproduced, written about, criticized and praised. The artist was already renowned for his portraits of beautiful women. He said in interviews that the personality of Lady Vandekar was more fascinating than her looks. She had inspired him, he declared. He regarded the portrait as his best work. Few, even among the most jaundiced critics, could disagree. Hugo had been knighted in the New Year's Honours List. It amused Alice to hear Lily calling her 'My Lady'; Lily got more satisfaction out of it than she did herself. Once or twice it grated and she'd say, 'Shut up saying that every other word, can't you? Don't be such a damned snob! What's wrong with "madam"?'

'Nothing, except it's not proper,' was the answer, and Lily got her way.

She liked the portrait. 'It does you justice,' she announced when it arrived at Ashton. She had infuriated the artist by trying to see the work before it was finished and making loud judgements upon it.

She didn't tell Alice that she'd travelled to London and queued for hours at Burlington House to see it in the exhibition. Alice would have laughed at her. Lily stood with Hugo and Fern and Richard as it was hoisted up into position. It was magnificent, she thought. You'd swear she might step down out of the frame any minute. That artist, puffed up little twerp of a man he might be in her opinion, but he knew how to paint her lady to the life.

'It looks well, doesn't it?' Hugo said. He was very

pleased. He was proud of the picture, proud of the public attention it had received.

'It's marvellous,' Alice said. Hugo had wanted her festooned with some of the magnificent jewellery he'd given her. The artist had refused to paint her looking, as he put it, like a Christmas fairy. Simplicity, a single ornament, perhaps, but the marvellous shoulders and arms must speak for themselves. Nothing should distract from the colour of flesh against a dark background. He was right, and Hugo admitted it. It was a major work of art.

Fern had come down from college for the weekend. She didn't come home often enough, Hugo thought. He missed her, but it wasn't his way to say so or suggest she give up whatever she was doing to spend time with him. She had matured and gained in confidence. She could have been extremely attractive if she hadn't affected the ragged-artist look. Unkempt hair, no make-up, clothes thrown on, and if every colour clashed, so much the better. Was it a protest against Alice, always so impeccably groomed, and who couldn't hide her irritation, or was it an attempt to blend with her fellow students? He wasn't sure, but he suspected that annoying Alice was the main motive. He didn't say anything and Alice had long since given up.

'It's very like you,' Fern said, choosing her words carefully and surveying the portrait with a practised eye. 'There's nothing wrong with the perspective and the background works well.' She paused and lifted her shoulders slightly. 'But it's so unoriginal, that's the trouble.'

'Well, it's not a bloody daub like the rubbish you do!' Richard had exploded. 'It's a lovely picture, and it's the image of Mum.'

He was so easy to goad – she could make him lose his temper and then slide out of range with the infuriating little shrug that was a permanent mannerism. She had a sharp, sly tongue, and Richard was no match for her.

'I never said it wasn't like her,' she retorted. 'I just said it was unoriginal, that's all. I'm sorry. I know I'm supposed to bow down and worship but, as an artist, I don't like the style. I can't help it.'

'Fern dear,' Alice decided to put an end to the contest, 'we all know a portrait has to have two heads and an eye on its chin before you like it. I'm delighted, Hugo darling. Thank you.' She gave him a brief kiss on the cheek. 'Now, why don't we have a drink before lunch?'

'Why not?' Hugo agreed. It pained him to see the antagonism between brother and sister. They couldn't be in the room together without bickering about something. But then Alice showed such a preference for the boy; Hugo couldn't blame Fern for being jealous.

Fern said rather loudly, 'Could we have champagne?'

'Of course,' he answered. 'We can celebrate the picture.'

Fern gave them all a long and triumphant look. 'We've got something else to celebrate. That's what I've come down to tell you. I'm getting married.'

Lily stood for a moment looking after them. Fern had led the way into the library, closing the door firmly in case Lily expected to be included among the family. Lily took a deep breath. In all her life she had only hated one person, and that was Fern Vandekar. To say that about the portrait, trying to hurt her mother . . . Jealous bitch. Thank God she was getting married. The sooner she was out of the house for good, the better. Lily had watched her over the years and suffered a superstitious fear that one day she would do her mother a real harm.

'Congratulations, and good bloody riddance,' she muttered under her breath, and went upstairs.

'But you've never mentioned anyone,' Alice protested. 'We've never even met him!'

'Well, you will,' Fern answered. 'I've asked him

185

down for lunch tomorrow. I thought it would be easier if I broke the news first.'

'It would have been easier if you'd told us you were serious about this man, whoever he is, instead of just dropping a bombshell like this!'

Fern blushed bright red. She had expected opposition from Alice, and she was geared up to do battle. But it was Hugo who was really angry. He was white with rage. He had told the butler to go away, so there was no champagne, no chance for Fern to be defiant.

'I won't allow it,' he said. 'I won't have this fellow asked down to my home without even being consulted. As for marriage, he'll have to satisfy me before there's any question of it!'

'Hugo,' Alice interposed. 'Fern is twenty-one. She doesn't need our permission, she can do what she likes. For God's sake, let's have a drink and talk about it sensibly.' She gave a warning look at Richard, who had opened his mouth to say something.

It was natural for Hugo to react like this, but she hadn't expected it. He was jealous. As I would be if it was Richard, she thought. I wonder if he realizes why he's making such a scene. I wonder if Fern knew how much trouble she was storing up when she set out to be number one in his life. Mentally, Alice imitated her daughter's habit and shrugged the thought away. What did it matter? She wasn't angry, she was more concerned that the girl wasn't making a fool of herself with someone unsuitable. Someone who knew a rich prize when he saw one. She said to Richard, 'Get Simpson, darling, and let's have the champagne. Now Fern, tell us about him.'

'His name, for a start,' Hugo demanded.

Fern's eyes filled with tears. If only it had been her mother she could have coped. But not her father. His cold anger, his accusing look – it was all too much. Her nerve gave way and she burst into tears.

It was Alice who went and put an arm round her

shoulder. 'Now,' she said, 'pull yourself together. Simpson will be in any minute. You've told the whole household you're getting married. What's he going to think if he sees you sitting here, crying your eyes out? Have this.'

Fern took the delicate handkerchief and blew her nose. She straightened, releasing herself from Alice's embrace. 'This is why I didn't bring him down to meet you first,' she said. 'I knew you'd be like this!'

'Then you realized we wouldn't approve?' Hugo inquired. 'Yes, come in Simpson. Thank you, no, just leave the tray, we'll help ourselves. Very well, Fern, let's hear about him. What sort of man is he, that you couldn't invite him down for a weekend like anyone else?'

'Got two heads, has he?' Richard couldn't resist it.

'Shut up,' Alice snapped. 'It's not the moment to be funny.'

'He's not like you and your dreary friends.' Fern rounded on him. 'He's sensitive and intelligent, and he'll be a great artist one day.'

Richard opened his eyes wide. He looked so like Alice that she could have jumped up and hit him.

'I'll open the bottle,' he said.

'Because he's sensitive and intelligent he wouldn't feel comfortable with us, is that right?' Hugo remarked. 'I don't see why not. Do you Alice?' His sarcasm was cruel.

'He's not like us,' his daughter protested. Her eyes were brimming again. 'He's got no money or anything, he's had to work to pay for college. He'd feel shy and uncomfortable even if you were prepared to be nice. Which you're not. None of you!'

'Wait a minute!' Alice got up. 'After all, he must know what to expect. He knows who you are, doesn't he?'

'Oh, yes,' Fern said, 'yes, he knows. He's read all about you, Daddy and Mummy. No one can help seeing your picture in the papers, can they? He's ready to come down and meet you all, but I said I'd rather tell you myself first.'

'What's his name?' Alice asked. 'How old is he?'

Fern wished she wouldn't ask the reasonable questions – she hated her for being calm and trying to mediate. Her father's chilling anger made her feel angry in turn. She'd imagined he would support her. She really had.

'He's twenty-four,' she said, 'and his name is Brian Kiernan.'

'Irish? He's not a Catholic, for God's sake?' Hugo gave a snort of disgust.

'So what if he is?' Alice interposed. 'Nobody in their right mind takes that stuff seriously. When did you decide to get engaged?'

'A few days ago. We're not engaged. I'm not going to have a ring. Brian doesn't believe in that sort of thing. We'll just get married, and that's how we want it.'

'Is anyone going to drink this or not?' Richard asked. 'It's just sitting here getting warm.'

Alice held out her hand. She made a face at him as he gave her a glass. Don't get your own back, it said. Not now. Otherwise your father will turn on you. He pulled a face in return. All right, I won't. But it was tempting. Alice lifted the glass and said brightly, 'Now, we're going to drink a toast. To you, Fern, and your young man, and let's all hold our horses till we've met him, shall we?' She looked at Hugo. 'Please?'

He didn't say anything. He merely nodded, and didn't raise his glass.

Fern turned away from him. She bit her lip. 'Thank you, Mummy,' she said.

'If we don't want this marriage,' Alice said later, 'we mustn't fight it. That's the one thing that will make Fern go ahead. You say I'm tactless and direct, but, my God, Hugo, you ought to know better.'

Fern had gone for a walk and Richard had loped off with one of Hugo's labradors to find a bit of rough shooting. The atmosphere was so tense, Alice didn't blame him.

'You don't care,' Hugo challenged her. 'You've never loved Fern, and you don't really give a damn if she makes a mess of her life or not. If it was Richard you wouldn't be so calm about it!'

'Richard wouldn't behave like this,' she countered. 'There's no need to pick on him because you're upset about Fern. And you're wrong – I do care. Not the same way as you do, but I don't want her to get caught by some fortune hunter, and that's what this sounds like to me. Hugo, the best way of driving her closer to this man is for us to be hostile to him. When he comes tomorrow I'm going to be charming, and if you've got any sense you'll be friendly and see what sort of person he is. That will take the drama out of it.'

'I can't believe she's kept it secret from us,' he said. He was showing more hurt than anger now.

Alice said kindly, 'She's very young. He's not what we'd expect her to marry. Don't be too disappointed. Wait until tomorrow, and keep cool.'

That evening she took Richard aside. 'Listen darling; one word of warning. No funny cracks tomorrow, promise me?'

'She's gone off her head,' Richard protested. 'She picks up some weirdo at this college and wants to marry him. I won't say anything, Mum, I'll be perfectly nice to him, but Dad's right. He'll have to stop it!'

'Dad's always right so far as you're concerned, isn't he?' Alice remarked. Hugo couldn't put a foot wrong in his son's eyes. It was sad and touching to see his admiration and loyalty. And to know that it was unappreciated. She smiled at him. 'Yes, he is right, Richard, but his approach is wrong. I've tried to tell him, and I just hope he'll listen. Anyway, you do your bit tomorrow, won't you?'

'Don't worry.' He gave her a quick squeeze round the waist. 'It'll be all right.'

*

189

'Don't be overawed,' Fern had told him. 'Just be yourself and don't take any nonsense from her. You'll love my father, he's so different . . .'

He wouldn't admit that he was nervous. Who the hell were these Vandekars anyway, just bloody rich bankers and social climbers. He wasn't going to be put down by them. Or let them bully Fern any longer. He was going to take care of her, and if her family thought he was after her money, they had another think coming . . .

He could see how anxious Fern was when she met him at the station. The Sunday trains were few and far between, so he had come early. She rushed into his arms, and he kissed her passionately, holding her so tightly she was lifted off the ground. Brian Kiernan didn't believe in hiding emotions. He didn't believe in deceit of any kind. 'How are you, Ferny? How did they take it? Was it bloody awful for you?'

'Not too bad,' she said.

'What about your mother?' That was the target he had been aimed at, and he was already mentally setting his lance for the charge. Poor little Fern, neglected and pushed aside by this cow of a woman. He boiled with protectiveness.

'Oh, she doesn't care enough about me to bother,' Fern said bitterly. 'My father was upset. But he was better by last night. Come on, we'll be late.'

The first sight of Ashton didn't affect him as Fern had expected. He leaned out of the car window and exclaimed in admiration. 'What a beautiful place! Jesus, what an architectural gem!'

'It's enormous,' Fern had said, 'so cold and huge, not a bit like a home.' His reaction surprised her. A worm of disappointment stirred inside.

He was an instant enthusiast, that was the trouble. If he liked something, he could find no fault. Equally, if he hated something or someone, there was no good to be found. 'It's the Irish,' he had said. 'Black and white – no greys for us.'

'I never thought it'd be like this,' he went on. He had blue eyes and they were bright with pleasure. He loved beauty in all its forms. That passion transcended envy or class consciousness.

He stood for a moment looking around him, and Fern had to tug his arm to remind him to follow her into the house. He had made a concession by dressing in corduroys and a sweater, instead of the jeans which were a uniform for all his friends, but that was all. He walked up the steps and through into the hall, where the butler met them, and Fern hurried him inside saying, 'That's all right, Simpson, my parents are expecting us.'

And then the door of the library opened and Alice came towards them. She saw a tall, thin young man, with unruly brown hair and a pale, fine-boned Irish fa e, standing with his arm round Fern.

Brien Kiernan saw one of the most beautiful women he'd ever imagined walking forward with her hand stretched out to greet him and a warm smile on her lips.

'Mummy, this is Brian. My mother.'

The cold, uncaring old cow, the American snob who'd discarded her daughter from the moment she was born. The lance came up and pointed at Alice's heart.

'I'm so glad to meet you. We've been looking forward to it. Do come in and have a drink. My husband is just coming in from the garden.'

It was the opposite of everything he had expected. There was no formality in spite of the grandeur. No hostility nor, more intolerable still, any hint of condescension. Fern's father was not the cuddly teddy bear of her description, Brian noted, but then he hardly would be especially to another man who'd carried off his daughter. The favoured brother was a drip, with his too good manners making small talk, but not unpleasant. What turned everything he had imagined upside down was Alice Vandekar. Formidable, yes, he'd been ready for that, and the glint in his eye warned her than he was ready to do battle on behalf of Fern if she threw down the gauntlet. Beautiful – that couldn't be argued about – but no dressmaker's dummy, preening herself and inviting admiration. She was as straight-talking as a man, quick-witted and witty – he found himself laughing before he realized it. And she exerted a curious magnetism that kept him watching her and listening to her from the moment they met. The only challenge she tossed at his feet was not to like her. Nothing was said about the impending marriage.

Fern had a feeling that the purpose of his visit would be lost if she didn't pull him back from talking to Alice. Hugo had said little; he watched Brian, and Fern saw him making mental notes. I don't care, she thought, I don't care what he thinks. I love Brian, he's wonderful. I'm going to marry him.

They were all being so natural and friendly, that was the trouble. She had prepared Brian for battle, half hoping to see him lash out in her defence if anything critical was said. But it wasn't happening that way. She felt overshadowed, her role supplanted.

Alice turned to her with a smile. 'Well, Fern, I expect Brian and your father want to have a word in private, so let's leave them, shall we? Come on, Richard.'

She had swept them out of the dining room and into her sitting room before Fern could protest. Brian stood up, hesitated, and then sat down again. The door closed on him and Hugo.

'You don't like him, do you?' Fern said.

Alice looked up. 'As a matter of fact I do. Are you trying to say I wasn't nice to him?'

Fern shrugged. 'That doesn't mean anything. I've seen you be nice to people you can't stand the sight of.'

'Not this time,' Alice answered. 'I think he's very

unusual. You're right about the intelligence – he's bright and he took the whole thing in his stride. That says a lot for him. It can't have been easy.'

'I wonder what they're saying,' Richard interposed. He had been very careful not to be flippant or give offence. Fern's boyfriend wasn't anything like the bearded freak he'd expected, but he was chippy and ill at ease. Mum had been marvellous, he thought fondly. She'd really won him round. It occurred to him that Fern wasn't pleased about it. He couldn't for the life of him see why not.

'I wouldn't worry,' Alice said. 'He's not going to ask Brian about his prospects.' She lit a cigarette and finished her coffee.

A penniless art teacher, scraping a living. Not enough money to buy the girl a ring. Alice understood now why there was no engagement. She rather admired that kind of pride. He could have been a fortune hunter; he was good-looking in a hungry kind of way, with a fiery romanticism about him that would sweep someone like Fern off her feet. Alice stubbed out the cigarette.

Except that she didn't believe it was true. I know about fortune hunters, she thought, and Fern was suspicious when she saw a brief smile come and go. I was one myself... He wasn't marrying Fern for money. For other reasons, maybe, and God knew what they were, but not for that.

'They're taking a long time,' Alice said suddenly. 'I hope it's all right and your father isn't being too difficult. I think I'll go and see.'

'I'll go,' Fern insisted. She jumped up, slopping coffee into her saucer. She paused at the door and turned back to her mother. There was a sense of drama about her that irritated Alice.

'Nothing's going to stop us,' Fern said. 'Not you, or even Daddy. We've made up our minds!' She shut the door so hard it almost slammed.

'What's the matter with her?' Richard asked. 'Anyone'd think you and Dad had chucked him out of the house.'

'Perhaps that's what she hoped would happen.' Alice's voice was very cold. 'Personally, if that boy wants to marry Fern, I won't stand in the way. I know she'd like me to, but I won't. And your father won't either in the end. He's too good a judge of character. He'll see that Brian is better than some chinless wonder who might have been around. From first impressions, I'd say she was lucky.'

She said the same to Lily when she was changing for dinner. Fern had driven Brian up to London. Hugo had shaken hands and kissed Fern. With Brian he was polite but stony, and it was Alice who sent the boy away with a warm handshake and an invitation to come again soon and stay next time.

'Did Sir Hugo give permission then?' Lily asked.

'Oh, Lily, don't sound so Victorian – nobody gives permission to a girl of twenty-one! He made some points about them being young and the boy not having a proper job, but that's all he'd tell me. He's too upset to talk about it. It's better not to nag. He's hurt, that's the trouble. She behaved in such a stupid, tactless way . . . I'll wear that green kaftan – it's just the three of us tonight.'

'It'll be the first wedding from here,' Lily mused. Pity it had to be that sly boots getting all the glory . . .

Alice said, 'I don't see either of them wanting a big social wedding, so don't start making plans. It'll be in London, I expect, and very quiet.' She stretched. 'I'm tired tonight. It was quite a strain, I don't mind telling you.'

'I imagine it was,' was Lily's answer. 'Still, you'll be able to relax tonight. It's so nice having Master Richard home.'

'It's his last term,' Alice said. 'God, Lily, how the time flies. He's nearly seventeen, and it doesn't seem a minute since he was toddling round this room!'

'Little devil he was,' Lily said fondly, 'getting into everything and poking around among your bottles and jars. I never could be cross with him though.'

'I know,' Alice said. 'Nor could I.'

'Well, he'll get married one day,' Lily said over her shoulder, hanging Alice's discarded dress over her arm. She didn't trust the young maid with pressing expensive fabrics. She liked to do that herself.

'Marry?' Alice stared up in surprise. 'He's just a baby, Lily. He won't marry for years.'

Later that evening Richard looked up from his book and said suddenly, 'Mum, I forgot. I met that girl Diana Brayley playing tennis the other day. She looked just the same.'

'Just the same as what?' Alice was watching a play on television. Hugo was dozing. 'The same as when we used to play together. You were pally with the parents at one time, weren't you? She was always coming over here.'

'Oh, yes, of course. I know who you mean. We tried quite hard with them, but he was rather a horrid man, I thought, and your father couldn't stand him, so we just dropped out. Their daughter can't be more than a child. What's she doing? Is she still at school?'

'She's in Switzerland,' Richard answered. 'She couldn't play tennis to save her life. She's jolly pretty though.'

'She always was,' Alice said, not paying too much attention. It was an interesting play. She looked across at her son and smiled. Again she had no sense of premonition.

'This wouldn't be happening,' Hugo said, 'if you hadn't given them every encouragement.'

He was tying his tie in front of the glass as he spoke. He saw Alice's reflection behind him. She was wearing a dark blue dress and a wide-brimmed hat that cast her face in shadow. The big diamond circle blazed in one lapel. She said, 'Nothing was going to stop Fern. All

I've done is try to keep the family together. You and she were always so close, why didn't she listen to you?'

'Because she's besotted with this man, that's why. And she knew she had your backing.'

'That's never made any difference before,' Alice retorted. 'Normally it made her go the opposite way.'

'It had a rarity value perhaps.' He turned away from the glass and slipped a white carnation into his buttonhole. He had an acid tongue, sharpened by the cut and stab of parliamentary debate. It was an unpleasant attribute that was making him many enemies. It couldn't hurt Alice any more. She responded with brutal frankness when he went too far.

'It's not Brian you object to,' she said. 'It's any man taking her away from you. Whoever it was, you'd find something to pick on, and it's lucky you can say he's poor and from a different background. It makes it more convincing. But you don't fool me, Hugo. Daddy's girl has grown up. Now we'd better go or we'll be late.'

It was a registry office marriage. One surprising development had been Brian Kiernan's parents refusal to come to the wedding. 'They're Catholic Irish,' Brian explained. 'It's not a marriage to them. I'm sorry, but they won't come. Maybe later they'll change their minds.'

He was upset, in spite of putting a good face on it – Alice could see that.

Fern didn't seem to notice. 'It'll be a bit late by then,' she declared. 'It's just mumbo-jumbo anyway.'

There were twenty guests at a reception in Hugo's flat. Alice had made the arrangements, deliberately keeping them simple. Hugo maintained a stony disapproval, refusing to discuss anything. And he was blaming Alice because it hurt less than blaming Fern.

In the car on the way to Marylebone, with Richard sitting in front, he said, 'It won't last, I'm sure of that. She'll come to her senses and he'll have to be paid off. That's what will happen.'

Alice ignored him. She understood his disappointment, his frustration at Fern's choice. A son-in-law
from a working-class background, a precarious
profession and no inherited money. It must be a
father's nightmare if the father was like Hugo. And a
mother's even more so. Except that she could view
Brian Kiernan dispassionately. Easy to do, when you
weren't emotionally involved with your own daughter.
Even relieved that she would be making a life of her
own. Alice could judge without prejudice, though
Hugo and Richard couldn't. They were in complete
accord about the unsuitability of Fern's husband.
Alice didn't agree with either of their views. Hugo saw
a self-important upstart, a racial and religious second-
rater, beguiling his daughter with sex. Richard
dismissed him as a chippy bore with a lot of pretensions
about art and beauty that were codswallop from start
to finish. Much as she loved him, that broad dismissal
of a mind more cultivated than his own annoyed Alice.

Brian Kiernan was the exception to the rules her
husband and her son judged other men by. There was
no humbug in him. Pride, but not arrogance. A sense
of spirituality which searched for fulfilment in his own
creative gifts. Devoid of envy, almost unselfconscious,
he was completely natural. With humour and spirit
and a capacity to talk that made a conversation
sparkle. And, of course, he liked her. She knew that.
Fern's efforts to prejudice him had suffered a series of
setbacks every time he and Alice met. Little by little
the barriers came down, though he was still defensive
about Fern. After three months, two weekends spent at
Ashton and one private lunch with Alice in London
where she tried to explain Hugo's objections without
hurting him, Brian had begun to turn to her as his only
ally, which was not at all what Fern wanted him to feel.

Her insistence on a hole-and-corner marriage had
hurt Hugo, not Alice. She couldn't trip Alice up,
however hard she tried. Everything she stipulated was
agreed to: no smart hotel for the reception, only two or

three close relatives, and their friends from college. Alice said yes, yes, yes, and refused to be goaded into a protest that Fern could turn into a row. The best wedding present I could give her, Alice thought, is the opportunity to go to Brian in tears and say, 'I told you so. I told you what she was like.' I haven't and I'm not going to.

It was a simple brisk ceremony. Fern had chosen pale green and carried a little posy of spring flowers. Brian Kiernan was ungainly in a cheap dark suit that didn't fit properly. He was very nervous. Even Alice had to admit that for once, as soon as the marriage was concluded, her daughter radiated happiness. The reception was a success. Hugo exerted himself to be pleasant, conceding to good manners what he didn't feel. Richard found himself amusing a little group of Fern's girlfriends from college. There was a lot of laughter, and when the bride and groom finally said goodbye, kissing Alice and Hugo, Richard announced that he was going off with some of the others to the pub to round off the evening. So she and Hugo faced each other alone, in the empty room with its flower arrangements, dirty champagne glasses and plates of staling cocktail snacks.

'Well,' he said, 'now that's over, what have you arranged for tonight? Do we go home or do we celebrate?'

There was a sudden sense of dreadful anticlimax. Alice found that she was close to tears. One more bitter or sarcastic word from him, and they would overflow.

'I had booked for the three of us at the Savoy,' she said. 'But Richard's gone off for the night I should think, and if you'd rather go home, I don't mind.'

He eased himself into a chair. After all the years since the war, he still suffered pain. 'For God's sake, let's get this mess cleared up,' he said. 'I don't know why they had to go out to a pub when they've turned this flat into the next best thing.'

Alice began collecting glasses. He looked up and

said irritably, 'What are you doing? Where the hell's Barron got to?' Fern had insisted that Hugo's manservant shouldn't appear. 'We'll help ourselves,' she'd said. 'It'll be so pretentious otherwise.'

'I gave him the afternoon off,' Alice said. 'Fern didn't want him here, I told you.'

'So you did. How pompous of her. I expect it was Brian's idea. Leave it alone – Barron can clear it. Let's go, shall we?'

'Go where?' Home?'

He hesitated. He looked suddenly tired and miserable. 'I'm going to miss her,' he said. 'It's going to be damned lonely without her. I don't feel like going down to Ashton tonight. Let's go to the Savoy. I haven't been there for ages.'

Alice swallowed. I love Richard so much, I must try and understand what losing Fern means to him.

'She'll come back,' she said. 'We'll make sure they see Ashton as a second home. You lose sons, Hugo, but not daughters. Cheer up, we'll have a lovely dinner and we might even drop into the Embassy Club for a nightcap. We're bound to see some chums there.'

'I'm sorry,' he said as they drove towards the Embankment. 'I'm sorry I've been so bloody disagreeable to you. It will be lonely without Fern but she'll come down and stay. You're right, Alice. As usual.'

5

'Come on Diana – we'll be late!'

The girl examining her side view in the looking glass said, 'I'm ready. I won't be a sec.'

It was an important dance, given by one of the new rich for their daughter. A dance in London at a grand hotel, with no expense spared to get mentioned in the newspapers. Diana had read about the thousands of pounds spent on flowers for the ballroom, the cost of the debutante's dress, the number of guests, the extravagant food and wines. She and her friends had been giggling over it that morning. The poor girl needed all the trimmings she could get, one of the cattier girls declared. She had a bottom as big as a double-decker bus. Diana thought that was too unkind. She was looking forward to the evening and dreading it at the same time. There would be the usual anxious post mortem from her mother the next morning, and the threat of her father's disappointment. She was having a season with the objective clearly defined for her. She was to find herself a husband and get married.

She knew how much they had spent on sending her to Switzerland, and that the cost of buying her dresses and giving a cocktail party to launch her was a strain on their resources. And she knew why they did it. The only way to stop a scandal was to get her married off. She wasn't vain; her time spent getting ready was as much anxiety as conceit. She was very very pretty, everyone said so. But she had to please. She had to dazzle the young men she met until one of them asked her to marry them. If she failed at the end of the season, her father would be angry. Sometimes she could hear voices echoing in her head. Especially since she had come back and was living at home with them.

'Oh, Bill, Bill, please don't! She doesn't mean it, she doesn't understand!'

'Like bloody hell she doesn't, taking her knickers down and showing herself. I'm not having my daughter end up a tart! Get out of my way, Anne. She's going to learn a lesson this time . . .'

'She's only ten . . . Children play these games they don't mean anything.'

Voices rising and falling, her screams as she was beaten. Sobbing in the darkness, her buttocks on fire.

'You dirty little girl, I'll teach you not to do a dirty thing like that . . .'

'Darling, don't cry. Daddy didn't mean to lose his temper – he was upset, seeing you do that. I've told you not to play with those boys – they're rough and nasty. Don't cry.'

Her father was cruel and he hated her. Her mother had tried to protect her, tried to believe her when she lied. There were no more beatings now. Not for a long time. Not since she'd been taken away from her boarding school and sent to Switzerland. The music teacher had been sacked. They hadn't found out about the odd-job man at home.

There were no boys in Switzerland, no means of getting near any – it was that kind of school. But there were girls, so Diana made do with them instead. Fear had taught her to be cunning. She wasn't found out. She came home at eighteen, pretty and sweet-faced as an angel, with a terrible ache in her body that couldn't be satisfied. Marriage was the only solution, her parents decided. If she didn't disgrace herself before it came about. The medical reports from Switzerland were not encouraging. They felt as if there were a time bomb in their rented London flat, about to explode and destroy them in horrendous scandal.

'Diana! Come *on*, can't you?'

'Yes, sorry, June, coming now . . .' She grabbed her evening bag and a flimsy shawl to put over her shoulders and hurried out of the bedroom. She mustn't think like that. She mustn't remember the shame and the pain and the ecstasy that made it all worthwhile. There had been two men since she got home. Both safe enough. Both much older with wives. They wouldn't say anything. It was the young men she had to be careful with. She had heard other girls talked about – 'She's a real little tart...' – and blushed with fear in case it was being said about her.

She was very popular. She had made friends with other girls. There was nothing spiteful or competitive about her. She was forgiven for her extreme good looks and her attraction for men because she was so genuinely nice.

One eligible young man had already proposed to her. She didn't dare tell her parents that she'd refused. He was pompous and ugly, and though she would have slept with him if he'd asked her, she shrank from the frightening commitment of marriage. He was rich, her parents' problems would have been over, but she couldn't bring herself to do it. There must be someone nicer. She believed in falling in love; her belief in romance had nothing to do with the compulsion to sexual encounter that had tortured her since she was old enough to understand what it meant.

Her body, quivering with outrageous desires, was only one part of her. Her heart hadn't been quickened by anyone yet. She believed and hoped that when love came it would appease body and soul.

They split up into little groups outside the house in Eaton Terrace. Two men were anxious to take Diana in their car. She smiled sweetly at both of them and said she didn't mind really who she went with, so her friend June made the decision.

'It may be pretty boring,' June said as they drove through the late evening traffic to Park Lane, 'all those thousands of people. I'd much rather have a small dance in the country. At least you might know someone.'

Diana murmured her agreement. She was pressed up close to the man on the outside of the back seat. She couldn't concentrate on anything else.

The ballroom was a splendid sight. It was fashionable to have a theme, and the chosen one was 'Spring in Paris'. The room was massed with imported spring flowers and murals showing Parisian landmarks had been hung round the walls. 'How original,' someone mocked. 'Isn't that the Eiffel Tower?' Poor girl, Diana thought suddenly. I wonder if she knows how nasty people can be. They shouldn't come and stuff themselves and have a good time, and make fun of her party like that.

She looked around her, seeing faces she knew here and there in the crowd. Someone took her elbow. It was the young man who'd been pushing his thigh so hard against hers in the car. 'Let's find ourselves a table,' he suggested. 'Tom and June are over there, they've grabbed themselves a place. Come on.'

She let him guide her. He squeezed her elbow and she liked that too. He was rather nice. Big brown eyes, quite tall... She forgot that he'd been very dull at dinner, with nothing much to talk about except his job in a London estate agency. They joined Tom and June, and then immediately Diana was taken off to dance. She danced for most of the evening. If I make an excuse and go home early, she thought, I might telephone John and suggest we go somewhere. I can say I went to a nightclub... John's wife was away in France.

Someone bumped into her back and she was bounced against her partner. She went scarlet and gasped as the impact produced an orgasm. 'I'm sorry,' she heard a voice say. She managed to get her breath back.

Her partner thought she must have been trodden on. 'Watch where you're going, can't you?'

Diana looked round and saw Richard Vandekar. He was dancing rather boisterously with a dark girl. 'I am sorry,' he repeated.

'That's all right,' Diana said. She smiled. 'Hello,

203

Richard. Nice to see you after all this time.'

He smiled back. 'Nice to see you too,' he said. 'Come and have a dance after this. Where are you?'

Diana said, 'June Fitzroy's table, over there. I'd love to.'

Her partner scowled. 'Clumsy lout,' he muttered, and tried to draw her close again.

Diana resisted. 'Let's sit down – I'm dying of thirst,' she said.

He scowled again as they left the dance floor.

He won't come, she thought. I remember making such a fool of myself trying to play tennis the last time I saw him. He was marvellous, hitting the balls like someone at Wimbledon. I looked such an idiot. He won't come. But he did.

Diana didn't telephone her middle-aged lover that night. She didn't sit at breakfast with her mother and invent a pack of lies to explain why she didn't get home until five in the morning. She stayed at the ball with Richard Vandekar until it was daylight outside and the last stragglers were leaving. She had never been so happy before in her life. He had spent the rest of the evening with her. He was taking her out to dinner, he had talked of theatre tickets for the Friday and of going down to Windsor for lunch on Sunday. She was in love.

Anne Brayley couldn't hide her anxiety. Sometimes, looking at Diana, she couldn't believe what had happened in the past. She was a sweet-natured, gentle girl, liked by the old as well as the younger generation. Anne's friends were always saying how charming and pretty she was. Was it possible that one of Bill's old friends had been caught fondling her when she was only thirteen and, when challenged, retorted that she had tried to seduce him?

Anne couldn't forget that day. Her husband had broken down. Diana had fled to her room in terror and locked herself in. Her father didn't go near her. He couldn't trust himself. Together he and her mother faced the dreadful truth. Their daughter was a nymphomaniac. Punishing her wouldn't help – he admitted that at last, after years of brutal treatment. Weeping with rage and shame, he told his wife if something wasn't done, he'd lay hands on her and kill her.

Anne had persuaded him to go to London and let her deal with Diana. There was a visit to a specialist. The poor, white-faced girl was questioned and examined. She lied and lied, convinced that a confession would bring a terrible retribution from her father. The doctor seemed nice and kindly, even sympathetic, but she couldn't trust him not to tell. She was given some tablets to calm her nerves. They made her feel dull and sleepy, and the devil in her body dozed. But it couldn't go on. The verdict was a special school in Switzerland, and a safe distance from her father. She would get regular medical treatment, and it was always possible that her impulses could be brought under control. Personally the doctor didn't think so, but he had to give the unhappy mother some hope. He had seen many cases of uncontrollable sexual hyperactivity, but seldom one more pathetic than that frightened child.

She looks so happy this morning, Anne thought. Often she caught a glimpse of the furtive look that meant Diana was lying. But not now. The dance was a success; she bubbled with enthusiasm about it. 'Did you meet anyone nice?' Anne asked.

She had asked the question so often, and been answered with a sly smile and an eager response. 'Oh yes, Mummy, they were all nice, I had a lovely time.'

'Guess what? I met Richard Vandekar again! We had such a lot of fun. He's taking me out to the theatre and then down to Windsor on Sunday. He's terribly good-looking too.'

'Diana.'

'Yes, Mummy?'

'You will be careful, won't you. Don't do anything silly with him, will you?'

Diana's big eyes opened wide. 'Oh, you know I wouldn't! That's all over, you know it is! You mustn't think things like that any more.'

'All right, darling. I'm sorry. I worry about you, that's all.'

'I know, but you needn't.' She came round to her mother and kissed her affectionately on the cheek. Thank God Daddy was still upstairs.

She said, 'I do like him. I really do. It's funny, we used to play when we were little. I remember the very first time we went over to Ashton and he swung me up on a swing so high I nearly fell off. I'll remind him of that. Now I must fly, I'm meeting some of the gang for lunch.'

Anne Brayley poured herself a cup of coffee. Richard Vandekar. She had never seen Diana so naturally happy. It was too good to be true. Nothing would come of it. And if it did, how long would Alice Vandekar be fooled? She looked up as her husband came into the room.

'Sorry I'm late,' he said.

She knew he avoided Diana as much as possible. Did he never blame himself, she wondered. Perhaps loving kindness and patience in the early stages might have helped. She regretted her disloyalty. She knew what he had suffered when their only son was killed, the hopes he had had that the little daughter might grow up to compensate. And the blind horror and disgust that drove him to cruelty. He was a simple man, with rigid views and little imagination. Diana had been too much to ask of him.

'Has she gone?' he said.

'She's getting ready to go out. She met Richard Vandekar last night. They seem to have hit it off. She was bubbling over this morning. Have some coffee, Bill. I'll make some fresh toast.'

'Vandekar,' he said. 'Son of that MP fellow with the American wife. Never liked either of them much. I thought he was a pompous prick.'

'Well,' his wife said, 'I don't think we need get excited. With all that money, the boy's probably got dozens of girls chasing him. Here, darling, have some toast. The honey's good.'

He looked up at her and suddenly reached out for her hand. He was not a demonstrative man by nature and she was surprised.

'God knows what I'd have done without you,' he said. 'You've been marvellous. I just want to get her off our hands. Then you and I are going to make up for all this and have some happy times again together.'

'I love her, Bill,' she said. 'I wish you could see there's sweetness and goodness in her. She can't help this dreadful thing.'

'When I look at her,' he said, 'I think of our boy cut down before he'd had a chance to live at all. She's like a curse come on us. And she's the last of us. Don't let's talk about her any more.'

'I remember that swing,' Richard said. 'I was really pissed off having to play with you. I was hoping you'd scream.'

'Well, I didn't,' Diana said. 'I loved it.'

It was so romantic of him to get a picnic and hire a little motor launch for the day. They had found a pretty place and moored the boat. She helped him unpack the food and wine. It was peaceful and private. She was so happy he hadn't asked anyone else. They had the launch and the isolated spot on the river all to themselves.

The gentle rocking was agony. It was agony to sit beside this beautiful man and not reach over to stroke him and guide him to stroke her. He mustn't know what she was feeling. She drank too much wine and giggled. When he started kissing her she nearly passed out with the ferocity of her response. But he mustn't know. He mustn't know what happened when she was kissed or touched, or just held too close.

Richard looked down at her. She was so pretty, so

amazing, with her little body quivering in his arms and her eyes closed as if he was the best kisser in the world. He was so excited by her he could have seduced her in five minutes flat. But he wouldn't. It would be a lousy thing to do, after she'd drunk so much wine – she was so helpless and unsophisticated. Some of the other girls he knew, no problem, but not Di. He called her Di, and she said it was sweet because no one else had ever called her that.

'We'd better stop,' he said. 'I'm out of control as it is.' He smiled, a little embarrassed by the admission.

'Are you?' He didn't see the look in her eyes – they were open now, staring at him. 'Let me see.'

'No,' Richard said. 'Come on, you're a bit pissed, darling. I'm going to start the engine. That'll take my mind off it.'

She sat up. She was damp with excitement, flushed and heavy-eyed.

'How many girls have you had, Richard?'

'Quite a few. Why?' The engine was throbbing. He wound up the little anchor of its chain.

'I just wondered. I bet you've had lots and lots.'

She found her bag and saw herself in the compact mirror. She powdered her face hastily, smeared lipstick on her mouth. Stop it, she told herself. You'll say something in a minute. You'll let him know... And he's not like the others. He's not John, who wants you to talk about it and gets driven mad when you pretend to be a first-timer. Richard is different. You love him. You want him to love you.

She plunged her arm into the icy river water up to the elbow.

Richard saw her and called out, 'Don't lean over like that. I'm going to open up a bit, you'll fall in.'

She laughed. 'I wouldn't mind,' she said. 'I've had such fun with you.'

He glanced back at her. 'I've had fun with you too,' he said. 'Do you want to stay and have dinner? There's a new restaurant opened in Maidenhead. Why don't we go there and try it?'

'Why not?' Diana called back. 'I was doing something else but I can phone and cancel him.'

Richard steadied the little boat. He frowned. 'Who's him? Anyone I know?' He was quite surprised to feel jealous. Of course she had other boyfriends. She was so pretty and such a funny little thing, she must have half London running after her. 'Anyone I know?' he asked again.

'I don't think so,' Diana answered. Not John tonight – John, waiting for her in his flat in Knightsbridge, with the whisky on his breath and the dirty pictures set out. He needed the pictures, he needed the little-girl dirty talk. Richard didn't need anything like that, she knew. He was young and beautiful. She loved his blonde hair and those blue eyes. He would be like a god to sleep with. 'He's rather a bore. I'd much rather have dinner with you.'

'Good,' he said. He was glad she had made little of the man, whoever he was. Glad he'd changed the plan from lunch at Windsor with friends who had a grace-and-favour house in the Great Park to a picnic on the river with just the two of them. It was one thing to see a girl with a crowd of others. Spending the day alone was different. How often he'd been bored. Not this time. She made him laugh. She was quaint, he thought – the old-fashioned word suited her. A good sport too, not spoilt, and never bitchy about anyone. He hated bitchy girls.

As much as he hated the greedy ones, who always asked for champagne and the most expensive things on the menu because they knew he could afford them. Di didn't seem to care what she ate. She was sitting by the side of the boat, trailing her fingers in the water, watching the little tides spreading out behind. His mother had liked her, he remembered. As a child, of course. She always said she was as pretty as a picture. It might be fun to ask her down to Ashton for a weekend.

Brian Kiernan's first major exhibition at the Waddington Gallery was a sensation in the art world. The serious critics hailed him as the new Graham Sutherland. The nastier gossip columnists hinted that he owed some of his success to the influence of his in-laws. Hugo had bought them a small house off the King's Road. He thought it was a dreadful, shabby district, but Fern insisted that Brian wouldn't accept anything in a smart location. The north-facing attic could be turned into a perfect studio. Hugo gave way, and Fern hugged and kissed him with her old fervour. He was so wonderful, he understood how Brian felt . . . She was so blissfully happy.

Except when she came down to Ashton. Even Hugo, who didn't trouble about atmospheres so long as the surface was calm, noticed how tense Fern became when her husband and Alice were together. They got on, that was the trouble, and Alice couldn't help overshadowing her daughter. She took the centre of the stage instinctively, leaving Fern a sullen spectator of the wit and the wordplay that went on between them.

Brian sparked Alice and she in turn sparked him. They argued, they disagreed, they debated, and their friendship grew. Hugo remained aloof, glad to spend time with his daughter, trying to revive their old intimacy. But she had changed. She had grown away from him and closer to her husband. It was difficult for Hugo to understand because he couldn't see that they had anything in common. Except sex. That thought displeased him. It diminished Fern in his eyes if she was subject to Kiernan because of that. He consoled himself with the thought that she was happy with him and he seemed devoted to her.

The only flaw in their relationship was her failure to make him hate Alice. 'Oh, come on, darling,' he'd say when she began a tirade about her mother, 'she's been very good to us. She's doing her best for you now.'

'Daddy's been the one,' Fern countered angrily. 'All she does is play up to you. She's so vain and self-centred. I never thought you'd fall for it.'

Then she would cry, and he'd be overcome with guilty feelings, which he resented afterwards. He loved her, but she was still so insecure. And possessive. He didn't mind that. He wasn't interested in other women. After five years of marriage he was just as much in love with Fern as ever. Closer, he felt, because he understood her so much better. And he owed so much to her support and enthusiasm for his gifts. She believed he was a great artist and her faith never faltered. One day he would win recognition.

She admired his ideas and tried hard to follow the intense intellectual approach he brought to his work. It wasn't easy, because she was not very clever. She never once suggested that he should seek help from her family connections. When his early work was hung in tiny galleries, he sold very few, attracted little notice. He went back to teaching, and Fern made a point of living on his salary. Her allowance accumulated unspent, and nothing Alice or Hugo could say would make her humiliate Brian by using her own money.

When the breakthrough came for him it was sudden and by chance. A major modern-art critic from the United States was staying with friends in London during the summer. The friends liked to patronize unknown painters, frequenting the fringe galleries and exhibitions. The critic suspected they were motivated by an inverted snobbery because so much of what they bought was worthless. Except for one exceptional nude that hung in his bedroom. He asked about the artist, contacted the gallery which had sold them the picture, and discovered Brian Kiernan. An introduction to the director of the Waddington followed.

There were stacks of canvases in the attic studio. Fern waited downstairs in a state of such apprehension that she put coffee in the teapot. The time passed – it seemed they would never come down. When they did, one look at Brian's flushed excited face told her that the news was good. The gallery would mount an autumn exhibition for him.

The critic began talking about him in New York. One or two articles appeared in select newspapers and magazines. By the time his connection with the Vandekars had been discovered, his pictures were selling on their own merits.

The private view was a triumph. It was only marred for Fern by the photographers who clustered round her mother. If only Alice hadn't come. Fern had hinted that it was really Brian's evening, and it would be awful if attention was taken away from him. But she couldn't have Hugo without Alice. And she wanted her father to see that Brian was a success. She knew how much Hugo valued achievement. She wanted her father to be proud of him.

She left her husband's side for a few moments, linking her arm thorugh Hugo's. She looked radiant with pride and happiness as she gazed up at him. 'Well, Daddy, didn't I tell you? Isn't it wonderful? Half the exhibits have been sold already. *Everyone* important is here!'

'I'm so glad,' he said. 'And you were right. He's very gifted.' He smiled at her. 'I still don't see it, but everyone says so. Anyway, you're happy, darling, that's the main thing. Look, there's Richard.'

Fern saw her brother moving through the crowd. He paused to look at one of the pictures. A small, very pretty red-headed girl was hanging onto his arm.

'So it is,' she said.

Diana Brayley again. She was staying at Ashton the last time they were there. Fern didn't like her. Not that Diana bothered her or Brian. All she did was follow Richard around. After the money no doubt. Everyone knew that the Brayleys didn't have a penny.

Fern turned away and went in search of her

husband. He was encircled by admirers. She paused for a moment. He was famous at last. Now they could begin to live well; he need never feel inadequate because she had money. And they could have a child. She had wanted a child very badly, but not until they could afford one. The thought of Alice sweeping in to interfere killed her maternal yearnings dead. There, she said to herself, she's over there with Richard and the girlfriend. She's happy now. She's got her baby boy under her wing. I haven't dared tell Brian about that. But one day I will. Then he'll see what she's really like.

'Darling,' Richard said, 'what did you really think of the pictures? Truthfully now.'

Diana pulled a face. They were having dinner in his flat after the exhibition. They had been lovers for the last three months and they spent every spare moment together. He was absolutely marvellous and she was beside herself with happiness. 'Truthfully, I thought they were pretty ugly,' she said, and he roared with delighted laughter.

'So did I. But all the arty people are raving about them, and I could see dozens of red stickers, so that's all right. Brian's quite a nice chap when you get to know him. I couldn't stand him at first, but he's really not bad. Even Dad rather likes him now.'

Like Alice, Diana had noticed how influenced Richard was by Hugo.

'Do you think he likes me?' she asked.

He grinned. 'He couldn't help it, could he? Of course he likes you. So does Mother.'

The most passionate, adoring, marvellous girl. She made him feel superhuman. She told him he was the most wonderful lover, and proved it every time he touched her. And she was the most sweet-natured person he'd ever met. She wouldn't even let him buy her a present. All she wanted was to be with him. And little by little he had learned that life at home hadn't been easy. She was frightened of her father. He had met Lord Brayley once or twice when he went to collect Diana and had found him grim and formidable. Her mother was nice, but she seemed a bit twitchy too. It made Richard very protective towards Diana. Luckiest of all, Alice genuinely liked her. After that first weekend at Ashton, she'd come to stay quite regularly, and the atmosphere was always relaxed and friendly. They had to be very careful, of course, but Diana was clever about sneaking along to his room when everyone had gone to bed and getting back to her own without anyone suspecting. He didn't like deceiving his parents and breaking the code of conduct in his own house, but he couldn't bear to refuse Diana when she begged him to let her come to him. She needed him so badly, to reassure her, as well as to make their delicious, protracted love.

'Di,' he said, 'I want to ask you something?'

She flushed. He thought it was adorable the way she blushed without any reason. Her heart did a jig with fright. What was he going to say? What sort of question, put like that without warning?

'Ask me what?' Oh, please God, I do love him. If I have to lie, help me . . .

'Can't you guess?'

He teased her sometimes. He was teasing her now. It wasn't serious, nothing had come to light. She smiled and shook her head. 'No. Go on, ask me, then.'

'Will you marry me?'

She gasped and, instead of blushing, all her colour drained away. 'Oh, Richard! Do you mean it? Do you really mean it?'

'Of course I mean it. I wanted to ask you for ages, but I couldn't until all this hooha about the brother-in-law and his exhibition had died down.'

She got up and came to him. Her eyes were full of tears. 'Oh, darling, darling, you know I will.' She clung to him and a tear slipped down her cheek. 'I'll make you the best wife in the world,' she whispered. 'I promise.'

*

'Richard, you can't be serious!'

Alice came up to him and put both hands on his shoulders. He was much taller and she had to look up to him. 'Darling, you're only twenty-two! Diana's eighteen – you're both far too young. You shouldn't have done this without telling us.'

'You'd have tried to stop me, Mother,' he said. 'That's why I didn't tell you. I want to marry Diana, and she's said yes. Being young hasn't got anything to do with it. People get married at our ages. It's not as if we hardly know each other.'

Alice stepped back. 'I must sit down,' she said. 'My God, what a shock you've given me. I don't know what your father will say.'

'The same as you, I expect. Mother, please. I'm sorry I've sprung it on you. She's the only girl I'll ever want to marry – I don't want to lose her.'

'You won't, not if she loves you,' Alice countered quickly. 'She'll wait if she really loves you.'

'Wait for what? A year? Six months? There's no point. We want to get married.' He sat down and lit a cigarette. Not next to his mother as he usually did, but opposite.

She saw how unhappy he looked and her resolution weakened. She said quietly, 'Richard, you don't have to marry her, do you?'

He went red. 'You mean, is she pregnant? No, she's not. If you're asking if we've slept together. I don't want to be rude, but it's none of your business.'

'No,' Alice said. 'You're right, it isn't. So we won't mention it again. I must say, I never thought you'd speak to me like that.'

He got up and stubbed out his cigarette. 'Don't you like her? Is there any other reason you're against it?'

'No other reason,' Alice answered, 'except loving you and wanting you to be happy. I've nothing against Diana – she's a sweet girl and you know I've always made her very welcome here. It's just that marriage is one hell of a commitment if you take it seriously, and

I'm sure you do. I'm sure she does too. You've just started your career. You've been around London and you know a lot of people, but that's not life, that's not experience. You haven't travelled, you haven't done anything to get a broader view. You're just marrying the first girl you think you're in love with. A year from now you could have grown out of it completely! You're not listening to a word, I can see that!'

'Yes, I am. I've always listened to you. And Mother, you know I've always done what you wanted. Now I want you to do something for me. I want you to say yes, you're happy about my engagement, and welcome Diana into the family. Will you do that for me? Will you, please?'

For a moment Alice didn't answer. He was her son, the child of her one love. From birth he had given her nothing but joy. And, as he said, he'd always done what she wanted. She broke down into tears.

He had never seen her cry since he was a little boy. He couldn't help himself. His anger and disappointment wasn't proof against that. 'Oh Mum, Mum, don't...' He put his arms round her and they held each other.

'You really love her?' Alice asked him. I can't refuse him... I can't make him unhappy.

'Yes, I really love her.'

She drew in a deep breath. She found a handkerchief in her sleeve and wiped her eyes. 'I'm sorry, darling. Maybe I just find it difficult to lose you so soon. But if you want Diana and you think she'll make you happy, then all right. I'm on your side. Forgive me?'

'Don't be silly, Mum,' he said. 'I'll tell Dad when he comes home tonight. I hope he takes it better than he did with Fern.'

Alice managed to smile at him. 'I don't think he'll be quite so difficult with you,' she said.

Alice wanted a spring wedding, but to her surprise

the Brayleys favoured a much earlier date. Diana and Richard didn't want a long engagement – she understood that, but there was a tinge of disappointment that her son's wedding would be in the winter. And not at Ashton either. Diana's father had vetoed that suggestion. Since their house wasn't big enough to accommodate the number of guests, a London wedding was the proper compromise.

Alice gave in gracefully, but she was irritated. If he was too proud to have his daughter's reception at Ashton, he hadn't hesitated to squeeze a handsome marriage settlement out of Hugo. And surprisingly, Hugo had been more than generous.

She in turn passed on the big circle of diamonds to her future daughter-in-law.

'I thought you'd leave that to Fern,' Hugo said.

'Fern never wears jewellery,' Alice retorted. 'Your mother gave it to me, and I've given it to Diana. I've got plenty of other pieces if Fern wants them. It's a bit large for the child, that's the trouble. She's rather swamped by the size of it.'

'I expect she'll learn to wear it,' was his answer. 'Most women come to terms with diamonds.'

Alice shrugged aside the sarcasm. As she expected, he had been indifferent to the point of boredom about Richard's wedding. When Alice expressed her worry that their son was rushing into marriage, he remarked that it was just as easy to make a mistake at thirty-two as twenty-two, and the reference was clearly to himself.

Lily was her confidante, the recipient of her doubts, and Lily did her best to calm them. 'They're young, yes,' she agreed, 'but they're head over ears in love, My Lady, and that's what matters.'

'Head over heels,' Alice corrected her irritably. 'He's too young, Lily, and she's very immature. Some girls of eighteen are grown women, but not Diana. I wish I'd realized it was serious and put a stop to it in the beginning.'

'You can't run everyone's life for them,' Lily said. 'Master Richard's a man – he's got a right to make up his own mind.'

'Oh, shut up,' Alice snapped, as she had done for nearly thirty years. 'And why get married in January? It's such a damned awful time of year. London in the rain!'

'But you like her,' Lily pointed out. 'What would you have done, if she'd been someone you didn't take to?'

'I don't know,' Alice said impatiently. 'Yes, of course I like her. She's a sweet little thing, there's nothing *not* to like about her. I'm just uneasy, that's all.'

And jealous, Lily said to herself. You've made an idol of that boy, not that I blame you, and it's hurting to lose him.

Then she had an idea. She made a suggestion that was to change the course of all their lives. She made it out of love for Alice to try to mitigate the loss.

'Why don't you give them a suite of rooms of their own here?' she said. 'They won't have a place in the country and it'd be nice for them. Let Miss Diana do them up for herself. There's plenty of rooms going begging. We don't use half of them.'

Alice smiled suddenly. 'Lily, what a good idea! Richard loves this house, and after all, they'll live in it one day. They'd spend most weekends here in the winter – he's mad on his shooting. And Diana would be happy – she's always saying she hates London. Lily, I'll do it! I'll tell them tomorrow. I'm sorry I told you to shut up just now. I didn't mean it.'

'Don't worry,' Lily said. 'After all these years, I'm used to it.'

It didn't rain in January. It snowed instead. The night before her wedding Diana and her parents stayed in Claridges Hotel. Her wedding dress had been delivered. Her father had said she must be married in

proper style. There was no paring of the costs. He sold
a block of shares and told her mother to spend what she
needed. With what was left of the money he had
booked a long cruise for himself and his wife. The dress
was beautiful, designed by Dior, the snowy velvet
trimmed with white mink. She had been lent the
Vandekar tiara; her own family jewels had been sold
off long ago. It was too large and too heavy for her, but
she didn't want to offend her parents-in-law by
refusing. Alice's big diamond brooch had to be worn
too.

They had dined with some cousins of her mother
and Diana had gone up to bed early. She was still
awake when Anne Brayley tapped on her door.

'Mummy? Come in!'

'I saw the light under your door,' her mother said.
'We've dropped Joan and Peggy back and your
father's gone down to have a nightcap. Can't you
sleep?'

'No, I'm too excited. Come and sit with me for a
minute.'

Anne sat on the bed. She looked so pretty, she
thought, sitting up with the red hair flaming against
the pillows. So pretty and vulnerable and young. 'You
are happy, aren't you, darling?' she asked. 'You really
love him, don't you?'

'Oh, yes, I really do. He's wonderful. I'm so
lucky.'

Anne reached over and took her daughter's hand.
'You've got every chance of happiness, Diana. From
tomorrow, it's up to you. You know what I'm trying to
say, don't you?'

'Yes.' She looked at her and the big grey eyes filled
with tears. 'I'm so sorry. I wish I hadn't been such a
worry to you. But everything is all right now.'

'Of course it is.' Anne held out her arms and for a
long moment she embraced her child. Tomorrow
Diana would be someone else's responsibility. She and
Bill would be on their cruise. There was a limit to their

capacity for anguish. They had done their best. Now, as she had said, it was up to Diana. She was not a religious woman, but at that moment she offered a silent plea to God, if He existed. Then she kissed Diana and got up. 'Good night, go to sleep, darling. You've got a big day tomorrow.'

Diana switched out the light and slid down under the bedclothes. She could see the white dress in its cellophane shimmering in the dark. Tomorrow she would be married. On the way to her honeymoon. Richard wouldn't tell her where they were going. Somewhere in the sun was all he'd say. It was only one night, after all. One night alone, and then after the wedding she would have Richard with her and they could make love over and over again, and she would never need another man.

'The Snow Bride,' the tabloids called her. People thronged round the church twelve deep to see the beautiful society girl marry her handsome millionaire. Snow flurried round them as they came out of the porch and stood for the photographers. The diamonds on her head and at her neck flashed and glittered. There were oohs of excitement from the crowd. She smiled and Richard smiled, their hands clasped tightly, and then the cavalcade moved off, and the photographers were busy again, snapping frantically as Sir Hugo and Lady Vandekar came into view, with Lord and Lady Brayley. It made the front page of every national newspaper.

The wintry weather lifted within the week. The rain Alice had predicted fell in torrents and London was slippery with mud.

'If they've got their own suite of rooms, then surely we ought to have some as well. After all, it's my home too.'

Alice had gone for a walk. Brian had offered to go with her and that had upset Fern. Richard and that simpering wife of his were upstairs with two-year-old

Nancy Alice. Diana *would* have a baby the first year, Fern thought bitterly, while we keep trying and nothing happens. Hugo looked up from his book. Weekends were precious when he could spare them from his constituency. He liked to read and be at peace. He loved his daughter but he could see that she was working herself up. She and her husband often quarrelled in public now, and Hugo found that distasteful and embarrassing. He blamed his son-in-law's lack of upbringing.

'Fern dear,' he said, 'of course this is your home, just as much as Richard's. If you want some permanent rooms here, then you shall have them. Why didn't you mention it before?'

She turned away and slumped down into an armchair. 'Because Brian wouldn't want to sponge,' she said. 'You know what he's like. I'd come home much more if we had a sitting room of our own. He likes to be independent. I don't think Mother will be too pleased though.'

She glanced at Hugo quickly. He had gone back to reading his book and didn't take the bait. She shifted restlessly. Why did Brian have to go out for a walk with her mother? He hated walking. They'd been gone for over an hour.

'Perhaps it's not a good idea after all,' she said.

'What isn't?' Hugo had thought the matter was decided.

'Being here as often as Richard and Diana,' she answered. Being with Alice was what she meant. She was sorry she had made an issue about the rooms.

'Why on earth not?' He laid the book aside. 'I like to see you. You know that, Fern.' He looked tired these days, and in the years since she had married he had become more withdrawn. Unlike Alice, whose energy and appetite for life never seemed to flag. Stamping round the countryside on a bitterly cold day... Fern was sorry she'd been difficult with him.

'I know,' she said. 'I love coming home, Daddy, and

I love being with you. I didn't mean to be demanding. It's just that everything's for Richard. Richard this and Richard that. And, of course, they've produced a baby and we haven't.'

'Now that *is* ridiculous,' Hugo protested. 'It makes not the slightest difference to me. I find the whole grandparent business a total bore, if you want to know. So don't get any nonsense about that into your head.'

She looked gratified. They exchanged understanding smiles.

'Perhaps I shouldn't say this,' she said, 'but have you noticed how much Richard drinks?'

'No, I haven't. Does he?'

'Like a fish. I'm surprised you haven't noticed.'

'I don't pay too much attention to Richard,' Hugo remarked. 'Your mother makes up for both of us. Why should he drink? He never did before.' He didn't sound very interested.

'I don't know,' Fern shook her head. 'I'm surprised Mother doesn't do something about it.'

'It's just a phase, I expect,' he said. 'It must be teatime. I suppose we'd better wait for Brian and your mother.'

Fern got up and came over to him. She bent down and kissed him on the cheek. Her reward was the rare softening of his expression as he looked up at her.

'If you want tea, then I'll ring for it,' she said. 'They can't stay out much longer, it's getting dark!'

The lights were on in the west wing. Alice noticed them as she and her son-in-law rounded the corner of the building. They'd walked farther and for longer than they intended. She had a plan for a folly at the far end of the lake. She wanted Brian's opinion of the site.

He loved Ashton, she thought. He seemed instinctively to appreciate and understand its beauty. And he had original views that stimulated her imagination.

'Well,' he said. 'I'd be happy to go and see this temple, if you'd like. The drawing looks fine, but a lot depends on the colour of the stone and the density of

222

the green. Copper can weather quite variably.'

'I'd like you to come with me,' Alice said. 'Hugo's so busy and he hates careering round the countryside at weekends. If I telephone we might even go over tomorrow morning.'

'I'd enjoy that,' he said.

They went into the house and through to the back cloakroom. Brian helped Alice off with her coat. 'You wouldn't do me a favour, would you Lady V.?'

Alice said, 'I do wish you wouldn't call me that. It sounds like a deodorant!'

Brian laughed. 'No, it doesn't. I can't call you Alice, Fern'd kill me. And I don't fancy trying to call my father-in-law Hugo!'

'I guess not,' she agreed. 'What's the favour?'

'Talk to Fern. Stop her working herself up into a state about getting pregnant. It'll never happen unless she relaxes.'

Alice sighed. 'You must know I can't talk to Fern about anything. She just thinks I'm interfering. Hugo might be able to. He's the only one who can get through to her. I'm sorry about this – it's such a waste of time. Children aren't always a blessing. Anyway, I'll see what I can do.'

'Thanks,' he said. 'So long as she doesn't know I've talked to you. She'd take it the wrong way.'

'That's a waste of time too,' Alice retorted. 'But it's nothing new. She's very lucky to have met you, Brian. I hope I don't lose my temper one day and tell her so.'

'I hope you don't too,' he agreed.

Alice said, 'You go in and have tea. I'm going up to see how Nancy is. She had a temperature this morning. I expect it's just a little cold, but that nanny is behaving as if she had pneumonia.'

She had never expected to love the child. She was pleased for Richard because he was so thrilled that Diana was pregnant within a few months of their marriage. She was happy for his wife, who still seemed so much of a child herself. But there was something about the tiny girl that touched her. The child didn't even look like her son, so there was no rational explanation. She had a thatch of bright red hair and a crumpled little monkey face. To her own amazement, Alice thought Nancy was adorable.

It seemed that the marriage was a success. Alice's worries had been unfounded. They made a perfect couple – her handsome Richard, his pretty little bride with the new baby. But that was two years ago.

She had lied to Brian. She wasn't going to the nursery. She was going up to see her son. It was ironic that they should have chosen the west wing. Their quarters were immediately above the room where she had nursed Nick back to health and sanity, only to lose him in the end. She never passed that door without thinking of him. And of his son, who had whisky on his breath at breakfast.

She was halfway up the stairs when she met Diana coming down.

'Oh, hello, Lady Alice!' Immediately there was the bright smile which Alice was learning to mistrust. 'I was coming to join you all for tea. Nancy's still a bit sniffly, so I thought she'd better stay in the same atmosphere. Nanny said –'

'Isn't Richard coming?' Alice cut across her.

'He's got a headache.' The answer was so quick she knew it was rehearsed. 'He may be getting Nancy's cold. He'll be down later.'

'I'll go and see him,' Alice said.

Diana didn't stand aside. 'He's asleep,' she said. 'I gave him two aspirin and he lay down. He was asleep when I looked in just now.'

It had been going on for a year. Too many drinks at night when they were spending a quiet evening. Too many drinks at weekends when Ashton was full of guests. Obviously drunk at shooting lunches. Diana appearing without him with some excuse. The smell of drink that couldn't be washed away the next morning. For a whole year Alice had said nothing, clinging to the hope that it wasn't serious. Just a phase some men went through. An exaggeration on her part. He was happy, doing well, in love with his wife and thrilled with his child. There was no reason.

She looked at Diana. There was a guilty colour in her face and the bright smile was fading.

'He's drunk,' Alice said. 'Don't lie to me. Get out of the way!'

He wasn't asleep. He was unconscious, sprawled out in a chair, his arms dangling, his legs stuck out in front of him, an empty glass on the floor. He was snoring. For a moment Alice stood and looked down at him. His hair was on end, his face pink and shiny with sweat. She had never imagined he could look repulsive to her, but he did. She felt a surge of disgust and anger. There was nothing to be done. In the cinema you threw a bucket of water over a drunk and that revived them. But this was real life. She turned away and locked the sitting-room door from the outside. No one must go in and find him like that. Then she went downstairs and joined the rest of the family round the tea table.

Fern was pouring in her place. Alice said, 'I'm sorry I'm late. I went up to check on Nancy.' She saw Diana's frightened gaze flicker. 'We had such a nice walk. Hugo darling, I think a folly down by the lake where that view opens up would be just perfect.'

She took a cup of tea. Anchovy sandwiches. She said she adored anchovies, they made a change from cucumber. 'Poor Richard's got the flu,' she announced. She spoke directly to Diana. 'He'd better stay in bed this evening. Don't let him come down to dinner.'

'No, I won't,' was the reply. 'He's feeling so rotten.'

She's an accomplished actress, Alice thought suddenly. Or do I mean liar? Nobody would guess from the way she said that that we were both lying.

As they separated to dress for dinner, Alice slipped her daughter-in-law the key. 'Keep him locked in,' she said under her breath. 'Tomorrow I want to see both of you.'

'Oh, Dick, Dick, why did you do it? What are we going to say to her?'

Diana was crying. It made him miserable when she cried. He'd done his best to sober up, but he had enough drink in his system to be instantly lit up by even a small shot. He hated her to cry. He hated himself even more, because it was his failure that was the cause of it all. His failure to match the endless, anguished demands for more and more sex that finally left him impotent and exhausted. At first a drink or two had helped. It made him feel confident, forget the miseries of the last attempt to satisfy her, try again. Even so, he had to fail in the end. He couldn't keep pace with her. Sometimes, lying beside her in the dark, before he anaesthetized himself with alcohol, he couldn't believe that the insatiable demands were made by the same girl who was sweet-natured, loving to her child and to him, still unspoiled in every other way. He felt he was being eaten alive.

But he still loved her. He loved her when he discovered that she was slipping away in the afternoons in London and seeing an old boyfriend. He only found out by accident, having seen her leaving a block of flats in Knightsbridge as he drove past in a taxi. She told a tissue of lies that evening when he asked her how she'd spent her day. He looked in her diary and saw the initial J and a scribbled '2.15' on the same date.

She had carried on lying, weeping and inventing, while he swallowed two glasses of whisky and kept on demanding the truth. In the end he had given up. She went to bed and sobbed herself to sleep.

He left without waking her the next morning. He went to the block of flats and took a note of the names on the index. He looked them up in the telephone directory and rang each in turn. Only one reacted when he said he had a message from Mrs Vandekar. It was a man. He hung up. He got drunk before he went home because he was so afraid he might beat her into telling the truth. She tried to make it up. She begged him to forget it, not to ask, just to believe she loved him more than anything in the world, and he'd never need to be jealous or suspicious because *nobody* meant anything to her except him. And Nancy. She clutched at the baby in desperation for forgiveness. She cuddled her and the little girl began to whimper. Richard took them both in his arms and wept with them.

He didn't follow her or pry again. He knew when she went to the flat in Knightsbridge because there was an aura of guilty excitement about her, and she would pour him a drink and make an extra fuss of him.

He dreaded going to Ashton. He dreaded his mother suspecting that he wasn't happy and blaming Diana. He fooled himself that he could control his drinking and for some time he managed to deceive them all.

But now the game was up. He said as much to Diana. 'It's no use, darling, I know my mother. You may lie to me, and I may lie about how many drinks I've had and where I've put the Scotch, but we won't get away with it with her!'

'What are we going to tell her? You won't say anything about me, will you? Promise me? Please, please, don't say anything, will you?'

'About our little problem? My little problem? It's not that little, is it? It was big enough when we started.'

'Oh don't,' she begged him. 'Don't say horrid things like that. You've had a drink, haven't you? She'll know. She'll know as soon as she sees you.'

'I won't tell her,' he said. 'I won't tell her you just can't have enough of it. And if I can't do it, you'll sneak off to someone else. Oh, for Christ's sake, do you think I didn't know? How's Knightsbridge? Haven't you worn him out yet? Sorry. Sorry, sorry... I shouldn't have said that. I wish we could tell her, Di. She'd know what to do. I wish you'd let me trust her.'

She sprang up. 'No! No!' she cried. 'I'll kill myself if you do. I'll kill myself! Dick, please, don't you know what would happen? She'd make you divorce me. She'd throw me out...'

He got up and went into the bathroom. There was whisky in the medicine cabinet. He reached for it and then hesitated. Better not. He had to keep his head. There were tears in his eyes. Mother could help us. I know she could. But she'd never forgive Diana. If I could stop the booze, we might pull ourselves together. 'If only she wouldn't lie' – he said it out loud in anguish – 'if only she'd tell me, and then we could try to talk it out. But she lies and pretends there's nothing the matter. I'm twenty-four and I'm impotent. I can't tell my mother that. I can't tell anyone what's happened to me...'

He came back into their bedroom. He took in a deep breath and steadied himself. 'When is she coming?'

'After breakfast,' Diana whispered miserably.

Richard said slowly, 'It's better if we don't sit up here waiting. Better we go downstairs and talk to her.'

'Oh, I can't... I don't want to...'

'Then I will,' he said. 'You stay here. She doesn't want to talk to you. I'm the one who's got to face her. If you start your fairy stories with her, she'll know we're hiding something. Leave it to me.'

'He's lying to me, Lily,' Alice said. 'I begged him to tell me if there was anything wrong, but he went on saying, "No, no, I've just got into the habit." It's not true and I know there's something the matter! But I *couldn't* get it out of him.'

Lily watched her in silence. Alice was pacing up and down in her agitation, asking Lily questions without waiting for an answer. Lily hadn't seen her so upset for years. 'It's not his work, is it?'

'No.' Alice dismissed that immediately. 'That's the first thing I thought of. I've asked Hugo in a roundabout way and he said how well Richard was doing. And he doesn't exactly praise him. If he's drinking like this, how long will that go on, I wonder? Oh God, Lily, I could smell the whisky on him when he came into the room this morning. He'd been drinking already!'

'If he's not worrying about the bank, then there must be something else,' Lily said, trying to be tactful. She knew how fiercely protective Alice was about her son, and that protection extended to his wife. Lily liked Diana – she was such a gentle, charming girl, and always pleasant to Lily. Pleasant to everyone who worked at Ashton. But a bit too sweet, perhaps . . . Lily suspected perfect people; she knew human nature just wasn't like that.

Alice stopped walking up and down. She looked hard at Lily. 'You think it's Diana?'

Lily retreated quickly. 'I didn't say that, My Lady.'

'But you think so? Stop beating around the damned bush and come out with it!'

'What else can it be?' Lily countered. 'Mister Richard's never kept anything from you in his life. He's never stood up to you either, except when he wanted to marry her. If they're not getting on, he won't say so to you. Why don't you talk to her?'

Alice said slowly, 'Because he'd never forgive me. I said something about Diana facing the problem with us, and he started shouting and saying he'd cope with it without worrying her and I wasn't to think of dragging her into it. Then he broke down. He sat there and cried, Lily, and said, "What do you think I should do about it, Mother? Help me . . ." I thought I was going to die, seeing him in that state.'

She swung round out of Lily's sight, but not in time to hide the tears.

'He's going to see a specialist,' Alice said after a pause. 'He's promised to do whatever he suggests. And I've promised to keep it from his father.' She cleared her throat and turned round. She was composed again, but there was a set to her jaw that Lily recognized. Whatever or whoever it was, she was going to fight it for her son's sake.

'If he and Diana are unhappy, I want to know,' she said. 'Can you find out for me, Lily? When they come down and stay, can you keep an eye on things?'

Lily nodded. 'I'll see what I can do,' she said. And then, as she had done so often over the years when Alice was in crisis, she added, 'Don't worry about it. Leave it to me.'

Diana was so lonely. Richard was going to be away in the nursing home for three whole weeks. She couldn't go down to Ashton at weekends because they were supposed to be on holiday. And she couldn't think of an excuse when Alice invited little Nancy and her nanny to stay with them while her parents were away. Diana was alone in the smart London flat.

Their friends were told a different story. Richard was travelling to America on business. Diana couldn't go with him because he had so much work to do. She was kept busy, with invitations to lunch and cocktail parties, a long weekend shooting in Norfolk.

She was still lonely without Richard, and sneaking into bed with one of the houseguests during the Norfolk stay didn't stop her missing him. She spent most afternoons at Knightsbridge, but sometimes John made an excuse not to see her. There was more and more sexual byplay needed to arouse him and her own needs were often left unsatisfied. She wasn't allowed to see Richard. He had to take the cure and cope with it on his own. Not even a telephone call. And always the worry that someone would mention seeing her and her father-in-law would wonder why they weren't abroad as he'd been told. Lies surrounded her – she lived with lies and the fear of being found out. And she lived with guilt: Richard was in that dreadful place in Hampstead because of her. She knew it, but it didn't stop her ringing up John and begging him to come round. It hadn't stopped her seducing a man in Norfolk and agreeing to see him secretly in London. The more guilty and tormented she felt, the more the ravening sexual need began to dominate her.

Richard was due home in three days. She had a spare afternoon and decided to go to the cinema. She became engrossed in the film. Then a man sat beside her and after a while she felt his hand touching her leg. She let him stimulate her, and she orgasmed. She couldn't help herself. And when he followed her out of the cinema she took him home. He couldn't do anything without the cover of darkness and furtiveness. She had to give him money before he would go.

Then she was afraid. He had been shabby, rather unclean. He knew where she lived. He might come back. Richard might be there. She shivered and burst into a fit of frantic weeping. What had she done? How low had she sunk to pick up a creature like that, let him fondle her, excite her, and then, in utter madness, bring him back into her own empty flat? He could have robbed her, murdered her even. There was nobody to turn to, no one to confide in. Her parents had long settled in South Africa, not that she could have told them. She was alone with a problem that had shown it was getting dangerously out of control. Frightened and isolated. When Richard came back he would be cured. No more drinking. No more miserable scenes when he accused and she denied. He loved her. She loved him. Her tears flowed in self-pity and self-hate. But love wasn't enough. She crouched on her big bed, hunched like an animal at bay before the truth of what her life was going to be. Richard wouldn't be enough. No man would be. She was doomed to deceive the person she loved best in the whole world. For a moment Diana was tempted to do something positive. To empty the medicine cupboard of every aspirin and sleeping pill, and just lie down and die.

It was such a strong impulse that she got up. Her hand was turning the handle of the bathroom door when the telephone rang. She stopped, shocked into reality by the sound. She let it ring. Then she turned with a cry of relief and ran to pick it up.

231

'Diana darling.' It was one of her best girlfriends. June Fitzroy, now happily married and living in the New Forest. 'Diana, how are you? It's ages since I've seen you...'

Diana answered, her voice a little thick but bright and enthusiastic. Yes, she was all alone. Dick was in New York. Oh, how lovely, she'd adore to come down and spend a couple of days until he came home. No, she had nothing arranged at all. She could drive down that evening if June could bear it. London was terribly dreary at the moment...

She packed as quickly as she could. How nice it would be to see June again. Her husband too. He was sweet. How wonderful to get out of the flat, out of the room, with its memories of that horrible, sordid man demanding money from her while he buttoned his trousers. She had so nearly done something terrible – lost her head completely. She was trembling as she packed. Still trembling when she ran out of the flat, looking round in case the man was lurking somewhere. Then she was in the car, driving to her friends and safety.

The pretty house on the edge of the forest was a beacon of light and hope. A warm welcome, kisses and embraces, a drink and a hot bath, June and her nice husband fussing over her. Poor sweet, fancy staying in London in that big flat all on her own... She should have rung up and asked herself down before. Life was sweet again. She had just panicked. In the cosy bedroom, lulled by friendship, Diana wondered how she could have been so hysterical. The cinema was a mistake. She wouldn't do that again. For all these years she'd coped with her particular temperament and managed to be quite happy. It was temperament again, not a problem. She fell asleep, looking forward to the next two days. And to Richard coming home.

6

'He'll have to divorce her,' Alice said.

She and Hugo had driven round the park. It was a beautiful spring afternoon. The eighteenth-century temple had stood at the far end of the lake for four years now, its copper dome shining green in the sunshine. It seemed as long as a lifetime to Alice since she had walked there with her son-in-law Brian and asked his advice on how it would look. A lifetime of hope and despair as she watched her son deteriorate. The rumours about her daughter-in-law Diana were not even whispered any more. Sooner or later the scandal had to break, and that moment had come. She was being named as co-respondent in a divorce.

Richard wasn't working for the family bank any more. That had been impossible for the last two years. His constant relapses into alcoholism made him unemployable. He went in and out of homes. He went to Zürich for a three-month cure and was drunk again before the New Year. But nothing else had changed. He was married, and he insisted that he was happy and he loved his wife. He was a drunk, and poor Diana had to suffer.

Hugo looked at her. 'He can't do that,' he said.

Alice turned the wheel. They moved close to the grass verge and she stopped the car. 'I don't believe it,' she said. 'I don't believe you could still say that. After what she's done to him?'

'He's done it to himself,' he answered. 'He's a hopeless drunk, and you won't admit it. No wonder she's had affairs. I don't blame her.'

'Affairs!' Alice exploded. 'She slept with anyone and anything, including her best friend's husband. June Hubbard is divorcing him – it's been going on for God knows how long! Lily says she heard gossip about her from the nanny when Nancy was a baby. She used to go out at night and not come home until all hours!'

'You may listen to servants,' he retorted, 'I don't. They can't get divorced. If your son is an alcoholic, that's not my fault. This business with Hubbard will cause a fuss and the bloody press will make a meal of it, but so long as Richard does nothing, it'll die down. And I'll survive. But not if there's a follow-on. No divorce, Alice. I'm not wrecking my political career on account of Richard. So don't encourage him. The consequences could be very serious.'

'What do you mean? How can you stop him?' she demanded. 'Why should he have his life ruined because of you? If he gets rid of her, he'll stop drinking. I know he will!'

'Maybe, but he won't inherit this house or a single penny from me. If you think it's worth losing all that, then go ahead.'

Alice said slowly, 'I never thought you could be such a bastard, Hugo. I never thought you'd threaten your own son. And what about Nancy?'

He didn't look at her. He stared ahead as he said it. 'With a mother like that, she's probably not even his child. And he's your son, Alice. Not mine. There's nothing in him I recognize.'

He saw the beautiful hands with the heavy diamond ring clench like a vice on the steering wheel, and he waited. But she said nothing. She never would, he thought. She'll die with that question unanswered. But her silence is an answer. We both know that.

'I shall leave everything to Fern,' he announced. 'With a life interest to you, my dear, of course. But nothing to Richard, if he loses me a Cabinet job. So you can explain that to him, if you like. If you do nothing, my guess is, he'll do nothing. He'll stay soaked in drink and she'll behave herself. For a time anyway. Now, don't you think we should go home? We've talked over our problems, which was why you suggested driving round, and we've seen the park. I've got some letters to dictate.'

Alice switched on the engine. She swung the car round into reverse and started back up the long road round the lake towards the house. 'I shall never forgive you' was all she said.

'I'm sorry to hear that, Alice. I feel we've had to forgive each other rather a lot.' He went into his private office and closed the door.

Alice went upstairs. 'Lily! Lily! Where the hell are you?'

'I'm here, there's no need to shout.' She came hurrying along the corridor.

Alice went into her room and Lily followed.

'He won't hear of it,' Alice said. 'I could kill him, Lily. I really could.'

'You'd better have a cup of tea. You're all upset.'

'How could he threaten to cut Richard off? How could he put his bloody political career in front of his own son's life?' She swung round, her face working with pain and anger. 'He'll die, Lily. He's got liver damage – he blacks out. He's only twenty-nine! And I'm supposed to sit and watch it happen. Well, I won't. I'll get rid of her. I'll *make* her leave him! Never mind the tea. Ring down and order the car for me. And tell Mrs Fry I won't be here to lunch, or probably dinner. I'm going to London. I'm going to see Diana.'

'It won't do any good, My Lady.' Lily said quietly. 'She'll never go. Everyone knows what she is. She wouldn't have a friend or a door open to her if she left this family, and I reckon she knows it. Go up and try if you like, but don't pin your hopes on it.'

'Stop crying,' Alice said. 'For God's sake stop it, it's not doing any good.'

It was all going wrong. She had met Diana in London at their flat, flint-hearted and determined to get rid of her and save her son. Prepared to bully, to bribe, to threaten. But it ended with her helplessly enmeshed in pity and horror. It was an unfair contest. Alice knew Diana was no match for her. Her love for Richard dismissed any scruple about that. But it wasn't in her nature to trample the defeated. And there was utter defeat and despair in the weeping girl.

'Don't lie to me,' Alice had flared at her when she pretended her innocence. 'One affair, my foot! You've been cheating on Richard since Nancy was a baby. You've made him an alcoholic, you've destroyed him. And you're not going to go on doing it. You've had your chance.. Now you're going to get out and stay out of his life!'

'I won't.' The moment of defiance was short-lived and pathetic. 'I won't leave him. You can't make me.'

'Oh yes I can,' Alice threatened. 'Richard will listen to me. If I tell him to get rid of you, he'll do it. I'll tell him he's been killing himself for nothing. I'll tell him what you really are!'

'He knows,' Diana said. For a moment Alice stared at her. The tears began to flow. She seemed to shrink into herself. 'He knows about me. I can't help myself. I've tried and tried... My father used to thrash me when I was little. I was sent away...'

At last Alice managed to stem the torrent of confession. She felt so shaken she was trembling. 'There must be something,' she said. 'There must be a cure.'

The answer was a whisper. 'There isn't. The Swiss doctors tried. They said if my father hadn't beaten me, it wouldn't have got so bad. I don't know. I wish I was dead. If I lose Dick and Nancy I'll kill myself.' It wasn't a threat. It was a statement. Alice bit back an angry retort. She wasn't blackmailing. She meant it.

I've lost, Alice thought. I can't have that on my conscience. And if it happened, it would destroy my son completely. She said at last, 'I wish he'd told me. Maybe I could have helped. Stop crying, Diana. For Christ's sake, stop. I've got to think. I've got to try and think what's best for all of us.'

236

At last she said, 'He loves you, that's the trouble.'

'I love him.' It was a whisper. 'I don't expect you to believe me, but it's true. Nobody else means anything. Let me stay with him. I beg of you, give me one more chance.'

'One more chance to do what? Get into another dirty mess, like the last one?'

'I won't,' Diana protested. She made a visible effort to calm herself. 'I won't ever do that again. I just let it happen, because he wanted it and there wasn't anyone else. June was my best friend. I felt so terrible all the time, but once I'd started I didn't know how to stop.'

'I need a drink,' Alice said.

Diana scrambled up. 'I'll get you one. What would you like?'

'Brandy,' Alice said. 'You'd better have one too.'

'I don't like spirits,' Diana said. She didn't drink, she hardly ever smoked. She was so abstemious compared to a lot of young women. Except in her appetite for men. Alice felt a spasm of real nausea. She of all women was supposed to understand. Was that ignorant brute of a father responsible? Or had he sought the age-old remedy for driving out a devil? It didn't matter now. She shuddered at the mental picture.

'Here you are, Lady Alice,' Diana said. Alice looked up into the wretched face, blotched and swollen with tears, and felt overcome with helplessness. I never imagined I could pity her, she thought. I came here full of anger and contempt to drive her out. But I can't.

She took the glass and sipped the brandy. It was the second time in her life she'd drunk it. The first was when Hugo came back to Ashton.

'If Richard doesn't stop drinking, he'll be dead before he's thirty-five,' she said. 'If not before. The last specialist said so. If I make a pact with you, Diana, you'd better keep it.'

'I will,' the voice was low. 'I will.'

Alice said, 'There's another cure we haven't tried. I

didn't want to because it's so cruel. He'll suffer so much. Do you realize that?'

Diana hid her face in her hands. 'Don't say that,' she begged. 'I can't bear it.'

'You won't have to, Richard will,' Alice answered. 'If it works, you and he must go away. Right away for some time. If he stays sober, Diana, and you keep yourself under control, then I'll support you. But if he drinks again because of you, then you're out. And I will personally see to it. Do you understand me?'

'Yes, I understand.'

'No second chance. Never. Just this once.'

She didn't finish the brandy. It wasn't helping. It made her feel sick all over again.

'What about Sir Hugo?' Diana found the courage to ask. 'He doesn't want a scandal. It would hurt him politically.'

Alice's tone was cold. 'I'm not concerned with that. I'm only thinking of my son. What's best for him. And Nancy.' Then, seeing the misery in front of her, she made herself say, 'And for you too. Say nothing to him about this. I'll think what's to be done and let you know. Before this bloody divorce case comes to court.' She got up. 'I'll see myself out. I'd do something about your face before he comes home. He might be sober enough to notice.'

'Dick?' He had been trying to read but his attention kept wandering away. Diana said again, 'Dick ... Dick, darling?'

He smiled at her. 'Hello.'

'Hello.' She reached across and pulled the rug closer over his knees. There was a cold wind even though the first-class deck was sheltered. Below them the seas swelled and rushed away in the wake of the great liner. 'I don't want to interrupt you,' she said. 'It's a good book, isn't it?'

'I suppose so. I keep forgetting who's who, that's the trouble.'

It was the tranquillizers, she thought. They had slowed him down a lot. He'd got very thin too, after the last treatment. Aversion therapy, they called it. They fed you pills and drink, and the pills made you so terribly sick you wanted to die. But they wouldn't stop. It had sounded so dreadful that she spent days in tears imagining what he was going through. He had missed the divorce, that was one mercy. She would never forget the shame, the misery of those press reports. June had done her best to disgrace her. She appeared before the world as a woman without morals or conscience, cheating her best friend.

It had been a frightful ordeal, but because Tom Hubbard hadn't defended it didn't last too long. Diana had stayed at Ashton, where the press could be kept at bay. She hadn't wanted to go there. Not after that encounter with Alice. She didn't want to face her or Hugo. But Richard had collapsed again, and she didn't have the strength to resist their terms. She was to stay at Ashton, with Nancy, and when the case was over and Richard out of the nursing home, they would go on a six-month cruise.

Sentence was pronounced and passed and, alone as she was, Diana couldn't resist. She was so cowed, even Alice pitied her. The lovely house was like a prison. She clung to Nancy, more like a child herself than a mother.

At last Richard came home. A wreck, but a sober wreck. That hateful sister was there with her little twins, smirking and self-satisfied because Richard and she had fallen from grace. Only Brian was kind. Kind and sympathetic. They all dined in the huge formal room, with footmen serving them and a stilted flow of talk in which she didn't join. Only Brian made an effort to treat her normally. He chatted about the cruise she and Richard were planning. They were driven away from Ashton in Hugo's car. They embarked at Southampton, and the cruise began. They were alone, exiled for six months, until Hugo's promotion to the Cabinet was through and the scandal had been forgotten. Hugo had made sure the press knew about the trip. It stopped any speculation about divorce. And they were oddly happy. She didn't trouble Richard – he was too weak and frail. Within a few days she had found a young ship's officer and a fellow passenger travelling alone. The rest of the time she nursed Richard and kept him company.

'I wish it wasn't so cold,' she said. She drew the rug over her legs. 'We'll be getting near the sun soon. You'll feel better then.'

'It's dull for you,' he said slowly. 'Thank you for coming with me, Di.' He reached over and clasped her hand. 'Thanks for sticking to me.'

'I'm the one to say that,' she said, 'After what happened. Anyone else would have thrown me out. You're not sorry I didn't leave, are you, Dick? If I'd been braver, I'd have done what Alice said. I'd have left you to make a new life for yourself. But I couldn't. I couldn't live without you and Nancy.'

'Bloody fat chance of me making anything of myself,' he said. 'Poor old Mum – she thinks everyone's as tough as she is. I never was. Never could be, that's the trouble. If you left me, Di, I'd drink myself to death in a month. I love you, you know.'

'I know,' she said, and bowed her head. 'And I love you. Whatever happens, that's the truth. That's real.'

'I can't read this bloody book,' he said. 'What's the time?'

'Nearly four.' She had arranged to meet the young officer at 5.30. 'It's time for your pill, isn't it?'

He shrugged. 'I don't have to take it. I could lay off for a couple of days and then try a drink.'

'But you won't, will you? Oh, please, please, Dick, promise me you'll go on taking them. You'll die, you know. Alice said so. You'll die if you start again!'

'Don't worry,' he squeezed her hand. He had been so handsome, she thought sadly. Now he was haggard and sallow, with great pouches under his eyes. He looked forty. 'Don't worry, I won't do anything silly. I'll stick to it. Maybe it'll work.'

'I'm sure it will,' she insisted. 'Come on, let's go to our cabin. It's getting miserable up here. You take your pill and the dopey one and have a snooze for a bit. There's a good film on after dinner. *Roman Holiday*. We saw it, do you remember?'

'Yes,' he said to please her. He had no memory of seeing any film. Or any stage play either. Very little memory of anything.

She helped him lie down and, bending, kissed him tenderly. 'Have your snooze, darling, and I'll wake you.'

Then she slipped out, leaving him to sleep. The young officer was waiting for her in an empty cabin. He was used to having women during these long cruises. Too many of them were middle-aged, but they gave good presents at the end of the voyage. He'd had a lot of young ones too, but never a bedmate like the Hon. Mrs Richard Vandekar. If he wasn't careful she'd leave him for dead.

'Well,' Fern said, 'I wonder how long it'll last.'

'What?' Brian asked her.

'Richard, of course,' she said irritably.

Brian picked up his drink and swirled the ice around. He knew that look only too well. And that tone of voice with an edge to it. She was a very attractive woman, but the meanness of spirit was showing in her face. How long had he thought of her like that, he wondered. When he had fallen out of love and seen what sort of woman she really was.

'He's been off the booze for a year,' he countered. 'Why shouldn't it last?'

She shrugged. He had grown to hate that mannerism. 'Maybe it will. I just don't think so. And don't tell me you think *she's* changed her spots!'

He put his glass down. He'd had a long day at his studio; he was tired and drained and in no mood to

241

listen to Fern carping on her eternal jealous theme. She was never content. She had everything. They'd bought a fine house in Portman Square; money was pouring in. He had more commissions than he could cope with. Two major European exhibitions in the next two years and a one-man show in New York. He was a famous artist, fêted wherever he went. She had had her longed-for children, a boy and a girl. She was her father's darling even more obviously since her brother had been banished. She even hinted that she might inherit everything and couldn't understand why he reacted so angrily. He was attentive, faithful and generous. But he didn't love her any more. Perhaps she knew. He hoped not. Where he once pitied her, he found the harping on her unhappy childhood an egotistical bore. Sometimes he wondered just how exaggerated all those stories about Alice had been. She sniped at her brother and the unhappy Diana at every opportunity. He had heard her poisoning Hugo about her brother and his wife, and had been disgusted by the malice that struck at them when they were down. And he had watched her gloat over Alice's proud agony. Perhaps that was the catalyst. The moment he stopped loving her.

'Why don't you stop it, Fern? Why don't you get on with your own life and let go? All you ever think about is putting the boot in to your mother and your brother. I'm sick of hearing it.'

She went quite white. It reminded him of his father-in-law, who paled like that when he was angry. White-livered, his mother used to call such people. Meaning dangerous, capable of anything in the grip of rage. His mother and father had come round after the twins were born. And he had insisted that the children were baptized Roman Catholics. Fern had resisted furiously. 'Daddy will have a fit! You can't be serious...'

'They're my children, not his,' was his answer. 'And my parents have as much right as he does. The kids will be Catholics and that's the end of it. The day you go to church you'll be in a position to complain!'

Alice had remained neutral, and he was very grateful for that. He knew she shared Hugo's prejudice, but for different reasons. It wan't snobbery. It was a total disbelief in any organized religion.

Brian had won, and his Irish parents came to the christening and there was a surface reconciliation. They came for a visit now and then to see the little ones, but Fern managed to make them feel uncomfortable without doing anything specific. They were proud and they understood that she didn't expect to see them too often. It was as much as he could hope for, but there were times when he was staying at Ashton surrounded by Fern's family that he felt a deep resentment.

He saw her get up. She stared at him, and again it was Hugo, cold and supercilious in his anger.

'I'm going upstairs to say goodnight to Ben and Phyllis,' she announced. 'I know they're not my mother's favourite like that brat of Richard's, but then you don't even care about that! Shall I tell them you'll be coming up, or are you going to sit there, swilling down the gin?'

Brian looked up at her. 'Why don't you fuck off?' he said.

At first she had cried when they quarrelled, and he was very soon contrite, begging her to make it up. He hadn't done that for a long time. She just said, 'Charming!' and went out, banging the door. He gave a great sigh of boredom and frustration. And there was no reconciliation in bed that night. He was getting tired of that too.

'Mummy, come and watch me.'

Diana smiled. The child was pony mad. She'd never gone through that phase when she was little. Nancy spent every spare moment with the new pony. It was Alice's birthday present. The docile old pensioner she had learnt to ride on was happily retired. There was a new star in the stable, bright chestnut, with a flowing mane and tail and a reputation won at show classes in the county. Alice and her granddaughter were a familiar sight at local shows. And Alice had seen the little chestnut heading the line so many times, it began to take her fancy. Nancy sighed and gazed at it, never imagining that the prize could be hers. Alice decided that she must have it. There was no gainsaying her when she had made up her mind. Diana tried; she was frightened the high-spirited little creature would be too much for Nancy to manage. Alice brushed the objections aside. 'The child who rides it isn't as good as Nancy,' she said. 'I'll get a proper groom, and she can teach Nancy. In fact I might try to tempt the girl who looks after it now.'

The pony and its keeper were tempted indeed by the price Alice offered. And it had been waiting for Nancy in the stable on her seventh birthday, with ribbons plaited into its mane. Alice spoiled Nancy. Diana couldn't stop her and didn't really want to. She hadn't been spoiled herself as a child. Where Alice loved she was overgenerous. So much of her love for Richard had spilled over to the little girl.

Richard was going into the bank twice a week now, not doing too much at first, but he was enthused by the idea of writing a book on the Vandekars. Diana was so happy to see him interested and alert again. Of course he would write the book, she insisted when Fern made some disparaging reference to the length of time he spent researching. You can't hurry these things. He'd get down to the actual writing when he had everything assembled. She loved him so much. She told him so, and it was a way of begging him not to ask questions or wonder why she made no attempt to revive their sex life.

She had made a promise during that long voyage. She was responsible for his loss of confidence and the drinking that followed. He must never be pressured again. She would deal with her own problem in her own way.

And so far fate had been kind. Her affairs were discreet and she had avoided the risk of becoming involved in a long-term affair with any married man. She lived a schizophrenic life, a loving wife and a fond mother at Ashton for part of the week, and the woman who slipped in and out of hotels and flats with a variety of men. She had matured, and at twenty-six she was a very beautiful woman. It wasn't difficult to find men. They gravitated towards her, scenting the sexual invitation that was implicit in everything she did. Their object was the same as hers. Luck was holding out so far. Richard was sober, Nancy was growing up into a lovely, happy child, and Alice, whom she had feared more than anyone in the family, had come down firmly on the side of the marriage once Richard had stopped drinking. Alice was her safeguard, and though she was never at ease with her, Diana was grateful.

She went down to the paddock to watch Nancy school the little pony. The girl was coaching her. Diana stood by the rail and watched. She didn't understand exactly what was happening, but there were rosettes in Nancy's bedroom to prove that it was working.

'Hello, Diana.'

She turned in surprise. 'Brian? I didn't know you were coming down? How nice to see you.' He gave her a friendly peck of a kiss on the cheek and she blushed.

'Fern wanted a break. We've brought the kids. How's the riding going?'

'Very well, I think,' she said. 'I never had a pony myself, so I don't know too much about it.'

He grinned. 'I didn't have a pony either! She looks good on it. I'm afraid horses are not my idea of fun.'

'Dangerous at both ends and unsafe in the middle,' Diana quoted, and they both laughed. After a decent interval they walked back to the house together.

Alice and Hugo went to the South of France that

summer, to the same rented villa. They had gone to Cap d'Antibes for the past ten years – Hugo disliked hotels. The villa belonged to a Greek shipping magnate. It was luxuriously furnished with a large staff and a magnificent swimming pool. The magnate had lent it to the Vandekars in the palmy days when tankers were at a premium. Latterly he wasn't so rich and was happy to take a generous rent from his old friends. Alice enjoyed it. She took Lily with her, who grumbled because she didn't like the heat but would never have agreed to stay behind.

Sometimes they invited friends to join them. It amused Alice to see how ambitious Hugo was and how cleverly he courted those who might support him. He had higher ambitions than a place in the Cabinet, and only she suspected just how high they might be. He could do it too. He was shrewd, determined, dedicated, and he could gather people round him when he wanted to. He was a noted and feared opponent in the House.

Alice was charming, amusing and hospitable to everyone who came to stay, and Hugo thanked her solemnly for helping him. When they were alone they were very companionable. No Fern to claim his attention, no Richard to wring her heart with worry.

We could be very happy in our own way, Alice thought that summer, reading side by side with Hugo at the edge of the pool. I loved him once, and God knows, he loved me. If there'd never been children. If there'd never been Nick. She put the novel down and closed her eyes. The sun was hot; she felt relaxed and sleepy. Nancy was coming out with her nanny to spend three weeks. That would be fun, Alice thought. She loved that child. She had to have the twins as well, because Fern would start creating and saying she didn't love them as much. But they were very small and quite sweet, which meant they didn't get in the way too much. She could take Nancy down to the Hôtel du Cap and swim in the sea. The pool would bore the child after a time and the sea was much more fun. Hugo hated it and wouldn't go near a beach because of his amputated leg. He even insisted upon swimming in the pool alone. The rest of the time he wore a long beachrobe and a slipper on the artificial foot. But he loved the villa and the climate suited him. He hasn't been happy, she thought. He's made the best of a bad job. Marrying me. Losing his leg. He's been brave, no one can deny him that. 'Hugo,' she said.

'Mm?' He was deep in the biography of Lloyd George.

'Why don't we make Stavros an offer for this place?'

'Why on earth should we?'

She stretched lazily. She had as good a figure as the day they got married. He noticed it, but there was no twinge of desire any more. 'Because you love it here.'

'Do you want it?'

'No, not particularly. Ashton is enough for me. I was thinking it would be nice for you. We could come out in the winter recess. The weather can be lovely here.'

'And why should you want me to give myself a present?' he asked.

She opened her eyes and smiled. 'Because you deserve one,' she said. 'For putting up with me for all these years.'

'I'll think about it,' he said, and went back to his book.

He found he couldn't concentrate. She still had the power to disturb him. To make him so angry that he could feel himself shaking inside. To say something outrageous and original that made him bark with laughter. And to move him, just as she had done now, by saying something thoughtful, even tender. He didn't love her any more. He didn't want to reach out and touch her though she lay half naked an arm's length away. He paid for that in London. No Celia Forbes, but an attractive professional who'd given up her other clients and lived in a flat in Regent's Park. He was her only friend. He paid for everything and she was the most discreet mistress he had ever had since he came back from the war. She had to be because of his position in the government.

But he wasn't proof against Alice. The worm of distrust had eaten into him until desire was dead, for so long that his whole core was rotted through. He kept hearing the pain-crazed accusations of the dying man in hospital cursing Alice for his fate. Hugo would never know whether she had given another man the love she had refused to him, whether the son he found on his return was the result of adulterous deceit or his own lovemaking before he left England. He had tried to make himself hate her and thought at times that he had succeeded. He knew how to strike at her, how to wound her as she had wounded him. He hadn't hesitated. But she could still say something that moved him.

'If you wouldn't mind leaving Ashton sometimes in the winter,' he said after a pause, 'then I might have a word with Stavros about this. But only if you'd enjoy coming here too.'

'I would,' Alice said. 'The winter doesn't bother me the way it does you, but it would do us both good.'

She closed her eyes again and fell asleep. They drew close together and, without putting it into words, they stayed close for the rest of the holiday. Neither of them was to know that their lives were about to change for ever.

Diana had slipped away to Portugal. 'You don't mind do you, darling? Just for ten days. Patsy's going – she asked if I'd like to join them. I know you don't want to go away just when you've started your book.'

'I don't mind,' he said. 'It is important not to stop now, it's taken me long enough to get started. You have a little break, Di. I'll go to Ashton and work there'.

'You're sweet,' she said, and kissed him. 'We'll plan something special for the autumn, shall we? You'll be well into the book by then. I'll have a look round

Portugal and see if there's anywhere you'd like. The weather's gorgeous there right up to October.'

She went to Ashton to see him settled with his tape recorder and his copious notes, and then flew off. She had a friend called Patsy Frewen who was going to Portugal with her husband and two children. But Diana wasn't joining them. She was going alone to a hotel on the Algarve where nobody would recognize her. She had promised there'd be no scandal. She would have ten days among the package tourists and the Portuguese who catered for single women on holiday. She'd done it in Spain in the spring, and nobody had asked awkward questions. Richard never did. He would be busy working on his book on the Vandekars at Ashton.

He didn't ask for an address and she promised to send postcards. They parted happily. It was a glorious summer. He had the house to himself except for a skeleton staff. He felt as if Ashton belonged to him already. He didn't hurry to begin the actual dictation. He played back the few hundred words of the first chapter and felt satisfied. Nobody except Diana really believed he'd write that book. Fern was always jeering. His father never mentioned it. Alice, being Alice, asked about its progress, but only because she wanted to encourage him. He thought of her and laughed to himself. She should have written it. She wouldn't have pondered and hesitated and put off starting. She'd have rattled away and finished the whole thing while he was still researching.

He took his time because there was such a lot to find out about the Vandekars. They weren't dull either. Solid, respectable Dutch merchants, but not above a little slave trading and smuggling in the early days. Good businessmen, steady churchgoers, who saw no sin in profit, only in waste. He had spent a lot of time on his great-grandfather, the founding father, as he headed the chapter devoted to him. Steely-eyed old bugger from the portrait and the many photographs

he'd gathered. Adam Vandekar. They owed it all to
him. The bank, the businesses in the States and
Canada, the gaudy jewels his grandmother had left
him which Diana couldn't wear. They were too heavy
and vulgar for her. Ashton, the ultimate jewel. It was
so beautiful, he spent the first few days wandering
round, taking long walks with his father's current
labrador for company. There was always a labrador,
one generation after another. Fine, affectionate dogs,
highly intelligent. He loved dogs. When Nancy was
older and could really take care of it, he'd buy her a
puppy. Might wean her away from that damned pony.
It was so peaceful and he felt calm and contented. He
must take a pull and go and start dictating. Otherwise
there'd be nothing to show Diana when she got back.
She'd be home in a week. He spent a lot of time
remembering. Happy memories. Walking with his
mother by the lake, learning to fish from a little boat
with his father teaching him. His father had been too
busy politicking to spend much time with him when he
was a boy, but he had taught him to fish. Playing tennis
with his friends during the holidays. Swimming parties
in the new pool. What bloody good times they'd been.
The place where the swing used to be. There was a
new, low one with a cradle round it, put there for
Nancy and the twins. He'd swung Diana up so high she
nearly fell out.

He must get down to work. It was fascinating stuff,
seeing what had made him and Fern. All those strong-
willed Dutchmen and their wives. His father had a lot
of the burgher in him. Richard grinned to himself.
He'd better not put that in. The old man wouldn't be
pleased. He might chance saying it into the machine. It
would make Diana laugh. He could erase it later. He
went back to the house, up the steps and under the
splendid porch. The big hall was cool and restful after
the heat outside. The tapestries still moved in a
draught no one could find. When they were little Fern
used to frighten him shitless saying there was a man in

the German armour with the pig's head. What a cow, he said to himself, and shook his head. Upstairs and to work. He felt quite inspired. He had a room with a desk and a filing cabinet for his documentation and letters – masses of letters from people all over the world connected with the family – his dictaphone, cigarettes, everything the writer could require. He put in a whole afternoon's work, and when he played it back, he was genuinely surprised at how good it was. Interesting, concise. Funny in parts too.

There was a knock on the door. One of the under footmen looked round. 'Sorry to disturb you, sir. Would you like tea now? It's nearly five.'

Nearly five. The time had sped by. 'No thanks, I don't think so. I've got some more work to do, John. But you could bring me a whisky and soda.'

He'd forgotten Diana was due back. He'd worked feverishly on his book, and listened to the playback, exulting in how original and amusing it was becoming. It was so easy now that he had the odd drink. It was commonplace for the young footman who looked after him to find him asleep in his clothes in the morning. Nobody knew what to do. They waited, because Mrs Richard would be home by the end of the week.

She drove up the drive and the stately house was like a pearl in the sunshine. She was so longing to see Richard. Longing to make a fuss of him and give him the presents she'd bought. She was very brown and very, very tired. Lethargic, after a sexual marathon with dozens of different pick-ups. From the moment the plane landed she shut Portugal out of her mind. It would be so lovely to see Richard and Nancy. She'd got a dressed doll for her that was so pretty.

She hadn't forgotten her promise to find somewhere they could go together in the autumn. The local travel agent had recommended a hotel inland which had been a private palace. It had magnificent rooms and terrace after terrace of ornamental gardens. Richard would enjoy it. She parked the car and ran in and up the stairs to their rooms to find him.

He was sitting by his desk. She didn't see the decanter and the glass at first. 'Darling! I'm back!' She hurried to throw her arms round him.

He pushed the chair back and tripped. 'Di!' He recovered himself. 'Di, darling! *Hello*...'

Diana froze.

He lumbered towards her, a beaming smile on his face. 'Did you have a good time? Did you have fun? I've had fun... I've been working and working... Listen, come and listen... It's bloody good, you know.'

He was drunk. Very drunk. She let him lead her to the desk, put her into his chair, and she sat while he switched on the tape. It was gibberish.

He leaned down and looked at her. 'What's the matter? Don't you like it? What's the matter?'

Diana got up. He was unsteady on his feet. 'Sit down, Dick,' she said. 'You've gone back on it, haven't you?'

'Not really,' he protested. 'Just one now and again. It hasn't hurt me. Don't you like the book?'

'Yes,' she mumbled. 'Yes, I like it. It's very good.'

She had to get him away from Ashton. Back to London. The servants knew, of course, but the house-keeper wasn't there, nor thank God, was Lily Parker. The young staff wouldn't dare say anything to Alice. She had to get him home. She couldn't think what to do beyond that.

He was amiable in drink. Affectionate and friendly, willing to do whatever she suggested. She drove him home that evening. He was sober enough to unpack and behave normally when they got in, but he went looking for a drink. Diana never kept alcohol in the flat. 'I'm just popping out for cigarettes darling,' he said.

She stood against the door. She was trembling. 'It's your punishment. God's punishment for what you've been doing.' Her father had shouted that at her often enough. 'God knows you're lying. He knows what you are ...'

'Don't buy drink,' she said. 'Please, Dick, I beg of you. Don't go out and buy it. Just for tonight.'

'Don't be silly, Di. There's nothing to worry about. I can handle it now. I promise you.'

'You can't,' she said in despair. 'You can't ever have a drink again. You know that! Oh, why did you do it? Why? Just because I left you for a few days.' She broke down in tears.

He shook his head. 'That's not why,' he said. 'Listen, darling, I'm not lit up now. Well a bit, not much. I didn't booze because you weren't there. I boozed because I wanted to. You're here and I still want to. If I don't get some tonight, I'll get it tomorrow.'

She went into the bedroom and locked the door. She didn't want to see him go out or be there when he came back. She had to have help. She had to stop him before Alice came back. She dialled the specialist who had looked after him before. It was a Friday and the Ansaphone gave a number to ring in an emergency. She rang it. A woman answered. Diana stammered in desperation. The woman on the other end was used to such calls. 'I'm sorry,' she said. 'My husband is up north. He won't be back till Monday. You can ring him in Harley Street at nine o'clock.'

'What am I to do?' Diana cried. 'How can I stop him?'

'I don't think you can,' was the answer. 'Just hold on till Monday. And try not to worry. Isn't there anyone you can get to come round?'

'No,' Diana said slowly. 'There isn't. Thank you. Goodbye.'

She put the phone down. She came out of the bedroom. The flat was empty. He had gone. There were times when he didn't come back for a day or more. Especially if she'd been upset or angry because he was drinking. He went and holed up in some bed and breakfast and drank himself insensible.

By nine o'clock Diana knew it was going to be like that this time. She had three weeks to save herself and Richard before Alice and Hugo came back from France. And she couldn't do it alone.

'Brian, it's so good of you to come.'

'No sweat,' he said gently. 'When did he get back?'

'Half an hour ago. He's in a dreadful state. I put him to bed. In there.'

He opened the door. Richard was lying flat on his back. He was unshaven and dirty, and the sickly smell of alcohol hung pungent in the air.

'He'd fallen down,' Diana said behind him. 'His trousers were torn and his knee was bleeding. He started crying when he saw me. It was so terrible to see him like that.'

'Not much fun for you either,' Brian remarked. He closed the door. Poor little thing – she looked so white and miserable. He had no sympathy with the rotten drunk lying in there. 'Thank God you called me,' he said. 'You couldn't possibly cope with this. Come on, why don't you sit down? I'll make us both a cup of coffee. Have you had anything to eat?'

'I couldn't,' she said. 'I felt sick with worry. I'm so sorry about this but I *had* to talk to somebody!'

He'd been kind when she was in trouble before. He was always nice to her in spite of Fern. She couldn't risk getting *her*, so she phoned his studio and by a miracle he was working even though it was Sunday. She burst into tears as she spoke to him. Richard had been missing since Friday night. She'd tried the police and the local hospitals but he hadn't been picked up. He was on a major jag. Brian didn't ask any questions. He just said, 'I'll be right round.'

She did as he told her and sat down. She was weak with misery. He came back with coffee and said, 'Drink this. I've made us some sandwiches. I haven't had any lunch either.'

'What am I going to do?'

He shrugged. 'Get him in somewhere and let them dry him out. That's the first step.'

'But he'll start again as soon as he comes out,' she protested. 'It's happened every time before. Brian, you don't know what will happen when Alice finds out he's drinking again. After eighteen months. She'll think it's because I left him alone.'

He saw despair and fear in her eyes. Fear of what? 'Why the hell should she blame you?' he demanded. 'She knows he's a hopeless boozer. How could you have stopped him even if you were with him twenty-four hours a bloody day? You never managed it before.'

'She will blame me,' she said. 'They'll kick me out. Hugo won't mind this time. I don't know what to do,' she repeated.

'You're not going to do anything,' he said. 'I'll handle this. I'll get him in somewhere tonight. You can't be left alone with him. And I can't stay because Fern would raise hell if I did.'

'Don't tell her,' Diana pleaded. 'Please, don't tell her.'

'I wasn't going to,' he answered. 'I've got a pal who's a doctor. We were at school together. Good old Paddy, like me. He's up in Harley Street coining money. I'll get hold of him.'

Richard was admitted to a private clinic that evening. Brian got him up, washed him and shaved him, changed his clothes. It upset Diana because he was quite rough. Richard submitted to everything, bleary and disorientated. Brian and she drove him to Putney. Brian's friend was waiting for them. He was a slight, spectacled man, with a Cork sing-song in his voice. He took charge of Richard, who willingly agreed to go wherever was suggested. It wasn't strictly ethical to admit him in that condition, but after what Brian had said Tim Flanagan wasn't going to bother about rules. The wife couldn't be left alone with that.

Outside the clinic Brian helped Diana into the car. 'You'll be all right tonight, won't you? I wish I could say come back and stay with us, but I can't.'

He saw her crying and said, 'For Christ's sake, don't upset yourself over him. He isn't worth it.'

'I'm so sorry,' she whispered. 'I'm so sorry for him . . .'

'Do better to be sorry for yourself. Look. I'll ring home and say I'm going to the pub. I meet my old friends sometimes and we have a few jars. Fern never comes, she hates pubs. I'll take you somewhere and give you dinner.'

He was being kind, Diana told herself. Helping her out because she was his sister-in-law. He was very much a family man. All the Irish stuck together. She gazed at him across the table. He had rather a beautiful face. Not classically handsome like Richard used to be, but sensitive, fine-drawn. And deep, intelligent eyes.

They went to a small trattoria in the King's Road. Not so full on a Sunday evening. They had a table in the corner. She wasn't really hungry but she ate to please him.

Fern was so lucky. He was kind and strong and took all the decisions.

She gazed at him with such intensity that he began to see her as if it was the first time. She was beautiful in a wistful way. Marvellous colouring with the red hair and a flawless skin. What a waste, he thought suddenly. Throwing herself away on that piss artist. A good hard kick up the arse was what he needed, instead of everyone running round after him. No wonder she'd got herself mixed up with that married man – what was his name? He couldn't remember . . . Pity she didn't go off with him and leave mother's boy. What a hell of a life she must have led.

'I better get the bill. The pubs'll be shut by now.'

'Is Fern very jealous of you?' Diana asked him.

He hesitated. 'Possessive, not jealous. She knows she

256

hasn't any reason to be. I've never looked at anyone else.' Until now, he thought, as he took her arm and walked to the car. She was light as a feather.

As an artist he knew that everyone has an aura. If you capture that, you've painted a true portrait. And Diana's aura was affecting him very powerfully. She breathed sexual attraction.

He drove her home and said goodnight at the entrance. He didn't trust himself to go up to the flat. She turned and lifted her face to be kissed. On the cheek, like a good sister-in-law. Her lips were slightly open.

'Thank you, Brian. Thank you for everything.' She reached up and kissed him full on the mouth. He didn't know how he managed to leave her and go home.

'I mustn't do it. I mustn't do it again.' Diana said the same thing every time. 'Richard's in that home, having treatment. I mustn't see Brian.' But she did. Each day she made the resolution when he left and the next day she broke it. He had done everything, taken the responsibility for the specialists and the nursing home, ordered her to stay out of the way. And taken her to bed as if he expected her to put up some resistance. 'I'm in love with you,' he said, and that had been enough. She hadn't had to touch him or seduce him. All she had to do was submit to his desire and let herself explode in unison.

He was a wonderful lover. She felt safe with him too. Fern mustn't find out. Her secret would be kept along with his. And he was helping her patch up Richard in time. 'He'll last for a bit, my darling,' he promised her. 'When he goes on the piss again, and he will, it's got to be right under their noses. You move into Ashton as soon as they come home.'

Diana said, 'Yes, darling,' and believed that she'd be strong enough to do what he told her. Alice and Hugo were still some days away. She forgot everything when he made love to her. In the end there were no more resolutions. 'I love you,' he said, and she began to say it back to him. It made the guilty feelings go away.

She went to visit Richard every day. He was restless and bored. 'I want to come home,' he'd say, and she'd do what Brian told her and persuade him that one more day wouldn't be too bad. He was so much better. One more day and the day after that. He was weak and depressed. Very depressed. He didn't think of discharging himself because Diana said he would be out on Wednesday anyway and she planned that they should go straight to Ashton. His parents and the grandchildren would arrive that evening. He'd be so much stronger and everything was going to be all right. And she loved him, she insisted, cradling the sunken head in her arms. She would never stop loving him. He knew that.

The day before they were due to go to Ashton her nerve failed. At least that was the explanation she gave herself. Just cowardice – fear of facing Alice and the chill eyes of Hugo. How could she pretend that nothing had happened? How could she hope to repeat the lie Brian had rehearsed her in so convincingly? Poor darling Richard had just got over a really dreadful bout of flu. That would account for the loss of weight, the low spirits. They wouldn't be deceived. Alice would suspect. She'd ask him. Diana worked herself into a state of panic.

She used to lie so easily, so fluently. But this time the prospect terrified her. She didn't want to go to Ashton, and if she hadn't telephoned Brian she probably wouldn't have done. 'You've got to be there,' she insisted. 'Stay for a week, see me through this. Darling, I can't face them on my own.'

'All right, all right, Diana, just stay calm. I'll suggest it to Fern. I don't know how I'm going to explain it, but I'll think of something. I'll call you. Yes, tonight. No, for Christ's sake, I can't come over, I'm in the middle of some work! I didn't mean to be nasty, darling, of course I didn't . . . Don't worry. I'll manage it.'

He hung up. He was sorry he'd lost his temper for a moment. She was more demanding than she realized. She didn't seem to understand he mustn't be rung up and interrupted and pleaded with to come and see her. But she was frantic with anxiety. Of course she turned to him, needed him. He felt selfish and guilty. It would help divert attention from her and from Richard if he and Fern and the children were there. The sooner that wimp blew the gaffe on himself and let Diana off the hook the better! He focused his frustration on Richard. He tried to - work for the next hour but his concentration was broken. He cleaned his brushes, closed up the studio and went home.

'Fern, I've an idea. Why do we have to wait to collect the kids till the weekend? Why don't we go down tomorrow and be there when they come back?'

'Oh, for God's sake,' Fern sighed irritably. 'When I suggested doing exactly that you said no, wait till Friday, I've got to finish the Leader picture. It's already behind schedule. So I made dates for this week and I can't possibly break them. I've two lunches and we've accepted a dinner tomorrow night.' She looked up at him and said, 'Why the change? It's only two days. Normally you make a performance about going down anyway.'

'I've missed the kids,' he said. 'You have too, I know. Never mind what I said. Let's scrap the dinner and the lunches. I won't finish the picture anyway. It's not been going right.'

'Oh? You didn't say so. Look, Brian, if you're worried about it and you want to see the children, Mother can send them up in the car. Why don't we do that? Then nothing has to be cancelled.'

He was caught. He tried to turn it round. 'Don't you want to go? You haven't seen your parents for nearly two months. They'd be pretty hurt just being asked to send the kids back by car. Come on, darling, let's do it. Tomorrow. Let's turn up and surprise everyone.'

It was unusual for him to insist. She didn't know

what to make of it. The twins had spent three weeks in France, along with Nancy, who was the real reason they had been invited. Fern wasn't fooled. Her mother tolerated the two little ones and Hugo liked them well enough, but it was Richard's child she wanted. And, to keep the peace, she had asked the twins as well. Fern thought her husband looked tired and ill at ease. It must be the painting. It was a very important commission. It had been going so well until recently. He had been quiet and withdrawn when he came home from the studio. That was unusual too. He was a gregarious man, outgoing and volatile. Fern was used to that. She understood and tempered her own needs to his artistic nature. To her, his work was all-important. 'Would it help if you got out of London, then? Is that what you think? Would it help to get your ideas in focus again?'

She never failed in her support. He had long taken her compliance for granted. At that moment he felt ashamed and guilty, but he went on to take advantage of it. 'Yes, it would. I'd like to get away.'

'Then we'll go,' Fern said. 'You look worn out. Have an early night. I'll get you a drink.'

'Glass of beer,' he said. 'Thanks. Thanks, love.' He sat there feeling contemptible. But he found a chance to slip upstairs and make a rapid call to Diana. 'It's OK. We'll be there.' He rang off before she could start a conversation.

It was a smooth flight back. Hugo was in good spirits. He looked brown and rested. Alice, careful of her complexion, was slightly tanned. The twins were brown as toast and, thankfully, sitting three rows back with their nanny to keep them amused. It was a very tiring age. Nancy was sitting with Lily, who hated flying and wouldn't sit near the window because it made her nervous to look out and see clouds floating by. She was happy to look after Nancy. It took her mind off the unnatural condition of being 30,000 feet above the ground. Nancy had a sore throat and a slight fever. Lily read to her till she dozed off.

The usual fleet of cars was waiting at heathrow. Hugo's Rolls and chauffeur, the Rover with one of the young footmen as driver for Lily, Nanny and the children, and the estate car for their luggage.

'Oh, won't it be nice to be home!' Alice exclaimed.

Hugo smiled slightly. 'That's a sure sign of a good holiday,' he said. 'It will be nice to get back.'

The cavalcade set off for Ashton as it had done so many times before. There wasn't a cloud in the sky.

7

Fern was delighted to have her children back. In contrast to Alice, she was strongly maternal. The weather was glorious, her father in a happy mood, so benevolent that he was even nice to Richard. Her brother looked awful, shrunken and pasty. It must have been a frightful bug to run him down like that.

Diana fluttered round him. They spent a lot of time in their own quarters, and Alice had decreed that Nancy must move into the main corridor and stay in the Print Room until she was better. Richard mustn't be exposed to any new infection. That irritated Fern because she knew how Alice doted on the child. She never went in to read or play games with the twins if they weren't well. But these were only pinpricks. She was glad she'd done what Brian suggested. He was still very tense, but if the picture was not coming quite right, it was only natural.

We've been having a bad patch lately, she thought, waking beside him. Everyone does sooner or later. It'll be over soon. And God, I do love him. She woke him to make love. He didn't respond. He stirred and turned over, mumbling about being tired. He pretended to be asleep. Fern knew he was pretending. She lay very still and after a time the tears began to seep down her face. They hadn't slept together for nearly three weeks. The fever of their first years had settled into a routine; they still took pleasure in each other, though she suspected her feelings were stronger than his. But he had never rejected her before. She felt degraded, not only by the refusal but the pretence that went with it. Something was wrong. Not just the strain of his work. It had never stopped him wanting to make love before. She didn't go to sleep again. She stayed beside him and listened to the fake deep breathing until the maid brought their morning tea.

She took the twins for a long walk. Brian didn't offer to come with her. She brooded; she nursed her humiliation. She said nothing; nor did he. But she watched him that night. They were in the library having a drink before dinner. She watched him with her mother, stung as always by their friendly intimacy. They were laughing at some joke and it grated on her nerves. She watched him with Richard, and was surprised at his antagonism. He had never thought much of him, but he was now positively hostile. It was like squaring up to a corpse for all the animation her brother showed. I bet he'd cheer up if someone offered him a drink, Fern thought acidly. He'd been off it for a long time now. Amazing. She hadn't expected or hoped it would last. Diana had a new dress. Very flattering, very expensive. Sea-green chiffon, with a short skirt that showed too much leg. And the Vandekar brooch blazing away on one shoulder. That should have been mine, Fern mused. I know Daddy wanted me to have it. Mother would give it to her, of course, just to please Richard. She makes me sick with that little girl act when she's been sleeping around all over the place. She even simpers round Daddy but he doesn't fall for it. I wonder who she's having it off with now...

Fern had been watching Diana without real interest. She avoided the sight of Brian deep in conversation with Alice. Alice got up – she was saying something to Richard. Casually Diana crossed the room. Fern watched her idly. She took a seat close to Brian. Everyone was occupied. Hugo half turned away from them. Alice perched beside her son, Fern herself sunk back in a big armchair.

Diana reached one arm across, lightly, carelessly, and Fern saw her fingers caress the back of her husband's neck. He didn't move away. He sat there while she fondled him in secret, drawing her long painted nails across the nape, just above the collar. 'Who is she having it off with now?' The question screamed in her head, no longer a malicious speculation.

And she had the answer. The erotic touch, and his acceptance of it. She had stroked him like that herself. Brian. Her husband and Diana. For a few seconds the room spun. The walls of books whirled round and round and the talk became a distorted hum. Fern had never fainted in her life, but for a moment it was very close.

'Fern?' She heard her father's voice. He was looking down to her. 'A little more sherry? It's rather good, I think.'

'Yes.' She forced herself to speak – it sounded strange. 'Yes, I'd love some. Thank you, Daddy darling.'

She was steady again. No crisis, no dramatic scene. She was shaking all over, and she drank the sherry quickly. Hugo was close by. She wished he'd move. She couldn't see them. Imagination. A trick of the eye. Diana was in view now, bending over Richard, murmuring some inquiry. Pretending to care, Fern thought. She wasn't near Brian, not looking at anyone but her husband. But Brian was looking at her. Watching her. No, Fern's heightened intuition argued, watching over her. I must hold on, she told herself. I must stay calm and make absolutely sure. I may be wrong, I may be seeing things that aren't there. I'm upset after what happened this morning. She smooches round every man. But she caressed his neck – I didn't imagine that. It's him I've got to watch.

Alice came up to her son. She was shocked at how frail and low he seemed. He'd better see a specialist in London. For a moment she and Diana looked at each other over his head. She was furtive, ill at ease. Alice knew what that look betokened. Another squalid liaison no doubt. So long as Richard didn't know, wasn't affected. She closed her mind and said to him,

'I'm going to feed you up, darling. You've got far too thin. It's such a good thing Diana brought you down to recuperate. A nice holiday would do you good.'

'We're going to Portugal next month,' he said. Alice had taken his hand. Poor Mum. Di was quite right. It would break her heart if she knew the truth. 'Di found a super hotel. How's Nancy?'

'Better. I went up to see her before dinner,' Alice said. 'It's just a bit of tonsilitis. It's easy to get it in France when it's so hot. Probably the damned pool. She'll be fine in a couple of days. Don't worry about her. I'll take care of her.'

He looked up at her. He squeezed her hand. Tears came into his eyes. 'You take care of all of us,' he said.

Dinner was announced.

On Sunday it was raining. Hugo went to morning service. Fern said she would like to go too. He was pleased but surprised. She usually went with her children and Brian to the local Catholic church in the village.

Diana said, 'I've never been to a Catholic service. What's it like? It's in Latin, isn't it?'

'It's been in English for years,' Brian answered. 'It's a nice little church.'

'Could I come?' Diana asked. 'It might be interesting to see. If Fern's not going with you?' She looked across at Fern.

'I'm going with my father,' she said shortly. 'He always goes by himself.' Alice was not in the room so it was safe to say that.

'Mum's an atheist,' Richard spoke up. 'Why should she go? It'd only be humbug.'

He was less lethargic, more alert. Or rather tense. Diana knew the signs. Sooner or later he'd break out. She didn't want to think about that. She wanted to be with Brian, to be alone with him. Perhaps they could slip away after this mass or whatever it was...

*

265

Guests were coming to lunch. Fern sat through the church service beside Hugo. She wondered if he ever prayed. She knew he felt it was a duty to attend service now and again. He read the lesson that Sunday.

St Paul to the Corinthians, Chapter 2, verses 12 to 19. She didn't hear a word. Diana and Brian. Three days of agony, watching him, watching her. Seeing the intimate looks pass between them, quickly veiled, but not quickly enough. The way Diana contrived to touch him at every opportunity. Brushing against him with a smile, resting her fingertips on his arm to emphasize something that didn't warrant it. Gazing at him with her limpid eyes, oozing sexuality as an octopus clouds the seas with ink. An octopus, Fern thought, hating her as she had never believed it possible to hate anyone. So powerfully that at times she felt choked with it, unable to breathe. An octopus with tendrils creeping, touching, entwining, devouring . . .

And Brian. Brian, whom she'd defied her father to marry, whom she'd supported and promoted and cherished because she believed in his genius. Who had held her hand as she gave birth to their twins, given her confidence in herself, love and feverish desire in those early years together. He was drugged with the creature. He couldn't take his eyes away from her, he was besotted enough to be almost careless. Fern hated him too, but it was a cruel mixture of love and jealousy as well.

She had gone with Hugo to the service for a purpose. In the car on the way back to Ashton she said she had to talk to him alone. After lunch, he suggested. Their guests wouldn't stay too long. They could have a chat then. Was it something serious, he added. She hadn't looked or seemed herself for the last few days.

'I think it's serious,' she said slowly. 'You're the only person in the world I can tell. And even you probably can't help me.'

They arrived at the house before he could ask any more questions.

266

Lily was in her sewing room. She was so glad to be back, out of that awful boiling sunshine. The food didn't agree with her either, and whatever was wrong with the water? You couldn't get a decent cup of tea. She was mending one of Alice's beautiful silk nightdresses, attaching a lace flounce with tiny stitches. Alice could still wear lingerie she had bought for her trousseau in 1934, she had kept her figure so well. Lily was proud of that. She knew what suited her lady and said so. Alice would tell her to shut up, but she seldom wore anything twice that Lily didn't like.

None of them was a patch on her, Lily considered. That daughter couldn't hold a candle to her, even though she spent a fortune on clothes and painted herself up. Funny, when you remember what a ragbag she was when she was a girl. Diana had the looks but she was a tart and, in Lily's opinion, it showed. No dignity, no presence. She might have a family going back to Agincourt, but she was as much a little tart as any girl standing around Piccadilly in the old days. Lily knew all about her. She'd seen her giving sly glances at a good-looking young footman once. It had made her sick.

Poor Richard. She would always think of him as the golden child she'd helped to bring up. He was a ruin now. Lily knew what drink could do – she'd seen it in friends and neighbours of her own family, It wasn't called a demon for nothing. But she didn't blame him. She blamed his wife. She'd driven him to it. He should have given her a good hiding and kicked her out the first time she had been caught and all that scandal had broken over the family. Mr Hugo stopped it. He wanted his Cabinet job and he didn't care if his son and her lady broke their hearts. Lily would never forgive him for that. It wouldn't go on for ever. She'd slip up and bring them all into the dirt again.

Lily came out of the sewing room to put the nightdress back in Alice's bedroom. She was a very quiet woman; she didn't make a noise when she moved about. She saw them in the corridor but they didn't see her. They were going into one of the empty bedrooms and shutting the door.

The nightdress slipped out of her hands. She stood there, so shocked she couldn't move. Diana and Brian Kiernan. 'Christ Almighty,' Lily whispered. Alice was out walking. Hugo and Fern were at church. Richard was reading the papers in bed. They had gone off with the twins, Lily had seen them. And come back early. She went back inside, picking up the nightdress, and closed the door. This would bring the family to total ruin.

'It's him, isn't it?' Richard said.

'Darling, please! I don't know what you're talking about!'

'Don't try to kid me, Di. I know you. I can tell by him too. You're really shitting on your own doorstep this time. And *don't* try to say I'm drunk. I'm not. Not yet anyway.'

'Why do you *say* that! You know how Brian's helped us.'

After the lunch party Richard had suddenly insisted on going out in the drizzling rain for a walk. Once out of earshot, he had rounded on her.

He's seen us, was her first thought. He must have done. She didn't know what to do but stand her ground and lie.

'He's helped you, you mean, and I know why. He treated me like shit in that bloody home. Told me he'd smash my face in if I came out and got pissed again.'

Diana went pale. 'I didn't know that,' she said. 'He shouldn't have done that . . .'

'It's bad enough my sister marrying a yob like him, but you . . . Di, how could you? How could you do this to me?'

She hung her head. The rain was getting heavy. Her hair was soaked and sticking to her head, the drops running down into her collar.

'I was desperate,' she said. 'Scared of your mother and what she'd do. You'd been missing for two days. I called him. I couldn't trust anyone else.'

He went on walking. She followed, pulling at his arm. 'You'll catch a cold,' she said. 'Come back, you're getting wet through.'

'I didn't know the others,' he went on, dragging her with him. 'I didn't know the bugger in Knightsbridge, and I must have met Hubbard but I couldn't put a face to him. I don't know any of the others. There must have been hundreds. They ought to make a film of your life, darling. A hundred men a night. But I know this one. Right under my bloody nose with my lout of a brother-in-law.' He stopped abruptly and wrenched away from her. They stood facing each other in the downpour. 'I think I've had enough. I think I've come to the end of my rope.'

'Dick,' she cried out. 'Dick, don't say that... Please!'

He walked on without answering.

She stood and let the rain drench her to the skin. He'd never said that before. He'd got drunk and accused her, but they'd ended clinging to each other in tears like the lost souls they were. He hadn't said anything for so long. She'd forgotten to be careful when he was there. Brian hadn't been careful either.

She ran after him but he had gone inside and locked himself into the bathroom by the time she got upstairs. She banged on the door and pleaded. She heard the water running, but he wouldn't answer. She stripped off her wet clothes and went to the twins' bathroom to soak in a hot bath herself. He didn't mean it. He couldn't. But she had to warn Brian. She had to see him that night.

Hugo sat down. He felt suddenly old and his leg ached.

'How far do you think this has gone?' he asked.

'I don't know,' Fern answered. 'Daddy, didn't you

notice, even going to the church with him this morning?'

'I did think it was odd,' he admitted. 'But I thought it was the sort of stupid, childish thing she would do, to call attention to herself. You're sure you're not imagining this?'

She dropped down beside him. 'No,' she said with the unhappiest sigh he had ever heard. 'I'm not imagining. He's not been his normal self for some time. He's home late, he's offhand with me – he says it's his new picture, but I don't believe him. I've seen the way they look at each other. She's always pawing him. There's something between them, I know there is!'

'I thought she seemed very shifty ever since we got back,' Hugo remarked. After a pause he said, 'I didn't connect it with Brian. Don't be proud with me, Fern. I love you and all I want to do is sort this out. Do you think they're sleeping together?'

She bit her lip, but it was no use. She couldn't help crying.

He slipped his arm round her and held her close.

'He doesn't want to sleep with me,' she mumbled. 'I think he's been with her behind my back. I don't want to lose him, Daddy. I can't lose him.'

He let her cry, giving silent comfort. He had never been so angry for years. How dare he! How dare Brian make Fern unhappy. Only the dregs of a Dublin slum would sink so low with his own sister-in-law. As for *her*, she should be locked up in a home.

'The twins,' Fern sobbed. 'How could he!'

Hugo said slowly, 'You don't want a divorce if it is true? You're prepared to forgive him?'

He hoped she'd say no. He hoped she'd admit at last that the marriage had been a dreadful mistake.

But she didn't. She looked at him with fresh tears falling and said simply, 'I won't lose him. I won't ever let him go. I couldn't face it.'

He had learned to accept the inevitable. He loved her too much to do more than regret her lack of pride.

'Help me,' she begged him. 'Get rid of her.

'My darling,' he said gently. 'I think the time has come when we must do just that. Now, don't cry any more, and don't say anything about this to anyone. I'll deal with it.'

Alice was dressing for dinner. Hugo insisted on changing – even on Sunday. She stood while Lily fastened her into a billowing silk blouse that buttoned up the back.

'There's something funny going on,' Alice announced.

Lily went on slotting buttons into their holes.

'There's an atmosphere you could cut with a knife.'

'Is there?' Lily muttered from behind.

Alice watched her reflection in the mirror. 'Diana and Richard aren't speaking. She's been trying but he just turns away. I've never seen them row before. Then she comes and says could she sleep near Nancy tonight as she's not very well.'

'Well,' Lily hid her reaction, 'that's not odd, is it?'

'I think so,' Alice retorted. 'She didn't leave Richard when Nancy was really ill with whooping cough. This is an excuse. For God's sake, haven't you done me up yet?' She was impatient, tapping one foot under the long skirt. Lily never fiddled normally. What was the matter with her?

'Sir Hugo looks like thunder, and Fern is as miserable as sour milk. I wish they'd all damned well go home!'

'There, that's the last one,' Lily declared. 'It's Monday tomorrow,' she said. 'Nanny told me the twins were going home, so *they'll* be gone too.' She couldn't bear to look her mistress in the face. That Irishman, sneaking off with his own sister-in-law . . . it was as good as incest, in Lily's eyes. And to betray her lady, after how good she'd been to him when he was just a penniless nothing . . . She felt rage so bitter that there was bile in her throat. Dirt, both of them.

271

Sleeping near Nancy, was she? To be able to sneak out and meet him . . .

'Lily,' Alice said, 'Lily, what's the matter with you tonight?'

I'll never tell her, Lily thought. She's had enough to bear. She'll find out soon enough, God help her.

She put on her stolid look, which Alice knew meant obstinancy. 'Nothing,' she said. 'Bit of a headache.'

'Then take an aspirin,' Alice snapped, knowing it wasn't true. 'Look at the time. You'll have to wait up and get me out of this damned blouse. I won't be late.'

She hurried out and down the stairs. She met Hugo limping ahead of her. He had refused to have a lift installed.

He stopped at the foot of the stairs. 'Alice, come in here a moment. I've got something to tell you.'

She followed him into his study. He closed the door. She frowned uneasily. 'What's the matter? Something wrong?'

'Very wrong, I'm afraid,' he said.

She saw the bloodless look and knew that he was very angry. 'What is it?'

He sat on the edge of an armchair. 'Diana and Brian,' he said. Alice gasped. 'What? Hugo! You don't mean . . .'

'I'm surprised you haven't noticed,' he remarked. 'You're usually so astute.'

'I don't believe it,' she said. She turned away from him. 'They couldn't. They couldn't do such a thing.'

'Why not?' He sounded acid. 'She is a degenerate. We both know that. And he's a guttersnipe who's no business in this family in the first place.'

'How do you know this?' Alice demanded. 'Did Fern tell you?'

'She came to me this afternoon. Things haven't been going well between them. She thinks Diana is at the back of it, and I believe her. She thinks it's been going on for some time.'

'Oh,' Alice said, 'oh my God. Hugo, are you sure

272

she's right? She's always been a jealous girl. Are you certain she's not imagining this? I haven't noticed anything – you said as much yourself...'

'You haven't been looking,' he reminded her. 'Nor had I. One doesn't expect to step into a heap of dog mess, so one doesn't look down. I have been watching them and I'm convinced that Fern is right. Diana is just a little careless at times. Not as deceitful as she used to be when she was up to something. She doesn't think we'd suspect. Brian is not very subtle at his best. He follows her round like a dog after a bitch on heat.'

The crudity disgusted Alice. She grimaced. 'You don't have to talk like that,' she said.

'I'm sorry. I know how fastidious you are about these things. But I'm not thinking about you, Alice. I'm thinking about Fern and the hell she's going through.'

'So am I,' she answered. 'And Richard. He looks so ill. They've been quarrelling. I noticed that. If anything starts him drinking again...'

'It would be this,' he finished it for her. 'And then your wrath would fall on her, wouldn't it, my dear?'

'It would,' Alice said. 'What are we going to do?'

'I know what must be done,' he said. 'I'm just considering the method. She's not going to ruin Fern's life.'

'She's already ruined our son's,' she said slowly. 'Hugo, have you got a drink in here? I don't know how I'm going in to face them and sit down to dinner.'

'I keep a drop of whisky,' he said.

Alice looked up at him. For the first time he noticed lines on her face that hadn't been there before.

Suddenly she said, 'I wish to God she was dead.'

'So do I.' He gave her a drink and took one for himself. 'But I don't think God is going to oblige us. Between us, we'll think of a solution. And whatever Fern says, I shall do my utmost to persuade her to get rid of *him*. Now, if you're ready, we'd better put a face on it and join them all.'

*

It seemed to Alice like the stage set in a play. The green and gold panelled dining room, lit by picture lights and candles. Silver sparkling on the table. Two liveried footmen on duty. A huge arrangement of chrysanthemums between the windows, bronze and gold and splashed with yellow.

The men in the family in smoking jackets, Brian in a polo-necked silk sweater. Fern in a mauve and silver kaftan, Diana ethereal in a clinging pale blue jersey dress. Wealth and health and beauty. The old toast came into her mind and it was like a curse. We sit here, playing the charade in front of each other, Hugo commenting on the wine, Fern pretending to eat and watching her husband and his lover under lowered lids. The guilty ones, trying not to glance too often, not able to resist a little smile across the table. Her son, her darling son, for whom she had hoped so much, sitting so close to her that she could have reached out and touched him, drinking the glass of water and trying not to follow the wine with his eyes as it passed him by. He was different that night. Edgy, irritable. The sad dejection had passed and, whatever the reason, Alice was glad for that at least. He had always, even in the worst times of his addiction, gazed with dependence on his wife, as if she were some kind of talisman. But no longer. Alice thought she saw a gleam of hatred when he looked across the table at Diana. But maybe not. Maybe, Alice thought, I'm seeing what I want to see. If only he didn't care about her. If only he could break the cycle of drink and guilt and infidelity that has destroyed him... She'll destroy that other fool, that talented fool who doesn't see through her. Hugo hates him and blames him, but it is old hatred and old blame that is only enhanced by being justified. Alice had to learn to hate him too, and she found she couldn't. It was a shock to Hugo to discover that Brian had fallen in love with someone else. But not to Alice. I pity her, she thought, catching a brief glance from Fern. But not as much as I should. Because I'd rather have Brian than her, in spite of everything. Brian would be ruined. Hugo's influence spread well beyond the sphere of politics and business. He was a patron of the arts, a man of such wealth that nobody wanted to offend him. He would pursue Brian Kiernan with remorseless vindictiveness because he had betrayed Fern. She heard Diana laugh. Such a pretty laugh, full of gaiety. I brought her into this family, she thought, remembering the little girl who had come to play with Richard because Alice was sorry she had missed his birthday party.

I remember that day so well, seeing her come up the steps with the sun shining on her red hair. Thinking, what a beautiful little child. How many intermarriages and cross-breedings had produced a genetic time bomb, destined to destroy itself and everyone connected with it. I don't know, Alice admitted. At that moment Diana gave her a sweet smile. I don't know and I don't care. I don't hate her. But I've no pity left. We can't afford her any longer.

My son, she thought. Nick's child, all that's left of his courage and sacrifice and hope for the future. I've let it happen. I've boasted of having guts, in the best American tradition, but I've given way to weakness, to pleading, even to the threat of his being disinherited. What use would Ashton be to him now?

They left the dining room at last. It seemed to go on for ever, one course, then another, the ritual serving, pouring wine, offering coffee and liqueurs. Richard watching openly as the brandy and the Cointreau came and went.

Alice stood up. 'I think we non-drinkers could go into the library. If you don't mind, Hugo? Come on, Richard, darling. We might have a hand of cards.'

As she intended, it released her son. She slipped her hand through his arm. It tightened against his side for a moment.

'Thanks,' he said. 'How did you know?'

'Because I'm not blind,' she answered. 'It'll never happen again. I promise you.'

'It doesn't make any difference,' he said.

They were alone in the library. Alice shut the door. For a moment or two they were alone. She looked up at him. 'You're all right, aren't you, darling?'

'I'm all right,' he said. 'But I'm not going to lie to you, Mum. I haven't had flu. That's bollocks. Sorry, but it is. I've been drying out.'

'Oh Jesus,' Alice groaned.

He went on, speaking very quickly. 'I'd promised not to tell you. Di was terrified you'd blame her. It wasn't her fault actually. Nothing to do with her this time. It's way beyond that. I was happy, working, loving being down here. I just decided to have a Scotch, that's all.'

'It *is* her fault,' Alice couldn't keep the bitterness out of her voice. 'I warned her if it happened again –'

'I know you did – she told me. It *was* her in the beginning. I was mad about her, you know I was. But I couldn't keep up. I just couldn't go on and on... I thought drink would help. Stop me worrying, failing. Then I found out she was going off with someone else. After Nancy was born I felt like killing her. But I didn't. I just got pissed out of my skull instead. Now, whatever she does, it's the booze that matters.'

'I'll help you,' Alice promised. 'We'll fight it together. But she's got to go!'

He put his arms round her and hugged her. 'No, Mum. Not this time. You've fought the battles for me all my life. I've got to win this one on my own. Maybe if I hadn't let you make it easy for me I'd have turned out better. I don't know. I'd like Dad to be proud of me for once. I've let him down more than anyone. And don't worry about Diana. That's my responsibility. Now, what do you want to play? They'll all come piling in any minute, so let's get the cards out, shall we?'

They played bezique. Alice kept her back to the

276

room and her attention on the cards. She played so badly that Richard won.

'There's a play on TV,' Fern said in a strained voice. 'Brian, darling, come and watch it with me?'

'If you like. What's it about?'

'It's a thriller about a Russian defector.'

'I've had the KGB up to here,' he said. He didn't move out of his chair.

'I'll watch it with you, Fern,' Hugo said. He seldom watched anything except news programmes or documentaries. He had never opted for the 'Sunday Night Play'.

'Thanks, Daddy, but I don't suppose it's any good. I'll read for a while and then go up to bed.'

Alice felt Diana's presence beside her.

'You said I could sleep near Nancy tonight,' she said, 'in case she doesn't feel well.'

Alice glanced up at her. 'The Pink Room is ready for you. There's nothing right next door, the beds haven't been aired properly.'

Diana said gently, 'Oh, that's so kind. I hope I haven't been a nuisance.'

'No nuisance at all,' Alice said coldly, putting the cards away in the box with the markers. 'There's always one room ready in case we have a guest unexpectedly. You know that.'

'Don't forget to order your glass of milk,' Richard reminded her. His face was pinched and bleak. Large black pouches had come up under his eyes. 'Diana always has milk before she goes to sleep,' he explained to his mother as if his wife wasn't standing there listening.

'Does she? She'd better tell Robert. He's about somewhere.'

'I'll tell him,' Diana said. She was blushing at the contemptuous dismissal.

Alice got up and turned her back on her.

'Good night, Dick,' Diana said.

277

He didn't answer.

She left the room and on her way out she chanced a pleading look at Brian. I've fixed it, I can come to you.

He didn't move, but one hand lifted an inch or so from the arm of his chair. It was their signal. He would get away from Fern. They had chosen their meeting place and fixed the time.

She went out closing the door quietly behind her.

'I'll see if Nancy's all right,' Lily decided. She was very fond of the little girl. She had her mother's horrible red hair, but she wasn't like her in any other way. More like her grandmother, with the same direct way of looking at you, the same sturdy courage. If that pony chucked her off, she was up and on its back to try again.

Lily made her way down the long corridor. She was restless and glad of the excuse to get out of her room and away from her own thoughts.

She wasn't a superstitious woman; she had a healthy distrust of the horoscopes and fortune-telling that obsessed some of the maids. But that night the great house was a place of foreboding. The atmosphere was charged with some evil to come.

She opened the door and saw Nancy sitting up in bed, reading.

The little girl smiled at her. 'Hello, Lily?'

'Hello, Miss Nancy. Feeling better? How's your sore throat – doesn't sound too bad.'

'It's not so sore,' the child admitted. 'Grandmother gave me some Disprin.'

Lily looked round. 'You're nice and comfy in here anyway. Can't have you giving the twins the sniffles. Do you want anything?'

'No, thank you, Lily.'

She had Alice's generous smile. It turned Lily's heart over to see it. Reminded her of the days when Richard was a boy. She felt tears come up into her eyes and blinked them angrily away.

'Well, you put your light out in a minute,' she said.

'It's past nine o'clock.' It was nearer ten, in fact. The child should have been asleep long ago.

Lily went over to the bed and on an impulse bent down and kissed Nancy. Nancy hugged her tight. 'Lights out,' Lily reminded her, 'or you'll get me into trouble.'

'I will. Just one more page,' Nancy promised.

Lily saw the title of the book. *Black Beauty*. She might have known. She went out, closing the door. Her lady. Richard, whom she'd helped bring up since he was a baby. The dear little girl in there. 'She's brought a curse on this family.' She muttered it out loud.

She was on her way back to her room when she saw Robert, the new under footman, coming up the stairs with a glass of milk on a salver. She stopped and said, 'If that's for Miss Nancy, I've told her to go to sleep.'

He went red. He was a gawky nineteen-year-old, recently recruited and still very unsure of himself. 'It's for Mrs Richard,' he explained.

'Then you're going the wrong way,' she said. 'Don't you know they're in the west wing?'

'No, Mrs Parker,' he answered. Lily, like the cook, was given the title of Mrs whether she was married or not. It ranked her at the top of the domestic hierarchy. 'Mrs Richard is in the Pink Room tonight. Near Miss Nancy. She told me to put this in there for her.'

'Oh.' Lily stood aside. 'Well, you'd better get on with it then.'

He hurried off, and she watched him go. The Pink Room. That's where she'd sleep that night. Nancy's young nanny was sleeping in the room next to Nancy, with a communicating door. It was an excuse. She'd be able to slip out and meet him during the night. The Pink Room. There were ten empty bedrooms leading off that corridor. She walked slowly back to her own room. She had lied to Alice about having a headache. It was true enough now.

★

'If you don't mind,' Hugo said, 'I think I'll sleep in my dressing room tonight.'

'Is your leg hurting?' Alice asked him.

'A bit. I don't want to keep you awake.'

'Do you want your painkillers?'

'Yes,' he said, 'I may as well take them.'

'Be careful,' Alice warned. 'You know how strong they are.'

'After all these years, I don't need reminding,' he answered. 'If I can't sleep I shall probably read.'

'Hugo,' Alice said suddenly, 'I think they've got some plan to sneak off somewhere tonight. She's never come to this side of the house before. That business about Nancy is just an excuse.'

'Of course it is,' he said. He stood by the door looking back at her. 'I knew you'd realize it. I only hope poor Fern doesn't. Are you glad you supported that marriage now?'

'There's no need to be cruel to me because Fern's being hurt,' Alice responded. 'Unless you want reminding about how little you cared about Richard. I never wanted him to marry her. If you'd backed me, he wouldn't have gone through with it.'

He turned the door handle. 'Then we're both to blame,' he remarked and went out.

Alice kicked off her slippers. Lily had helped her to undress. She looked so pale, with her eyes screwed up against a headache, that Alice sent her off, refusing to let her put the clothes away. It wasn't just concern that motivated her; she hadn't wanted Lily near. She was glad Hugo had left her to herself, although she didn't believe his leg was troubling him. Like her, he wanted to be alone. To come to terms with a situation that could wreck the family. And try to think what to do to stop it. Richard had gone to his rooms in the west wing; Diana had slipped upstairs to the Pink Room. Fern and Brian had said good night and gone off together. If a rendezvous was planned, Brian would have to get away without Fern suspecting. Alice wondered bitterly how he was going to do it. Her daughter took sleeping pills. She disapproved, but she knew Fern kept them in case she couldn't sleep. He'd sneak out later.

I love him, Fern was thinking, lying in bed waiting for Brian to come out of the bathroom. I love him and I hate him. I hate him so much for what he's doing, and I don't even want to lie beside him. I don't want him to move and touch me even by accident. But he's not going to leave me. He's not going to show me up and let everyone know he doesn't love me any more. Nobody knows about it except Daddy. I couldn't bear it if Mother knew . . . She's no better, no wonder she gets on with him. She did the same, cheating on Daddy when he was away at the war. I've never forgotten that time when I caught her with that man Armstrong. She's a liar and a cheat, like my bloody husband. I hate them both . . . But I love him too. I might be able to forgive him, if only that wicked little bitch wasn't around any more. Every time I see her, I'll think of her and Brian, doing the things we did together. I wonder if it's back to front. She'd be on top, she's too small to take the weight of him . . .

Her mind ran wild with obscene images, torturing herself in a frenzy of jealousy. She threw the bedclothes back on an impulse, ran across the room and tried the bathroom doorhandle. 'How long are you going to be?' she called out.

'I'm coming,' Brian answered. Behind the locked door he had delayed and delayed, nerving himself to face her, to suggest, insist even, that she drugged herself to sleep so he could get away and join Diana. He had felt the atmosphere very keenly and was alarmed. They couldn't know. Nobody could know. They were ganging up on Diana, treating her with coldness and contempt, because she was alone among them. However they carped and manoeuvred internally, they were a tribe and Diana was not a member, any more than he was. Whenever it suited the Vandekars, they could turn in unison and step on either of them. Even Alice, who he'd hoped was above such an attitude, had been guilty. Diana needed him, and he wasn't able to refuse her. He wanted her too – he went hot at the thought of making love. His wife was outside, rattling the doorhandle as if he were a schoolboy being bidden to bed. He hadn't wanted to touch her; he had no overspill after Diana. He thought for the first time, perhaps I should get out of this marriage. If I can feel like this about someone else, it's over anyway.

Fern didn't get into bed. She moved round the room, touching things, putting them back. Photographs of the twins at every stage in their growing up. Photographs of herself and Brian in the old happy days. She'd tried to personalize this bedroom, to make it a part of their lives. She drew back the curtains.

It was a very dark night, but the life-sized marble figures of Cupid and Psyche were spotlit until the main lights were put out. It was her mother's conceit to illuminate them. She would. They must remind her of something, those naked figures in their erotic pose...

She dropped the curtain back as Brian came into the room. They got into bed together. He said casually, 'You look tired, Fern. You said you didn't sleep well last night.'

How could I, she mused, when I was thinking about you and her?

'Take a Mogadon tonight.'

'You're always saying I shouldn't,' she countered.

'Well, I think you could do with a good night's rest. You don't want to make a habit of it, that's all.'

He sounded so natural. Any other time she would have been touched that he was thinking about her.

'Here,' he said, and got up. 'I'll get them for you. Just one. That'll do the trick.'

She took the tablet from him and the glass of water. She palmed the sleeping pill and took a long drink. 'Thank you, darling,' she said.

'I'm going to read for a bit,' Brian announced. 'You

282

turn over, I won't keep the light on for long.'

Fern did as he suggested. The sleeping tablet was clenched in her hand. He wants me knocked out so he can go to her. She's waiting for him, down the corridor. When the light went out she began to breathe deeply and regularly. Nothing happened. So far as she knew he was asleep. The doors were bolted, the night lighting system switched on. Cupid and Psyche would be in darkness now . . . She dozed off without realizing it. When she woke with a start later, the bed was empty.

Two o'clock. It would be safe then. No one to see him slip outside and hurry down the long, ill-lit corridor. Not to the Pink Room. That was a risk they dared not take. If Nancy woke and wandered along to find her or if the nanny decided Diana needed to be roused if the child suddenly got worse, Diana could explain her own absence. Brian would find an empty bedroom and keep a watch for her at two o'clock. He hadn't slept. He'd listened to Fern's heavy breathing thinking the Mogadon must have knocked her out.

He had a feeling of fierce excitement as he made his way to the rendezvous. He tried a door, far away from the child's room. It was locked. For a moment he hesitated, swore and then moved on. Nearer than he liked, but this one was open. He stepped inside, shut the door and felt for the lightswitch. It was strange to him. There were so many rooms in that vast house. Twin beds stripped down, covered with white dust sheets. Red and green silk on the walls. It was cold and he shivered for a moment. He searched for the thermostat and turned it on. The heating hummed gently. It would soon be warm. She mustn't catch a cold. He looked at his watch. Ten to two. He switched the light off and opened the door a little way so he could look out, down the corridor towards her room. The element of risk combined with a rising sexual excitement. At last he saw the white-draped figure moving under the intermittent lights along the corridor towards him. She was so light, so quick, she seemed to float. He put his head out and called to her in a hoarse-sounding whisper.

'Diana, in here, darling...'

He opened the door wider and she slipped inside. He closed it, turned the key, and took her in his arms. The negligee and nightdress were stripped off, drifting aside like thistledown. He carried her naked, lolling in his arms like a doll, and placed her on the bed. She gave a whimpering cry of ecstasy.

The child shut her door and hid in terror under the bedclothes. The watcher she'd seen had stood in the shadow and listened to the sounds of the man and woman locked in the bedroom making love. And then the figure had moved away, keeping out of the pools of light along the way, and no one saw where it went.

They had lost track of time. Wild words were spoken in the heat of that passionate encounter, more passionate, more consuming for him than anything he'd ever imagined. Promises, vows, commitments that Diana echoed without thinking or caring whether they would stand the light of the coming day. At last, reluctantly, she left him. He was the man. He was her salvation... She felt exhausted and exhilarated, without a trace of guilt. No guilt at all. For the second time in her life she was in love. She wrapped the negligee around her and slipped out. A quick glance assured her that all the world was asleep. She made her way back as quickly and silently as she had come, and very gently opened the door of the Pink Room.

The screams could be heard all down the long corridor and down the huge stairwell. They brought the menservants running up and the bedroom doors opening in alarm. Seven-thirty and the first early-morning trays were being brought up. A weeping

284

parlourmaid was being comforted outside the door of the Pink Room. The dropped tray with smashed crockery and a river of spilt tea was lying in the middle of the room. The curtains were drawn back. Diana Vandekar lay back on her pillows. Her face was blue-grey and her jaw sagged. She had been dead for some hours. The body was already stiff.

Hugo had been called first. He barred the way to Alice. Lily, sallow and bleary-eyed, had followed after them.

Nancy's nanny was dispatched to keep the child in her own room and the door closed. Hugo persuaded the hysterical maid to go downstairs. The doctor was telephoned. Hugo locked the door and kept the key. He saw Alice standing in the corridor with Lily close by. She didn't say a word. No question, nothing. She just stood and looked at the scene in silence. Hugo took her into their bedroom, closing the door firmly on Lily. Alice was as white as her own nightgown.

'Hugo...' she began.

'It seems the good Lord has solved our problems for us,' he interrupted. 'She's dead. All that kerfuffle was Simpson finding her. I've sent for Gradder. Sit down. You look faint.'

'I'm not,' Alice said. 'Dead in bed. How terrible. What a terrible thing.'

He said, 'What's terrible about it? You've never been a hypocrite before – don't be one now. It's a godsend, a way out for all of us.'

Alice looked at her hands. They twisted in and out, turning her wedding ring over and over. 'It must have been a heart attack,' she said. 'There'll be an inquest...' She might have been talking to herself. 'How am I going to tell Richard?' Then she looked up at him. 'They'll find it was a heart attack, or something like that, won't they? Natural causes?'

'My dear Alice,' Hugo answered, and it seemed that he was mocking her, 'what else could they find?'

★

It's like a stage play again, Alice thought. Act III, Scene iii. The final scene of the last act. The library. Only it isn't, it's my little sitting room, and they're all crowded in here – my poor darling son, my daughter Fern, and my son-in-law looking as if the world had blown up in his face. And my husband Hugo. Cold and in command, giving them the details.

'There's been a family tragedy. As you all know, Diana has been found dead.' He might be addressing the House... Quite unmoved, my husband... He had a heart once, human feelings. I've killed them, that's the truth. The family must keep its dignity and its calm.

There was a sharp cry of protest from Brian, which was choked back. A strange satisfied look on Fern's face. Richard, vacant-eyed and silent.

'Dr Gradder has examined her. He can't be sure without a post mortem, but at first sight he thinks it was an overdose. She did take sleeping pills, isn't that right, Richard?' The disdainful look at his son. Richard nodded, not raising his eyes. 'We must hope it was an accident and not some dreadful act of folly. There'll have to be an inquest. Most unfortunate. I'm afraid we'll all have to put up with a lot of publicity...'

When is he going to stop, Alice wondered. When is he going to get off the centre of the stage and stop pouring out these cynical platitudes? Nobody believes him. We all know the truth. She's dead and some of us are glad. Not Kiernan – he's shattered and beyond pretending. My son – I don't know... he was so strange when I told him. He seemed stunned. But not surprised. He went backwards into himself and turned away. He didn't want comfort; he didn't want anything except to be alone. I expected to find him dead drunk when I went back later, but he was just sitting there, and he was perfectly sober...

'... No press interviews,' Hugo was saying. 'Whatever you do, don't be tricked into making any comment whatever. Fern, I think it would be a good idea if you and Brian took the twins back to London immediately and let us cope with the rest.' He turned away as if that was the end of it.

Alice stood up. Hugo looked startled and then angry; she ignored him. She made her voice strong.

'I've something to say to all of you,' she said. 'We've got a scandal as well as a tragedy on our hands. Diana's dead and nothing can alter that. Personally,' and she stared directly at her son-in-law, 'I'm not sorry. I don't have to explain why because you all know. We're adults, and we'll get through any unpleasantness that may be coming. If we don't, then that's too damned bad. But there's one person nobody's mentioned, and that's Nancy. Nancy is not going to know anything about this except what I tell her. I want that clearly understood. Especially by you, Fern. One word, one hint that hurts that child at any time, and whoever does it will have me to answer to.

'I'm going to see that she's protected. Whatever the verdict on this turns out to be, Nancy's not going to find out until she's old enough for me to tell her.

'And one more thing –' She looked round at them in turn. There was a high colour in her face and a fighting set to her jaw. Every one of them recognized it. 'When this is over, life at Ashton will go on as if nothing had ever happened. It won't be whispered about – it will never be mentioned again. No, Hugo, *I'm* going to talk to the staff. I want them to know where they stand too.'

She walked out and left them all staring after her.

'You don't have to drive like a maniac,' Fern snapped. 'We've got the children in the back, you might remember that!'

Brian didn't answer her. He had packed in silence, bundled the twins and their nurse into the car and driven away from Ashton at top speed.

Fern glanced at him. He was very white-faced. Shocked, no doubt, she thought bitterly. Not the expected aftermath of a night making love.

He didn't know she knew. When he had crept back into her bed, she had pretended to be asleep. He was too exhausted, too sated, to make sure. She had lain awake and listened to him snoring.

There would be no more prowling round the house at night for him now. No more lies about being with his vulgar Irish cronies in the pub when he was screwing that insatiable bitch... Diana was dead.

Fern looked out of the window; she didn't see the country roads flashing past. The image of Diana, gently scoring his neck with her long painted nails, mocked and tormented her. She's dead, but I'll never be able to forget it. I thought I would when it was over, but I'm not sure now. Perhaps she'll always be between us. Even if he forgets her, I'm the one who'll be haunted by what happened. When he touches me, I'll think of him doing the same to her. And because she *is* dead, I'll never be sure he wouldn't have left me for her in the end.

When they reached their London house Brian heaved the cases out, carried the children's up to the nursery and then shut himself in the drawing room. Fern was upstairs, organizing. He could hear her voice admonishing someone about something. He got up and poured himself a large neat whisky. Diana. He couldn't believe it.

He could see her, feel her close to him. Imagination taunted him with the strong individual scent she wore. Gardenias. The room was full of that sweet pervasive smell. 'I don't believe it,' he said. His eyes filled with tears.

'Good night, darling... I love you...' the light voice murmured in his ear.

The door opened and then closed loudly. He looked up and Fern was standing there. 'Do you have to drink at this hour? It's not eleven o'clock yet.'

He said slowly, 'I'm a bit shaken. I'm surprised you're not.'

'About her? Why should I be? I never liked her – she

was just a scrubber, that's all. Richard's better off without her. We're all better off.'

'You're glad,' he said. 'I can see you are.'

She turned aside. There was an odd smile on her lips for a moment. 'I'm not sorry,' she said.

'I don't believe she killed herself.'

He saw her hesitate, then she looked round at him. 'What do you mean? She took an overdose. Gradder said so. You're drunk, Brian –'

'Not yet,' he answered. 'You don't believe it either. None of you. I saw it the night before, the way you all treated her. That rotten pisshead of a brother of yours wouldn't even speak to her. Sentence was passed on her, wasn't it? The Vandekars wanted her out.'

Fern said quietly, 'I'd be careful if I were you. You don't know what you're saying. How much whisky have you had?'

'Not enough,' he answered. 'Oh, it'll be covered up. The tame family doctor will see to that. But I know the truth and so do you.'

'I'm not going to listen to you,' Fern said. He thought how like her father she sounded. 'You're talking gibberish.'

'There'll be an inquest,' he remarked. He swallowed the whisky down. 'That'll be interesting.'

For a moment she stared at him. He saw a dark hatred in her eyes. 'Then that's your opportunity. Why don't you give evidence. If you've got anything relevant to say?'

Then she left him, slamming the door shut. He refilled his glass. There was nothing he could do. Nothing that wouldn't involve telling the truth about their last night together. Wrecking the marriage, disgracing his children for the future. Nothing. He would be part of the lie for as long as he lived.

As Hugo predicted, there was a lot of publicity. The less squeamish newspapers dredged up the Hubbard divorce. A reporter flew out to Cape Town and tried to get an interview with the dead girl's parents.

The verdict was suicide while the balance of her mind was disturbed. A massive dose of barbiturates had been found at the post mortem. The coroner heard evidence that Diana Vandekar had been in excellent health, but she was morbidly worried about her daughter who had a mild infection, and had changed bedrooms to be close to her. Otherwise there was nothing to account for swallowing a fatal dose of sleeping pills. The residue had been found in the empty glass, in the dregs of the milk. The young footman Robert had given evidence at the inquest. He had brought the milk at her request.

The pathologist also reported recent sexual intercourse and marks on the body consistent with lovemaking a few hours before death. Richard Vandekar swore under oath that he had visited his wife earlier that night and then returned to his own suite of rooms. The coroner gave a long opinion and managed to slip in a few reflections on the transience of wealth and beauty, as if an unhappy girl killing herself was some kind of retribution.

At last it was over – the photographers and reporters abandoned their siege of Ashton. The picture of Alice walking away from the coroner's court in a black hat with a thick veil, arm in arm with her son, was printed throughout the world. There was a general feeling of satisfaction that the Vandekars had been given a kick in the teeth at last, just to make up for what they had and who they were.

Diana was buried in the churchyard at Ashton. It was a private service, without flowers or letters of condolence. There was a wreath of red roses from Richard and one from Nancy, Alice and Hugo which Alice had ordered. Fern sent nothing. The unmarked sheaf of white carnations came from Brian Kiernan, and everyone in the family knew it. It was a simple service; the vicar spoke movingly of the young life blighted so tragically. The Vandekars sat in their pew;

not a handkerchief was produced even for form's sake. The vicar was shocked by the coldness and lack of grief. He had never liked Sir Hugo. He thought him patronizing and supercilious, while his wife never attended the church. The servants sitting behind them were more human than the immediate family. Several of the younger girls were in tears.

At the graveside only Lady Vandekar and her husband stayed on to see their daughter-in-law buried. That shocked the vicar too. When it was over they shook hands with him, thanked him formally and walked to their car to be driven the 2 miles back to the house. He watched them go with distaste. He paused for a moment by the new mound of earth. The wreaths and flowers were laid on top, a brilliant splurge of colour against the dark clay. He stood and said a personal prayer for Diana Vandekar. He had no doubt she had died unhappy and alone among them all.

From the day of the funeral Diana's death was never mentioned. Two of the staff at Ashton were sacked because they were reported by the housekeeper for gossiping, and Robert the footman gave notice. He couldn't pass that Pink Room door without feeling she was somewhere about and it was getting on his nerves.

'I want to take Richard away,' Alice said.

Hugo took off his glasses – he was busy reading. Parliament had reassembled and he had a great deal of work to do. 'If you wait,' he said, 'I might be able to go with you. But I don't want to leave Fern alone at the moment.'

'How can you go?' Alice was surprised. 'You can't possibly take the time off now.' He opened and closed the spectacle case, opened and closed it again until she said, 'Hugo, what's the matter?'

'I saw the PM.' He sounded almost casual. 'It was all done very nicely, of course, but the feeling is that after this businesss I would be rather a liability in an election year. So I offered to resign, and it was agreed that the right timing would be just before the Christmas recess.

No one wants it to look as if I've been forced to go.' He gave a sour smile and put the glasses away at last.

Alice said, 'I'm so sorry. It's so damned unfair. What happened wasn't your fault.'

'I've often wondered,' he said, 'whose fault it was. Haven't you?' He saw the shut look come over her face.

'I don't know what you mean. She did it herself. And, thank God, Richard hasn't touched a drink since.'

'If you're satisfied that's what happened,' he remarked, 'then well and good. Personally I was very relieved by that verdict. It could have been quite different if the coroner hadn't been such an old fool. Richard bore up very well. As you say, he hasn't even consoled himself once.'

'Why do you hate him?' she asked. 'He's never hurt you. He always loved you, always wanted to please you. The last thing he said to me the night she died was how sorry he was that he'd let you down and how he wished he could do something to make you proud of him.'

'Perhaps he has,' Hugo said. 'Perhaps he has. I shan't mind retiring from politics. There'll be plenty of other things I can do.'

'You will mind,' she countered. 'You wanted the top job and I know it. If you'd stop lashing out at me, I might be able to help you bear it.'

'I think that's a very nice thought,' he answered, 'but not very realistic. I'll find plenty to occupy my time, don't worry. I won't be under your feet. Now, I really must get on with this. Let me know if you decide to postpone your trip. That is, if you'd like me to come with you. I don't want to be in the way.'

'Even if I didn't want you, and I do,' she said, 'Richard would be thrilled. I'm sorry about what's happened to you, Hugo, but I'm not going to stand here and listen to you being sorry for yourself. OK, you're not going to Number 10. You won't even be leader of the Opposition, because I think your lot are going to be thrown out next year. But other people have to face disappointment. For Christ's sake, pull your socks up!'

To her amazement he burst out laughing. He laughed for quite a long time until water stood in his eyes. 'My dear Alice,' he said at last, 'my dear Alice, what an incredible creature you are! Nothing gets you down, does it? I believe you're indestructible,' and he began to laugh all over again. 'Pull my socks up, you say. You're the one who should be Prime Minister. Suicide – if it was suicide – all the dirt thrown at us... Most women would be shattered. But not you. Oh no, not you.'

'What's the use of giving in?' Alice demanded. 'Life goes on, it has to. You might tell that to Fern by the way. If she keeps on nagging the soul out of Brian, he's going to walk out on her.'

'That's what I hope,' he countered. 'I've been encouraging her to feel aggrieved. You see, you're not the only ruthless member of the family.'

Over her shoulder Alice said to him, 'I've known that for a long time. As God made us, darling, he matched us.'

8

Alice didn't go away on the planned trip with Richard. Hugo resigned on grounds of ill health just before the House went into recess for the Christmas holiday. It was understood that he would be made a life peer in the New Year's Honours List. The Prime Minister wrote him an official letter in which he expressed his deep regret at losing a friend and colleague who had devoted the last thirty years to public service, and emphasized how much the nation owed him. Richard had it framed for him as a Christmas present.

Richard himself was sober. He had begun to work on the family history again. Alice kept going on from day to day in hope, and she felt her judgement had been right. Without Diana, he had pulled through the crisis. And what crisis could have been worse than his wife being found dead and the medical evidence that she had been with another man only a few hours before? Looking at him sometimes, Alice wondered. She wondered how he had managed to go into the court and lie to protect the family and his dead wife's name with a coolness that was so untypical. He had never been strong-willed. There was no steel in him, and the lack of it had puzzled her over the years. He wasn't Nick's son in that respect. He had always been easygoing, friendly, anxious to please. Not tough like her, or ruthless either. But the sight of him in that witness box haunted Alice. Immediately after Diana's death he had been stunned, shocked into a silent withdrawal. But he didn't drink. In the greatest crisis of his life, he bore it in his own way and without trying to escape. It was odd, but she was too anxious about how long it would last to question it. She never mentioned Diana. He never spoke about her. He wouldn't let Nancy cling to him; he stood aside while Alice took over the role of both parents to his child. He retreated into a world of his own, with his book on the family and long solitary walks regardless of the weather. He had bought himself a labrador, in imitation of Hugo, and the dog was his constant companion. He refused, very politely and with grateful thanks, his mother's offer of a trip abroad. He wasn't in need of a holiday. He was busy on his book, quite contented, thank you, and didn't want to interrupt the work. As Alice said to Lily, she didn't know what the hell to make of him. But so long as he stayed away from the bottle, she wasn't going to question. He was there at Ashton, but not there in a way. Not the Richard she knew, whom his father despised and his sister hated because she was jealous of him. He had shut them all out, including Alice.

He consulted his father about the family history and Hugo was cooperative but distant. He didn't think about Richard or ponder the change of personality that had taken place.

Immediately after the funeral their friends had rallied round with sympathy and support, but, led by sections of the press, there was an undercurrent of criticism and it began to touch on Hugo's political career. Articles appeared assessing his performance in the Cabinet. He had made enemies over the years. Now the victims of his lacerating tongue and his pursuit of personal power exacted vengeance in a campaign of smear and innuendo. One article in a prestigious political monthly bordered on libel.

Alice reacted predictably. She thought the attacks were cowardly and despicable. 'Sue them,' she advised furiously. 'You've got the money – you can break them, Hugo!'

'No,' he answered. 'They'd love a court case, more scandal, more opportunity to throw mud. And we have a lot to hide, remember. If I sue Mollins, he wouldn't let it rest at my political career. He's got friends in the gutter press who'd help him out with a very different kind of muckraking.'

'It's only because we never invited him here,' Alice retorted. 'He's just a miserable little blackmailer. If you'd licked his boots like some of your colleagues, he wouldn't be attacking you now.'

'And would you have liked having David Mollins in the house?' he asked her.

'No,' she admitted. 'And I'm not sorry we didn't. He's the worst kind of leech.' Miserable little man, she thought angrily. As a political journalist and self-styled pundit, he had undoubted power and influence. He had long been an enemy of Hugo Vandekar because he hadn't been invited to the gatherings at Ashton.

'You mean you're going to sit and take this sort of character assassination? Don't do it on account of me, Hugo. Or Richard, or what happened with Diana, or anything else! If you want to fight them, I'm right behind you.'

'I know you are,' he said. 'But I know the way these people work. They thrive on publicity, on controversy. It makes them big. It only ends by diminishing their victims even if they win the legal battle. I shall ignore it, Alice. But not because I'm afraid, I wouldn't want you to think that.'

'You don't have to say that,' she answered. 'One thing about you, Hugo, you've never been afraid of anything. It just makes me sick to see scum like Mollins sniping at you and getting away with it.'

'They'll lose interest. They'll pick on someone else after a time. What a dreadful year it's been.' He glanced up at her. 'You're smoking too much,' he said. 'You've been told to cut down.'

'I know. Don't nag. It helps if I'm worked up.' She stubbed it out. 'I've got an idea,' she said.

'Now that's far more alarming than Mollins at his worst,' he countered. 'I know you when you're in this mood. What is it?'

Alice sat down facing him. 'It's a year, as you said, a

year since Diana died. You've left politics, OK. I still think it was bloody unfair. But we've been taking it lying down, Hugo. We've been keeping a low profile as if we had something to be ashamed of – I reckon it's time we came back on the scene, and back in a big way. I want to throw a party – we'll find a reason, some birthday, anniversary . . . something – a party that will have everyone fighting for invitations and make every newspaper in the country. We're going to show them that the Vandekars are people to be reckoned with. What do you say?'

Hugo smiled in his unwilling way. 'What I said to you before. You're an incredible creature, Alice. Indestructible. Go ahead. I rather like the idea.'

They spent Christmas in the South of France that year. Hugo had bought the villa and the winter weather was exceptionally cold and wet. A new government had been elected, and it wasn't Conservative. Hugo had a succession of colds, and it was her idea that they should pack up and go to France where it could be pleasantly mild at that time of year.

Richard resisted coming with them. He had finished his book, which was being typed and prepared for submission. An old friend with a prestige publishing house had commissioned it on a first chapter and draft, more because he hoped to ingratiate himself with the Vandekars than because he felt it would be commercial. Richard had become more and more solitary. Most Sundays he went off alone to morning service and could be seen sitting by himself at the back of the church. He didn't want to go to France with them for Christmas, but Alice wouldn't go without him.

'Darling,' she said, 'don't be difficult. Your father's run down and needs the change. I've got to have Fern, God help me, and the children – Brian's spending Christmas with *his* parents – and what about Nancy? You can't *not* come with us!'

He said at last, 'All right, Mum. I'll come. I'll come

297

if it'll make that much difference to you.'

Alice hugged him briefly. She felt sad so often when she was with him these days. Happy about his recovery, but also sad, as if she had lost him somewhere on the way. 'You know it will,' she said. 'You know I'm always happy when we're together. I wish –'

She stopped, and he said gently, 'Wish what? Come on, tell me what you wish.'

'I wish you wouldn't spend so much time on your own,' she said. 'Day after day shut up in your rooms, coming down for dinner if we're lucky.'

'I'm working,' he reminded her.

'Not now,' she said. 'You've finished. What do you do with yourself, darling? And now this business of going to church . . . What's got into you?'

'I'm not sure,' he said quietly. 'That's what I'm waiting to find out. Don't worry about me, I'm really very happy.'

Alice bit her lip. He knew the mannerism. She always did that before saying something that embarrassed her. 'You don't miss Diana, do you?'

His eyes were calm and clear. He shook his head. 'No. I don't miss her. I hope she's found peace. Don't think anything like that, will you?'

'I'm glad,' she said. 'We won't talk about it again. I didn't mean to mention it. I'll tell Nancy you're coming. She's getting excited about Christmas already. Try and spend some time with her while we're there, will you? She's taken it so well, poor little thing, but I think she needs you, Richard.'

'I'll do my best,' he said. 'But you're the one that matters to her. She won't miss Diana so long as she's got you.'

It was strange being away from Ashton. Alice felt restless. She was irritable with Lily, who grumbled and managed to get a bad cold in spite of bright, sunny weather. It didn't feel like Christmas. Fern was sullen and hostile to her; Alice shrugged her off. Hugo didn't seem to notice and mother and daughter maintained a cool politeness when he was there. The children found it all very exciting. The twins were obsessed with their presents, counting them and picking them up until Alice longed to smack them for being so greedy. Nancy dogged her all day long. She seemed afraid to be without her grandmother, and, sensing the reason, Alice kept the child with her as much as possible. They went for walks in the hills above the villa and for excursions into the town below. But all the shops were still and shuttered, a holiday resort closed up for the winter, and they retreated feeling depressed. I won't do this again, Alice decided. It's not fair on her. She misses her pony and all the familiar things of Christmas at home. She would search out Richard and make him walk with them. If he liked striding around with his dog at Ashton, then he could damned well keep his little daughter company. She had never been critical of him before. There had always been an excuse for him in the past, but not now, particularly if he was selfish with Nancy.

The great family feast of loving and giving came and was celebrated in a kind of exile. The same standards of luxury applied, as if they were in England. Alice made sure of that. But she longed to get back to Ashton. Hugo was in better health and spirits. The three children looked well and spent a lot of time scrambling round the gardens and climbing the hillside. Fern tried to monopolize her father, but there was nothing new in that. Richard read a lot and seemed content in his remote way. With a child's intuition Nancy sensed that he didn't want to be disturbed and, although he was kindly and attentive when she approached him, she did so less and less.

It would be the New Year soon. A new year in every way, Alice had made up her mind about that. No more regrets, no more recriminations. Life was for living. That was her motto, and with all the force of her energy and nature she set about making it a life full of vitality and challenge. It would begin with the most lavish party given since the war. The successor to the great ball at Ashton on the very eve of the war. If the world thought Alice Vandekar was licking her wounds and keeping out of sight, it was in for a surprise. The ball would celebrate her sixty-fourth birthday.

On 29 December there was a storm. Torrential rain swept over the South of France and the temperature plunged. It was time to go home.

The date was set for June, on the Saturday of Royal Ascot week. The preparations began three months before. If the press were against you, then you had to win them over. Fighting them was useless – Hugo had convinced her of that. She engaged a public relations firm to start the publicity off and continue it. And, to everyone's surprise, she agreed that the climax of the party should be an auction in aid of a children's charity. That way, it was explained, she would deflect charges of extravagance. She could spend without limit on decorating the superb house and its setting. She could lavish food and wine on her hundreds of prominent guests and, provided the charity benefited, the ball would come out smelling of roses.

The idea of extracting treasures from their rich friends appealed to Alice's sense of mischief. 'Lily,' she said, 'I'm going to badger them till the pips squeak! Think of old Harvey Watson – he's so mean he wouldn't give you mouseshit! It'll kill the old devil to give something good and he won't dare not to, because everyone's name is going on the programme. Lily, don't you think it's a great idea?'

'You won't have many friends left,' Lily countered. 'Especially the mean ones.'

'Oh yes we will. They'll have a wonderful evening and a lot of good press, and they'll love it. And the people we haven't asked are going to be sick as cats.'

'Parrots, My Lady,' Lily corrected.

Alice laughed. 'Cats,' she insisted. 'I'm not a footballer.'

She looked so well, Lily noted happily. For a long time after that business she'd been poorly, not her bright self at all. All that blood pressure was due to worry, no doubt about it. Lily always referred to Diana's death as 'that business' to herself. And then she'd add, Good riddance, good riddance to bad rubbish. She's cost the family dear as it is. Lord Vandekar losing his job, the nasty things written about him since. And Richard going queer and spending his time in that damp old church every Sunday. He's made his mother unhappy too. Lucky she has Nancy. She and that child dote on one another. She is letting her dress up and come to the party. She never did anything like that with either of her own children at ten years old.

Pity about that red hair. Lily wished it hadn't been that colour. But otherwise the child was her grandmother to the life. Lily always smiled when she thought of Nancy. Dear little thing, but full of pluck. Not like those twins. They weren't staying up. Always bickering and crying about something. Mind you, the parents were to blame. They spoiled them and they used them against each other. Fern and him were always fighting. Or not speaking when they did come down. Lily hated it when they were there. He had no right to cross the door after what he'd done.

Quite often he didn't come with them but stayed in London. Then *she* would mope round the place with a face on her like a boot, for ever ringing up to see where he was. Hoping to catch him out. Marriage, Lily snorted at the idea. If that was what marriage was, thank God she'd had the sense to stay single. She was excited about the ball, although she had to grumble because it annoyed Alice. Annoying Alice and Alice responding with the inevitable 'Shut up, Lily,' had become a game they played for their own amusement. It stimulated their relationship. It stopped Alice from treading on Lily, and Lily from admitting how much she depended on Alice in order to be happy. No one else understood the way they talked to each other or why their ways hadn't parted years ago. Even Hugo, hearing them shouting over some trivial detail, was bemused at times.

Lily was consulted about Alice's dress. She came to London for the fittings, criticized and made suggestions, to the fury of the couturier, but Alice insisted that she was there and often took her advice. Lily remembered the other dress, the green chiffon with the touches of embroidery that she had worn to the ball in 1939. It was still hanging up in the back of the cupboard. Her figure hadn't altered. She could still have worn it. She had been so beautiful, Lily mused, her mind going back in time as the preparations reminded her of that other party. She was beautiful now, with her blonde hair a silver-white and hardly a line on her face. The dress was blue, the same colour as the sapphire necklace His Lordship was giving her for her birthday.

And what a guest list. Lily was a self-confessed snob. She had a reverence for titles and grandeur which was quite unaffected by her own self-esteem. She was Lily Parker and proud of it. She didn't have to envy anyone, thank you, and that left her free to admire them if she liked.

She knew Alice and understood that there was a very different motive from the obvious one in giving such a lavish and highly publicized party. The country wasn't in a good state either, with high inflation and everyone going on strike. Taxes were sky high too. It wasn't vanity or extravagance that prompted Alice Vandekar to give a ball at Ashton and invite every celebrity in every sphere of public life that she could think of. She would no more have a charity auction at her own birthday party with all that upheaval and running around than fly, except she had another reason. Alice's response to charity appeals was to write a handsome cheque. Lily knew that she was embarking on a new career. No longer a politician's wife, no longer privy to the highest circles of government, she was determined to establish herself, her husband and their great house as the centre of fashionable society. She was going to be the most famous hostess in England, and the ball was her opening salvo in the battle.

'What's the weather forecast?' Alice demanded. It was the Friday evening before the ball.

'Sunny, clear, normal temperatures.' Hugo had memorized the television report.

'Thank God for that. Let's hope they've got it right for once.' She swept out again before he could say any more.

Her energy was astonishing. A huge marquee draped in green and white had been built out at the back of the house below the level of the terrace. The guests would dance there after the auction. The items donated were already laid out and Alice's efforts had been well rewarded. So well that a team of security guards had to be employed throughout the night and the next day to make sure nothing was stolen. There were pictures, porcelain, bronzes, jewellery, trinkets and treasures of every kind and the chairman of one of London's best known auction houses had agreed to act as auctioneer. He was an old friend and the Vandekars were faithful clients. There were banks of flowers in every room, garlands festooned round the suits of armour, draped the staircase, blazed a profusion of colour and scents from every corner. A green and white striped awning spread from the portico to the courtyard below the entrance. Flambeaux were ready to guide the guests up 2 miles of twisting, turning drive. There was a live orchestra and the inevitable disco, for the young and some of the middle aged who pretended they weren't. Hugo deplored that, but gave way because Alice argued that they weren't giving a party for geriatrics. She and he didn't have to patronize it, but it had to be there.

She had invited thirty for a private dinner before the

party started, and secured a royal duke and duchess, with three very senior ambassadors including a charming newly appointed millionaire representing the United States. The doyen of Shakespearean actors was another trophy. Alice had never cultivated the stage before, but she relied on a meeting the previous year and issued her invitation. It was accepted with alacrity. Politics were represented, and carefully chosen from all sides of the House. No one guilty of the slightest criticism or disloyalty to Hugo, regardless of rank, was included in Alice's list.

The gossip columnists were primed and salivating at the amount of copy she was providing. Money and power have their own peculiar fascination; accompanied by personal charm, they can be irresistible. At a quarter to eight on that Saturday in June, Alice was dressed and ready to meet the first of their important guests. There was a knock on the door. Lily stood back, admiring the picture, and called out, 'Come in.'

Nancy opened the door. She came forward and then said, 'Grandmother. You look lovely!'

Alice smiled at her. 'Thank you. You look very pretty too. Isn't that dress a success, Lily. Aren't you pleased with it?'

Lily had made it herself. None of that awful green people associated with redheads or anything like a strong blue. White organdie with some touches of colour – pale turquoise ribbons. The child was delicately pretty, with a very pale skin and mercifully few freckles. Lily had designed the dress, and the result was a charming, old-fashioned costume which neither she nor Alice realized was out of date.

'Come here, darling,' Alice said. 'Turn round. The back's perfect too. What do you say to Lily?'

Nancy's face flushed pink with excitement. 'Thank you, Lily. Thank you so much,' and she reached up and clasped Lily round the neck and kissed her.

Over her head the two women looked at each other and exchanged a smile. Grandmother and granddaughter went down the staircase hand in hand to where Hugo waited for them and took their positions to greet the guests.

It was a long evening – the sky was bright blue overhead when the last cars disappeared down the drive. Nancy had long gone up to bed, worn out with excitement. On her way up with her new French governess, she came face to face with her Aunt Fern. 'What's that child doing up at this hour?' she heard Fern say.

The new French governess was nice, but too new to know about Aunt Fern. 'I'm sorry, Madame Kiernan, but she's been with Lady Vandekar.'

'It's disgraceful. She ought to be in bed.' And then Fern swept past them, and the little cloud over Nancy's happiness went downstairs with her.

Alice spent the next morning in bed reading the morning papers. The ball had been a huge success. The sum raised for charity made a second headline in some of the national dailies. £50,000. A record. The party of the decade. Photographs, anecdotes, reports of who was there and what was worn, and what the famous said to each other. And pictures of Alice and Hugo, welcoming their royal guests at the top of the steps, with the little girl in her party dress peeping from behind them.

'It's a success,' Alice called out.

Hugo came out of the bathroom. He looked tired, but there was a faint air of satisfaction which he couldn't quite hide, although he scorned to read all the copy or do more than glance at the photographs.

'Of course it is,' he said. 'Congratulations. It was a triumph of organization.'

'And fun,' Alice prompted. 'Say it was fun, can't you, Hugo?'

He said gravely, 'Great fun, Alice. I enjoyed it. I particularly enjoyed the people we left out. I think we settled a few old scores last night.'

'Well, it's going to be fun from now on,' she

declared. 'We're going to have the best parties in England. We're going to be famous for them.'

'If that's what you've decided,' he said, 'that's how it will be.'

The next eighteen months seemed to run on at roller-coaster speed. Hugo had given up shooting because he couldn't walk the distances or stand for a long time at the butts. But none the less they leased a grouse moor and migrated to Scotland for the Glorious Twelfth.

'Why is it called that?' Nancy asked. Alice had come up to say good night. Nancy was excited about going to Scotland, and she'd spent the afternoon looking at pictures of the Highlands with her governess, who was going along too. There were lakes, called lochs, which sounded like someone coughing and made her giggle, and beautiful mountains and little castles like nesting birds in the wilderness.

But nobody knew what made 12 August glorious. 'God knows,' Alice said. 'After all the years I've lived here, I've never understood the English. What's glorious about shooting a whole lot of grouse beats me. But we'll have fun anyway. And there'll be some children your age to play with – we've a mass of people coming up.'

Nancy hesitated for a moment. 'Is Daddy coming?'

'No.' Alice made it sound casual. 'No, not this time. He's going to Scotland, but it's not near us. Now go to sleep. OK?'

'OK,' Nancy echoed, and slid down under the bedclothes. 'Good night, Grandmother. Where are you going?'

'Out to dinner. Over at Castleford.'

'You look very nice.' The big eyes were fixed on her.

Alice came back into the room, over to the bed and bent down. Richard wasn't going shooting with them. Richard was going to Scotland, but he was never coming back. She had insisted that she tell the child herself.

She stroked the hair back off Nancy's forehead and kissed her lightly. 'Stop trying to make me late,' she chided. 'Go to sleep!'

She went down the corridor. She passed the Pink Room. It was locked permanently now. Her step faltered and she gave a bitter glance at the shut door. 'Damn you,' she said under her breath. Then she quickened her pace and hurried down the corridor to the stairs.

Dinner at Castleford. One of the great ducal houses, open to the public now like so many, but with private apartments that were wallpapered with priceless old masters, and Their Graces, while bemoaning the rigours of life under the Labour Government, still dined off gold plate if they decided to be formal. Weekend parties throughout the summer season; invitations to Cowes week, as guests of the Commodore of the Royal Yacht Club; the Derby, where Hugo, who was becoming interested in racing had a box; letters from every prestigious charity asking for their patronage – no first night was complete now without Lord and Lady Vandekar attending. They were becoming known patrons of the arts. Hugo himself had joined committees and raised substantial sums of money for selected charities. He concentrated on ex-service organizations. He left the arts to Alice. Occasionally he took part in a debate in the House of Lords, but she couldn't resist the jibe about the Upper House being the ultimate proof of life after death, although it wasn't an original remark. They were busy, courted and flattered, and the circle of intimates who came to stay regularly were known as the Ashton Set. They were credited with more influence than they could possibly have had, but Alice didn't mind. They cultivated foreign politicians and tycoons and mixed them with artists and opera singers and actors.

And then, at the end of that long, frenetic summer, Richard had come down to breakfast one morning and announced to them both that he was leaving home for good to live in the Western Isles. As a lay brother in a High Anglican monastery.

Hugo was the first to speak. He put down his knife and fork very deliberately, wiped his lips with a napkin and said, 'You are going to do *what*?'

'I'm joining a religious order,' Richard said quietly. He had heard his mother gasp, but hadn't looked at her.

'Are you completely mad?' Hugo asked.

'No, I don't think so.' The reply was spoken calmly.

'Richard –' Alice had found her voice. 'Richard darling, you can't be serious...'

He turned to her then and smiled. It was a gentle smile. 'Why not, Mother?' It had been 'Mother' now for a long time. 'Why shouldn't I be serious? It's a very serious decision. I'm sorry if you think it's mad, Father. I think it's the first sane thing I've done in my life.'

'Richard,' Alice was pleading – there were tears in her eyes. 'You're sober, you're happy, your books have been published... What's wrong with your life?'

'It's empty,' he said.

Hugo snapped, 'You mean, it's idle. If you'd got a decent job and done something useful –'

'Like you, Father? Making money – going into politics? I'm not like you, I never was. I'm not like either of you. I don't want to be unkind but I'd say both your lives were pretty empty. From now on mine is going to have a real purpose.'

'What sort of purpose?' Alice argued. 'Hiding away with a lot of misfits for the rest of your life. Richard, for God's sake...'

'You've just said it,' he answered. 'For God's sake. That is my purpose, Mother, and nothing is going to stop me. I've had plenty of time to think about it. Ever since the night Diana died. You asked me once if I missed her, remember?'

Alice said, 'Yes. I know I did. You said no. I believed you.'

'It was true. I didn't miss her. I didn't miss the

misery and the lies. I didn't miss getting blind drunk either. It's not a happy state, you know. But that didn't mean I pushed it out of my mind. I kept thinking there must be something more to life than the way we lived. Otherwise nothing made any sense at all. It was just a bloody awful mess. I couldn't find any answers here. I found them in the church. Not your church, Father, going once in a blue moon and reading the lesson for form's sake because you live here and it was a duty, like Mother opening the British Legion fête every year. Things began to make sense to me at last. I didn't think you'd understand but I hope you'll try.'

'And what about your responsibilities?' Hugo demanded. 'What about Nancy?'

'Nancy doesn't need me,' he said. 'She needs a mother. She needs love and security, and she's geting all that here.'

'Richard,' Alice said, 'Richard, what are you running away from?'

'I'm not running away from anything,' her son answered. 'I'm running towards something. It's an enclosed order. We don't leave the abbey until we die. It's in the most beautiful spot in the world.'

'When did you decide this?' she asked him. 'When did you go there?' And then in anguish, 'Why didn't you tell us? Why do all this behind our backs?'

'Because I didn't want you to try to stop me, and you're a very powerful lady, Mother. I had to make up my own mind. I saw the abbey when you were at Deauville in April. I had a long interview and I stayed there for a week to see what it was like. I've never been so happy in my life. I knew it was what I had to do.'

'I suppose you'll be expected to make a financial settlement on them?' Hugo said.

Richard ignored the sarcasm. 'That's the great thing about it,' he said. 'No possessions. No money, no personal things, nothing. You were generous to me, Father. I've made arrangements to give it all back to you. Do what you like with the money. The abbey doesn't want it. Mother, please don't cry. Try to be happy for me.'

He looked at them both and gave each the same distant smile as if he were a benevolent stranger who had wandered in and would soon wander out again. When he was gone, Alice gave way and wept.

Hugo got up and came round to her. For a moment his hand rested comfortingly upon her shoulder. 'Don't upset yourself,' he said. 'If he's fool enough to make this kind of reparation, then he must get on with it.'

She raised her head and looked at him. 'Reparation? What do you mean?'

He didn't answer. He just said, 'Come along. Don't cry any more. It's probably for the best. And you have got that child to make up for it.'

It was a happy summer for Nancy. Two of Alice's guests had brought their children at her suggestion, so she had companions. They all went exploring the great purple moors, paddled in streams as clear as glass and had picnics every day. Sometimes they were allowed to watch the guns, but Nancy didn't like to see the birds being shot out of the sky, and the mountain of feathered corpses at the end of each day was even worse.

There were huge shooting lunches, outside if the weather was fine enough or back at the lodge. It was a wonderful time for the children because they roamed for miles, and Nancy's young governess, Mademoiselle Druet, was a sporty girl who encouraged them all to climb some of the hills and didn't fuss about their getting dirty.

Nancy decided that, next to riding at home, she loved Scotland the best. And it helped her understand why her father wanted to go and live there. Alice had explained it in a practical way, leaving the spiritual aspect out of it as much as possible. She couldn't have

310

made it convincing anyway. He needed to live very quietly, and he'd found a place where other men got together because they felt the same. They did some praying, and they worked in the gardens producing their own food, and they had flocks of sheep. It all sounded peaceful and rather like a very long holiday.

'When will he be coming home then?'

It had taken all Alice's self-control to answer that. 'Not for a long time, I think. It depends on how much he likes it. We'll see.' And she had hurried Nancy off to do something before she could ask any more questions.

But Nancy noticed, that although her grandmother was always busy and surrounded with people, she looked funny round the eyes after Nancy's father left, as if she had been crying. And she had to stop smoking because the doctor said it was bad for her. And Lily was fussing round her too. Nancy liked Lily, but she was secretly a little scared of her. Lucille Druet was talking to the twins' nanny one day and Nancy heard her say, 'I wouldn't want to get the wrong side of her... She's a right old battleaxe.'

There was a letter once a month from Scotland. Alice read it to her. Sometimes they came addressed to her.

Her father was very happy. It was a wonderful place to be, and he prayed for her and for all the family every day of his life. Nancy couldn't imagine him kneeling down like that. He began to fade a little, and sometimes there weren't letters for months. But she agreed with Mademoiselle about Lily, because it was Lily who persuaded her grandmother that it was time Nancy stopped living for horses and went away to a proper school.

And that was the first time she had ever seen her grandmother Alice break down and cry, as she said goodbye to her at Waterloo Station.

And it was the first time that Nancy, blinking back tears in case any of the other girls should see them,

311

thought her grandmother looked an old lady. An old lady in a long mink coat and hat, waving a handkerchief as the train moved out.

The rumours began with the servants. The Kiernans had been quarrelling for years – everyone had heard the voices raised inside their room and sensed the atmosphere. They led a cat-and-dog life, those two, though they had to behave themselves when Her Ladyship was about, and nobody dared upset His Lordship. Often Mr Kiernan didn't come to Ashton at all. The staff took bets on how long it would be before they got divorced. The sooner the better. Those children were badly brought up and allowed to be rude to the staff, and Fern was so abrupt and temperamental that nobody felt comfortable when she was staying there.

But that Christmas there was a crisis. It began on Boxing Day, when Dr Gradder was called in to see Fern. The husband stayed downstairs, socking into the whisky in the library, and His Lordship came down with the doctor. He had a face like thunder and he went into the library and slammed the door. Nobody dared hang around outside to listen in case they were caught, but the household knew in a matter of minutes that something very serious was up. They knew for certain when the husband called for his car and loaded a suitcase and drove off. It looked as if they had finally bust up.

'Do you think I should go up and see her?' Alice asked.

'She's been given a sedative,' Hugo answered. 'Gradder says she'll sleep. It was dreadful to see her in that state.'

'Did you throw him out or did he go?'

'Both. He said he was leaving her and I said he was to get out immediately.'

Alice sighed. Hugo was very shaken. It didn't do him any good to get angry at his age. He was remarkable for a man in his seventies, but just the same... She wished she could feel sympathy for her daughter. She wished she had been able to run upstairs and offer comfort instead of hanging back and leaving it to Hugo. But she couldn't. If Brian had finally left Fern, she only had herself to blame. Alice didn't say so to Hugo. I must be getting old, she thought suddenly. I'm learning to be tactful.

'What brought it to a head? Has he got someone else?'

'I expect so. But it wasn't that. He finally admitted about Diana.'

'Oh my God,' Alice said in exasperation. 'She's been goading him for years. Why does all that have to be brought up again?'

'She may have suspected he was with Diana that night, but he actually told her he was. Boasted of it, she said. He said terrible things to her, Alice. She was completely devastated.'

'You know how long Diana's been dead?' Alice said suddenly. 'Six years. And still something happens to bring it all back again. For Christ's sake, why can't she stay buried!'

'Perhaps Richard's not saying his prayers hard enough,' he remarked. There was silence between them. He cleared his throat.

Alice felt overcome with irritation. 'Why do you always do that before you say something?' she demanded.

'I'm sorry. I know it gets on your nerves. I must engage a good divorce lawyer for Fern. He won't get a penny, I'll see to that.'

'He's never money-grubbed,' Alice pointed out. 'He's rolling in money himself. His portraits sell for twenty thousand. Why don't you stay out of it? You won't get any thanks for interfering.'

He looked at her. His expression was coldly unpleasant. 'You're very consistent, aren't you, Alice? You've never altered in your selfishness and dislike of that poor girl. You can keep out of it – I'm going to help her cope with this. She wouldn't come to you even if you offered.' He got up and walked out of the room.

For some minutes Alice remained looking at the empty chair where Hugo had been sitting. Fern's always come between us, she thought. I'd forgotten he could look at me like that after all these years because of her.

She opened a drawer in the library table. She kept a packet of Marlboro cigarettes hidden there for emergencies. She lit one and had a few puffs. 'Stupid,' she said to herself. 'What the hell do you care after all this time. Put it out and go and get it off your chest. Lily will be delighted. She always hated her.'

Lily was confined to her room with flu. No amount of arguing and answering back deflected Alice's determination that she should stay in bed and take the medicine prescribed for her. There was one brief outburst during which Alice simply shouted her down, and then Lily gave in and admitted that she was ill. It embarrassed her to have Alice come in and sit on the bed and chat to her as if she were an equal.

'You'll catch it,' she answered. 'And you'll be laid up yourself.'

'Rubbish,' was Alice's retort. 'I'm never ill.' Which, as they both knew, wasn't strictly true.

'She's not coming back here to live, is she?' That was Lily's first reaction.

'Not if I can help it,' Alice said. 'She won't want to – she's got a lot of friends and a busy social life in London. What a fool. What a fool she's been. Nagging and bitching at him for every little thing. I don't know how he's stood it for so long.'

'I'm surprised he didn't pack up and clear out long ago,' Lily said.

She glanced quickly at Alice. I've kept my secret, she thought. I've never let her know what I saw that day. And thank God for it. He's gone, and thank God for that too. *She* had it easy, dying like that. At least he's gone on paying.

And Alice, playing with the fringe on the bedcover, twisting it in and out of her fingers, thought much the same thing. The only secret I've ever kept from Lily. I couldn't bring myself to share that, even with her. Hugo and I are bound by it for ever, just as Richard is and Brian will be, whether he leaves Fern for good or not. Perhaps Lily guessed. She misses nothing that goes on in this house. Or this family. But she'd never say. Just as she never said anything about Nick and the baby.

'I'd better go,' she said, and got up. She drew the cover back and smoothed it down.

'Oh, don't do that, My Lady,' Lily protested.

'Why shouldn't I? You've been doing it for me for thirty odd years. Hurry up and get well, Lily. I miss having you around.'

It was a bitter divorce. As Hugo said, it was one thing to suspect, another to be told in cruel and wounding terms that Brian had been in love with Diana, as well as being her lover. If Fern had ever loved him, she forgot it. She was consumed with jealousy and hatred; and fear, because she was going to be alone. There would be other men, her friends consoled her, but she rejected the idea. She couldn't tell the truth, so she invented drunkenness and mental cruelty, hinting that sometimes it had gone even further. She got a lot of sympathy, and Brian was surprised to get invitations from one or two of Fern's friends suggesting he come round for a drink. She had made him sound rather exciting with her tales of violence. There was no need for Hugo's divorce solicitor. Brian wanted nothing except his freedom and he agreed to any terms suggested. But he insisted on joint custody. And that was where Fern decided to fight him.

And Hugo backed her. Alice watched the contest and saw her grandchildren growing more fretful and uncertain, because Fern didn't hesitate to tell them what a wicked man their father was and how unhappy he had made their mummy. And Alice forgot her own advice. She hated to see children suffer, and the twins were miserable, poor things. 'Mother love, my foot!' she exploded to Hugo. He didn't rise to her outburst. He wouldn't discuss Fern with Alice, and the subject hung between them, a fragile taboo destined to be broken. And broken it was one day when Fern had come to Ashton with the children. She had brought them, she announced, because she didn't trust Brian not to try to kidnap them.

Alice's patience was in short supply whatever Fern said or did. She lost it completely at the absurdity and injustice of that suggestion. 'I've never heard such rubbish in my life! Brian wouldn't do anything of the sort! You're just making a drama out of the whole lousy business. Take those poor children home at once. You ought to be damn well ashamed of yourself!'

Fern also lost control. She had always been afraid of Alice. But adversity had made Fern strong too, and suddenly she faced her mother as an equal. And an enemy. 'You would stand up for him,' she accused. 'You don't care what he did to me. No wonder you both got on so well together! You cheated my father with Armstrong, just the way he cheated me with that filthy little nympho!'

She stopped and took a deep, deep breath of relief and triumph. It was out. After all the years of nurturing her secret, feeding on hate and frustration, Fern had struck back at her mother. And what a blow – in all her poisoned imaginings she'd never hoped to see Alice falter as she did then. Lose colour, clamp one hand to her breast as if she were having a heart attack.

'I saw you,' Fern went on. 'I was only a little girl and I came to this very room and opened the door and there you were. You were so busy kissing him you didn't hear me. I'll never forget it. I was sick all over the floor outside.'

316

Alice didn't move. The pain in her chest made it impossible to speak for a moment. And for that moment the hate-distorted face of her daughter blurred in front of her.

Then it was gone. The pain stopped and her breath came back.

'You're not even going to deny it, are you?'

'No,' Alice's voice sounded hoarse. 'No, I'm not. You saw me comforting a sick man. What you made of it doesn't bother me one good goddamn. Now take your children and get out of my house.'

'One day I'll tell Daddy,' Fern said at the door.

'You do that,' Alice said. 'Hurt him as you're hurting Brian. And your children. It still won't make anyone love you. Now get out.'

When the door closed she sank onto the sofa. The pain had stopped but there was a persistent ache and niggling pain down her left arm.

She couldn't have seen us. I locked the door myself. It must have been before, before we became lovers and I had anything to hide. I don't care. I don't care if she tells Hugo. Nothing can hurt Richard now. He's gone from all of us. He's gone into his silent world and he might as well be dead. I don't care about anything any more except living to see Nancy safely grown up.

It was a long time before she felt well enough to ring for Lily.

Fern didn't tell her father. It wasn't a serious threat; reflection advised caution. He might not believe her; he might not forgive her for telling him if he did. She rang her friends and told them her mother had refused to take her and the children in, and everyone agreed that Alice was an inhuman bitch, and if poor Fern needed somewhere to stay she could always borrow their house in the country, villa in Italy or whatever refuge was available. Fern sobbed into the telephone and refused all offers but they made her feel better.

The next day she wrote Alice a short envenomed note. 'I have thought it over. I don't want to hurt

Daddy. When I do come home in future, it will only be to see him. Fern.'

Alice read it and tore it up. Thank God for that, she said. Let's hope it's not too often. She had an appointment with a specialist in London for the following day. And not even Lily knew why she was going.

9

'I was eighteen,' Nancy said. 'I'd finished school and I was going up to Oxford to read modern languages. I hadn't spent Christmas at Ashton that year. A group of us went to Gstaad to ski. It was great fun and I was rather good at it.'

'I bet you were,' David said. He'd woken and found that she'd got up early and gone out walking in the grounds before breakfast. It made him uneasy. Already she had slipped away from him, engrossed in the family and the past. They hadn't made love that night. His plans for a celebration dinner as the lead-up to asking her to marry him had gone awry. He couldn't reach her, and they had drifted to sleep lying close but very much apart.

She had come back from the walk looking too bright and didn't respond when he kissed her. They went down to breakfast in the splendid green and gold dining room, and it was peopled for him with the ghosts of Nancy's past. He felt ill at ease and unhappy. He wasn't used to such feelings. He reached out and held her hand under the table.

'Let's go for a walk,' she suggested. 'There's so much to show you and so much I haven't told you yet.'

'All right. I'm ready when you are.'

'I went walking with her that day,' Nancy said. 'Down here towards the lake. It was very cold, and there was a bit of snow about. I remember telling her about the skiing. She wanted to know everything; she had this gift for making you feel important and that everything you did mattered to her. She said to me, "Isn't this the loveliest view? When I came here to look at the house with your grandfather, we came down here, just on this spot. That's when he said he'd buy it for me. He knew I loved it. I've tried so hard to show him I was grateful, Nancy." I was horrified, David, because her eyes were full of tears. I'd hardly ever seen her cry. It scared me, because she was so strong you couldn't imagine anything getting the better of her. I didn't really understand what she was talking about. Maybe that's why she said it. She'd kept so much bottled up for all those years. "He did love me you know. He wasn't always like he is now. Things have gone so wrong for him. I wish I'd done more to try and make up for it all."

'I didn't know what to say. She turned and looked at me and smiled. "Poor Nancy, you don't know what I'm talking about do you? Never mind. You will one day. Come on, let's walk. It's getting chilly."

'When we got back to the house she took me into her sitting room. "I've got something for you," she said. "I want you to keep it and not open it until I tell you. It's very special to me and I want you to have it." She took an envelope out of her desk drawer. It was sealed and it felt like a book of some sort. She said it again, "You promise you won't open it till I say so?" I promised. Nothing in the world would have made me break that promise, David.'

'What was it?' he asked her. He couldn't imagine himself as an eighteen-year-old resisting taking a look.

'I don't know,' Nancy said. 'I never opened it. It's still in the flat with the other things she left me. I haven't looked at any of them. Let's walk back. I want to show you the secret garden.'

Other couples were strolling past them in the bright sunshine. The rainstorm of the night before had cleared completely, leaving everything fresh and green. He took her arm and held it tightly.

What was a 'secret' garden? He didn't ask, but let her lead him to it. He understood when they rounded a long path through a shrubbery and came upon it suddenly. It was enclosed by walls of clipped yew and anyone inside was quite invisible.

'There were statues and a line of little ponds with fountains, and we used to play hide and seek when we were little. There were places to sit where you couldn't be seen. I loved this garden. Let's sit here for a minute, shall we?' She led him to a deep marble seat in the shelter of the tall yew hedge.

He said, 'You love this place. The house, the gardens, the views... I can see by your face when you talk about it. This place and your grandmother. What happened to make you walk out on all this?'

'I didn't walk out,' Nancy said. There was a pause and then she looked at him. 'I was driven out.' She stood up. 'The sun's gone in. Let's go back.'

'Wait a minute.' He caught hold of her. There was a bright flush on both cheeks, as if she had a fever. 'What do you mean, driven out?'

'Three weeks after we went for that walk, my grandmother died. The day after her funeral, my Aunt Fern turned me out. "Your father was a bastard and you don't belong here. God only knows who *your* father was!"'

Nancy started walking, walking so rapidly that he had to pull her arm to make her slow down. 'I was eighteen,' she said. 'I'd been left my grandmother's money as well as a legacy from my mother. I was independent. I didn't stay another night. I packed up and left. That was ten years ago. I've never been near Ashton until we drove up here last night.'

He said slowly, 'Where's your Aunt Fern?'

'She's dead,' Nancy answered.

'Pity,' he remarked. 'I'd have liked a word with her. You've got cousins, you said so.'

'They're dead too,' she said. 'They were going to Switzerland to ski. Fern and Ben and Phyllis. Do you remember there was a terrible plane crash in the Alps about six or seven years ago? They were all killed, all the passengers. My Uncle Brian died a couple of years afterwards. He never got over losing them – his children. I heard he just drank himself to death.'

'Don't expect me to say what a shame,' he said. 'Do you really give a shit about people like that? Who the hell knows who's who or cares any more? You're you. That's what matters. So you're a Vandekar or you're not a Vandekar... What that old cow said doesn't count. Why don't you stick two fingers up and take your own name back and forget the whole thing? Put it behind you, darling.'

'I can't,' she said. 'I tried. I changed my name, I ran away, but it never really worked. It's not what my aunt said. I've learned to live with that. It may be true, it doesn't really matter now.'

'Then what is it?' he asked her.

'Come back to the house,' she said.

They went up to the first floor, to the long connecting corridor.

'Down here,' Nancy said, and turned away from their room.

Every room had a name: 'Print Room' was on the door in a little gilt cartouche. Nancy tried the handle – it was open. She went in and a maid looked up and said, 'Oh, good afternoon, madam, I'm just getting the room ready ...' She was smoothing the bedcover down and a pile of used linen was heaped in one corner. 'Please have a look round, I won't be a minute.' The staff were used to guests inspecting other rooms. It was part of the hotel service. 'It's such a pretty room, isn't it?' She had a pleasant smile.

'Very pretty,' Nancy said.

David wasn't interested in the decoration. At first he thought the massed prints covering the walls were wallpaper.

The girl gathered her burden of dirty linen and left them, leaving the door open. 'If you wouldn't mind closing it when you leave,' she said. 'The new guests are coming around teatime, I think.'

Nancy said, 'Thank you.'

David came close to her. 'You're as white as a sheet,' he said. 'What is it?'

'I was sleeping here that night,' she said. 'I'd had tonsilitis and my grandmother moved me downstairs from the nursery. She didn't want the little ones to catch it. This was a guest room. I remember feeling very grown up and grand sleeping in here. She used to come in and read to me or play cards. I'd fallen asleep reading. Something woke me, David. I don't know what it was, but suddenly I was awake and the light was still on. It's so clear, I can feel it all coming back as if it had just happened.'

'What happened?' he prompted.

She didn't notice the question. 'I don't know what made me get up. It must have been a noise. It was very late, I remember thinking that. I opened that door there, David. It's a heavy door but I opened it and I looked out. Like this.' She moved across the room and opened the door into the corridor.

'I heard the clock downstairs strike two,' she said. 'I was frightened. I'd never been awake in the middle of the night before. And then I saw my mother. It wasn't lit like it is now. The lights were kept low and only a few were switched on.'

'You saw your mother? What was she doing?'

'She was walking down the corridor towards me. She had an odd look on her face. A guilty look, but excited somehow... It was horrible. I'd never seen anyone look like that. And then I heard something. I heard a man's voice. I was terrified she'd see me, she was so close, then I heard this voice. "Diana – in here, darling."

'I opened the door a crack just as she passed. I saw her but she couldn't see me. She was wearing a floating sort of negligee. I was only a child, David, but I knew that whatever she was doing it was wrong and I wasn't supposed to see. I didn't dare to shut the door in case it made a noise. I was frozen, crouching down, peering through the crack. I couldn't see where she went or who had called her. Not my father, I knew that. It wasn't his voice, and their room was the opposite end of the house.

'But she wasn't alone. Someone else was out there, watching her. I saw them. I saw them in the shadows, creeping after her.' She stopped and shivered.

'Who was it?' David asked.

'That's what's so terrible,' she said at last. 'I don't know. I just saw this shadow moving, and that's all I can remember. It passed by my door just as she did, but I couldn't see. It was semi-dark, my mother was easy to see because she was wearing white... I don't know whether it was a man or a woman who followed her. I think I was so frightened I shut my eyes...'

She closed the door and leaned against it. 'She was found dead the next morning.'

'Christ,' he muttered.

'Dead,' Nancy repeated. 'David, whoever was watching her, tracking her down the corridor, I knew they meant something evil, something that was going to hurt her. That's what made me so frightened, that sense of danger... I shut the door at last and went back to bed. I never told anyone. But I've dreamed of it. It's been a nightmare all through my life, and I couldn't ever tell anyone what I saw.'

'How did she die?'

'An overdose. Sleeping pills. That's what the inquest said. Of course, I didn't find that out until years later. Suicide, while the balance of her mind was disturbed. But she didn't kill herself. Not after a night spent with whoever the man was. She was killed, and I saw the murderer.'

'Christ,' he said again. 'What a trauma for a kid. How old were you?'

'I was eight,' Nancy answered. 'I didn't understand what was happening at the time. Grandmother made sure of that. The children stayed upstairs in the nursery – we had a nanny and a governess. Anyone mentioning

324

a word about it would have been sacked on the spot. I heard someone say that but it didn't make sense to me. I never saw a newspaper and the radio was taken away. To be repaired, they said. But I knew something terrible had happened – children feel atmosphere. I remember I was very restless and nervy. My cousins were sent back to London. People seemed to go round on tiptoe. The house was full of whispers, full of fear. I can feel it now. But there was nobody to ask. Just Grandmother coming upstairs every day, making a fuss of me, taking me out for rides on the little pony she gave me. I told you about that . . . having me down to tea with her alone. And all the time she looked so strange, as if she were holding herself together. I could feel the anger in her and it scared me. I knew it wasn't meant for me, but I was still frightened. Things happened when she was angry and everyone was scared of that.'

'Your mother,' he said, 'didn't you know she was dead?'

'No, not till Grandmother told me. She was often away, and so was my father. I didn't see them for days or weeks sometimes. They lived their own lives. It was different for children then.'

'What did she say?' he asked. 'What did she tell you?' He was trying to visualize the world in which she had grown up, where it was possible to hide a mother's death from her child.

'She took me on her knee,' Nancy said slowly. 'She never usually did that sort of thing. But she held out her arms and said, "Come here Nancy, come and sit on my lap. There. Now you've got to be a brave girl. Will you be a brave girl?" And I said, "Yes, Grandmother," and felt myself starting to cry because I was so frightened. And she held me, David, and rocked me in her arms.

'"Your Mummy's gone to Heaven," she said. "There, try not to cry. Be brave like you promised. She's gone to Heaven and she's very happy, so you mustn't be sad, Nancy." I can hear her voice, just as if she was saying it now. And then I said, "Where's Daddy? Has he gone to Heaven too?" And there was that tight look round her mouth. "No darling, he's here. He's just tired and the doctor said he should stay very quiet and rest. So you won't see him for a while. But he sends you his love and a big kiss." She adored him. He was very good-looking. I've got the old newspaper cuttings of his wedding to my mother. They were both young and glamorous. Mother was nineteen, he was twenty-one. I've got the other cuttings too. "Vandekar heir's wife found dead."'

David put his arm round her. 'I want to see them. I want to read them with you. Then we'll burn them. That's a promise.'

She didn't seem to hear. 'My grandfather didn't like me,' she said. 'He would visit my cousins and talk to the nanny about them, and pat them or ask Ben, the little boy, how his lessons were getting on, but he didn't take any notice of me.'

David said, 'Is that why you never mention him? It's always her – she's the one you talk about...'

'He didn't like me,' Nancy repeated. 'I heard my grandmother say to him once at Christmas, when I was very little. "Hugo, you shouldn't make it so damned obvious that you prefer Ben and Phyllis. She's not stupid, you know..."

'"I like them because they're mine." That's what he said. I didn't understand it, but I felt there was something wrong with me, and I used to keep in the background when he was near, so I wouldn't be noticed. Not that it happened often. We saw very little of him, thank God.

'I was sent to Ireland with my governess before the inquest on my mother. We stayed in the depths of the country. There were no papers, no radio, not a chance that I'd hear anything. I remember having a lovely time staying in this big house with a river running close by. I can't tell you who the people were – friends of the

326

family I suppose. It was Grandmother's way of protecting me until she knew what was going to happen.'

He saw the tears suddenly well up and overflow.

'Poor little thing. I see her in that dream, and it's hateful and sickening, but I remember her as she was. So pretty, like a doll, with big eyes and a sweet face. She'd come and kiss me good night. And if they'd been away she'd have presents for me. Even when I was little I felt she was more like a child than one of the grown-ups. You wouldn't think that a child could feel protective, but I did. Grandmother was strong – she was what made the world safe. My mother was like that fairy you had to shout out loud that you believed in or else she'd die. We went to a pantomime once and all the children had to shout as loud as possible to save the fairy.'

'I didn't go to pantomimes,' he said.

'She left me that brooch,' Nancy went on. 'And her money. She didn't have much, but there was a settlement when she married my father. Her family insisted on it. They were giving the Vandekars the bloodline and the Vandekars had to pay for it. What they didn't realize was that along with the pedigree they were getting the legacy as well.'

She didn't wait for the question. She answered it quickly and defiantly before he could ask. 'My mother was sick,' she said. 'She couldn't help it. She had to have men. Any man. That's what my Aunt Fern told me when she threw me out of here. "You could be anyone's brat," she said. "Not even the boot boy was safe from her." She was twenty-seven when she died. For all these years I felt I've failed her. I've blamed myself for saying nothing, pretending she'd killed herself when I know in my heart she didn't.'

She had turned away from him. He knew she was crying. He turned her round and put his arms round her. 'I'm a bit of an ordinary guy and a lot of this sounds like a bloody nightmare, if you ask me. It's not my world, and sure as hell they're not my values or the values I grew up with. But what matters is what it's done to you. You're the most special lady in the world so far as I'm concerned. If you want to know what really happened to your mother, then we'll find out together, OK?'

'Help me,' she said. 'I can't go back now. I've got to know the truth. If it's not too late to find out.'

'It's not,' he assured her. 'There are people alive who were here when it happened. We'll find them. And we won't go away without answers, I promise you. Now give me a kiss, sweetheart, and then I'm going to get the bill and get the hell out of here.'

He drove her away from Ashton at speed. For all its beauty, the great house was full of rottenness. He couldn't wait to get out and take Nancy away from the place. All that money and snobbery and misery.

They didn't talk much during the drive. He put his foot down and just said, 'We'll be home soon, darling.'

She nodded. 'I'll be glad.'

He took her back to his house in Holland Park and as soon as they were safe inside he felt better. It was as if he'd shed a heavy weight. They were back in his environment; he felt master of the situation for the first time since they went away.

He turned Nancy to him. 'Glad to be back?'

'Yes, very glad. You've been wonderful, David, you know that?'

'I'm always wonderful,' he retorted, and was thankful to see her smile. He kissed her and she responded, opening her lips to him, grasping him close to her. He wasn't deceived and he didn't mind. The passion of despair, not desire. It wasn't time for that, not yet. He eased her away and said, 'You put your feet up, and I'm going to get you a nice gin and tonic.'

'David –' she began.

But he wouldn't listen. 'I won't be long.'

They'd have got on, she thought, imagining him and Alice together. Alice valued loyalty above

328

anything else. It was a quality she possessed in abundance herself. Loyalty and courage.

He came back with the drink and sat beside her.

'She must have known she was going to die,' Nancy said suddenly. 'My grandmother, I mean. She'd made a will only a few months before. When she gave me the envelope she knew. The will mentioned it and said I was to open it after her death. I try not to think about that day, David. It was as if the world had come to an end. She was having tea in her sitting room – that lovely Wedgwood room I showed you – and suddenly she collapsed. I wasn't there, but I heard my grandfather shouting, and everyone came running. I saw her lying on the sofa. There was a look on her face as if she was in terrible pain. My grandfather was kneeling beside her, holding her hand, and poor old Lily had hobbled in – I could hear her sobbing. Then the expression on my grandmother's face changed. It just stopped, like that. Wiped clean. She was dead.'

David said gently, 'Don't cry. She doesn't sound the sort who'd want you to, after all this time.'

'She'd had a bad heart for years,' Nancy said slowly. 'Nobody knew about it. I remember she stopped all the parties and rushing around and I realized afterwards it was because of that. She said it to me one day. "I want to see you out in the world. Up at university, making your life. After that, I don't think I'll worry too much."

'I think she was afraid for me, David. She knew what might happen if she wasn't there. And she was right, it did. I think she kept herself alive as long as possible for my sake. My Aunt Fern came down that night. I'll never forget that either. My grandmother was taken upstairs to her bedroom. Fern went up on her own. She didn't stay more than a few minutes and then she walked down the stairs and into the hall. There was a look on her face I can't describe. I thought at the time, she's not crying. She's glad. She said to me, "Where's my father?"

'He'd been desperately upset. I couldn't imagine

him showing his feelings about anything, but when he saw Alice die he broke down and wept. She told me he'd loved her, and I believed it then.

'"Where is he?" my aunt said. I said, "He's shut himself up in the library. He's in an awful state. He won't let anyone come near him."

'"He won't grieve for long," was what she said. "He won't waste any tears on her. Not after what I'm going to tell him!" And she marched up to the door and walked inside. I heard her say, "Daddy darling, don't . . ." and then she closed the door. I went to my room, David. I didn't know what to do. I couldn't imagine that I'd never see my grandmother again.

'I went to find poor Lily – I knew what losing Alice meant to her.'

'What happened to her?' he asked.

'She was kicked out the very day of the funeral. She was old and rather feeble, but that didn't stop Fern. She was out, bag and baggage.'

'What about your grandfather? What did he do about it? Didn't he try and stop your aunt?'

'Stop her?' Nancy echoed in bitter irony. 'They stood side by side with his arm round her while the poor old thing was driven away to the station.

'Before I left I went in to see him. I'll never forget it. If he'd said one kind word or shown me any human feeling, I might have stayed and tried to fight Fern, but he didn't. "I'm leaving," I said. "After what my aunt has said, I feel I can't stay here another night." In my heart I hoped he'd try to stop me, David. I was very young and I was so lost. He was sitting in the library in that big leather chair by the french windows. He was reading a book, and he put it down, took off his glasses and looked at me. "I think that's a very wise decision." That's what he said. "I think Fern and I deserve to have our home to ourselves, now that Alice is gone." That's all. I wouldn't break down and cry. I remember thinking, damn you, damn you, I won't let you see how hurt I am . . .

'Lily knew what my aunt had done. The night Alice died and Fern went in to my grandfather, he came out a different man. He looked like a stone. He went through the funeral without a flicker of feeling. All he did was stand by the graveside holding on to my aunt's arm. He never spoke a word to Lily or to me. We just stood by ourselves. Lily was crying. I couldn't. I felt as if my whole life had come to a stop. I walked back to the house with her. She said to me, "She's done it at last. She's waited all these years to put between them and blacken her own mother. Much good it'll do her!"

'It didn't do my grandfather any good either. He didn't live very long after Alice died. I saw the news item about his death in New York and the sale of Ashton. That's when I changed my name, David, and made up my mind to start a new life. I wanted to bury it all. I didn't know who I was any more. I had no real identity. Fern had seen to that.

'I know who you are,' he said. He put his arm round her. 'I love you, do you know that?'

'Yes,' she nodded, 'I do know.'

'All right then. Now I'm going to tell you what we do. Tomorrow we get to work. We go round to your flat and we go through the cuttings you told me about and we open the old lady's envelope. That's a start. By the way, when did Lily die?'

'She's not dead,' Nancy answered. 'I traced her when I moved back. I just wanted to make sure she was all right. She's in a nursing home. They told me she was bedridden and senile. She doesn't even know her own name any more. I've got lots of family albums and all the press cuttings in a box at home. Fern sent them on with the rest of my things from Ashton.'

'That was gracious of her,' David said. 'We'll make a start tomorrow. I've got a theory of my own about what really happened, but I'm not saying anything yet. I want you to have a good night's sleep first.'

Nancy turned and put her arms round his neck. 'I'm

331

not tired,' she said. 'I want you, David. I want you so
badly.'

His arms locked round her. He didn't speak for a
moment. He didn't quite trust his voice. At last he said,
'I thought you'd never say that to me again.'

'Where's that envelope?' David asked her.

'It's in that box,' Nancy said. She touched him and
said, 'Darling, would you mind if we left that to last? I
don't want to open it just yet.'

He didn't argue, he just nodded and said, 'We'll
wait then. You might like to read whatever it is on your
own.'

She hesitated. 'No,' she said, 'I wouldn't. You're
part of my life, David. We'll open it together. Let's
look through these first.'

There were heavy leather-bound photograph albums
laid out on the floor. She opened them, and for David
the people she had talked about came to life. Pictures
of Alice as a young woman. Even in the unflattering
prewar fashions she was amazingly beautiful. Hugo
Vandekar. Yes, he was seeing him properly now. A
cold eye, a hard mouth, good-looking, impeccably
dressed. Different in the elaborate wedding photographs. He looked young and smiling, full of a
triumphant happiness. It was the only time, except in
snaps taken with a plump little girl in his arms. Fern
and Hugo, 1938.

And there was Lily Parker. He was fascinated to see
her. Sturdy, quite a big girl, with a strong, plain face.
Dark dresses, everything so neat and functional, beside
the glittering, ethereally slim Alice Vandekar. He
thought suddenly, I wouldn't like to have got on the
wrong side of Lily.

And Nancy's American great-grandmother, Phoebe.
Pretty, smiling, quite different from her dazzling
daughter. There were lunch parties and shooting
parties, and parties labelled Ascot, Henley, the
Derby ... Groups taken on holiday in the South of

France, the men in old-fashioned one-piece bathing suits, the girls long-legged and covered up, wearing ugly bathing caps which looked like helmets. Golfing pictures, tennis pictures, pictures of picnics with everyone grinning self-consciously at the camera with glasses in their hand. Photographs of Hugo on a series of hunters. He looked an arrogant sod, David thought, imagining the child Nancy being ignored, the bereaved Nancy being coolly turned out after Alice's death. Fern again, with a stolid nanny clutching her on her knee. He tried to see something in the round, flat little face that might indicate the woman she grew into, but it was anonymous, a child like every other child. She wasn't even pretty.

Then the war. Alice, and Hugo in uniform. Ashton, with nurses and VADs in their distinctive outfits, posing with groups of convalescents on the terrace in front of the portico. Men in khaki, men in RAF blue, Alice posing with them. 1940. 1941. 1942. There was the newly born Richard Phillip Vandekar in his mother's arms. Swathed in a shawl, with the legend 'Christening at Ashton Church, January 1943,' written in ink underneath.

They turned the pages and the children grew. Fern, in school uniform, holding tightly to her father's hand. Not so plain now, promising to be a pretty girl, but with a shut-out expression as if the face were painted onto the print. The boy Richard, a toddler, one hand clutched by an invisible keeper, to help him stay on his feet.

David said to Nancy, 'He's blond, isn't he?'

'He was always blond,' she said. 'He had Grandmother's hair and eyes. They were the same bright blue.' She closed the second album. 'I haven't looked at these for years,' she said.

He said to her suddenly, 'There's a missing piece in this story, darling. What happened to your father?'

Nancy answered after a moment. 'He died while I was in New York. The abbot wrote to the solicitors and they sent me the letter. "He died in the Peace of Our Lord of Jesus Christ." That was all.'

She lifted a slimmer album, bound in morocco leather, with an elaborate coat-of-arms embossed on the front cover. 'This was my mother's,' she said. 'It's a scrapbook too. I put the old press cuttings I found afterwards in here.'

'So you did,' he answered. 'And I said we'd look at them together and then put them on the fire.' He put his arm round her. They opened the album and Nancy's mother, Diana Brayley, smiled at them from the very first page.

David looked at the photograph and then turned the leaves one by one. Diana as a girl, arm in arm with Richard at their engagement party. Diana in her long white wedding dress, and the heavy tiara framing her wistful face. Very pretty, childlike, but with something secretive and knowing in the eyes. Diana with Nancy in her arms, Richard posed behind her. David recognized one of the tapestries from Ashton in the background. He looked at Nancy. She was pale and strained, gazing at the pictures over his shoulder.

'You know something? You're not at all like her. If it wasn't for the colouring I'd never think you were related. Isn't that you riding the pony Alice gave you?'

'Yes,' Nancy said. 'It is. I remember the show – we came second. I was so disappointed. David, I don't want to look at these. I don't want to read the press cuttings and the coroner's report. Please.' She leaned over and closed the album.

He said, 'Tell me what you're afraid of, darling.'

'I'm not afraid of anything. It's just so upsetting. I didn't think I'd mind, after all these years, but I do. Forget it. Let's forget all about it.'

'No, Nancy,' he said, 'we can't stop now. You can't stop. You're shit scared of something. That's why you want to pull out now. Why don't you open that envelope and see what's in it?'

It was difficult to tear the flap – it had been sealed in

three places. David slit it open with a kitchen knife. There was a cheap little notebook inside and a small white envelope marked 'Nancy'. A sheaf of faded press cuttings fluttered to the ground.

David picked them up and gave them to her. She set them aside. 'I want to see what she wrote to me,' she said.

A single sheet of writing paper, embossed with the word 'Ashton' at the top. No date.

'My darling Nancy,' The handwriting was bold and strong. 'I've lived longer than I hoped, but not as long as I'd have liked. This little book was written for me by someone I loved very much. The press reports will tell you all about him. I think you'll be proud to know he was your grandfather. I hope you'll understand and not judge me. You must never try to judge him. I know that my daughter Fern will say things to hurt you. They will be lies. This and the little notebook are the truth. My own mother said to me once, "Love is the most important thing in any woman's life. One day you'll find it." I didn't believe it would ever happen to me, but it did. When it comes to you, be brave. Don't hesitate. You won't regret it. I never did. Think of me sometimes. My love always, Grandmother.'

Nancy handed him the letter. She picked up the press cuttings and started reading from *The Times* out loud. 'It was announced in London yesterday that the George Cross has been awarded posthumously to Flight Lieutenant Nicholas Armstrong, RAF, for his part in directing the successful bombing mission on the Gestapo prison at Lyons in May this year. The mission resulted in the escape of Resistance leaders from German custody.

'Flight Lieutenant Armstrong had been captured and tortured by the Gestapo on a secret mission the previous year and, after escaping back to England, volunteered as soon as he was medically discharged from hospital to go in the leading aircraft and pinpoint the exact target areas. He had been held in Lyons himself as a prisoner. The citation emphasizes that, without him, the mission could not have been accomplished.

'The aircraft, with its crew and Flight Lieutenant Armstrong, was shot down on its way home and there were no survivors...'

'David? David, look at these.'

He read the other reports. They said the same thing, carried the same photograph of a dark, thin-faced man in a peaked RAF cap.

He looked at Nancy. 'This must make you feel pretty good. He must have been a hell of a brave man. Why don't you keep the notebook and read it later yourself? I don't think anyone else was meant to see what he wrote to her.'

'You know, David, I don't think she'd mind if it was you. But I'll look at it first. Thank you, darling. What a relief to know at last.'

'You know *something*,' he answered. 'But you still don't know who followed your mother that night and put pills in her drink. But I think you do know, Nancy, and that's what's scaring you. Maybe you did see who it was and you've spent your life forgetting it. Except when you were asleep, and you kept dreaming it, and waking yourself up before the truth came out. Listen to me. Isn't that it? Isn't that what you ran away from, all the way to America when your grandmother died? You could have gone to Oxford. You had money of your own. But you put three thousand miles between yourself and what had happened. Because Alice was dead and you'd have to face the truth.'

The verses were passionate and tender. Nancy felt embarrassed, as if she were spying on lovers.

It was strange to think of Alice inspiring a man to write like that. 'To my darling, who made my darkness light' – the dedication on the flyleaf, Ashton, 1942. The year her father was born. How cruel it had sounded when Fern taunted her. 'Your father was a bastard and you don't belong here ...' There was nothing sordid about the love affair between the man who wrote the verses and the woman they were written to.

How wise her grandmother had been to give them to her. She could be proud now of her father's father. Proud of Alice too, because she hadn't been afraid to love him and take the consequences. As she, Nancy, was afraid. David was right – everything he said touched a nerve. She was hiding something from herself.

'I won't go on about it,' he said. 'I'll let you think it through. But you know I'm right, darling. You'll never be happy, and we won't be either, until you get rid of this guilt feeling for good. We both know what you're scared of finding out, don't we?'

'Don't say it, David,' she protested. 'I don't want you to say it!'

'All right. You're the one who's got to do that. I'll go into the office and I'll call later. You'll make up your mind, won't you?'

'Yes,' she said. 'One way or the other.'

He loves me and I love him. But I can't make a commitment. I've never really made one with any man. The married lover in the States was safe enough. I knew he wasn't serious, just having a bit of fun on the side. I made a big thing about it because it let me off the hook. I didn't have to fall in love with anyone where there was any future. I could go on pretending to be someone else, with my phoney name and my career-girl image. But my conscience wouldn't let me get away with it. It made me dream, it made me hold back from really giving myself to anyone. If I don't face up to it, I'll lose David in the end.

Nancy put the little notebook away with Alice's letter folded inside it. 'I know what you'd have done,' she said out loud. 'You said it in that letter. "Be brave."' She reached over and picked up the telephone and dialled David Renwick's office.

*

It was raining hard. The wipers flashed at full speed across the windscreen, just as they had done that night all those weeks ago when David drove her to Ashton. But it was daylight now, and there was no risk of her being lulled to sleep. The London traffic crept down Fulham Road. They seemed to catch every red light. Nancy knew how much David hated delay. He fretted and swore under his breath and then said, 'Sorry, darling. It drives me crazy crawling along like this. Every time it rains the whole of London gets jammed solid.'

'It doesn't matter if we're late,' she said. 'They said any time between five and six.' He glanced down at her and squeezed her hand. 'Stop worrying,' he said. 'If it's no good we haven't lost anything.'

'You've spent so much time and money already,' Nancy answered. 'Private detectives, advertisements, travelling all over the place to see people, and we haven't got any further. If this is another dead end, then I'm not going on with it!'

He didn't argue with her. They'd found the housekeeper and the footman Robert; the agency had tracked them down. The housekeeper had retired to a bungalow in Haslemere. She had nothing to add about the night Nancy's mother died. David and Nancy had the impression that she didn't want to help or get involved. The habit of discretion was ingrained in her.

Robert had left domestic service. It took a long time to find him. He ran a garage in the West Country. A long trip down there brought little more than interviewing the housekeeper.

He remembered Diana. 'Can't forget that red hair,' he said. 'Lovely lady your mother was. Same to everyone.'

He remembered that evening and the coroner's court. But he had nothing new to tell them, though David questioned him closely.

'What was the feeling in the house – about the verdict? Did anyone think it wasn't suicide?

Robert hesitated. For a moment their hopes rose.

'I wasn't sure,' he said. 'She wasn't much older than me. I often wondered... Why should she do a thing like that? But she didn't seem herself that night. Not when she ordered the milk. Not smiling or anything.'

'She did order it? It wasn't suggested by anyone else?' Nancy asked him.

He was definite. 'Oh no. She came out and called me and asked for it specially. Told me where she'd be sleeping. You know, it's funny. After she died I couldn't stay on there. Got on my nerves. If it hadn't happened, I'd still be carrying trays in and out. Now I've got a nice little business of my own.'

He stood up and held out his hand. Nancy took it. 'Sorry I can't help any more,' he said. 'She was a lovely lady.'

On the long drive back David had said, 'We've got one chance left. Lily Parker.'

'That's hopeless,' Nancy protested. 'I told you, darling, she's completely gaga. The nursing home said she wouldn't recognize me if I went to see her.'

'Maybe,' he agreed. 'But there's no one else. Old people remember the past, don't they? I had an old aunt once and she could tell you everything about thirty years go, but she didn't know what day of the week it was. It's worth a try anyway.'

And so they were on their way to the nursing home the other side of Putney Common, where Lily Parker had lived in the twilight of senile dementia for the past seven years.

The rain was so heavy they had to use sidelights. At last they crossed Putney Bridge and the flow of traffic quickened slightly. Nancy felt the familiar lurch of apprehension as they turned down a wide street towards the nursing home. The same sense of sick unease before they found it all came to nothing. As this would, she felt sure. But she was still nervous.

'It's quite a place,' David said. 'Must cost a bomb to stay here long term.'

They passed through tall ornamental gates. There was a short drive, bordered by well-kept shrubs and lawns. They stopped in front of a big, Victorian Gothic house.

David took Nancy's arm as they went up the steps and into the reception hall. 'Don't worry,' he said again.

It was stiflingly hot inside. Nancy glimpsed a few very elderly people sitting in a room with the door half open. There was a bright patch of colour from a television set. The hall was panelled in a dark wood, with armchairs and a sofa. Out-of-date magazines were neatly laid out on a big table in the centre of the room. There were green houseplants standing sentinel.

A nurse came to meet them. She was a smiling, lively figure in the gloom. 'Mr Renwick? Miss Percival? Good afternoon. Isn't this rain terrible?'

'Yes,' Nancy said. 'It makes the day so dark.'

'Well, I told Miss Parker you were coming to see her, but I'm afraid she didn't take it in. She's bedridden now, poor thing. Come this way – her room's on the first floor. She has a very nice view of the grounds. The gardens here are really lovely.'

'I'm sure they are,' Nancy murmured.

David whispered to her as they climbed the stairs. 'Who pays for all this?'

'My grandmother left Lily quite a lot of money. She wanted to make sure Lily would be independent.'

'Here we are,' the nurse said.

She opened a door and went in ahead of them. She raised her voice slightly, as people do when dealing with the old, even if they're not deaf. 'Hello, dear. You've got a nice surprise today. You've got visitors.'

She motioned Nancy forward. She said in an aside to David, 'I'll bring you some tea. I hope your friend won't be disappointed. She won't recognize her. If she shouts or gets fretful, just ring the bell. It's by the bedside.' She gave him a quick smile and went out.

Nancy walked towards the bed. She didn't know the woman propped up on the pillows. Her hair was white and her face had collapsed into folds of wrinkled skin, with bleary eyes peering out either side of what had become a prominent, bony nose. Her mouth was slightly open, showing an ill-fitting top denture.

Nancy swallowed. Lily Parker. She remembered her as a tall woman, plainly but impeccably dressed, very much the power behind the throne with everyone in the house. She couldn't identify her with this shrunken mummy in the bed.

She made herself lean close and speak. 'Hello, Lily. It's me, Nancy. I've come to see you. How are you?'

No answer, no response. The old turtle eyes were fixed on her but there was no gleam of awareness in them.

Nancy turned back to David. 'It's no good,' she said. 'It's hopeless. Let's go, darling. It's so awful to see her like this.'

He came and stood close to the bed. 'You remember, Nancy,' he said loudly. 'You remember Alice, don't you? Alice Vandekar –'

'It's hopeless,' Nancy insisted. 'Come on, please.' She caught his arm.

'You're dead – I'm not afraid of you!'

It was a deep croak. The eyes were alive now, glaring at Nancy. 'You're dead and you can't come back,' the croaking voice went on. The feeble body heaved itself a little upright, away from the supporting pillows. 'You can't frighten me . . . I knew what you were up to! Ruin My Lady and the family . . . I wasn't going to let that happen. Not ever! I'm glad I did it! I'm glad . . .'

Nancy gave a loud gasp.

The old woman faltered suddenly, the burst of energy exhausted. She fell back on the pillows. 'My poor Lady,' she mumbled. A thin tear streaked one side of her face. 'The dead don't come back . . . You get away from me . . .'

341

'It's the hair,' David whispered. 'She thinks it's your mother.'

The eyes half closed and the mouth fell open. Lily snored loudly.

'Here we are,' the nurse said behind them. 'Two nice cups of tea . . . Oh dear, she's gone to sleep on you. That does happen a lot now. I'll put the cups down here.'

David had his arm round Nancy. 'No thanks. I think we'll just go now. Thanks for the tea, but we won't hang around.'

The nurse saw Nancy's face. Funny, she looked quite white and poorly. 'Never mind, I'll have a cup myself,' she said. 'I'll just settle the poor old dear, she's slipped right down in the bed. You know your way out?'

'Yes, we can find it,' David answered.

The nurse said to Nancy, 'Don't be upset. She's quite happy in herself. I always say it's worse for the relatives than it is for them.'

They walked down the staircase into the stifling hallway and past the room marked 'Residents' Lounge'. Someone had shut the door. It was very silent until suddenly a telephone began to chirrup from inside an office marked 'Staff Only. No Admittance'.

David heaved the front door open and hurried Nancy down the steps and into the car. The rain had stopped. There was a smell of wet laurel and earth all around them. He put his arm round her.

'You thought it was Alice . . . That's what's been at the back of it all. You thought she'd poisoned your mother.'

'It was Lily– it was Lily following her that night,' Nancy whispered. 'Oh David! Thank God you made me come!'

He looked down at her and smiled. 'You're a bit shaken now, sweetheart, but there'll be no more nightmares. Lily did it. And you can live with that.

Now we'll go home. It's all over. You'll be a different girl tomorrow.'

He put the car into gear and they began to move, turning in the short sweep of drive, out through the gates and down the long tree-lined residential street into the busy main road round the common.

'David,' she said suddenly.

'Yes, darling?'

'I thought it was my father,' she said. 'Not Alice. I knew she wouldn't do a thing like that. I thought he killed her, and that's why he went away and spent the rest of his life in a monastery. That's what I've been running away from.'

He hid his surprise. She'd had enough shocks for one day.

'Well, you don't have to run any more,' he said firmly. 'I think your grandmother would be proud of you.'

'She'd be proud of you too,' Nancy answered.

It was going to be a quiet registry office wedding. Nancy didn't want a lot of fuss. Just their closest friends and a private lunch afterwards. When they returned from their honeymoon David planned a very big party.

He had never seen her so happy. She was so full of energy and high spirits. Full of plans for enlarging her own business. He didn't argue about that. He let her have her head, confident that when the time came to choose between Becker & Percival and a family, she'd choose the family.

No doubt about it, the grandmother's phenomenal drive had been inherited by Nancy. Only the burden of fear and guilt had kept it shackled. Other inhibitions had disappeared. She was passionately in love with him, and told him so. Ever since that scene in the nursing home she had bloomed into a vital, confident woman.

343

He left her to make the arrangements. He had business in the States. Important business, which could lead to a share in one of the biggest property consortiums in New York State. Nancy came to Heathrow to see him off. Concorde waited on the tarmac, sleek and menacing, like a great silver bird of prey in the sunshine.

'Goodbye, darling. Have a wonderful trip. I'll miss you!'

'I'll call you from New York,' he promised.

She kissed him and watched him go through the departure lounge. He turned and waved once more.

The flight was smooth and fast, aided by a strong following wind. He disliked the cramped seating and the high-pitched engine noise, but the time saved was invaluable. He loved New York. He loved the bustle and energy of the great city. It must have been a lonely place for Nancy when she first came. He booked into the Waldorf and for the next five days was immersed in business meetings and trips to see various projects for development. He telephoned Nancy every evening. All was going well. She'd booked a private suite at the Ritz for lunch after the wedding. He laughed and refused once more to say where they were going for their honeymoon. She was happy and missing him. He was missing her.

At the end of the trip he felt a deal was likely to be concluded. It would make him very, very rich, even by American standards. But he didn't fly home. Instead he took the shuttle down to Washington. A car was waiting and it drove him through the city and into the smart Georgetown residential area. There were embassies and fine private houses. It was reserved for the rich and the diplomatic. The car stopped before an elegant house set back off the road. It wasn't a big house, but it had age and charm.

'I won't be more than an hour, I expect,' he told the driver. 'Then back to the airport.'

'It's very nice of you to see me, Mrs Wallace.'

She had a charming smile. She sat upright in her chair – she had once been very striking. Elegant still, with fashionable clothes and painted nails. She smoked a cigarette in a neat little holder. It gave her a quaint, old-fashioned air.

'Not at all, Mr Renwick. You've come a long way. And I was intrigued by your letter. It's funny, people still want to know about him after all these years. I was approached only last year by someone researching for a book on SOE in France.'

'I'm not writing a book,' David Renwick said.

'So you said,' she answered. 'Then why have you come to see me? Isn't it about Nick and the heroics?'

There was a bite in that last word. He was surprised. But then she might not appreciate the subtlety of a foreign language. She still had a strong French accent after forty years of living in the States.

'In a way,' he said. 'I know you married again. I'd like to talk to you about him, but I wouldn't want to upset you.'

'My dear Mr Renwick, you're very kind. I wouldn't be in the least bit upset by talking about Nick. I have been very happily married to my husband since 1943. Sadly, he died eighteen months ago. My marriage to Nick lasted less than two years. Since you have taken the trouble to find me and come all the way from England, you must ask any questions you like. Cigarette?'

'No, thank you. He spent time at a place called Ashton, convalescing after he escaped from France. People called Vandekar owned it.'

There was a change in her expression. Then she visibly chided herself. 'I went down there. Mrs Vandekar invited me. She became very famous, didn't she? I used to read about her and her husband in the American papers. She was American, of course.'

'Yes,' David said. 'Did you know she had an affair with your husband?'

'I suspected,' she replied. 'I didn't care then and I

345

don't now. I had left Nick and was living with Chuck. She was madly in love with him, that was obvious. I almost felt sorry for her.'

Almost, David thought, but not quite. They'd have squared up to each other on sight. Janine Wallace was quite a personality.

'Why sorry?'

She shrugged slightly, stubbed out her cigarette and expelled the stub with a practised twist of the holder. 'Because she would be hurt, as I'd been hurt. I didn't leave him for nothing, Mr Renwick. We had a lot to bind us together. We met in France where I was also working for the Resistance. Nick was nice-looking, dashing, very brave...' She shrugged again as if decrying her own stupidity. 'Of course, we became lovers, and on leave in England we were married. I had lost my nerve, Mr Renwick. I wanted to stay in England and try to live a normal life. Relatives of mine had been taken by the Gestapo and killed. Friends too. I was twenty-three years old and I couldn't stand any more of it. Nick thought I was a coward.

'He went back to France and I lived through hell for three months without word, wondering what had happened to him. And imagining the worst, of course. But he came back, full of stories, reproaching me for resigning from the Service. Not in those words, but everything he said, every reference to other people working under cover that we both knew – they were all reproaches. Even now I can remember feeling so unhappy, begging him to give it up, to go back to flying if he was so desperate for excitement and danger. I wanted to have a child.'

She looked at David and sighed. 'Such a long time ago, and such a waste when you think about it. We were not suited and we were not happy. I left him, just before he went on the mission where he was captured. I had met Chuck at a party, and it was just like that between us.' She snapped her fingers. 'I had been living with a man in love with heroics. I found a man who loved me instead. Nick was very bitter. I think he hated me at the end. He was very brave, I'm not denying that. And that's what Mrs Vandekar admired I expect. A real hero figure, and he ended up in the blaze of glory he always wanted.'

'It sounds to me as if you hated him,' David said. And still do, he thought, in spite of telling yourself you don't mind any more. 'Just as well you didn't have a child.'

'There was no chance of that,' she said. 'He told me after we were married. He made a joke of it. Can you imagine? He'd had this illness – mumps – when he was already grown up. He could never have children. He was sterile. I sometimes wondered whether it affected him. Whether he was trying to make up for it in some way.'

After a pause she said. 'Mr Renwick? Is there anything else you want to know?'

'Nothing else, thanks very much. You've been a great help, Mrs Wallace. You've cleared something up for me. Something I've been bothered about ever since I heard it.'

'Can I ask what it was?'

He stood up. She was intelligent and poised but he didn't like her. He had a mental picture of the bomber going down in flames and her epitaph for Nick Armstrong. 'The blaze of glory he always wanted.'

'I'm sorry, but it's not connected with me. And it's nothing to do with you either now. Thank you for seeing me.'

He didn't shake hands before he left.

'David,' Nancy said at last. 'Why didn't you tell me? Why didn't you say anything?'

'Because I didn't want to start the whole business up again. You were happy, you'd got rid of all the hang-ups. But I wasn't satisfied myself, darling. I wanted to know for sure. If I was wrong, then I wouldn't have said anything about it to you. But I had a gut feeling about this. From the minute I saw your father in those albums. When he was grown up. You wouldn't see it, and your grandmother wouldn't because she was convinced of something else. But he was the spitting image of Hugo. Everyone said he looked like Alice because he was fair. You said the same. But it was a blind. I looked at him and I looked at Hugo, and I said they're father and son. They must be.'

Nancy twisted the diamond engagement ring round her finger. 'Poor Grandmother,' she said quietly. 'She went through all that for nothing. She died believing that lie.'

'You've got it wrong, darling,' he said. 'She loved Armstrong and she loved your father. She wanted him to be Armstrong's son.

'I said to you that day at Ashton that it didn't matter who or what you were. Vandekar or not, what the hell . . . I remember saying it, sitting in the garden with you. I'll never forget how upset you were. It made me bloody mad and you said afterwards, "I don't know who I am, I've no real identity." That's the real reason I went to Washington to see her. In case I could find out something to clear it up for good. The past's the past. You can put it all behind you now. You're Nancy Vandekar, and in three days you'll be Nancy Renwick. I think it suits you better.'

She looked up at him. 'I think so too.'

A Selection of Arrow Books

☐ No Enemy But Time	Evelyn Anthony	£2.95
☐ The Lilac Bus	Maeve Binchy	£2.99
☐ Rates of Exchange	Malcolm Bradbury	£3.50
☐ Prime Time	Joan Collins	£3.50
☐ Rosemary Conley's Complete Hip and Thigh Diet	Rosemary Conley	£2.99
☐ Staying Off the Beaten Track	Elizabeth Gundrey	£6.99
☐ Duncton Wood	William Horwood	£4.50
☐ Duncton Quest	William Horwood	£4.50
☐ A World Apart	Marie Joseph	£3.50
☐ Erin's Child	Sheelagh Kelly	£3.99
☐ Colours Aloft	Alexander Kent	£2.99
☐ Gondar	Nicholas Luard	£4.50
☐ The Ladies of Missalonghi	Colleen McCullough	£2.50
☐ The Veiled One	Ruth Rendell	£3.50
☐ Sarum	Edward Rutherfurd	£4.99
☐ Communion	Whitley Strieber	£3.99

Prices and other details are liable to change

ARROW BOOKS, BOOKSERVICE BY POST, PO BOX 29, DOUGLAS, ISLE OF MAN, BRITISH ISLES

NAME..

ADDRESS..

....

....

Please enclose a cheque or postal order made out to Arrow Books Ltd. for the amount due and allow the following for postage and packing.

U.K. CUSTOMERS: Please allow 22p per book to a maximum of £3.00.

B.F.P.O. & EIRE: Please allow 22p per book to a maximum of £3.00.

OVERSEAS CUSTOMERS: Please allow 22p per book.

Whilst every effort is made to keep prices low it is sometimes necessary to increase cover prices at short notice. Arrow Books reserve the right to show new retail prices on covers which may differ from those previously advertised in the text or elsewhere.

Bestselling Fiction

☐	No Enemy But Time	Evelyn Anthony	£2.95
☐	The Lilac Bus	Maeve Binchy	£2.99
☐	Prime Time	Joan Collins	£3.50
☐	A World Apart	Marie Joseph	£3.50
☐	Erin's Child	Sheelagh Kelly	£3.99
☐	Colours Aloft	Alexander Kent	£2.99
☐	Gondar	Nicholas Luard	£4.50
☐	The Ladies of Missalonghi	Colleen McCullough	£2.50
☐	Lily Golightly	Pamela Oldfield	£3.50
☐	Talking to Strange Men	Ruth Rendell	£2.99
☐	The Veiled One	Ruth Rendell	£3.50
☐	Sarum	Edward Rutherfurd	£4.99
☐	The Heart of the Country	Fay Weldon	£2.50

Prices and other details are liable to change

ARROW BOOKS, BOOKSERVICE BY POST, PO BOX 29, DOUGLAS, ISLE
OF MAN, BRITISH ISLES

NAME..

ADDRESS...

....

....

Please enclose a cheque or postal order made out to Arrow Books Ltd. for the amount
due and allow the following for postage and packing.

U.K. CUSTOMERS: Please allow 22p per book to a maximum of £3.00.

B.F.P.O. & EIRE: Please allow 22p per book to a maximum of £3.00.

OVERSEAS CUSTOMERS: Please allow 22p per book.

Whilst every effort is made to keep prices low it is sometimes necessary to increase cover
prices at short notice. Arrow Books reserve the right to show new retail prices on covers
which may differ from those previously advertised in the text or elsewhere.

Bestselling Thriller/Suspense

☐ Skydancer	Geoffrey Archer	£3.50
☐ Hooligan	Colin Dunne	£2.99
☐ See Charlie Run	Brian Freemantle	£2.99
☐ Hell is Always Today	Jack Higgins	£2.50
☐ The Proteus Operation	James P Hogan	£3.50
☐ Winter Palace	Dennis Jones	£3.50
☐ Dragonfire	Andrew Kaplan	£2.99
☐ The Hour of the Lily	John Kruse	£3.50
☐ Fletch, Too	Geoffrey McDonald	£2.50
☐ Brought in Dead	Harry Patterson	£2.50
☐ The Albatross Run	Douglas Scott	£2.99

Prices and other details are liable to change

ARROW BOOKS, BOOKSERVICE BY POST, PO BOX 29, DOUGLAS, ISLE
OF MAN, BRITISH ISLES

NAME...

ADDRESS...

....

....

Please enclose a cheque or postal order made out to Arrow Books Ltd. for the amount
due and allow the following for postage and packing.

U.K. CUSTOMERS: Please allow 22p per book to a maximum of £3.00.

B.F.P.O. & EIRE: Please allow 22p per book to a maximum of £3.00.

OVERSEAS CUSTOMERS: Please allow 22p per book.

Whilst every effort is made to keep prices low it is sometimes necessary to increase cover
prices at short notice. Arrow Books reserve the right to show new retail prices on covers
which may differ from those previously advertised in the text or elsewhere.